BENEATH
THE
DARKEST SKY

Also by Jason Overstreet

The Strivers' Row Spy

BENEATH
THE
DARKEST SKY

JASON
OVERSTREET

Kensington Publishing Corp.
www.kensingtonbooks.com

DAFINA BOOKS are published by

Kensington Publishing Corp.
119 West 40th Street
New York, NY 10018

Library of Congress Card Catalogue Number: 2017951326

Dafina and the Dafina logo Reg. U.S. Pat. & TM Off.

ISBN-13: 978-1-4967-0178-7
ISBN-10: 1-4967-0178-X
First Kensington Hardcover Edition: February 2018

eISBN-13: 978-1-4967-0179-4
eISBN-10: 1-4967-0179-8
First Kensington Electronic Edition: February 2018

10 9 8 7 6 5 4 3 2 1

Printed in the United States of America

This book is dedicated to the memory of Lovett Fort-Whiteman.

"An American, a Negro; two souls, two thoughts, two unreconciled strivings; two warring ideals in one dark body, whose dogged strength alone keeps it from being torn asunder."
—W.E.B. Du Bois

Acknowledgments

To my family: I love y'all! Thanks, Frank Weimann, Selena James, Lulu Martinez, James Fugate, Ben Jealous, Vanny Nguyen, Deborah Burton-Johnson, Anne Saller, Gabby Gruen, and Ryan Herr. All of you have been so kind and supportive.

Thanks to the helpful folks at UCLA's Charles E. Young Research Library. A writer has never felt so at home. I'd be remiss not to mention how indebted I am to Professor Mark Hamilton for setting me on my creative path. And finally, I want to acknowledge the passing of a dear friend and artist, Deanna Hamro, who we lost in 2016. All of us love and miss you so much, DD!

BENEATH
THE
DARKEST SKY

1

Moscow, Russia
August 1937

I SAT AT THE DINING ROOM TABLE WITH MY FOURTEEN-YEAR-OLD TWINS, James and Ginger, waiting for my wife to come home for dinner. Six o'clock turned to seven and then eight. No sight of her and no telephone call either.

I'd asked the children to go ahead and eat their pot roast and vegetables from the Torgsin grocery, but they couldn't muster up an appetite, consumed with worry over their absent mother. In the twenty-plus years we'd been together, she'd never been late for a planned dinner. I knew something was wrong.

When the clock struck nine, I sent the children to bed. Shortly thereafter was a hard knock on the door, and I rushed to answer. Two large NKVD policemen, "blue tops" we called them, stood there stone-faced. Both mustached, one five-eleven and stocky, the other six-three and broad shouldered.

"Is your name Prescott Sweet, and is this your residence?" the stocky one asked in Russian, which I spoke fluently.

"Yes, Prescott Sweet. That is me. What is the problem, officers?"

They looked at each other, obviously a bit surprised that I'd responded in the Russian tongue, something they hadn't expected from a colored American.

"Come with us," the tall one said, reaching out and grabbing my arm.

I flung it free and stepped back into the living room. "Tell me what this is about," I said. "Where is my wife? Loretta Sweet! What have you done to her?"

"She has been jailed for being a *counterrevolutionary*," he said. "Now . . . come with us."

"She is no such thing!" I said.

They both rushed me, and I swung at the stocky one, connecting to his jaw and dropping him, his hat rolling across the floor. The other took his baton and rapped me on the side of my head, cutting my left ear open. Before I could move again, both were on top of me, cuffing my wrists behind my back within seconds.

"This is a fucking strong black baboon," said one, digging his knee into my spine. These were two of the most physically imposing and robust men I'd ever encountered. Two of Stalin's finest.

"Daddy!" cried Ginger from the front hallway.

"I'm fine, sweetheart," I said, still speaking Russian, as both of my children were also fluent. "They've made a terrible mistake and I'll clear it all up. Daddy will be right back. Wait here with your brother."

James came storming down the hallway from his back room and tackled the tall one.

"Stop, son!" I yelled, as the blue top grabbed him around the neck and threw him to the floor so easily it was as if he were throwing a sack of potatoes. Then he cuffed him, yanked him up, and led him outside.

"Don't you dare hurt my boy!" I groaned.

The stocky one, still on top of me, jumped up and grabbed Ginger by the arm, leading her out as well.

"Don't worry, sweetheart!" I shouted, rocking back and forth on my belly, wrists cutting at the metal cuffs, chin held up from the floor, blood pouring out of my ear. "Daddy will be there to get you right away. You hear me?"

As I lay there on the floor alone listening to the painful sound of car doors slamming outside, my instinct still had me trying to break free from the cuffs. But this was only causing more injury.

"Come!" said the returning tall blue top, yanking me up by my extended arms, damn near dislocating my shoulders.

"You sons of bitches!" I screamed. "Don't you lay a finger on my daughter!"

"Come!" he repeated, leading me outside and to the backseat of his parked black vehicle. With my son sitting next to me, I turned and watched the other blue top get in the car behind us, where Ginger had been placed. I was numb. I was helpless.

"Where are your passports?" said the tall one, so quickly his Russian was hard to pick up. He stood there holding my door open. "All of your family's passports! Where?"

"They are in a brown leather bag," I said, grimacing, blood streaming down my cheek. "In the back room on the left. They're inside the closet."

"Podozhdite!" he said, slamming the door.

Forty-eight hours later, having spent them in an eight-by-eight dark closet of a jail cell at Taganka Prison with my son, James, hugging me and crying nonstop, we were escorted to a train in the cover of darkness. We had already stood in front of a three-person panel of Soviet officials, a "troika" the guard who'd opened our jail cell had called them. They'd informed us that we'd been officially sentenced to ten years of prison for our involvement in counterrevolutionary activities. A complete fabrication!

The lights streaming above and along the tracks were bright, and the line facing our train car was made up of distraught and petrified men, all of them white, perhaps a few of them foreign like us, but most probably Russian. Not a woman in sight.

"ON YOUR KNEES!" shouted a blue top policeman, his vicious canine growling up and down the line. "And keep your heads down."

All of us did as he said. On our knees we remained for a good hour, waiting for God knows what. With my blue suit pants digging into the rocky dirt, I noticed the bloodstains on the sleeves of my white dress shirt from the cutting cuffs that night. Staying still, I could see in my periphery that there were hundreds of men in both directions waiting to board the other cars as the NKVD surveyed all of us like animals about to be herded into a slaughterhouse. NKVD was simply the joint law enforcement agency for all of the Soviet Union. Whether policemen, military soldiers, intelligence agents, traffic directors, border and prison guards, firefighters, etcetera, they all fell under the NKVD umbrella. Most people just referred to any and all officials as NKVD, mainly because, regardless of title, they each acted without limitation and were part of this mysterious authority machine.

We could hear the blue tops roaming about, perhaps inspecting the train and checking individuals for weapons. I figured if anyone even hinted at trying to stand they'd shoot him. Perhaps this was a simple test. Finally, the officers began poking individuals with their guns one by one and telling them to stand and get in line.

"You . . . give me your papers, *zek*!" he said, the tip of his rifle digging into my shoulder.

The troika had given me a document, so I reached into my pants pocket and handed it to him.

"You're an American! Do you have your passport?"

"Yes."

"Give it to me!"

Again I dug in my pocket and handed it over.

"Is this your son, *zek*?"

"Yes," I said. "Give him your passport and papers, son."

James did as I said and the officer read.

"Both of you, stand . . . now!"

James and I got up and rushed to get in line. At least the blue tops had some kernel of humanity within them, because I hadn't been certain they'd allow the two of us to stay together. Still, I kept my fingers crossed, hoping this would remain the case.

As we stood in line, a guard walked the line and checked all of our passports once more. He wrote each of our names down on a list. I assumed it was for later roll calls.

I made quick observations as I boarded the car. To the right was a compartment with a regular wooden door. It was open and inside was a bunk bed, an NKDV uniform hanging on the wall, and two cushioned seats, obviously the living quarters for this car's guards.

Returning my focus straight ahead, it was fairly dark, the windows to my left along the corridor covered with heavy curtains. It stank of sweat and tobacco throughout. A few lit lanterns hung along the corridor wall, but most remained off. There were compartments to our right, six wooden seats in each—sets of three facing one another.

I counted ten compartments total, or cages, if you will, as the only thing separating them were heavy, black chain-mail curtains. As we continued down the corridor, the smell of urine and feces became intense. Just as I began to cover my nose, an officer far ahead in front yelled for us to stop. I had been so consumed with studying how they'd reconstructed the car for the sole purpose of transporting prisoners that I bumped hard into the man in front of me. James and I were now standing in front of compartment eight, and the corridor was completely full.

"SIX TO A COMPARTMENT!" yelled the blue top. "QUICK!"

I held James's arm and led him to the far seat on the right next to the curtain-covered window. I sat next to him in the middle seat. It wasn't long before the two officers began sliding shut the ceiling-high metal fences that separated all of the compartments from the corridor. They then locked them with bolts. This entire setup was obviously designed to make sure the guards could see us at all times.

"LISTEN!" yelled a blue top. "You hold in your shit! You hold in your urine! When it is time, you can use the hole at the end. We will let you go once in the morning and once at night. You go on yourself and you will get this hammer on the head!"

He began banging it against the fencing.

"Don't ask for food!" he said. "We will give you your ration when it is available. The less you eat, the less you will have to shit. The less you drink, the less you will have to urinate. You are all lousy wreckers and pigs and saboteurs, so sit in your seats and keep your mouths closed. If you talk, I will use this to knock the teeth out of your mouth and give you a pretty pig smile."

After he'd given his orders, the lanterns were turned off, and we sat on the train in silent darkness for two hours. Finally, as we began to move, the faint sound of sighs and whimpering from a few men could be heard throughout. I wondered if the officers considered that "talking."

I wrapped my arm around James. He had no tears left and was motionless. All I could do was be strong for him. Where we were heading was beyond all of us.

2

Port-au-Prince, Haiti
Four years earlier

IT WAS GOOD NOT LIVING A LIE WITH MY WIFE ANY LONGER. A DECADE of truth can do wonders for a man's sanity. And our ten-year-old twins knew only a father of complete transparency.

The *cause* behind the spy work I had done in Harlem, ostensibly for J. Edgar Hoover, still pulled at my soul, but I had to find another way to seek equality for my colored brethren. Nine years in Paris teaching college engineering courses to French students part-time had hardly been the answer. But it appeared I was destined for a life of lecturing, at least until my good friend Bobby Ellington came to Paris in 1929 to serve as the U.S. Embassy's First Secretary. He'd brought with him his new wife, Dorene, and their son and daughter. The family was delightful and a joy to spend time with.

During his three-year post, we'd reconnected, discussing everything—from our past Bureau days dealing with J. Edgar Hoover and my killing of the four British Intelligence men—to Marcus Garvey's arrest, Adolf Hitler's rise, the spread of global communism, etcetera. He also tried to convince me to come work alongside him as an embassy consultant whenever his promotion and new post came about.

As fate would have it, his call from Haiti to be U.S. Counselor came in 1932, shortly after Momma passed away. The loss of her, Loretta's need for a new cultural experience, and my desire to do politically centered U.S. Government work was all the reason we needed to join the Ellingtons in Port-au-Prince. I also had this burning desire, a yearning, to somehow be a *part* of my America, even if from afar.

I was hired under a personal service contract as a safety engineer consultant for the embassy, and Bobby had also arranged for me to work as his interpreter. "You can have a lifelong career as a diplomatic interpreter," Bobby had said back in Paris, "and it will allow you and your family to see the world." I'd become obsessed with languages the moment we'd arrived in France, so I was now fluent in French, Spanish, Italian, and German. It had all been born out of paranoia and a fear of having to move my family out of Paris if British Intelligence ever discovered my whereabouts.

It felt like a lifetime ago that my name was Sidney Temple. I was now comfortable with my relatively new one—Prescott Sweet—and having been posted in Port-au-Prince for a year at this point, I realized how freeing it could feel getting lost in a sea of black faces, a luxury Paris hadn't provided. I was the perfect embassy employee for Haiti, a colored American who spoke French and was well-educated. Most of the people, especially in rural areas, actually spoke Haitian Creole, a language based largely on eighteenth-century French, so I'd quickly mastered it, too.

Unlike the white embassy staff, Bobby included, the Haitian people accepted me, and I was determined to help them cope with being subjugated to an American occupation that was now eighteen years in the making. It was a bit ironic, considering I, too, was a U.S. Government employee, but still, I was not working as an "official" Foreign Service officer like Bobby.

Save for a gentleman named Clifton Wharton, I didn't know of any American coloreds in the world who were actual FSOs. Every other who'd served abroad, men like Frederick Douglass and James Weldon Johnson, had been appointed directly by a sitting president. As for me, all I knew was that Bobby insisted he'd keep me employed for as long as he continued to rise through the ranks.

The social climate in Port-au-Prince was volatile to say the least. The U.S. controlled the customs, collected taxes, and ran many governmental institutions, all of which benefited America. There was reason to believe that U.S. soldiers would soon be ordered home by President Roosevelt, but part of my job was to go out into the streets and convince the angry locals of such, to assuage feelings between those willing to accept employment from us and those who'd rather stick a knife in us. I was a peacemaker. Luckily, our twins attended the private American school, which kept them insulated and oblivious to all of the surrounding cultural noise.

Loretta had grown comfortable with Port-au-Prince. So much of the strife and upheaval in the area was feeding her artistic appetite. Remnants of Africa, in terms of color, clothing, musical rhythms, food, and art, were very present throughout Haiti, so she anxiously soaked it all up. She was much tougher these days, and had many friends who enthusiastically shared their stories with her, most of which involved violence and unrest, along with diatribes about "puppet presidents" from years past.

Between 1911 and 1915 alone, seven presidents were assassinated or overthrown, one having been beaten, his limp body thrown over the French embassy's iron fence before an angry mob ripped his body to pieces and paraded the parts through the streets.

These horror stories, and how they'd shaped these women, made Loretta more invested in the community. She was becoming somewhat of a political artist, less concerned about the fact that her career hadn't taken off in Paris, and she had also found some joy and extra income leading painting workshops.

She'd sold a few paintings here and there, and many Parisian aficionados of art had praised her work, but in terms of a household name, she was still chipping away at that dream, a dream Bobby's wife believed would eventually come true. He had said

as much during the long ship ride over from Le Havre the previous year in August. Not only had we discussed that, we'd also
had an extensive back-and-forth about our Haitian mission.
He'd seemed resolute about its purpose, and I'd gotten the distinct impression that he was certain Roosevelt would be elected
that November, a result that Bobby believed would bring about a
policy change in Haiti.

"Make no mistake," he'd said, as we'd dined and looked out
over the glistening Atlantic, "we are going here to put an end to
this disgusting, paternalistic occupation, but it can't happen
overnight. We have to creatively, patiently, and calmly use our
diplomatic skills to help at least get the ball rolling. Then, once
Mr. Roosevelt takes office, the groundwork we will have laid . . .
the exit strategy we'll have implemented . . . will shift into over-
drive."

"Is Dorene still on the campaign trail with Roosevelt?" I had
asked, cutting into a delicious porterhouse.

"Yes, joyously so. The whole lot of them are in Ohio as we
speak. Columbus."

"Are the children with her?"

"No, they're in Nantucket with her parents. She will be bringing them with her to Port-au-Prince sometime in December
once the election is over. Once she's finally spent more money
than God knows . . ."

"Stop it," I'd said. "She's putting it to wonderful use."

"I realize that. It's just that the woman spends her money like
a Rockefeller."

"You're complaining?"

"You're right. Forget money. No, on second thought, speaking of money . . . regarding your personal service contract . . .
what the State Department will be paying you won't suffice the
way I see it. I shall pay you extra—cash—the first of every month.
Out of our family's private account. Consider it done and do not
argue. It's the least I can do considering your education and the
fact that State makes it next to impossible for coloreds to enter
the Foreign Service."

"What if I try to argue?"

"You'll be wasting your time," he'd said, cutting into his steak. "Of course, you could return to Washington and take the exam if you want to be an official Foreign Service officer. I could try to pull some strings and get you hired as an attaché."

"I'm not about to go back to D.C. and subject myself to the background checks."

"I don't blame you."

"For all we know," I'd said, "the same British Intelligence mole left Hoover's bureau and is now firmly planted inside the State Department."

"You don't think Hoover ever pegged him?" he'd asked.

"Actually, I still can't help but also wonder if it was Hoover all alone in cahoots with the Secret Intelligence Service."

"Hmm."

"Think about it, Bobby. Hoover wanted to imprison Marcus Garvey. But SIS wanted to kill him. You don't think Hoover was willing to give them carte blanche in order to do so?"

"Impossible to rule out," he'd said.

"What did he have to lose . . . besides my black ass?"

"Plausible," said Bobby.

"More than."

"Back to your contract," he'd said. "I couldn't do this Haiti job without you and your language skills. Dorene knows that. And she respects the hell out of you. The State Department may not be in the business of hiring colored FSOs, but Dorene and I are damn sure in the business of paying *you*, my friend, as if you were one."

"I appreciate this, Bobby."

"I'll see to it that you're treated with the same decorum as an official diplomat. However high I rise and wherever I'm posted in the world, you'll always have a job with me."

I'd lifted my glass of water. "Thank you . . . future Ambassador Ellington."

"I only wish," he'd said. "But it better happen someday soon or Dorene will surely leave me for a more worldly and accomplished bloke."

"Stop."

"I kid. But it *is* her dream as much as it is mine. If only Eleanor, her idol, were as keen on Franklin becoming president as he himself is. It's certainly his dream and not hers."

"Well, all I know is you're leaving your mark on history, Bobby."

"We both are, Prescott. Whether you're official or not, we both are."

3

Somewhere in Russia
August 1937

MY OBSESSION WITH RAILROAD MAPS DIDN'T LEAVE ME WHEN I
left America. And as my son and I sat in our sweaty, wooden,
triple seats, having survived the first three days of this horrific
journey across Russia, I couldn't help but wish I had a map with
me. Perhaps I'd be able to bring a touch of comfort to James by
showing him the different towns we were traveling through, perhaps along the Mongolia border. Then again, even if I had one,
how could I point out locations? None of us knew where we
were going.

All I knew was that we'd been traveling for three nightmarish
days in darkness, the curtains so heavy we never knew when the
sun was setting or rising. No hot meal. No bath. No good sleep.
The train made the occasional stop, so that officers could refill
the water buckets, I assumed, and buy themselves tobacco and
real food. Common sense told me they had to be stopping for
inspection as well. Still, we never knew which remote town we
were in.

One bit of information a blue top had relayed was that we
were riding on car twenty-eight. There were fifty in total. I assumed ours was like all of the others—disgusting. So far, the
guards had done as promised and let each compartment out

separately in the morning and at night to visit the hole at the rear of the car after turning the lanterns on. And that was exactly what it was, a hole cut out in the wood floor in a tiny closet. When not in use, it was covered with a filthy rug.

I'd tried my best to ignore the various moans, hallucinations, and cries throughout the car. On more than one occasion, the lanterns were turned on, the fencing opened, and the brutal sound of someone being pulled from their compartment, taken near the rear, and beaten, could be heard. How vicious the beatings, none of us knew. Fortunately, no one in our compartment had made so much as a peep.

The gash on my ear had scabbed over, as all they'd done was tape some gauze over it at the jail, no stitches, which were needed. I hadn't been able to see the cut but could feel the lobe split apart when I'd first checked that night. I figured it had scabbed over now because it itched like crazy. But I hadn't removed the gauze, choosing to leave it taped on for as long as possible.

We'd been given nothing to eat but a small piece of black bread twice a day and a thirty-two-ounce canteen of water to share amongst the six of us. The canteen was refilled each morning and night, but the water was very warm and did little to quench one's thirst. We craved something hot to eat. Anything. Grain, soup, or even gravy.

Day three turned to day ten with nothing changing for us prisoners except a deeper feeling of agony, all of us having become immune to one another's unpleasant odor. To say we were hungry is too simple. We were ravenous.

Trying to describe what hunger feels like is akin to trying to explain what being stabbed feels like. Unfortunately, I could now say I'd experienced both. When James and I had first been taken, all I was consumed with were thoughts of my wife's and daughter's well-being. I needed relief, to know that they were at least safe. But as the days passed, those thoughts, those very instinctive ones, were overtaken by the desperate feeling of hunger.

It's not that my concern for them subsided; it was simply supplanted by science. My body had been deprived of nutrients and had gone into protective mode, trying to conserve energy at all costs. And make no mistake, the simple act of *thinking* about someone's well-being consumes a lot of energy. There is not a human being on this earth who, when faced with the overwhelming pain of hunger, doesn't become selfish, wholly consumed with survival.

After these ten days of travel, I realized that starving someone had to be the cruelest form of punishment. It leaves one feeling nothing but ache in every fiber of their being, right down to their bone marrow. I wouldn't wish it on my worst enemy. It only takes a few days of having nothing substantive to eat to make you totally aware of the fact that you are already starting to die, your body decaying with each passing hour, the hunger siphoning every ounce of clear thought from your brain, save for the one telling you that your body is eating itself.

Accompanying all of this mental anguish was the physical reality of our situation. We'd been sitting on wooden seats in tight quarters with little ventilation for ten days—unable to move about, other than the brief visits to the hole. My back ached—from neck to pelvis. My head was throbbing. My legs felt numb. My skin was sensitive to the touch. My muscles were tender.

Perhaps the twenty years I'd spent doing Kodokan Judo had all been in preparation for this journey into hell, this no-end-in-sight test of will. I'd kept my hand on James's thigh for most of the time, choosing to simply see him as a literal extension of my body, a third leg if you will. I'd convinced myself early on in the trip that my internal strength would flow through him this way. My meditative training would touch his soul. My physical presence and tough veneer would cocoon him.

It was on the eleventh day that, much to our surprise, the train came to a stop and a guard said something new, prompting me to wonder if maybe this would be the day that a substantive meal might actually await us.

"Wake up, you filthy wreckers!" he yelled, as the lanterns were turned on. "We are going to let you off the train to walk outside. You can stretch. You can shit. You can drop dead if you want. You will get a little bit of food. We don't want you to die before we even *get* to the last city."

The guards began to laugh after those words had been spoken. Each of them spoke Russian with deep, menacing voices. I could feel their hate with each word they uttered.

"All of you walk slowly!" he yelled, as the fence began to slide open. "One of you makes any fast move and I will shoot you through the fucking eye."

Once we were outside, the temperature around sixty-five degrees Fahrenheit, we all stood there for a period just adjusting to the painful light. Then I squinted in both directions at the sea of prisoners. There was a river behind us and we'd just crossed a large bridge. Was I dreaming? My eyes still not even half-open, I looked up at the sky and peeked directly at the sun for a while, my face wrinkled up, the first time I'd done this in my life. I didn't care about the pain in my eyes, the burn. I kept squinting, wanting every ray to recharge my mind, revitalize my spirit. There was life in these rays, and I knew I needed to stay alive somehow, someway.

Slowly peeling off the tape and gauze from my ear, I closed my eyes and contorted my face several times, just trying to awaken my senses. I looked down at my brown patent leather shoes. Had purchased them in Paris back in 1929. How far they'd traveled!

I looked left and then right. Nothing but barren land in all directions, save for one shabby log building close by—some type of maintenance post it seemed, a place to resupply goods and inspect the train. Perhaps a few kind souls inside had made us a decent meal.

I gazed at the other men in my compartment group. The six of us had grown more attached to one another than we'd realized, because though we were free to roam about along the river, we remained huddled up, even standing in the exact arrangement of our seats. We had our eyes barely open, but we weren't actually looking at one another. It was as if we were staring straight ahead at the past and what we'd left behind. The old man who'd been sitting in the middle seat facing me began to cough—so heavy that I worried about him surviving the journey itself.

"*Vy nuzhna voda?*" I asked him, reaching out and offering what little warm water was left in the canteen, as it was my turn to have the last sip.

"*Nyet!*" he said, refusing to take it, closing his eyes, the wrinkles on his tan face full of grime.

The short young man with the blue newsboy hat who had been seated across from James seemed rather interested in the water. But if the old man didn't need it, I'd best keep it for now. I casually pretended to ignore the young man's stare.

"Is there anything I can do to help you, comrade?" I asked the old man in Russian.

"I am okay," he said, squinting, his khaki shirt and pants damp with sweat. "My name is Abram. You should give the water to your boy there. If I die it's normal. Your boy is too young to die."

"He *can't* die," I said, as Abram began violently coughing, his white hair soaking wet.

"I have five children," he finally said, his voice trailing off at the end of every sentence. "Three are in Leningrad, two in Poland. My wife died of stomach sickness two years ago. Do you have a wife?"

"Yes, her name is Loretta. I also have a daughter named Ginger. They were put on the trains the same day we were."

"They went on the train north then," said the old man. "I'm certain. You should hope you can see them again."

"You won't!" said the young man. James and the other two prisoners stayed quiet. "We are all going to die. Such is the will of Stalin. I counted sixty people on our car. The blue top said there are fifty cars. That means three thousand dead. They tell me I was arrested for taking a trip to Berlin."

"For simply taking a trip to Berlin?" I said.

"Yes, that is what they do. Stalin has taken what Marx and Lenin and . . . Trotsky—"

"Shh!" said Abram, waving his frail hand. "Don't say his name. They will shoot you on the spot."

"I know this," whispered the young man, his healthy white skin closer to olive than pale. "What I am trying to say is that Stalin has taken something pure and perverted it. Communism at its core is pure. They are arresting people for simply visiting other countries because they claim we have been tainted by out-side influences. We can no longer be *trusted.* We are to be re-placed by a select breed of proven Stalin loyalists. What constitutes *proven* is a mystery to all of us. I'm sure the list of so-called loyalists is not written in ink."

"How old are you?" I asked. "And what is your name?"

"I am twenty-two. My name is Yury. I had just been hired to write for the state newspaper, *Izvestiya.* Your name . . . age?"

"Prescott. Forty-three."

"I can only hope they shoot me while I'm not looking," said Abram, coughing again. "But every time one of the officers comes walking by our compartment, I fear that this is going to happen while my eyes are wide open. They know an old man like me is of no use to them. They hope I die before we arrive at wherever we're going."

"They will not shoot you, Abram," I said. "You've given them no reason. So don't give them one going forward. All of us are going to be okay as long as we listen and do as they say."

"You can tell you're an American," said Yury. "Your Russian is excellent and quite . . . how should I say . . . quite *Russian,* but your optimism is quite American."

"I *have* been accused on more than one occasion of being naïvely hopeful. Yes!" I turned to James. "Are you feeling okay, son?"

He nodded, his lips powdery dry. His cream-colored, long-sleeve, repro chambray shirt was still tucked into the brown her-ringbone pants Bobby's wife had purchased for him in London.

I knew he was in shock still, the look on his face hollow. But I'd made sure he'd eaten his bread and water. And I had a good feel for his well-being. He'd always taken his cues from me. As long as I projected strength, he'd be okay. Did I want to shield him from all of the horror around us? Of course. But that was now an impossibility. I'd have to fix later whatever trauma he'd experience. He was going to become a hardened man overnight.

"To think," said Abram, coughing, "that this train, known as the Trans-Siberian Railway, all five thousand eight hundred miles of it, the longest in the world, would be used for such evil. You see . . . I was born in 1866, so I was there when everyone believed that the *idea* alone of building the railway was absolute insanity. Construction was ordered by Tsar Nicholas II in 1891, and not completed until 1916. Twenty-five years! A marvel to the world! Built and rebuilt over and over again because of ungodly terrain having to be exploded, snow and rivers having to be dealt with, only to now be used to torture its own. My God!"

Abram closed his eyes and made a cross on his chest, then looked to the heavens. He was truly distraught at what had become of his country.

"Look!" said Yury, pointing to the car behind ours.

We watched as three guards began pulling a dead prisoner off of one of the many long metal spikes that had been placed under the cars. He'd obviously tried to escape through the toilet hole while en route, only to have the stake driven straight through his stomach. The officers were having a difficult time removing the poor soul—his limp body slouched over the long, bloody rod like a dead man on a horse.

"Don't look at this, son," I said to James. "Look at the river. Think of Paris. Think of your mother and sister and the good times we had. They will come again."

"This part of their master plan seems to be working," said Yury, as the rest of us watched the blood ooze from the dead man's stomach. "They don't seem to miss a thing. I wonder if it was Stalin himself who came up with this . . . this . . . how have I heard you Americans say it . . . this *doozy*. This is truly barbaric. Quite the appetizer for whatever food they plan on serving us."

"And to think," said Abram, coughing, "I actually thought of jumping through that toilet hole several times. I think they *want* us to try such things. I think they enjoy coming up with sick ways to kill us. They don't want to grow bored."

"How could they?" said Yury, pointing at the river.

We all watched as a tall man sprinted toward the river about one hundred yards away. Where in God's name did he possibly think he was going? An officer casually followed, as the prisoner entered the river and tried to wade across. None of the officers were yelling for the runner to stop. They just watched, as their fellow officer calmly walked after him.

I pulled James in tight and covered his eyes. The prisoner hadn't made it five yards across before the officer raised his rifle, took aim, and shot the man in the back of the head. It was a kill shot and his body was left floating there, no one ever attempting to retrieve him.

I watched the prisoner's beige newsboy hat drifting downstream, a symbol of a life taken far too soon, of a man's hopes and dreams buried at the bottom of a mysterious river. I stayed fixed on the hat until it was out of sight. Who would find it? And when he did, might he wear it, never knowing that it belonged to an innocent man who'd likely left behind a young family, a family who would never learn of their loved one's true fate?

"I'm going to protect you, son," I said, my hand still covering both eyes, his head pressed against my ribs. "Put all of your trust in me. You don't have to worry. You will always be safe because I am your daddy. Think of this as a nightmare. Do you remember what I've always told you when you've had nightmares?"

He nodded into my shirt.

"That you always wake up from them."

The rest of us were still looking at the body as it began to sink. It was difficult to not see ourselves in this man. And I wanted to believe what I'd just told James. But I wasn't so sure that our nightmare would end any differently than this escapee's had. Maybe it was just a matter of whether we'd take our bullets from the front or from the back.

"Not all of the train cars have seats or compartments," said the old man, breaking the silence. "Many are just cattle wagons. We are fortunate in that sense."

"LISTEN UP, CAR TWENTY-EIGHT!" yelled one of our car's officers. "There is beet and cabbage soup here for you. You get one ladleful per person. One! And a piece of bread! After you have eaten, you are to remain outside. Feel free to walk over to the river and wash your filthy selves. There are rags near the rear of the car for you to use. You stink like pigs! And if you want to join that piece of dead waste floating in the water over there, just try to cross the river. But, if you want to live and get back on this train, stay at the river's edge. Do you hear me?"

"*DA!*" we collectively said.

"And one more thing before you line up here, *zeks!*" he said. "You worthless scum need to squat lower when you shit down the hole inside. The floor is a mess. If you can't squat because you have old, bad knees, lay down on your back with your ass over the hole. And you better fucking get on your knees when you piss. That toilet rug is filthy. I hope you understand all of this because we are going to have to start watching you relieve yourselves until we find out who the clumsy shitters are. Now! Line up!"

"I've been meaning to ask you something, Abram," I said, as the six of us squeezed into the line of desperate souls. "What exactly is a *zek?*"

"There really is no appropriate translation," he said. "It is, in essence, a person who is a forced-labor camp prisoner, I guess you would say. But a *zek* has come to mean more than that even. It has intrinsic qualities . . . is deep-rooted. It is so unique to the Soviet Union. If you want to tell Americans one day about your horror story, assuming you live, you can translate most of it from Russian to English, but certain words like *zek* shouldn't be translated. A *zek* is a *zek*. The word is wholly painful, an ungodly amount of death and pain associated with it, and must be respected as such."

"I see."

The soup was barely warm. James and I stood at the river's edge sipping it, just the two of us now. I'd told him not to gulp it down. We had to savor each drop. They called it beet and cabbage soup, but there weren't many beets or cabbage. Maybe a couple of root fragments in my bowl at best, and only a few rotten-looking strands of cabbage. I could taste a hint of beef stock, but it was basically warm pink water with a lot of salt. I hated beets, but the moment the officer had mentioned the soup, I was craving it.

"Swish it around in your mouth, son," I said. "Don't swallow it fast. Let it soak into your tongue."

He nodded and did as I said. We hadn't eaten our black bread yet, as I wanted to spread the meal out for as long as possible. I knew that this paltry meal was only a preservation measure on the part of the officers. They didn't care how healthy we were, but they also didn't want us to drop dead too fast. Giving us some small amount of nutrition every week might be the qualifying minimum in their eyes. But they didn't seem to know anything about vitamins and calories and dehydration. They were experimenting at best, and we were the test rats.

"You need to come with me, big *zek*," said an officer approaching James and me.

"What about my son?"

"He can wash up while you come. Don't ask questions. Don't talk at all. Come!"

I looked at James and reassured him as best I could with my expression. Then I followed the officer over to the train car. It took everything for me to simply leave my son one hundred yards behind me, but I had no choice.

"Come inside the car," he said while we walked, many of the surrounding prisoners trying not to stare at us.

As soon as we were inside he pointed for me to enter his compartment. I noticed how clean it was, how thick the mattresses were on the bunk bed, how stocked the food supply was—canned sardines, mustard, loaves of bread. There were two chairs.

"Sit," he said, and I did. "Don't talk, *zek*. Don't say a fucking word. I mean it. I just want to give you a good meal. Don't ask questions. Just eat it."

He handed me a fork and a plate with a mound of grated vegetables on it. I was so hungry that I began eating immediately. Upon first taste, I recognized the dish as *herring under a fur coat*. It's basically a layered salad made up of salted herring that is covered with boiled, grated vegetables. I could taste eggs, carrots, potatoes, and onions. And the dish looked like a fur coat because the top was covered with beets and mayonnaise, giving it a white-on-purple look. It was the best meal I'd ever had, and again, I'd always hated beets.

After I'd completely devoured it, the tall, olive-skinned officer who'd been standing over me the entire time handed me a bottle of beer. I guzzled it down within twenty seconds, never stopping to question why he was giving me this special treatment.

"You can go back outside and wash yourself now," he said.

"Comrade Officer," I said, putting the bottle down and standing, "would it be okay to bring my son inside for a bite? I must tell you that I am a close associate of an important American diplomat who—"

"Shut your fucking mouth, *zek*!" he said, poking me in the chest with the tip of his rifle hard enough to move me. "I told you not to speak. That is your last warning."

I did as he said and exited. Trying to guess what this offering of food had been about was futile at this point. It meant something, but I hadn't the energy to try to guess. I just knew that the next two days' ration of my black bread would go to my son. I certainly had enough in my belly to last a good while.

On my way through the crowd again, I could see that the four others had joined James by the river, a sight that pleased me. I looked upstream and could see bare-chested prisoners washing their shirts in the water. They would rather wear wet, clean clothes than dry, dirty ones. I hadn't really taken the time to concern myself with how the officers had arrested us that night, never allowing us to bring a single item with us. All we had were the clothes on our backs and our passports.

"You've returned," said young Yury, holding his blue newsboy hat at his side, his thick head of brown hair soaking wet, as he'd obviously dipped it in the river. "What did he want with you?"

"He wanted to discuss my passport."

Why I was lying I didn't quite know. I just knew that whatever the reason behind the meal would reveal itself at some point. Perhaps I could find a way to get James a serving next time. Or would there even be a next time?

I looked down at James, his shirt off, sparkling beads of river water dancing in his frizzy hair, the sun warming his soft, cocoa skin. He had removed his brown soft leather shoes and socks as well. Seeing him in this condition—hungry, exhausted, and tormented—made me think about what had initially prompted me to leave our safe haven in the Montmartre section of Paris.

Back there I felt as if we were immersed in an international artists' community that had *run away* from the real world. Our day-to-day way of life, particularly amongst us American coloreds, felt temporary, like we were all cognizant of the fact that we needed to get back into the arena and fight for real structural and systematic change, the kind that would affect everyday Negroes, ones who couldn't afford to run to Paris and play pretend, ones who were forever entangled in the long-existing and carefully woven web of institutional racism.

That is what I believed then. But my current predicament had me questioning this decision. My son and daughter hadn't cared about any of this high-minded, critical thinking, this sociological examination of sorts that I'd been dead set on continuing. They'd been too busy playing with their carefree friends—oblivious to whatever frowns might have come their way from the occasional Parisian bigot.

I put my arm around James and pulled him close, looking downstream again at where the murdered *zek*'s hat had drifted. His son, if he had one, would forever wonder where he was. The agony that child would have to endure was unfathomable. It was a pain I couldn't dare let my boy experience. I had to stay alive.

4

Cap-Haïtien, Haiti
Three years earlier

AMERICA'S OCCUPATION WAS FINALLY COMING TO AN END. BOBBY and I stood along the pier in Cap-Haïtien as the USS *Houston* approached with President Roosevelt aboard. There was an excitement in the air, and many locals cheered and waved, hoping to get a glimpse of the president. He was visiting the island to put an end officially to America's occupation. Later that evening, Bobby and I actually joined the president and his staff for a private dinner. I didn't say a word. I just sat there and marveled at the way Bobby was able to so freely interact with Roosevelt's inner circle.

A lot had changed for Bobby and me. Not only had he been selected for a post as Minister-Counselor to Moscow, Russia, he had also asked me to come along as his personal assistant. He'd first learned of the possibility in September of last year, and the official news had come down this March. Per his orders, I'd spent the last ten months inundated with studying Russian. It had been an arduous task to say the least, but I'd made considerable progress and now considered myself semi-conversational. "A God-given gift for world languages," Bobby liked to say I had.

A few days later we arrived in Pétion-Ville, not far from Port-au-Prince, and convened for dinner at the beautiful little Hotel

Kinam, a white-on-white gingerbread house that had been around since the turn of the century. We sat down to eat on the veranda just before sundown and I marveled at the design of the place. I knew that most of Port-au-Prince's gingerbread houses had been built by just three architects: Joseph Maximilien, George Baussan, and Léon Mathon, all of whom were Haitian but had trained in Paris. And though we were in Pétion-Ville, I wondered if they'd built this nine-room hotel as well.

With the sun setting in the distance beyond the almond and palm trees, I envisioned myself having a go at building such a home for Loretta and the kids. The latticework was central to its theme; it was wrapped around the porches, doors, and windows. Victorian in style, the home felt wide, high, and open, and the tall turret roofs looked like snow-cone cups, the pointy tops seeming to tickle the clouds.

It was homes like these that made me pause and delight in the fact that I was an engineer. I sipped from my wineglass, wanting to dwell on pierced frieze boards, board-and-batten shutters, sawn balusters, braced arches, and scrolled brackets. But for now, I needed to be present at dinner.

We dined over chicken and cashew nuts, pickles, fried pork, crab and lalo leaf stew, rice with black mushrooms, and goat head. As we were all to depart for Moscow in two weeks, the dinner being treated as a bon voyage celebration. It was a table of eight, both of our wives in attendance, along with both sets of children.

"It's good to see you feeling better, Grant," I said, referring to Bobby's nine-year-old son. He'd previously been dealing with a bout of the chickenpox, an illness his eight-year-old sister, Greta, hadn't caught yet.

"He likes to sleep all the time," she said, biting into a chicken leg, as Grant rolled his eyes and half smiled.

"Do not," said Grant. "You do more than me. I'm just resting like M. . . . like Dr. . . . like Dr.—"

"Dr. Madison," said Dorene, rubbing the top of little Grant's blond head, a color he'd inherited from her.

"Yeah . . . him!" said Grant, spooning his rice.

Dorene doted on her children the way Loretta did ours. She was also similar to my wife in build, tall and thin with delicate features and a gentle disposition befitting an heiress. A calm, introspective woman with a stoic posture, a pristine etiquette.

"I would like to propose a toast," said Bobby, picking up the bottle of Bordeaux and filling our four glasses. He then pretended as if he might pour some in the children's glasses. "James, Ginger . . . Grant, Greta . . . would you like to join us?"

"Have you gone mad?" asked Dorene, all of us laughing as she took the pitcher of water and began refilling their glasses.

"Ah, come on . . . I want to try some wine," said my son, James, demonstratively tilting his head to the side and acting disappointed. He had a flair for the dramatic. "Mom, can I try some wine . . . please!"

"Yes, in about ten years," answered Loretta.

The children laughed, particularly his twin sister, Ginger, while James continued playing heartbroken, all the while doing so only to attract more attention, which he craved. But he always knew when to quit and not push it to the point of disruption. He was a good boy.

"In due time, dear James, my boy!" said Bobby, lifting his wineglass with a smile, his cheeks a bit pinkish from the two reds he'd already consumed. But he was the picture of good health, his dark brown hair fixed in the style of Clark Gable, his physique as trim and fit as it was back in our Bureau days.

"Yes," said Loretta, raising her glass, "in due time, my son."

Dorene and I lifted ours as well, and the children followed suit.

"To the Soviet Union!" said Bobby. "To Moscow, in particular! A place that can only be described as the great unknown! May she welcome us with open arms, keep us safe and warm through frozen winter with her sheepskin coats, and provide plenty of snow for these youngsters . . . so they can throw snowballs in Gorky Park while wearing their *ushankas*!"

"Yay!" said the children collectively.

"Hear, hear!" I said, all of us leaning over the candlelit mahogany table and clinking glasses.

"Eh, Comrade Sweet!" said Bobby, holding his glass against mine a bit longer, looking at me the way a happy younger brother might show his affection to the older. At this particular time, and in this particular place, we were *all* happy.

After the children had finished their dinner, Sissy, the Haitian nanny who'd been with the Ellingtons throughout our posting, whisked the four of them off to their respective hotel rooms so they could ready themselves for bed. It gave the four of us a chance to dive into a more substantive discussion.

"I'm going to miss this hot weather," said Bobby, taking a drag from his cigarette, his white linen shirt still clinging to his sweaty skin. "These veranda fans make it feel just about perfect. Having said that, I can't help but worry about the many throughout this land with no way of relieving themselves from it."

"That is why I married this man," said Dorene, striking a match and lighting her Dunhill, then Loretta's. "He is always thinking of others, never completely able to bathe in his own reverie."

"So your father has finally given you his complete blessing?" said Bobby, taking her hand and kissing it. "Her father would have preferred she marry McCormick Bradington. We both were at Columbia law school together, but unlike his parents, mine don't own the entire state of Maine."

"You're from Ohio, Dear," said Dorene, furrowing her brow before smiling. Her bright white teeth were almost too perfect, as if an accessory to her coral linen dress.

"Notice how she didn't object to my claim of McCormick's considerable wealth," said Bobby. "She's wonderful at deflecting, Press."

"Where I'm from we call that good-natured," I said, having grown used to him calling me both Press and Prescott.

"Thank you, Prescott," said Dorene. "I chose this man because of his passion. And my father knows this. His passion for foreign service is as valuable to my family as any amount of wealth."

"I thought you said I had no more than six years before I needed to secure an ambassadorship," said Bobby.

"I love how you twist my words," she said. "I said I'd be surprised if it took you longer than that, Dear."

"Word twisting is a skill this one here has mastered as well," said Loretta, bumping my leg with the side of her knee, as she took a drag and then a sip of wine.

Dorene's father was the founder and chairman of Stanfield Gas and Electric, one of the major American utilities companies. To say she came from a considerable amount of wealth would be a gross understatement. But she was progressive in her thinking and completely at ease around common folk. Let's just say she gave the word *rich* a good name, if that's possible.

"I think they've both gotten worse at it, though," said Dorene. "This . . . word twisting. Since we've been here on the island, I mean. Do please take this as a completely innocuous comment, boys, but you may be making yourselves susceptible to the island's voodoo. Beware in particular of the *pati gason* hex. American men are quite susceptible. You can be completely oblivious and then . . . wham!"

"Yes," said Loretta, knee tapping me again. "Twisting your wife's words opens you up to it."

"Wow," I said, "I could have sworn I was just sitting here minding my own business. Should I take cover?"

Dorene and Loretta held back their laughter, shaking their heads in the affirmative while Bobby gave me a look of empathy.

"I believe," said Loretta, "that the curse is designed to make a man's marriage slowly fall apart. Right, Dorene?"

"Yes, a sorcerer . . . or *bokor*, to be specific, could cast one on you without you even participating in a ceremony."

Bobby and I were still listening and playing along, but the way our wives were working in tandem had our eyebrows raised. It was as if they were able to finish each other's sentences or thoughts on cue.

"That's enough," said Bobby. "We get your point."

"Do you?" said Dorene, playfully. "You've been twisting my words since I've known you. It is just part of being an American man, I believe. Don't forget, I've traveled the world many times over and find that this word *manipulation* is unique to you American boys."

"Designed to make a man's marriage fall apart, huh, Loretta?" I said.

"You heard me, handsome man. I've learned a lot from my gals on the island. They run this country, boy. Once you are given the *pati gason* hex, your natural word twisting gets worse, then turns to flat out compulsive lying, then, dare I say, turns to rampant cheating. The wife then has no choice but to leave the bastard for a new, faithful man. Do you have anything to add, my dear sister, Dorene?"

The two clinked glasses.

"Only that the final stage of the curse, which happens even after the man is left alone and without family, is that a significant body part of his begins to decay and eventually fall off."

"Oh God!" Bobby and I said in unison.

They both inhaled and looked at each other, giggling, obviously inebriated in the most endearing way.

"Touché!" I said, picking up the bottle of wine.

"Yes," said Bobby. "Touché!"

I began refilling all of our glasses while the three of them lit a new smoke.

"Don't ever twist her words again, Bobby," I said.

"Oh, believe me," he said, playfully nodding, "I'll try not to."

"Good," said Dorene.

"But if I fail and do, may these splendid little digs at our maleness continue aboard your father's yacht next week."

"They shall," she said, the two of them kissing.

"Wait," I said, "we're not traveling on—"

"No!" said Bobby, excitedly. "Change of plans. The new agenda is for the yacht to pick us up at Cap-Haïtien around noon on the fourteenth. From there we will steam to Miami, then up the east coast to Nantucket, where we'll spend four days at her parents' estate."

"Oh my gosh!" said Loretta. "This sounds absolutely fantastic."

"It is a treat of all treats," said Bobby. "Believe me. Dorene doesn't mind my boyish excitement when it comes to traveling on the *Trumpet*. The first time I stepped aboard the ninety-six-footer, I ran around it like a child who'd stumbled upon Neverland. It is a pristine ship."

"And I really want to make this special for the four children," said Dorene, looking at Loretta. "Let's let them each have their own room."

"Well . . . okay!" said Loretta, surprised at all of it.

"We will depart for France from New York City aboard the *Ile de France*," said Bobby. From Le Havre we'll board the train to Moscow. Then our work begins, Prescott. It will be time for you to break out those Russian words for real."

"I still can't believe your acumen for languages, Prescott," said Dorene. "To say you are indispensable is not enough. Have you thanked him every day, Bobby?"

"Of course. But it's not just translating. I haven't had the opportunity to speak with Ambassador Bullitt yet. He's, of course, already been posted at Spaso House, but it sounds as if there are a myriad of technical problems with the house, and once Bullitt learns of Prescott's engineering skills, he'll likely be inclined to put him on a personal service contract as a technical consultant."

"But then how will you survive the city without your right-hand man, dear?" said Dorene.

Bobby turned to her. "Maybe you can learn Russian and take his place."

"I just may."

"I'm actually looking forward," I said, "to seeing if we coloreds are indeed treated as well in the Soviet Union as so many have claimed. According to an old friend of mine, Claude

McKay, he damn near forgot his skin was black while there. Du Bois has called their social experiment promising. Maybe I can bottle it and take it to America. Could it be that we and our children might find it a country that can offer us something altogether new?"

"Not even Paris offered us that," said Loretta. "Almost! But not one hundred percent!"

"No!" I said. "And we want our children to feel equal one hundred percent of the time. Not sixty or even seventy percent of the time! Not *only* in certain sections of certain towns! Am I being greedy?"

"Of course not!" said Dorene.

"There were times in Paris," said Loretta, "when we ventured out of our little community and I felt *less than*, or like I had wandered into the wrong place. And it was always, in some less than straightforward way, made clear to me by somebody that I should have *known better.*"

"Really?" said Dorene. "Even in Paris, Loretta?"

"Yes. Only in certain areas, but . . . there were times."

"But make no mistake," I said, "it pales in comparison to the systematic horror that exists in the U.S."

Bobby shook his head. "I was born in the wrong era for a white man, because for the life of me, I've never been able to wrap my head around racism. I truly haven't once, since the four of us have been sitting here enjoying one another, thought about the fact that you two have darker skin. I can only hope, as I set about my quest to become an ambassador, that President Roosevelt has an ounce of this same feeling in his bones."

Dorene seemed concerned. "Well, I know that the first lady has those sentiments personally. And if the president cannot get all the way there politically, well, then, shame on him. The United States of America can never consider itself whole and just until absolute social equality is felt by every single one of its citizens."

"Can I ask why you didn't run for president?" I said.

"Because I'm a woman. And as farfetched as this may sound, I believe a black man will become president of the U.S. before a woman does. But women's rights is certainly an issue the first lady is championing. We live in a time where real social change is on the horizon. At least I choose to believe that."

"You're so decent," I said. "Both you and Bobby are rare. You spoke earlier, Dorene, about my acumen for languages. Part of the reason I'm obsessed with languages is—"

"You're obsessed with everything," said Bobby. "And in a good way. Prescott doesn't like when I go here, darling, because he doesn't like to toot his own horn, but he knows a lot about literature, art, geology, cooking, sport, opera, theater, geography, history, and, of course, politics."

"A real renaissance man," said Dorene. "And you're an engineer."

"I want my entire life to be a renaissance . . . a revival of learning, a renewal of spirit, of vigor."

"Oh," said Loretta, "let us not leave out his interest in fashion and horticulture."

"Horticulture!" said Bobby with a look of bewilderment while Loretta nodded.

"There's a simple reason for all of this," I said. "When you're a Negro in this world, it is certainly in your best interest to be a jack-of-all-trades. And I try to be at least a master of a few. I think of that Negro of yesteryear . . . or of today. When he is constantly told by the powers that be that he is basically nobody and hasn't the right to do anything . . . he spends a lifetime trying to prove that he *is* somebody, and that he can *perhaps* do everything."

I sipped and watched the three of them smoke. I felt that I could say anything around the Ellingtons. I was completely at ease.

"I think it's a subconscious thing, though," I said. "I'm not actively trying to *prove* anything to myself or anybody. But you grow up hearing stories about ancestors, slave stories, and then you feel a lot of this racism yourself, and even though you've accomplished a lot in the way of education, you're aware that the general consensus is that *your type* is nothing. Such ignorance breeds a burning desire in you to try to soak up every single thing this world has to offer that is free. Learning is free."

"And you love it," said Loretta. "I've never gotten the sense that you're trying to prove anything, so that part is indeed a subconscious thing." She turned to Bobby and Dorene. "I think he gets inspired by the characters in the novels he reads."

"Let's just say I'm very hirable," I said, provoking laughter.

"What about the subject of law, Prescott?" asked Bobby.

"Now that . . . I hate."

The two ladies laughed at Bobby, knowing he'd worked hard to earn his law degree. But, as always, he took it in jest.

Dorene held up her glass. "All I know is that we are the two luckiest women in Haiti, married to two gorgeous men. Bobby, my dear, you do know how perfectly handsome you remain, don't you?"

"Thank you. I try."

"You do more than try, dear. You run every day." She began rubbing his chest. "And it shows on all six feet of you."

"I just wish I were a wee bit taller, say six feet two, like my translator friend there. Does he remind you often how fit he is, Loretta?"

She rolled her eyes. "You just don't know. The man loves one thing more than me. A mirror."

"Stop!" I said.

"He's always posing and primping and strutting around the bedroom. He *was* six-two when I met him, but I think he continues to grow because he stretches himself every day after doing that stuff with the kicking and the punching and—"

"Kodokan Judo," I said. "And don't make fun. Perhaps Dorene would like to know more about the benefits of meditative, physical routines."

"He still does it every single morning without fail," said Loretta.

"You'll have to show her on the yacht," said Bobby. "You'll have quite the captive audience. I would love to see my wife learn hand-to-hand combat. This trip to your parents, dear, can't come soon enough."

5

Vladivostok, Russia
September 1937

THERE HAD BEEN MORE TRAIN STOPS ALONG THE WAY, MORE BLACK
bread, an occasional cup of soup, and yes, a few more private,
hearty meals for me with the guard. We'd been traveling for
weeks now, and had finally come to the end of our journey, at
least all of us prisoners thought so upon hearing the guard's initial words to us. "The train is stopping for good now that we are
near Vladivostok," he said, the lights coming on inside the car,
as he stood outside of our compartments. "There is no more
land to travel. The train cannot keep going into the Sea of
Japan."

He and the other guard snickered at his comment before he
continued.

"But this is not your final stopping point. This is a transit
camp. Don't ask how many days you will be here because I will
hit you with the hammer again. Some will leave sooner, some
later. It is not freezing season yet, so you will be okay to stand inside the fences until we take you to the ships. From there we will
take you north to Kolyma. Then you will be finished traveling.
When you are not in the barracks or in roll call line, this transit
camp is wide open for you to walk and sit and pray and cry and
die. No! Don't die! Too many scum have already died on the way

here because they were too weak. And now . . . we don't want to have to shoot anyone because you try to run away over the fence. Do you hear me?"

We all let out a rather weak, collective, *"DA!"*

"Good!" he said. "Many out there are political prisoners, counterrevolutionaries. And others are rapists, murderers, and robbers. It doesn't matter to us. You are all in there together. And don't worry about your filthy smell. It rains a lot here this time of year. You will get a nice, long bath when the clouds come."

Moments later we filed out into a vast, flat area. There was mostly dirt under our feet, but off in the distance in all directions was green vegetation, and I could smell the sea. Perhaps this portion of oak wood trees and ginseng plants had been carved away just for prisoners like us. We couldn't yet see the camp and were told to line up parallel to the train. I had my eyes almost completely closed, as the morning sunlight was excruciating.

"Listen, *zeks!*" said one of the guards. "You are car number twenty-eight for the entire time you're at this camp. You will be assigned to a specific barracks, too, once we are inside. Beginning later in the day, when we release you from the lines, you can walk around and try to build some strength. But if you hear the horn, you must line up for roll call."

After he finished lecturing us, he took roll and checked our papers and passports. Then our group, along with the other few thousand, began to walk toward the rear of the long train. When we were able to, we crossed the tracks and walked east, along a trail lined with oak woods. Once we were out in the open again, we could see wooden structures in the distance and dots of men. The closer we got, the more unbelievable the scene.

There were an astounding number of prisoners already waiting inside the holding camp, some of them in rows, some wandering about. It was a shock to my eyes, this sprawling corral of men that seemed to stretch to infinity. I wouldn't have been surprised if the number were close to a hundred thousand. It was a massive collection of filthy, hungry, emaciated souls.

As we were herded inside the barbed wire, I focused on the many wooden barracks beyond the *zeks*. There were rows and rows, but perhaps not enough to house us all. I wondered where some of us would sleep when it got dark, but then I realized I was doing the one thing a prisoner here should avoid—trying to think rationally about our circumstances. We were of course going to lie down right on the ground and sleep, or at least attempt to.

Once we were about halfway inside this so-called *tranzitka*, we were told to stop. I was struck by the uniformity of all the prisoners. The long, perfect rows of downtrodden souls resembled those one might see on a military base.

"Listen to me!" said our guard. "I've just been informed that you have been given barracks number twelve. But you are to remain in line here until further notice. Once we take roll again you will be free to move about. But you are to stay away from the barracks until nightfall. When we release you here shortly, you can use the latrine. Remember, later when the horn sounds, you better be in line for roll call. No one better be shitting or pissing then. That will be very bad for you . . . very bloody for you!"

The rest of that day was miserable. We never were allowed to move about, as we were forced to stand in line until dusk and watch the other prisoners near the barracks, those who'd been here a while, roam around freely. The only positive was that it felt like good exercise just being able to finally stand for a long period of time. We were getting the blood out of our asses, the numbness out of our backs and legs. The only time we were interrupted was when some nurses came by and examined our teeth and pinched our buttocks for dystrophy. They were obviously checking to see which of us were still suitable to work.

Studying the camp, I noticed a long fence that separated the right set of barracks from the left. I was guessing that our guard had lied to us, and that these were two separate zones, one for political prisoners and one for common criminals.

With the sun about to dip below the oak woods in the distance, we were finally led to barracks number twelve. Inside the dark, filthy room that smelled of vomit, wooden bunk beds—each set stacked five high—lined the walls. After we all used the latrine and ate some rye dumplings with herring, I secured a bottom bed for myself, and one for James just above me. There was no talking on this night, only a long attempt to sleep through the filthy smell of the thin, sticky, straw mattresses and the itchy bites of mosquitoes and bed bugs. Nightmares would come easy, but sleep most certainly would not.

The following morning, after lining up for roll call and finally being allowed to walk about, the six from our train compartment walked north toward the farthest barrack.

"I would rather be a cow or a horse," said Yury, walking beside me. "At least they have proper stalls and barns. And I bet hay tastes better than the black bread or the urine soup they give us."

"I, for one, am looking forward to the soup," I said. "Let's try to think positive. Maybe we can salvage our sanity for a little while longer, Yury."

"You Americans!"

"I'm starving," said Mikhail, dragging his feet.

"So am I," said Boris.

"Listen to me," said the old man Abram, his Russian rather raspy, his old body damn near completely withered away. "Besides the boy here, James, we've all spent decades eating food, filling our bellies to maximum I'll bet. So now it is time to overcome this feeling of hunger. It's just that. A feeling! Overcome it! Think of the thousands and thousands of meals you've eaten, and imagine they were all consumed so you could survive this day, this week, this month, these years. Our lives have been a feast, and now we must accept this nothingness for a while and not succumb to it. It will all balance out in the end, this life of feasting and starving. We are loaded with nutrients, equipped to survive the torture. At least you all! My battle is with age."

"You seem to be walking just fine, Abram," I said.

"Because I was a runner." He coughed. "Even when I was teaching history at the university in Leningrad for all of those decades, I'd run every day at lunch with a colleague. In fact, he's the one I was visiting in Moscow when we were both arrested. Where he is now, I don't know."

"What did you do for work, Prescott, when you were free?" asked Yury.

"I was an engineer and a teacher, and I worked for a diplomat. I was—"

"Look!" said Yury. "There are women in that camp on the other side of the barbed wire fence in the distance."

The six of us looked to the north a couple hundred yards away.

"You told me the women went north from Moscow, Abram," I said.

"No women came on our train," he said. "Those women have been here. They came on different trains."

"I want to see Mommy!" said James, crying and beginning to walk fast toward the fence.

"Stop, son!" I yelled, running after him, clutching his arm and giving him a hug. "Your mother is not there!"

"She is!" he said, trying to break free from me. "I know she is! I want to see her!"

"You will, son. You will. Just not right now. You hear?"

Sobbing, he nodded into my chest. He felt so light, and his cry was barely audible. His body was too worn down to make tears.

"I'm here, son. I love you. Nothing's going to happen to you. But don't run away from me again. Understand?"

Once more, he nodded.

"It's okay!" said Abram, approaching and putting his arm around James. "You will see your mother again, boy. I am an old man who knows this. Look at me."

James pulled away from my clutch and gazed up at the old, wise Russian.

"I miss my children, boy. I know you are scared." He coughed. "But you have a strong father. Trust him. Stay by his side. All of you . . . come!"

The six of us all huddled together.

"We are in hell," said Abram. "Stalin's hell! But we can stick together and support one another . . . keep each other alive. Try not to think of tomorrow. Try to think of only right now. Help one another with kind words and encouragement. Our spirits won't die. You, Boris . . . who did you leave behind?"

"My mother and father," said the blond-haired twenty-something-year-old who'd been sitting to my left the entire trip. "But they are in Sweden. I was studying at Moscow State University. I learned Russian there."

"Think of them," said Abram. "And don't stop. You will see them again. And you, Mikhail . . . you have been sitting to my right for a month and I've heard you weeping under your breath. Whom do you weep for?"

"My wife," said Mikhail. "My parents have been dead for years. My sister lives in Paris, so she is alive and well. But my wife is still home in Moscow where I worked as a clerk. She is pregnant. My child will be born in weeks and I won't be there. I will never see my child and wife again."

The tall, handsome, olive-skinned Mikhail stiffened his arms at his sides, closed his eyes, and began to cry. He didn't hold back, and the anguish on his young, angular face helped tell the story. He was maybe thirty, but the gray specks in his black hair and thin beard suggested he was aging rapidly.

"Be strong, young man!" said Abram, touching his hand to Mikhail's shoulder. "You must stay alive for your yet unborn child and lovely wife. She will be waiting for you. I don't care if you spend all ten years in the camps, you must stay alive."

"It's important to watch each other's backs," I said, scanning the population. "There might be some real animals in here. Zones be damned! It's not enough to simply stay mentally strong. We have to stay mentally alert as well."

"You and Boris are the only ones imposing enough to defend

yourselves," said Yury. "In fact, Comrade Sweet, you look like a sportsman. How have you managed to maintain your large build during this journey? Are you Americans all like this, like machines that don't need food." He looked at James. "Of course not! Your son looks like me. He looks weak and thin. But you, Comrade Sweet . . . you look very alive."

"I began the trip in very good condition," I said. "I had built up a lot of muscle and it has served me well, I suppose. But it will atrophy soon enough. Muscle isn't immune to the negative effects of being sedentary, not even mine."

"When I used to hear stories five years ago about the prisons," said Abram, "I heard that they separated the politicals from the murderers and rapists. And I still believe it's true. The guards just told us that story about monsters in our midst to further torture us. No! The real animals are in the zone on the other side, waiting to go to Kolyma where *then* we'll have to avoid them."

"Maybe," I said, "but we should be cautious nonetheless. Maybe those on the other side are just the ones getting ready to leave first. We can't be sure. Are you feeling okay, son?"

"My stomach is swollen," he softly said, his Russian words nasal-sounding from his emotional episode.

"Mine feels the same way, James," said Boris. "Yet I am still starving. It must be normal."

"It is," I said. "It's just water retention in your gut, son. Bloat from a lack of protein. Try to ignore it."

I had some extra bread in my pocket that I wanted to give James, but figured I'd wait until the two of us had a moment alone.

"Negro *zek* Sweet!" said the familiar guard approaching. "You need to come with me now."

I looked at him and then at James. Was he here to take me for another private meal? Maybe. But the tone in his voice sounded different this time, more urgent. I couldn't help but feel real concern over leaving James.

"Can my son come with me?" I boldly, and perhaps stupidly, asked.

"No! Come! Now!"

Abram nodded at me, telling me with his sunken, droopy eyes that he'd watch over my boy. The old man even put his arm around James to further ease my panic. But my instinct told me I would be leaving my boy for more than a few minutes this time.

"Please!" I said to the guard, pleading with my eyes, hoping the private meals I'd eaten in front of him had somehow led to him taking a personal liking to me. But they hadn't. He frowned at me, raised his rifle, and struck me in the stomach.

"Daddy!" cried James, as Abram held him back.

I leaned over trying to catch my breath.

"Toropit'sya!" said the guard, his voice getting angry.

I took the bread from my pocket and handed it to James, hoping it wouldn't further draw the guard's ire. It did not. He stood there holding his rifle. As I began to move, he turned and led me south, past the long stretch of barracks again, the hungry, aimless, wandering *zeks* oblivious to us.

We exited the camp and headed toward the train. Waiting beside the tracks was a black vehicle, two unfamiliar officers sitting up front. As we approached, my accompanying guard opened the back door.

"Get in!" he said. And I did.

The car started moving, just the two officers and me inside. I was not scared. I was worried about James but did not fear for my own life. And as the hours passed, and this long drive toward some newer version of hell continued, my nerves stayed calm. Call it faith. Call it experience. Call it bravery. All I was certain of was that a sudden calm washed over me as we began to enter a new type of terrain. We were driving deeper and deeper into a thick woods—so thick that the afternoon sunlight began to fade away. The fir, spruce, and oak seemed to grow taller with each passing minute, the road a little more rugged.

6

Aboard the Trumpet yacht
Three years earlier

ALL FIVE CABINS ON THE *TRUMPET* WERE NAMED AFTER AFRICAN wild animals. On that continent, the most impressive and elusive of all of those roaming the land are categorized as the Big Five. They include the lion, elephant, buffalo, leopard, and rhinoceros. Loretta and I were staying in the Lion's Den on the lower deck.

Dorene's father wasn't a hunter but had visited Africa on several occasions and had taken some impressive photographs of the Big Five, all of which decorated the walls of the respective cabins. We hadn't been aboard the beautiful boat for a minute before James and Ginger begged to have the Rhinoceros Cabin. Something about the animal's long, pointy horn captivated them.

We had dined on the main deck both nights so far—trout on the first, duck on the second—and had all watched the sunset each night before winding down with butter half cake and tea. The ship's crew was at our beck and call around the clock.

Upon first laying eyes on the beautiful white yacht, I suddenly had a sweet tooth, as its design reminded me of a big bowl of vanilla ice cream with caramelized almonds sprinkled on top. The round windows dotted along its hull were framed with dark mahogany, and its two decks and railing were made of cedar.

For Loretta and me, the trip up the Atlantic toward Nantucket felt like a second honeymoon, our first having been a simple weekend in Montpelier, Vermont. As I lay on the bed in my white T-shirt and underpants watching her wash her face at the sink, her white silk nightgown shining in the cabin light, I realized how completely attracted I still was to her after eighteen years of marriage.

"Can you imagine getting used to this, Love?" she said, turning to me while pat-drying her face with a washcloth. "I mean, I'd like to think I'm a changed woman, having seen what I saw in Haiti. I certainly consider myself much more of a woman of conscience now. But, still, could you ever see yourself living like this, like a king?"

"All right, Miss Princess and the Pea!"

"No, I'm serious. Could you?"

"In all my life," I said, hands behind my head on the pillow, legs straight and crossed at the ankles, "I've never even taken the time to imagine such luxury."

"Well, I, for one, Mr. Sweet, am a woman who would *like* to get used to it." Her voice sounded playful. "I wish this big ol' yacht would just keep going and going around the world until our children are all grown up. I'm half joking, but then again . . . on the serious side . . . they're so safe on this boat, so jubilant and carefree. I know it's a vacation, not the real world, but it's just special to see all of us so completely together and bonded as a family unit. I'm trying to take it all in, knowing that we are very fortunate to be experiencing this exact moment in time. I feel like you're the captain that's keeping us protected. I find it beyond attractive."

"I'm your captain, huh?" I said, watching her brush her long hair.

"You are my captain, Love. You are the only man on this yacht who could fix it if it broke down . . . because the helmsman and crew darn sure seem to value your opinion more than I'd expect. And don't think I haven't seen the way you've been explaining to Bobby how the mahogany was used throughout to offset the white exterior, and how the planking was laid, and the type of fuel—"

"And the hydraulics, the propulsion, the electrical system, the wheel room, the—"

"Stop it, Mister!" She hurried over and jumped in the bed, pretending as if she might land on me.

"That was too close for comfort, lady." I pulled her close and we lay on our sides face to face. "Sorry I talk like that. You *did* marry an engineer."

"No, I married a very *sexy* engineer."

"*Ty krasivaya,*" I whispered in Russian, running my fingers through her long hair.

"What did you say, love?"

"You are beautiful."

"Thank you."

"*Ya lyublyu tebya,*" I said, our noses nearly touching.

"And that means?"

"It means 'I love you.'"

"I love you, too."

"Why do you brush your hair at night again?"

"Because it pulls the natural oils from my scalp into my hair, and that's very healthy for it while I sleep."

"Sleep? Can't that wait?"

"Oh yeah, love." She spoke softly. "It can wait a long time."

She began kissing me and we stayed like this for a while until I ran my hand along her thigh and she opened herself to me. I reached farther under her gown and pulled her black panties off with one hand as she straightened her legs to help me. There was a natural smell to her skin that wasn't always present—one that I believed indicated how intimate she was feeling. Of course, maybe I just wanted to believe that—my ego at play. Whatever the case, there would be no foreplay tonight, no setting the mood, for I saw in her mirroring eyes what we both were desiring.

Scooting off of the mattress, I stood at the end of the bed and removed my underpants while she remained on her back.

"Leave my gown on," she said, sliding toward me a bit and lifting her long legs up for me to grab. I took both of my hands and placed them on her ankles, pulling her to bed's edge, where I would remain standing. I slid my hands down to her under-knees, calmly pushing her bent legs back, her gown bunched up at the waist. I leaned forward, my hands still cupping her knees while I entered her. She cried out softly. Once again I felt us be-coming one. And I would try to prolong this oneness for as long as possible tonight. My mind had a singular thought: This was the only woman I would ever love.

Weeks later, on August 1, as our train approached Moscow—having chugged from France through Belgium, Germany, and Poland—the eight of us looked out of the windows and I tried to imagine what this new world might be like for us. I thought of the men I'd known who'd been here and had said such positive things. Men like my old poet friend Claude McKay, and my idol, W.E.B. Du Bois. What was the essence of this place that had so captivated these colored gentlemen?

Even the famous poet Langston Hughes had been here just two years earlier. I'd read where he had said of this place: "Folks went out of their way there to show us courtesy. On a crowded bus, nine times out of ten, some Russian would say, '*Negochanski tovarish*—Negro comrade—take my seat!'"

Maybe there was something powerful going on here, some ap-proach to changing unjust societies for the better good that I could use to help my people overcome their continuing plight against global, racial injustice. Might the still-burgeoning revo-lution that was taking place here serve as the blueprint for other countries? Perhaps the world needed a revolution. A young col-ored essayist I'd read a blurb about while in Haiti, a Mr. Richard Wright, seemed to believe so. And if he was back home in Amer-ica feeling this way, who was I, an expatriate, and not by choice, to dismiss him? I needed to learn more.

I looked across the aisle at Dorene. I could have been more forthcoming with her on that festive night back in Pétion-Ville. I could have told her that there was a spiritual element behind my insatiable appetite for learning. For I seek to learn nothing merely for myself. I do it to honor that Negro of long-ago days. Perhaps he might have been lashed to within an inch of his life had he so much as dared to even open a book. I do it for him because I am able. How could I not? Even when I get angry at these ignorant men of today, I hear him whispering to me. He's saying, *No matter how tired your mind grows . . . how saddened your heart . . . how troubled your spirit . . . push forward in honor of me, you unshackled king!*

During the last portion of our train ride, as we entered the outskirts of Moscow, I took in the scenery. James and Ginger looked about as if experiencing a new world. Upon first sight, my perception of this part of Moscow wasn't positive. It was a rugged place—gray, dim, and harsh, even under a clear blue sky. Yet, I was struck by the fact that so many women were everywhere doing what we in the Western world considered men's work—cleaning streets and driving trolley cars, many of them in padded overalls. It was forward-thinking equality on full display. Once we had disembarked at the station, we hopped on a trolley car and headed toward our destination—the Hotel National—where the chancery was staying. My daughter seemed particularly fixated on our stout, female driver. For reasons I could only imagine.

Perhaps Ginger was not only struck by the job this woman was doing, but by her appearance as well. She had a pretty face, and resembled what I'd seen of most the women here so far. They were huskily built, dressed in oversized, weathered, dark clothing—their skin drab. Dorene and Loretta stuck out like sore thumbs, as the Muscovite women wore no makeup or jewelry. Maybe my daughter was struck by this new-to-her-eyes representation of womanhood.

I, on the other hand, was taken by the architecture. I'd heard that the Red Square was pristine, but so far, as we drove through residential areas, all we'd seen were a bunch of log houses and dirt roads. I couldn't wait to see some stone structures, to lay eyes on the old Czarist architecture I'd read so much about.

But the people hustling about had a pep in their step, the men dressed in wrong-sized suits and bulky, square shoes. Taste in attire didn't seem to be an option. It was as if everyone had picked from the same pile of identical suits and garments, lucky if they'd picked the correct size.

As we continued through the city, my perception began to brighten and the sprawling city came alive. The people seemed happy in this bustling place. I could see the golden church domes in the distance and felt as if we were traveling on Moscow's only wide boulevard, as if we were in the middle of a maze made up of narrow cobblestone side roads.

Taking note of how the streets were dominated by trains of three-car trolleys, I turned to Bobby, who was sitting next to me. "What is the schedule for the rest of the day?" I asked.

"It depends," said Bobby. "Do you have to do your damn two-hour Kodokan exercise routine still? You haven't had a chance to do it today." He slapped my shoulder. "I'm just razzing you, Press."

"I'll do it first thing in the morning as always. It beats running, believe me!"

"Unbelievable." He shook his head. "Anyway . . . the schedule. We'll get the ladies checked in at the Hotel National, and then you and I will head over to Spaso House. Ambassador Bullitt has put aside a few minutes to receive us."

"Remind me what he's like again," I said.

"A perfectionist. Rather serious-minded, but knows how to kid. Likes the finer things. Much finer! Even drives a sports roadster. Comes from a very influential family in Philadelphia. A Yale man. He's made quite a reputation for himself over the years by establishing relationships throughout Europe. He even met Lenin back in 1919."

"You're kidding."

"No, he was part of the U.S. delegation to the Paris Peace Conference, but he visited Soviet Russia on a hush-hush mis-

sion. He was long thought to be considered for a posting whenever America and the Soviet Union continued relations."

"I wonder how he's taken to Stalin."

"I shall soon find out," he said. "I'm sure he's made every effort to establish a relationship. Bullitt is a workaholic. I'm not
sure he's much of a delegator, as he's prone to doing everything
himself. He's damn smart. But I'm anxious to see how the staff is
functioning. Anyway, he and I have a good relationship, one established off and on over the last ten years."

Moments later we headed down Mokhovaya Street and approached the hotel, which was on Manezhnaya Square, across
from the Kremlin. The entire area was breathtaking, a far cry
from the log houses, dirt roads, and cobblestone alleyways we'd
ridden past. This was the heart of Moscow, and every building
looked ancient, powerful—even magical.

"I heard," said Bobby, "that Lenin actually made his home
here at this hotel for a few days back when the Kremlin was
being repaired from damages. He stayed in room 107. As you
can tell, I have been in constant communication with staff members here since before we left Haiti, trying to learn all I could
before we arrived."

"Well, stop. You're getting my history bug all worked up."

"Okay, Press." He pointed to a five-story building next to the
hotel. "That building is called the Mokhovaya. It is where all of
our embassy staff has apartments and offices, our brand-new
chancery. I'd heard it was finally complete, but now I'm not
sure. Looks like they're still working, at least on the exterior. Apparently Bullitt is in negotiations to have a permanent embassy
and chancery compound built on some beautiful property
called Sparrow Hills."

"I wish we could walk for a while," I said. "My legs are so stiff.
I want to get the blood flowing and really feel this place."

"We can. Spaso House is about a mile down. We have an open
window to meet the ambassador between three and five. We'll
walk around a bit, at least head toward the Kremlin to get a

quick taste of the area, and then we'll catch a ride over to meet William."

As soon as we walked into the lobby of the hotel, a middle-aged colored woman dressed in a lovely gold dress and high heels greeted us. She had the air of a performer, her stance quite erect, her makeup, gold purse, polished nails, and perfect bun-style hair all like something out of a movie.

"You must be Prescott and Loretta Sweet," she said with a beaming smile, shaking both of our hands. "My name is Coretta Arle-Titz. I'm an American. The colored colony here in Moscow got wind of your pending venture this way some months back. Our journalist brother, Homer Smith, told us all. You didn't think we'd let a lovely colored family like yours travel all the way to this foreign land without a contingent of your people being here to greet you, did you?"

"Why thank you so much, Ms. Arle-Titz!" I said. "These are our children, Ginger and James. And these are our close friends, Bobby and Dorene Ellington, along with their children, Grant and Greta."

"Hello to you all!" she said, nodding her head to say hello. "Very nice to meet you! Listen, Mr. Ellington, you don't mind if we borrow the Sweets for about a half hour or so, do you? We have a group in the bar waiting to meet them. We won't keep them long. Promise!"

"Of course not," said Bobby, tapping me on the shoulder. "Look, Press, why don't you four go say hello and we'll get us all checked in. Then you and I can take our little walk. Sound good?"

"Appreciate that, Bobby. See you in a bit."

We followed Coretta through the lobby and into the restaurant bar. There had to be at least thirty colored men and women waiting for us. And as soon as we walked in they began to clap.

"Everyone!" said Coretta. "Our *colony additions* have arrived!"

We began shaking hand after hand as we walked through the group, many of them saying "welcome" and touching us on the shoulders. It was so warm and heartfelt, a lovely surprise to all four of us.

"Now listen!" said Coretta, handing Loretta and me some full glasses of wine from the bar and two glasses of soda to our children. "The Sweets are very tired, as I'm sure we can all imagine, having made that long-ass journey from the States ourselves, so they don't have time to meet you all today. However, I'd like for some of you who have been living in the Soviet Union for a while to tell them what brought you here. Maybe your stories will enlighten them, show them how truly free we feel here, as opposed to America. I'll start!"

"Go on now, girl!" shouted somebody, as if he'd been drinking for a while.

"Let us hear it, sista!" said another.

"I came before the Bolshevik Revolution," said Coretta, looking at Loretta and me. "I graduated from both the Leningrad and Moscow conservatories of music. I'm married to a piano professor who is Russian. And no one so much as bats an eye. We're free to be a mixed couple. And even when it comes to my wonderful husband, I make no bones about the fact that I was in a fabulous relationship with a czar before the revolution. Those were the good old days! Before they ran him out of town!"

"Hush!" said an imposing chocolate-skinned man who was sporting a big grin. "Lord knows who might be listenin' around the corner over there, Coretta girl!"

"Since you're the one hushin' me, Wayland," said Coretta, "why don't you go on and tell 'em about you." She jokingly fanned her face with her purse, as if she were hot. "Let me quit up in here! While I'm ahead, Loretta girl!"

She put out her hand for Loretta to grab and the two giggled.

"You forgot to tell 'em about how you got your start in Harlem," said Wayland, "and about how you are the best damn singer in Moscow. Our Coretta is being way too humble. Girl can sing in four languages!"

"Thank you, darlin' Wayland. Now go on and preach!"

"I ain't nobody!" said Wayland. "But I suppose I'm still trying to be. My name's Wayland Rudd. I came over in 1932 as part of the Negro group of twenty-two who'd been pegged to make a film about America's race problem. The film was to be called *Black and White.*"

"I heard about that," I said. "Much was written about the film project in all of the papers. Wow! You were a part of that, Mr. Rudd?"

"Yes, sir! But it never got to be made. President Roosevelt put pressure on the Kremlin to refrain from all propaganda against the U.S. Our race film qualified as just that, so Stalin axed it. He needed America's machines and technology more than he wanted to expose America's race problem. So, when all the other actors in the group headed home, including one Langston Hughes, I stayed here. I'm still trying to make it as a stage actor. But believe me, it is as hard here as it is on Broadway."

"You're not the only one from the group who stayed here," said a handsome brother from across the room.

"Shame on me!" said Wayland. "How could I have failed to mention my brother over there. That's Lloyd Patterson, y'all. He was with Langston and the group, too."

Lloyd just smiled and humbly waived.

"That film would have been groundbreaking," said Coretta. "We'll have to tell you four more about it later. I'm sure you're tired. We plan on having a much larger and lengthier gathering for you all soon. We just wanted to welcome you and let you know that you have plenty of family in this . . . damn near . . . other-planet-of-a-country. We all wish Emma Harris were here, too, to welcome you. She's back in the States now. Moved back last year. She had lived here the longest, since 1905. An outstanding concert soloist!"

"We called her the Mammy of Moscow," said Lloyd. "She would have cooked y'all a big Southern meal. She was from Kentucky. She cooked for every Negro in Moscow. Made us ham hocks, fried chicken, corn bread, hash, butter beans, cabbage! And she wasn't ashamed of being part of the czarist times when she had butlers and a wealthy Russian companion."

"Shoot!" said Wayland. "By no means was Mammy bashful about being a part of that czarist ilk. She would boast about that life right in front of these Stalinists, with their anti-bourgeois sentiments. And they left her alone, as they all admired her, too. She would straight up tell you, 'I'm like a cat with nine lives, honey. I always lands on my feet . . . been doing it all my life wherever I been. These Bolsheviks ain't gonna kill me.'"

"I remember," said Lloyd, laughing, "when Mammy was talking about being frustrated with having to live in a rundown apartment because of the Bolsheviks. She said, 'I would just love to be Stalin's cook. I'd put enough poison in his first meal to kill a mule.'"

Everybody shouted with laughter, including Loretta and me. James and Ginger just smiled and sipped their drinks.

"But Mammy actually knew Stalin and he liked her," said a man from the back. "I'm Oliver Golden, by the way. And since we're doling out professions, I happen to be an agronomist."

We waved at him and he continued.

"Mammy could get all kinds of food that no one else could find. She had her connections, probably from the peasants who still hadn't had their land turned into collective farms. They still knew her from the czarist days when she would purchase from them. The collectivization system is one that might leave you newly arrived Sweets wondering why we still like the Soviet Union so much. Simple. They treat us Negroes with such respect. Period."

"Go on now, Oliver," said Coretta. "Tell it."

Oliver cleared his throat. "I feel for the peasants, but still, it's okay for us to be selfish here in Russia and only see things from our perspective after over three hundred years of American slavery and oppression. Yes? At least that's what George here and I think. Say hello to our new kinfolk, Comrade George."

"Hello, Sweet family! I'm George Tynes from Virginia."

"Hello," we said.

"I'm an agronomist, too, but don't mind me. I'm not one to carry on about myself. I'm not so natural at it like my singing and acting comrades and sisters here. Just wanna say welcome! Oh, and I agree . . . I miss our Emma's cooking, too! No one like her!"

"Nope!" said Coretta, shaking her head the way one does when they miss somebody. "It just ain't the same here without our Emma, the Mammy of Moscow."

After our meet and greet, Loretta and I headed upstairs and got the kids settled. Then Bobby and I began our stroll south toward the Red Square. All I could smell was a mixture of engine and cigar smoke. But I marveled at the colorful buildings along the area between our hotel and the Kremlin.

"It feels so surreal finally being in this country," I said, "in this place that only seventeen years ago was home to the Bolshevik Revolution. I'm looking at all of these old buildings and trying to visualize Lenin and Trotsky leading their army of peasants against the powerful czars and overthrowing them. Hard to imagine."

"Also hard to imagine Lenin approving of Stalin's current treatment of Trotsky," said Bobby. "Having him expelled from the country and all. I'm pretty sure it was Trotsky whom Lenin wanted to have succeed him, not Stalin. Lenin definitely didn't trust Stalin. Even wanted him ousted as secretary general. John Reed would be quite upset were he alive today."

"Mmm, I don't know, Bobby," I said, studying the white stone building to my right, as our stroll continued. "I've read different accounts. Even though Trotsky was Lenin's right-hand man during the revolution, Lenin wasn't too fond of him, either, when it came to leading the country. He thought he was the most capable of all the candidates, but believed he was too arrogant. In reality, he wasn't too fond of anyone succeeding him. He wanted to increase the size of the governing body, the Central Committee, so that no *one man* would have too much power."

"Where is Trotsky by the way, Press? I ask because I'm only guessing you might know. Who am I kidding? Go ahead."

"Reports in April said he was forced to leave Barbizon, France. Hang on a second."

I touched Bobby on the arm and we stopped, taking a moment to look through a store window at a display that was set up. It was a bunch of loaves of black bread and mustard. I looked further into the store at the shelves that looked empty, save for a few that had more mustard and loaves of bread.

"Odd," I said, as we kept looking inside.

"Indeed."

"Like I was saying, and I should whisper this. He was forced to leave Barbizon because police could no longer guarantee his safety. Too many Russian spies."

"A life on the run."

"Stalin truly seems to want this man gone," I said. "Trotsky still has so much international support that Stalin probably fears he could return to Moscow someday and regain power."

"Speaking of power," said Bobby, "I think it's vital that Roosevelt project such to the world for as long as he's in office. Our work here will play a role in that. After all, we are only fifteen years removed from the Great War."

"I hear you," I said, "but, selfishly, I also have to always believe that the work we'll be doing, in whichever country, will in some way be helping coloreds, particularly colored Americans."

"It will be," he said. "Look at it this way. The work we're doing is critical. It involves massaging old wounds. If we can play even a tiny role in keeping this country and ours on good enough terms to influence the temperament, or even the *nerve*, of our enemies, it could prevent another war from breaking out. That, my friend, is helping the Negro by keeping him, quite bluntly, from dying along with the rest of America. That's just reality."

"I hear you," I said.

"Besides, Press, if I can eventually rise up and be an ambassador, and then maybe even a senator . . . hell . . . the president . . . I'll be in a position to influence those social issues we want addressed. Just stick with me and always take comfort in knowing you're playing a vital role and that you're doing all you can, Press. Jim Crow is not going to last forever. No way!"

We began walking again, crossing a wide road that long ago had been a big moat filled with water, which made the Kremlin an inaccessible fortress. I could feel the energy of this place and it felt good. Not one person had taken a second look at me, completely oblivious to my being colored. And it was genuine obliviousness. It was the first time I'd ever felt somewhat invisible, but in the most beautiful of ways.

"Can you believe these massive churches . . . the onion domes?" said Bobby as we began walking along the stunning, high, redbrick wall that outlined the massive triangular fortress known as the Kremlin. "Everything's so colorful, Press. But what do they have against broccoli or asparagus? Only onion domes I see!"

"Amazing," I said. "It truly is the 'city of a thousand churches,' most designed and built by Italians. Hard to believe they're all closed, museums essentially, per Stalin's orders, not to mention the many medieval churches that were built by Russians. Those were actually blown up . . . destroyed, also per his orders in 1929."

We continued walking along the wall, maybe fifteen feet high at some points and perhaps sixty at others. Finally arriving at Spasskaya Tower, we entered through the famous gate that Napoleon had actually passed through when he occupied Moscow in 1812.

"Look up at the big clock," I said once we'd walked through. "Spasskaya Tower's chimes have been way up there since 1852. The clock itself has been there since the days of Czar Michael Romanov, and I believe that was from 1613 to 1645."

"You're too much, Press. But thank you. Who needs a tour guide with you around?"

"Hey, you told me to learn as much about the Soviet Union as possible."

We made our way to the center of the Kremlin and stopped at Cathedral Square. Neither of us said a word as we marveled at the Cathedral of the Dormition, Cathedral of the Archangel, and Cathedral of the Annunciation.

"All three have shiny, gold onions on top," said Bobby. "Wonder why?"

"Don't know why they're gold, but there is widespread belief that the onion shapes themselves are supposed to symbolize burning candles. Focus on Dormition because it's the oldest cathedral."

"Which is the Palace of the Facets?" said Bobby. "I've read of its being very old, too, perhaps the oldest secular building . . . where the czars held banquets."

"It's the one in between Dormition and Annunciation," I said, pointing. "Let's go get a glimpse of Corpus Number One before we have to leave."

We headed toward the massive yellow and white building, where all of the powerful State officials had their offices, including Stalin. But when we arrived, no one was allowed to enter, so all we could do was stand outside and marvel at the neoclassical Corpus Number One. I was imagining what I'd read about the inside—the statues, magical courtyard, and stunning oval halls. Even from the outside, it reeked of power, of secrecy, and it somewhat resembled the Capitol Building in Washington, D.C., save for the lack of a very high dome.

"A colleague in Paris said that Stalin's office is a corner one on the second floor," said Bobby. "He said men get very nervous when called to the so-called Corner as they are all petrified of Stalin."

"It was designed in the 1770s," I said, looking in every direction, trying to remember what I'd read. "Lenin's old apartment is in there somewhere."

Bobby took in my comment and looked down at his watch. Our quick glimpse of the old buildings would have to suffice for the time being, because it was time to catch a ride to Spaso House. I was looking forward to eventually getting a formal tour of the Kremlin. I was also a little bit nervous about meeting the ambassador. And I didn't know why.

7

A Far East Forest, Russia
September 1937

I HAD BEEN AWAY FROM THE TRANSIT CAMP NEAR VLADIVOSTOK FOR about two weeks now, hidden away in the woods at Camp Z with a few hundred other male prisoners. We'd been tasked to cut down pine trees from dusk 'til dawn. No talking allowed unless it involved logistics. All of the men here were robust and fit, and most had a vicious air about them, many covered in tattoos and scars. I'd come to learn that a large percentage of Soviet prisoners convicted of violent crimes were covered in ink. They could easily double as pirates.

Unlike my rather tame, scraggly beard, theirs were messy-long and caked with sawdust. They were young and muscle bound, as they were getting plenty of lifting exercise and hadn't been deprived of food or water. Yet! Still, for the time being, one of the advantages of being stuck out here in the woods was getting to eat three hot meals a day.

I was beyond worried about the well-being of James back at the transit camp, or wherever else he might be, but chose to believe Abram was looking after him as he'd promised. Still, I wondered whether or not the old man had finally succumbed to malnutrition. If he had, perhaps Boris or Yury was watching over my boy now.

I tried not to think about what forms of brutality Loretta and Ginger might be suffering somewhere on this grand continent. Imagining their condition was too much to handle. I knew that no matter their circumstances, my wife and daughter would remain strong. Believing all of this was the only thing keeping me from falling further and further into Stalin's perfectly assembled abyss.

As I stood next to a tall pine tree, holding my end of a long, two-man chainsaw, my partner and I began to cut through the thick trunk—woodchips spraying our brown sleeveless coveralls and white undershirts, sap spitting at our goggles. I was holding the end with the levers, my partner the handle portion. As the rotating chain continued ripping through the wood, he and I braced for the big fall.

"DEREVO PADAYET!" we yelled, as the tree began to tip and fall downward.

Both of us took a big step back and listened to the big pine crash into the shrubby hillside. Looking past its top, I noticed two shiny black automobiles approaching on the dirt road at the bottom of the slope. They parked near the guard's barracks and six men in pristine uniforms got out.

"PUT DOWN YOUR CHAINSAWS!" yelled the guard who'd been tasked to watch over the six of us in this immediate area. "Time for lunch. When you are finished, you are to convene at the peeling yard. One of our commanders wants to speak to all of you *zeks*."

The guard led us down the slope and past a line of big trucks loaded with fresh-cut logs. It hadn't taken me long to realize that a major part of Stalin's prison system involved forestry. I'd heard from other mates, however, that up north in Kolyma, *zeks* were not tasked to do logging. They were sent out to mine for gold. It sounded as if Stalin had established an elaborate enterprise, all of it seemingly designed to line his own pockets while *zeks* across the land did his slave labor, hardly part of Karl Marx's original plan.

We finished eating our fish and beets at the food barracks and convened on the peeling yard, the perimeter lined with gun-carrying NKVD men. There wasn't a second of the day when an armed unit of guards wasn't watching our every move. And thankfully so, as I was certain there were savage murderers among us.

The peeling yard was a large plot of land where freshly cut pines were dumped. It was here where the nubs were sawed off, the bark peeled away, and the trunks turned into usable logs. There was no visible dirt or vegetation on the yard, as it was completely covered with sawdust, aromatic pine needles, and bark peels.

The most grueling part of being at Camp Z was having to pull trees down from the hillside to the road. Before pulling them, however, the treetops and most of the thick branches were sawed off. Then a chain was wrapped around the trunk, a thick rope tied to it. From there the trees had to be dragged to the road and loaded onto a low, flatbed trailer using a winch. The trailer was hauled away by a truck to the peeling yard. Pulling trees down the slope was excruciating labor, a team of men clutching a resin-covered rope and using every bit of strength just to move it a measly foot through the thick shrubs.

Most of the labor on this camp was done by way of sheer man power. There was only one bulldozer and a single skidder at the camp, both located at the peeling yard. The first was used to clear and haul excess, the second to load peeled and ready logs onto the transport trucks. Luckily, because I could operate heavy machinery, I'd had more than my fair share of opportunities to man the skidder.

If a *zek* were lucky, he'd get maintenance detail. This involved repairing, refueling, oiling, and cleaning the chainsaws at the tool barracks. It also meant removing resin from the handheld bark peelers with gasoline before sharpening them. Another routine job was that of a finisher. This person's job was to receive the trunks at the peeling yard, saw off the remaining branches, and then peel off the bark.

In the end, regardless of what job one had, the days passed

quickly. None of us was immune to getting an inordinate amount of splinters stuck in our fingers and arms, or blisters on our glove-covered palms. I'd also swallowed plenty of sawdust.

As we finished filing into the peeling yard, I noticed a make-shift, shallow, wooden stage that had been assembled. And on it, sitting side-by-side, were the six men I'd seen exit the two black vehicles earlier. Joseph Stalin was not amongst them, but each had the same air as the communist dictator. Their uniforms were adorned with medals, and they sat very erect, half smiling, as if they were looking out at us with a certitude regarding our ultimate fates.

The guards had positioned the few hundred of us *zeks* directly in front of the stage in rows of twenty-five. We hadn't a clue what this meeting involved, and the looks of curiosity on the tired, black-oil faces around me begged for clarity.

"REMAIN STANDING!" yelled an NKVD officer from the stage. "You are some very lucky *zeks* today! Sitting on this stage are six of the top men in charge of our Great Stalin's Far East Logging Company. This is one of many logging camps, but you are supposedly the most robust *zeks* in this part of the country. These bosses have come to judge who among you is the best ex-ample of strength and determination. Who among you is the greatest fighter? Perhaps one of you is worthy of having your sentence reduced by two years. Or, for you monsters, your life sentence cut to twenty years. Is any one of you out there such a man?"

"*DA!*" yelled all of the *zeks,* many of them foaming at the mouth at this surprising news. The screaming and hand-raising continued for at least a minute, as the men were desperate to hear their names called.

"QUIET DOWN!" the officer finally yelled, and we immedi-ately did so. "Calm yourselves, *zeks*! You all don't know this, but we have been monitoring some of you for a long time, even from the time you were initially arrested. You were all selected to do logging because of your size and strength. But once you arrived here, we began comprising a list of the men we believe are truly the most impressive."

He took a sheet of paper from inside his jacket and prepared to read.

"When we call your name, please come to the stage. And let me be very clear! If selected, you will be expected to fight each match until one of you can no longer move, either because of death, or because you are unconscious. If you stop before that . . . you will be taken away and shot! Now! Listen for your name!"

All of the prisoners looked around at one another in anticipation. Not a single *zek* among us was afraid to fight if it meant a sentence reduction. I prayed they'd call my name.

"Anatoly Ivanov!" he read aloud. "Bogdan Smirnov! Vitaly Petrov! Viktor Fedorov! Prescott Sweet! Leonid Nikita! Baldric Falke! Ziegler Hoffman!"

I was standing in the back and began approaching the stage with both anxiousness and concern. All of these selected prisoners were at least six-foot-two like me, or taller, but they were thicker men, more muscular. The air of each suggested they were more comfortable with death. Perhaps many of them didn't have a family back home. What we all likely had in common was that we had killed before, albeit most of them looked as if they'd used their bare hands. Their victims probably hadn't been on the receiving ends of bullets as mine had back in my Bureau days.

"These are the eight men we have selected to do battle tonight!" said the officer. "We are giving you all a reprieve from work early today so you can have a good meal and enjoy the entertainment this evening. There will only be three more hours of work for you today! Then you can feast on chicken and potatoes!"

The men bellowed as if they'd been offered a million dollars. The eight of us stood facing the six bosses, our backs to the crowd, while at the same time sizing one another up. The bosses smiled at us in a disturbing fashion, as if we were a line of prostitutes they were sizing up before making a final selection. And I'd seen this smile a lot on the faces of powerful Soviet men, particularly one Joseph Stalin. It was basically half smile, half frown. I liked to call it a "smown."

"Turn now and face your comrades!" said the officer, and the eight of us followed suit. "Two of these men at a time will dual each other. We have five Russians, two Germans, and one American. Who will win? We believe that one of our Russian comrades will take the trophy. They must! No German or American can win!"

He locked eyes with the bosses. All of them nodded and smowned at him from under their hats with approval.

"They have to win because they have Russian blood!" he continued. "Actually, we believe the *zek* from Leningrad standing on the far end over there will be triumphant. Are we correct, Leonid?"

The massive Russian nodded with confidence. He was at least six-four and riddled with tattoos. He had dark black hair, and his messy, long beard covered most of his dirty, square face. His legs looked like tree trunks, his arms, like legs.

"This will be like our own private Olympic Games," said the officer. "Maybe our Negro American can win the fights the way his comrade Jesse Owens won the races last year in Berlin. You think yes, American *zek*?"

He studied me and I nodded, not knowing if confidence was something I should show.

"You are big, but not the biggest," he said to me. "But you look like a perfect specimen. Very fit. If Leonid is our finest physical man, perhaps you are America's. Who wins?"

The prisoners began to yell different words, but it was unclear what they were saying.

"QUIET!" shouted the officer, and the crowd hushed. "I am talking to the American."

The officer turned to the bosses, then back to me. My being an American took center stage for the moment. My country obviously drew the ire of these men. Or, maybe the fact that Jesse Owens had dominated at the Berlin Games had the whole of the Soviet Union pining to prove their might. After all, they hadn't participated in the Games. But it was Germany who'd won the most medals. Why were they fixated on me? I could only guess it was my color.

"Which country is better, you American?" he continued, completely disregarding the other fighters, particularly the two Germans. "This is not about communism versus capitalism. This is about Russian blood versus American blood. What you eat and breathe and drink and pray to on your soil, versus what we eat and breathe and drink and pray to on ours. You pray to Jesus . . . to God! We pray to our Dear Comrade Stalin, who is the Father of Nations, the Guiding Star. So! We shall see!"

Later that night, with the peeling yard's perimeter lined with officers, the entire camp population assembled once again, this time in a large horseshoe formation, the open end occupied by the shallow stage. Large logs had been placed in the shape of said horseshoe, serving as the only barrier between the fighters and the crowd.

The *zeks* had been instructed to sit on the ground, while the bosses sipped vodka from their seats above. Poles had been placed in the ground along the perimeter of the entire horseshoe, behind the prisoners, ropes attached from one pole to the other. Hanging from them were several gas lamps that illuminated the entire area.

The eight of us fighters were being kept in an adjacent work shed. Surrounded by hanging chainsaws, large oil and gas cans, tools, and spare peeler blades, all we could do was wait and listen.

"WELCOME BACK, *ZEKS*!" the officer yelled from the stage outside. "GET QUIET AND LISTEN! We want you to scream and cheer for the combatants, but make no mistake . . . if you stand up, you will have your teeth knocked out immediately. Stay behind the logs! And if you stand up and try to move inside the ring, you will be shot. We don't want to have to kill any *zeks* tonight. The only men who should die . . . maybe . . . are the ones who lose inside the ring. If one of the fighters falls into the crowd, just push him back inside. Now! Are ready to see some blood?"

"DA!" they screamed.

The eight of us sat in different areas of the gasoline-smelling shed and listened to the crowd hoot and holler. They'd been set ablaze upon hearing the word *blood*. I wasn't making eye contact with any of my opponents. I just sat on a metal work stool in the corner, my knees apart, forearms resting on my thighs, head hanging down, as I stared at the oil drips decorating the wooden floor.

"Vitaly Petrov and Leonid Nikita!" said an officer entering the shed. "You two are up first. Let's go! You are to fight until Officer Kozlov calls the match off from the stage. No exceptions. If you surrender before then, it will not be good for you. That goes for all of you. You are fighting to have your sentence reduced. Don't forget that."

About an hour later I was still waiting to be called for my fight. The other three brawls had already finished, and I was to take part in the fourth against one of the Germans, Baldric Falke. The winner of our match would join the other three who'd already won, the massive Russian, Leonid, being one of them.

No one had been killed so far, but the three who'd lost had been dragged back inside our shed, saturated in blood and pummeled beyond recognition. The victors were now being housed somewhere else. Why these horribly wounded men hadn't been taken to Camp Z's hospital was a mystery. And not a single nurse had been called to the shed. The beaten men were being left to die.

One of the battered *zeks*, Vitaly Petrov, had suffered the most gruesome of injuries. He, unlike the other two, wasn't moaning because he was unconscious. According to what I'd heard the officers say upon dumping him near a pile of rusted winch cable, both of his testicles had been ripped away from his body. The officers had also laughed about the Russian's ungodly misfortune before they'd exited.

The sudden horror surrounding me was unspeakable. The shed felt like a blood-dripping slaughterhouse, and I had visions of waiting to be thrown into a meat grinder. My body ached and throbbed and I hadn't even been touched yet.

I closed my eyes and tried to counter the grotesqueness by thinking of my sweet wife and daughter, the tenderness of their simple smiles, the softness of their gentle touch, the kindness in their every word. I pictured my son doing his best to stay alive, his innate and beautiful optimism being put to the ultimate test. I kept my eyes closed until finally they came for me. It was time.

My opponent and I walked toward the ring, as the crowd, now worked into a complete frenzy, began to roar even louder. I gazed at the stage and the vodka-guzzling bosses. They'd had their appetites plenty wetted at this point and appeared all the more ready to see more violence.

The men in our path gladly moved aside, creating an opening for us. We stepped over the log and entered the ring. My eyes were fixed straight down and I could see blood splattered everywhere. Many of the bark peels were dark red now, and some of the sawdust and pine needles had been turned into bloody clumps. There were even pieces of human tissue scattered about, evidence that the combatants had bitten each other. But none of this distracted me. I was focused on James, Loretta, and Ginger. Nothing more. Nothing less.

We stood in the center of the horseshoe, the hanging lamps beyond the crowd illuminating an otherwise pitch-black night. Baldric Falke had white-blond hair and was my height. And like all the other fighters was covered in tattoos. He stood there bouncing up and down, all the while his knees bent and butt down like a wrestler. His face was twisted up into an intense frown. Even with his mouth closed, I could see some of his rotten teeth through his mangled cleft lip.

"*BORBA!*" yelled Officer Kozlov from the stage.

He had yelled for us to fight, and Baldric charged immediately, aiming for my midsection in an attempt to tackle me. I moved aside and he whiffed, still managing to keep his balance, however. I was focused on breathing, on not wasting any movements. Every punch I threw needed to be efficient, every kick I attempted, precise.

"KILL THAT AMERICAN!" yelled someone, as the two of us stood five feet apart, circling.

He lunged at me again and I went belly to the ground, grabbing both of his legs in the process and tripping him as he continued forward with his momentum. We were both on the ground now. I wasn't about to wrestle him, so I jumped to my feet again before he could secure me in his grasp. He rolled over and up onto his knees but didn't get to his feet fast enough. I kicked him square in the jaw with my heavy boot. I'd hurt him, even feeling a sharp pain in my own foot.

The big German stayed on all fours shaking his head, trying to get the dizzy out, but the kick had landed in the sweet spot and he was struggling. I moved forward and delivered a heavy uppercut to his face, dropping him flat on his back. As the crowd shouted, I turned to the stage. The bosses showed no reaction. They simply waited for Baldric to get up. I watched him struggling, coughing up blood until it covered his face. I didn't want to kill this man. I had no ill will toward him. But he damn sure appeared willing to kill me.

I looked again at the bosses, assuming they wanted me to charge Baldric and finish the job. We were like Roman gladiators brought back from the past to fulfill these Soviet monsters' sick, perverted fantasies. All of this was being done for their pure entertainment. It was evil. Yet I knew there was no choice, for if I refused to fight, they'd shoot me. Regardless, I looked at them and held my hands out, palms up, suggesting as best I could for them to call the fight off and drag this wounded man away. But they only sat there stone-faced, the crowd summoning, "KILL, KILL, KILL!"

But Baldric wasn't ready to die. He jumped up as if injected with some powerful stimulant. The *zeks* shrieked even louder at his display of determination. I was now questioning my decision not to have jumped on him and finished the job. But in my defense, I wasn't trained for this barbarism. I would have to learn quickly. This was kill or be killed.

We circled again. I watched him trying to get his balance in order. He blinked his eyes several times forcefully, and I could see them watering. This was a lumbering brute who was simply too slow to deal with my quickness. Again he lunged forward and I sidestepped him, hitting his nose with a right hook in the process.

Turning to face him again while he wiped at his nostrils, I decided to maintain the same tactic, to play the waiting game and let him be the aggressor. I knew this was a wounded man running on pure will.

I stood with my fists balled up in a boxer's stance and looked over his shoulder at the bosses. They were likely surprised that I hadn't so much as a single scratch. Their plan of seeing the Jesse Owens–like American take a beating was falling apart. At least so far.

With blood covering his entire face, Baldric staggered forward from about ten feet away. I waited. The crowd grew louder with every step he took. It was time to finish him.

As he began to speed up, I took two fast steps forward, leapt in the air, and kicked him square in the mouth with both feet at the same time, a maneuver I'd never executed before but had seen in pictures. The force lifted him off his feet and he fell back, all of his weight crashing flush into the ground, his torso hitting first, his twisted up legs following. This time he wasn't moving.

A hush came over the men, and I saw one of the bosses nod toward stage right. Within seconds, four officers entered the ring. Two grabbed his arms, two others, his ankles. They then carried him through the crowd and off to the shed.

"That was most impressive, American!" said Officer Kozlov. "Do you all agree?"

"DA! DA! DA!" they began screaming.

Another officer entered the ring and stood beside me.

"That was quite a display of physical and mental strength,"

Kozlov continued. "You have one more battle tonight. And if you can manage to win it, well, then . . . we will all be excited to see you in tomorrow night's final match. Take him away!"

The officer escorted me to the food barracks. Sitting at different tables sipping water were the three other winners—Leonid, the big Russian; Ziegler, the remaining German; and Anatoly, the other, less imposing Russian.

I took a seat at an open table and poured myself some water. My body was still shaking, but I had to regain my focus quickly. My goal was to get through the next fight without sustaining a severe injury, as the bosses would expect me to fight again tomorrow night regardless.

Accompanied by several guards, the four of us sat there for about twenty minutes before an officer entered. "Leonid Nikita and Ziegler Hoffman!" he said. "Let's go!"

The big Russian and German both eagerly pushed back from their tables and stood. Neither appeared to have any wounds, save for a few minor cuts. And again I was reminded of the sheer size of these brutes. God help me if either were to get me in their grasp. This was going to have to be a mental exercise of epic proportions.

The next day, fresh off of my semifinal victory and feeling very sore, I was relieved to learn that I had been given the entire day off from work to rest up for the late-night championship fight against Leonid. Anatoly had put forth a valiant effort in my second match, using his stamina and quickness to keep me from finishing him quickly.

We had done a lot of dancing around the ring, both of us reluctant to engage in a wrestling match. But once we'd danced to the point of exhaustion, we'd finally come to the center of the ring and boxed, both of us landing several effective jabs. One that he delivered to my left eye had me now barely able to see out of it, the swelling quite intense. I had landed a shot to his neck, and when he'd begun choking for air, I'd leg swept him, tripping him flat on his back. From there I'd straddled the bullish Russian and face-punched him until he was motionless. The bosses had tipped their hats at me, signaling I'd won.

But that was all behind me now. I had to lock in on my final opponent. I spent most of the day lying in bed, conserving energy. I ate. I drank. I prayed. I thought about the other bit of news that was spreading across the camp: Two fighters, Ziegler Hoffman and Vitaly Petrov, had passed away during the night. And both had fought none other than Leonid Nikita.

8

Moscow, Russia
August 2, 1934

BOBBY AND I ARRIVED AT THE AMBASSADOR'S RESIDENCE AND headed up the walkway after showing our credentials to a U.S. Marine who was standing guard at the gate. He then told us to walk to the driveway on the right side of the house.

Spaso House was a huge, gray stucco mansion on about one acre of land. It was neoclassical in design. The façade was expressive, the front featuring a semi-rotunda with columns. There were also widely spaced, paired columns along the entire front.

When we got to the doorway at the left of the drive, which was under an archway, a butler welcomed us and we entered a rather small, high-ceilinged foyer decorated with Empire-style furniture and paintings. Even the arched ceiling was painted with some type of Empire theme. Bright color was everywhere, save for the dark green columns directly in front of us that separated the foyer from what looked like a lounge. Decorative columns were an obvious motif at Spaso, both externally and internally. They were beautiful.

"We have an appointment with Ambassador Bullitt," said Bobby. "He's expecting us. I'm Bobby Ellington and this is my aide, Prescott Sweet."

"Ah, yes," said the tall, brown-haired butler in a French-sounding accent. "This way, gentlemen."

We followed him through the foyer and into the lounge. Heading to the right, we walked up a long, shallow stairway, which was covered with wine-colored carpet. The pristine white walls were decorated with framed pictures of various American dignitaries, and the white-painted railing looked impeccable. The wine against white everywhere was pleasing to the eyes.

As we finished climbing and landed at what was essentially an upper lobby, another set of stairs could be seen straight ahead. I assumed they led up to the sleeping quarters. To our left was one of the grandest chandelier rooms one could imagine. It was massive, with a high, arched ceiling and columns decorating the entire room. An old, czarist-looking rug covered the wood floor, and the chandelier hanging in the middle of the room was truly grand.

As the butler turned to the right into another impressive section adjacent to the chandelier room, we stopped, still caught up in admiring the glistening, hanging centerpiece.

"Ah, yes," said the butler. "That is the largest chandelier in all of Moscow. It is made of bronze and crystal."

"It's magnificent," said Bobby.

"Shall we, gentlemen?" the butler said. "The ambassador's study is this way."

We turned and followed him to the right, and then again to the left, into an impressive room with a stunning fireplace. Standing at the window was a handsome man—thin, medium height, intense—a cigarette in his hand. Sitting on the floor next to him was a small white dog.

"Mr. Bullitt," said the butler, "your guests are here."

"Ah, Bobby!" said a smiling Bullitt, turning and approaching, the two shaking hands. "It's wonderful to see you again."

"Great to see you as well, William," said Bobby. "This is my assistant and interpreter, Prescott Sweet. The man I told you about who was so vital to all of us in Haiti."

"Ah, yes," said William." We shook. "It's a pleasure. Welcome, Prescott."

"Thank you, sir," I said, noticing his receding dark hair.

"Please, both of you, come and sit," he said, as the three of us made ourselves comfortable around his desk. "Don't mind the dog. It's my daughter Anne's West Highland Terrier. Name's Pie-Pie. Anne is at the Moscow Children's Theater right now at a rehearsal. Anyway, enough about that. Bobby tells me, Prescott, and only recently, that you're a man of many languages . . . and of many technical skills. I should send you straightaway down the hall to help those idiots who are doing measurements for the new ballroom. And I'm serious."

"Well," said Bobby, "Press, here, is my ears and mouth for at least—"

"Your own fucking personal interpreter, Bobby?" said William, taking a drag. "I'm the damn ambassador."

"Yes, you are, sir."

"Months ago I told you that you could hire whomever you wanted as a personal secretary, but had I been made aware of his acumen for languages up front, I may have tried to hire him for myself." He turned to me. "It was only two weeks ago, Prescott, that I learned of your translator skills. I should still hire you away from Bobby immediately."

"I was told," said Bobby, "that you already had Charles and—"

"I kid, Bobby," said Bullitt. "My interpreter, Mr. Thayer, is fine. And I've also got a new aide who's great at shorthand and typing. Italian American named Carmel Offie. But these two assistants are not colored like your man Prescott, Bobby. That will certainly be looked upon favorably here in Moscow. And I mean it sincerely. Stalin is actually—"

Bullitt stopped talking and held up his finger for us to wait. He then jotted something down, a rather long something. He finally handed it to Bobby, who read it before handing it to me. It read: *Stalin is actually recruiting American Negroes to come study here and work in the factories. They're being told to leave America's bigotry behind and come be a part of a truly equal society. It's a real propaganda coup for him.*

"Sounds promising," said Bobby, while I just nodded and placed the paper on the desk.

"But seriously," said Bullitt. "We should all be so lucky to have an assistant with your skills, Prescott."

"Thank you," I said.

"And I want to be on hand when the locals first get a glimpse of a colored American speaking Russian. He'll be a star, Bobby. You'll probably have to hold court so they can get a good glimpse of you in action, Prescott."

I was reminded once again of my color. Bullitt didn't feel like an out-and-out racist, but he had quickly made sure to remind me who I was. I was accustomed to such casual, even unintentional barbs back in America. But I had enjoyed being away from them for years in Paris. It was so American. And Bullitt continued.

"There's a colored American columnist named Homer Smith who I've visited with several times here at the embassy. He seems to be trying to report on the Negro situation overall as it relates to living conditions in Moscow versus America. I'll have to introduce him to you, Prescott."

"Thank you," I said, halfheartedly, wondering why I should be so inclined to make this stranger's acquaintance. "I would love to meet him, Mr. Ambassador."

"It would suit you to know," said Bullitt, "that Mr. Stalin and . . ."

Bullitt, once more, put his finger to his lips, signaling for us to remain quiet. "I like to keep this handy," he said, opening his desk drawer, pulling out a slip of paper, and passing it along to us again. It read: *Sometimes I forget where I am. This room probably has camouflaged wire recorders hidden somewhere. Maybe even behind the walls. We believe the cleaning people are in on it. Found one in the garden last month. Hell, the damn light fixture above may be an actual recording device. After all, they built this house long before we ever arrived. Let's go take a drive.*

He stood and held his arm out, signaling for us to go before him, which we did, as Pie-Pie lagged behind. Once outside, he walked us to a black Lincoln parked in the driveway. "Hurry," said Bullitt, "before my chauffeur, Stewart, arrives. He's a U.S. Marine. But I have them dress in civilian clothes."

He'd barely gotten the door open when a gentleman in a black suit came running from a distant, smaller living quarters. "Where to, Ambassador Bullitt?" he said, half out of breath.

"I think I can handle this one, Stewart," said Bullitt.

"But, sir, I was—"

"You don't mind driving, do you, Prescott?" said Bullitt, ignoring the chauffeur. "I'll direct."

"Not at all," I said.

"Good. Listen, Stewart, can you make sure my little roadster is washed and waxed while we're gone? I want to take it for a drive this weekend."

"Certainly, sir."

We hopped in the Lincoln and I took the wheel, the two of them sitting in back so they could chat.

"Back out and take a right, Prescott," said Bullitt. "Then I'll point you where to turn a few times so we can get to Smolenskaya Naberezhnaya Street. We actually just call it 'Smo Nab Street' to avoid biting our tongues off. Such is the case with many of the street names. Anyway, from there we'll make our way to where we can get a nice view of the Moscow River."

I nodded, looking at them in the mirror.

"How is Dorene?" he asked Bobby, handing him a cigarette. "Has she already begun to complain about the lack of fashion here? She will not be able to do an ounce of clothes shopping."

"She'll make do," said Bobby, lighting up.

"Ah, you say that, but she'll be on the first train to London within weeks for a vacation. If *I* am finding it necessary to get out of town so much, she certainly will. I can't tell you how much I'd rather be in Paris."

"Moscow doesn't suit you, William?" said Bobby.

"Not particularly," he said, leaning forward toward me. "You know, Prescott, Louise Bryant, my ex-wife and mother of my ten-year-old daughter, was in love with the *idea* of this place. But she was actually just in love with Jack Reed, who was indeed *authentically* in love with Russia. So, you see . . . love, love, love."

"And you?" I said.

"I love Paris," said Bullitt, pointing. "Turn here, Prescott. I have hope for this place, but it frustrates me. Trying to make inroads with Stalin is like trying to find a good steak in this city. And Maxim Litvinov, the People's Commissar for Foreign Affairs, is all the more difficult. He's smart, but his integrity could use some work."

As Bullitt continued smoking and talking, it was as if he were venting his frustrations, thinking out loud. I could sense the weight he was carrying.

"Mr. Litvinov is acting as if the financial debts they owe America, along with their agreement not to interfere in our domestic affairs, are subjects we never discussed when our two countries initially met last year. Those agreements were signed when we reestablished relations. Why the hell does he think the president agreed to send me here?" He touched my shoulder. "You're not a spy, are you, Prescott?"

"*Ya ne shpion,*" I said in Russian. "No."

"I like that," he said, leaning back again. "I'm going to steal him from you, Bobby. Maybe I'll use him to find out where these damn Soviet spies are planting their hidden recorders. Can you find this out, Prescott?"

"Sir?" I said, pretending I hadn't heard him.

"I think Sergei, the caretaker who lives in the basement, is working with NKVD," said Bullitt. "His room remains locked and we have no access. I really don't care, actually, as we know the entire house is littered with hidden wire recorders. We just try to always make sure we're saying nice things about our hosts when inside Spaso House. We're actually just being honest, a foreign concept to them, one that will continue to puzzle them, as they only deal in suspicion."

"Does Sergei act suspicious?" said Bobby.

"Not particularly. Turn again here, Prescott. But you have to remember, gentlemen, when we reestablished relations last year, they had plenty of time to install whatever they wanted in Spaso before we moved in. God knows what's behind the walls. One of our third secretaries, George Kennan . . . you know him, don't you, Bobby?"

"Yes, I met him once in Washington."

"Brilliant fellow who's also fluent in Russian. Anyhow, he and I have spent hours at night trying to find a secret door that leads somewhere. Nothing. I know there's one, though. I believe this because when I first met with Stalin last year, he gave me the option of two different places that could serve as the ambassador's residence. One was Spaso. The other was an old Supreme Court building that looked like a prison. He offered me these two as options because they'd perhaps been remodeled as spy buildings."

"Just your hunch, though, right?" said Bobby. "You've seen nothing specific, have you?"

"No, it is indeed just my hunch. But my hunches are good. I believe they can plant recorders behind the walls, ceilings, and floors in the morning and remove them at night without any of us knowing it. Don't know how, but would like to find out! And I believe the new chancery they just finished next to the Hotel National is even more riddled with recorders. We may as well have had our staff move into the Kremlin."

"This sounds like a major problem," said Bobby. "Is there anything—"

"It's not a major problem. They just still don't trust us. That's what happens when you've had no relationship for sixteen years. I figure the less suspicious we act, the better. We've been tasked with a mission by the president to reestablish good relations with these people. We'll do our part and do so honorably. All of our staff simply leave the house when we want to carry on private conversations."

Bullitt paused for a moment and then continued.

"Hell. Who am I kidding? This car probably has a wire recorder hidden somewhere. Probably turns on automatically when the car door is opened. Can they do that sort of thing yet, Prescott? Technologically, I mean."

"I would think . . . yes," I said. "But I haven't spent a great deal of time studying recording, much less recorder activation. I do know this: Just because something isn't on the open market, doesn't mean it hasn't been invented. And as it relates to the Soviet Union, I recall reading somewhere during my research of this country that a Mr. Neill Brown, who was the U.S. minister in St. Petersburg back in the mid-1800s, said of this place, 'Secrecy and mystery characterize everything. Nothing is made public that is worth knowing.' "

"I'll be damned," said Bullitt.

"The truth of the matter," I said, "is that advancements in wire recording, as we Americans know them to be, are fluid, to say the least. But someone would have to have regular access to your Lincoln, sir, in order to remove any hidden device once it's full. And, of course, to plant another one."

"I see. Well, my vehicles are always locked, and I have the keys, so we need not worry about this conversation. And I have six U.S. Marines on guard detail at Spaso. One of them is even my courier who goes to the Kremlin regularly. He's very discreet, a real secretive sort, if you know what I mean." He pointed. "Make another turn here, Prescott."

"But you do sound a bit worried, William," said Bobby.

"That's because—and this goes to Prescott's point—they are working on new types of recording devices in this country like no other. They are absolutely obsessed with technology and the idea of finding new ways for their NKVD to spy on people, all the while believing every foreigner is a spy as well. They have even asked me questions about our American scientists back home, wanting to know about any new advancements in recording. As if I'd dare tell!"

"Obsessed with finding new ways to spy, huh?" said Bobby.

"Obsessed! And they're so indiscreet. I believe Stalin is pouring more and more money into their scientific institutions. They're opening the Institute for Physical Problems here in Moscow, and there's the Physical Technical Institute in Leningrad."

"You mentioned the caretaker," said Bobby.

"Yes," said Bullitt. "I don't know anything in particular. We just have our suspicions. This Lincoln vehicle was made at the Ford plant here in Moscow, but I have it thoroughly inspected regularly by Carl Lock, one of our staff who fancies himself an auto mechanic. The last inspection was a week ago. Still, I always wonder if the NKVD have found a way during the night to bribe one of the marines and plant a device in here somewhere."

"Those marines are too honorable," said Bobby.

"But they're so young," said Bullitt. "And I saw the way they blushed around the young Russian girls during a recent social event we hosted at Spaso. They're susceptible to bribes I believe. NKVD is using these beautiful girls, young ballerinas, to soften the men up."

We continued our drive along the river. All this talk of new types of recording devices had me wondering what technology the Soviet scientists were actually on the cusp of.

"That river is beautiful, isn't it, gentlemen?" said Bullitt. "Pull over up here to the left, Prescott. I'd like to get out and stretch my legs."

I pulled over and waited for the ambassador to get out. But he just sat there for a moment smoking and staring at the river.

"I'd like to have a private moment with you, Bobby," he finally said. "We'll be right back, Prescott. Keep it running."

I nodded as they exited and made their way to the rear of the vehicle, both of them lighting fresh cigarettes. My window was up, so I couldn't hear them, but my confidence was up as well, so I rolled it down just a bit. My desire to eavesdrop on their conversation overrode any type of honor one might suggest I exhibit.

"There is an apartment for you and your family at the Mokhovaya, Bobby," said Bullitt, essentially whispering. "But I think it's in the best interest of everyone to have Prescott and his family find a more suitable living space."

"Sir!" whispered Bobby, obviously taken aback.

"I'm not trying to hide him, Bobby, but I think it's best to keep other staff from making him feel uncomfortable. I know we're in the Soviet Union and race relations are progressive, but most embassy staff still see the issue as it is back home. They most certainly aren't comfortable with race mixing, in terms of living arrangements."

"But you and I talked," whispered Bobby. "In Haiti, embassy staff were completely fine with Prescott living—"

"This is not fucking Haiti . . . or Africa . . . or the Caribbean. You know there's not a single Negro FSO in our entire Moscow chancery. There's a reason for that. It's the way things are within the State Department still. For that matter, there's not a single female FSO here either."

"We're not like this, you and I, William."

"No, we're not. And I believe relations will change. Listen. I agreed to have you serve on my staff, at a very high level at that. And I know that Dorene's influence with the president and first lady didn't hurt. Franklin all but demanded I take you on. So you're here. You'll be an ambassador yourself very soon. That should be your focus."

"Prescott is a man of great integrity. And as my career grows, I intend to have him by my side for as long as—"

"You can have him by your side here, too. We're simply talking living arrangements. I agreed to let you hire whomever you wanted as your personal aide. Shouldn't that be enough? He's got embassy clearance at least, and he's on a personal service contract. But let's be clear, he's basically no different from the Russian builders I hired for the ballroom, a contractor hired by the embassy."

"I understand that," said Bobby, sounding quite disappointed. "But if—"

"He's a fucking assistant, for Christ's sake! Essentially a servant! They're plentiful. And like all the others, regardless of color, there won't even be a record of him having ever existed at the chancery here. That's just plain old reality."

"Prescott is one of the most brilliant, loyal—"

"So is my new Italian aide, Mr. Offie," said Bullitt.

"But Prescott will eventually be an FSO. I intend to see to it.

And he, like the American gentleman who's now Consul in Las Palmas, will eventually completely break through these archaic barriers."

"Dammit, I, for one, know this Negro Consul you speak of. His name is Clifton Wharton, Sr. And I really like and respect him. But he wasn't sent to Moscow."

"But perhaps he could have been."

"That's enough on the subject, Bobby. I'm sure Prescott is bright, and I meant what I said earlier about having him work with the Russian contractors on the new ballroom as a technical advisor. And your office at the chancery shall be his office as well. But let's find him a suitable apartment. Come! I'd like to get going."

I casually rolled my window back up as the two rejoined me, lit cigarettes still in hand. I wasn't going to let this living situation deter me from working with my friend, because I believed that he would one day see to it that such arrangements wouldn't have to be made. In fact, I intended to relieve him of even having to bring the issue up. I planned on telling him that Loretta wanted to live amongst some of the local artists, wherever that was.

"Let's continue on to Kutuzovsky Street, Prescott," said Bullitt, exhaling smoke. "I'll show the two of you Stalin's private estate. It was just built. It's called Blizhnyaya Dacha . . . his *nearby* dacha. The house is heavily guarded and difficult to even see, but you'll get a sense of the place. Construction is actually still being completed on it."

"Sounds fantastic," I said, knowing that Bobby's sour mood would lead him to remain quiet.

"I'm hoping," said Bullitt, "that Stalin keeps his word on something. He promised me I could build a new embassy chancery on a place I desire. It's a piece of land on a beautiful bluff in the Sparrow Hills overlooking the Moscow River. I've had an American architect draw up some plans. It could be like Jefferson's Monticello."

No slaves, though, I hope, Mr. Ambassador! I said to myself. I wouldn't have dared said it out loud.

"I would like to take this opportunity to be frank, gentlemen," said Bullitt. "I'm merely thinking out loud. As I hinted at earlier, Prescott, perhaps you could work with the Russians I just hired to build the new ballroom. Be our American electrician! The Soviet government forced me to use Russian contractors, but we need at least an American consultant on board. Then you could dig a little and find out where they're hiding their new gadgets. The electricity will have to be shut off periodically and you'll maybe have access to areas in the attic and behind the walls of the mansion—all thirty rooms."

I looked in the mirror at Bobby. His face was beet red. I was hoping that he could at least wait until we were alone to blow his top. I didn't want him to lose his job on the first day.

"You're being colored, Prescott, and speaking Russian will allow you to ingratiate yourself to the workers without raising any eyebrows. They simply find it almost a communist calling to treat coloreds with complete deference . . . as if how they treat you all is the ultimate test of their allegiance to Marx's manifesto. Is that too blunt, Prescott?"

"Blunt is quite preferable to vague, sir," I said.

"Indeed. You can have him most of the time, Bobby, but perhaps he can work on the ballroom for the first couple months here. Don't worry about desperately needing Prescott to translate for you for the time being, Bobby, because you're probably not going to leave your office very much in these early days. I need you to help sort out the passport mess our consular has on his hands."

"Yes, sir," said Bobby.

"He's overwhelmed. Hundreds of Americans have lost theirs. When Mr. Stalin initially promised them work over here, somehow their passports magically disappeared within the first few weeks of their arrival. Some, I know, threw them away as a protest to America's Depression after they'd been promised Soviet citizenship. They've told us as much. Now they're homesick and want them back."

"I'm here to serve you, Mr. Ambassador," said Bobby.

I hated hearing my friend have to suppress his own feelings and bow down to his superior, but such was the way it had to be. Besides, other than perhaps Paris, there wasn't a place on this earth where a colored man like me wouldn't have to deal with race-based inconveniences like this.

The thought alone made me start to miss our home city. Again, there, only when we'd ventured into high-end areas had Loretta and I so much as sniffed hints of well-disguised bigotry. Paris as a whole was the most accepting place on earth I could imagine when it came to treating coloreds well. And I actually wondered at times if even the bits of racism I felt were a result of the issue being so engrained into me back in the U.S. that I assumed it was there when it wasn't. Maybe those odd looks from wealthy Parisians had had more to do with class than color.

While teaching at the University of Paris, I was actually encouraged to try to earn my PhD and become a full-time professor, but I'd declined, knowing I didn't want to be a lifelong lecturer. But, still, the administrators never even batted an eye at my being a Negro. Even the *idea* of treating me as if I were *less than* was anathema to them. And outside of work, I was always invited to private functions or parties. Our social life was not just limited to attending events that took place within Loretta's little Montmartre artists' colony.

Looking back, I realized that the reason I'd always felt the need to leave Paris and pursue something else was born out of my desire to help my American brothers and sisters feel what I'd felt in France. Unless all of them could be free, too, my happy bones still ached for them. And if working for a potential U.S. ambassador meant having a hand in shaping a more compassionate foreign policy, one that might eventually teach our government to treat its own people with the same dignity and respect that it shows citizens abroad, I had to do it.

"In many ways," said Bullitt, lighting a new cigarette, "this might be one of the worst days in history. I failed to mention the news I received earlier. German President Paul von Hindenburg died today. God help us! Chancellor Adolf Hitler has just become the absolute dictator of Germany. He's calling himself *Fuhrer*. All that means is 'leader,' but I fear it will come to mean 'savage murderer' to the rest of us in the civilized world."

Again I looked at Bobby in the mirror. He was wiped out. This made me both sad and happy. Sad that he was hurting, but happy to know he cared so deeply about me. This was a friend, a brother—a man I'd follow to the ends of the earth.

9

DARKNESS HAD COME QUICKLY AND THE MEN GATHERED ONCE
again. They sounded even louder this time, unaffected by the
long day of work they'd just completed, starving to see more
blood. And as Leonid and I entered the ring, I had the distinct
feeling one of us was about to die.

"SILENCE!" shouted Officer Kozlov, turning away from the
bosses. "Most of us gathered here in the middle of this vast forest are Russian. We are proud Russians, too! And although we
men up here are free and you *zeks* out there are not, we all share
the same history. I say that to say this: Make us proud, Leonid
Nikita!"

The crowd roared all the way up to the star-filled sky. The
bosses smowned with pride at their great Russian beast, and
Leonid nodded back at them, assuring each that he'd heard
their message loud and clear and would heed it. I was alone. I
was surrounded. I was an American.

"*BORBA!*" yelled Officer Kozlov.

Leonid lumbered forward in attack mode and I tried to evade
him. My only hope was to make this a game of stamina. He
lunged again. I dodged.

With my back facing the stage, he moved in once more and I

jabbed his eye, ducking his sweeping counter right as the two of us switched places. His eye had been cut open pretty well. I jabbed again with my right and he caught my fist, pulling it in and biting it, taking the tip of my thumb off in the process. Then he bit down on the webbing between my thumb and index finger, ripping away more flesh like a rabid wolf. Blood oozed down my arm, as he still had it in his grasp.

Before he could chew any more of my hand off, I groin-kicked him and he released me. The visual of this beast growling at me now and chewing my flesh—fresh blood covering his lips—was a haunt for all times. He clutched his crotch and smiled, waiting for me to make another move.

"NIKITA! NIKITA! NIKITA!" the throng howled.

I held out my hand to have a look, all the while backing up. He'd taken off two substantial chunks. I tried to ball up my fist again, but the pain made it next to impossible.

Leonid rushed me once more and this time was able to grab the left shoulder strap of my coveralls as I turned away. He pulled me close, bear-hugging me, lifting my feet off the ground, trying to squeeze the air out of me.

I gasped for air and he began to run with me as if I were a mere child. As we neared the stage, he shoved me into one of the thick log beams that held up the platform. I fell to my knees and shook my head, desperately attempting to stay conscious. I could see a blurred image of him readying to kick me with a kill shot and I began to crawl. His foot still caught my left bicep, however, the force feeling like it had fractured my humerus.

"KILL! KILL! KILL!" the *zeks* belted out while I continued crawling on all fours.

He wound up for another kick, but I rolled away and got to my feet. The *zeks* screamed with approval, happy to see the battle continue. I was still woozy, my legs wobbly. Facing him and circling, I tried to buy time, praying with each second that my senses would return.

Leonid stood strong with his mammoth arms flexed and he grinned at me, his teeth appearing to be completely rotten, even with the pink of my blood covering them. Each time he stepped forward I backed up, vigorously shaking my head in the process and breathing deep for oxygen. I needed to think, to outsmart this giant. My only hope was to use his aggression against him.

I purposefully circled back around to the stage and backed up. He swung big and I dodged it, waiting for the next one. He kicked at my groin and I sidestepped, his foot crashing into the beam while I spun around, his back now against the stage.

The *zeks* laughed at his miss and a look of frustration came over him. I backed up and again we danced center ring, both of us breathing heavily. The blood from my hand and his busted-up eye had decorated both of us, creating a scene of complete savagery. His arms spread like a bird's, he lunged at me again, and once more, I was quicker. There was no doubt he wanted to wrestle, to get me on the ground and muscle me to death. And it was a smart strategy on his part, because he had to weigh at least 270, much heavier than my even 200. The time had come to stop evading him.

I looked over his shoulder at the stage platform, studying how high it was—no more than three feet, I figured. I began circling until again my rear faced the stage. Then I slowly began to back up, measuring my steps carefully, judging exactly how far I was from the platform—calculating every move. I would need to be precise in order to execute this final maneuver.

As I'd anticipated, he bullishly rushed at me once more and I dipped down real low, grabbing him around his upper legs, my face pressed against his stomach, all the while allowing his force to continue through me as I lifted him and he drove me straight back, my feet off the ground now, both of us suspended in air. Instead of banging my back against the stage beam, I arched my spine, continuing to use his momentum and weight to drive his head straight down now and into the platform's edge, splitting his face open, snapping his thick neck, killing him instantly.

We both lay there as a silence came over the crowd, dust swirling around us. Leonid's body had me completely blanketed, all of his weight bearing down on me like a dead grizzly's. I rested there for a moment, trying to feel for something that might be broken, but his head had taken the full brunt of the fall. I had surprised him with the all-too-quick tripping maneuver, so much so that he hadn't been able to extend his wing-positioned arms properly in time to brace himself and save his face.

My left arm felt fractured and was limp, so using my mangled right hand, I pushed at his chest and scooted out from under. I surveyed the silent crowd before turning toward the bosses, the anger on their faces suggesting I'd just murdered their wives. The American had won. The American was still alive. I closed my eyes and waited. It had been fourteen years since my life was embroiled in violence. Those years had been a reprieve from having to question how to simply stay alive.

I opened my eyes and looked at the black night beyond the quiet *zeks*. I yearned for the simplicity of everyday, normal life. I realized that my current predicament had been born out of a desperate yearning to transport some nonexistent model of freedom back to America, some philosophy that might take hold there and transform the lives of my people. I'd been suckered into believing that the Bolshevik Revolution had created a completely equal society based on certain principles, ones that could serve as the blueprint for solving America's racial woes, ones that would show U.S. blacks and whites how to live in peace and harmony, ones that President Roosevelt was viewing from afar and basing his New Deal on.

I kept staring at the night sky and realized that my life's purpose seemed to be cheating death over and over again, all in my impossible quest to finally reach this imagined utopia. Why hadn't I settled on a simple life in Paris? The answer: God had placed deep inside of me a compass that was always turning toward freedom, guiding my every move, forcing me to disregard logic and pursue that intangible, elusive something that represented fairness for American Negroes, even if it was merely some abstract semblance of it. I imagined that slave of long ago, of my ilk, being told that he might be able to buy his freedom if he plays his cards right. He could only turn to his master and say, "Unless I can buy everyone's, each and every one of my brothers' and sisters' freedom, what difference does it make?"

Continuing to stare beyond the crowd at dark nothingness, I wondered if my sentence would indeed be reduced to eight years. Even if it was, I wasn't about to serve it out without doing everything in my power to get released sooner. I feared that, at this rate, every member of my family would be dead within a year or two.

Again I turned to the bosses. And once more I waited. But no one said a word or lifted a finger as I stood there bleeding and shaking. They could only stare at their fallen Goliath. I was tired and beaten and sad and lonely. But I still had hope.

10

Moscow, Russia
September 1934

I'D BEEN IN MOSCOW FOR A MONTH NOW, MY FAMILY LIVING IN A wonderful apartment on Arbat Street, only a few houses down from where the famed writer Alexander Pushkin had once resided. This neighborhood's living quarters were quite different from others in terms of aesthetics, as the buildings were made of stone and brick. It was nice not having to live in one of the many one-story log row houses available to most tenants.

Bobby had helped us find the apartment. It was part of a large, white four-unit building—two apartments on the second floor, two on the first. Our unit was on the left side, first floor. We figured the entire building had once been a czar's fancy house. Perhaps after the revolution it had been remodeled to create four apartments. Whatever the case, our two-bedroom unit was plenty spacious.

Our stay at the National Hotel had lasted only a week. I never told Bobby that I'd overheard his conversation with the ambassador regarding his desire not to have my family live at the chancery with the other staff. I'd preempted any pending discussion on the matter by simply expressing to Bobby my preference to live in a place large enough for Loretta to do her painting and readily host artists for events. This prompted Bobby to raise my level of pay, allowing us to easily afford the apartment. I was happy to have eased his private worry over the matter. Initially, I had refused to accept his side money, prompting him to spill his soul a bit to me.

"Please don't make an issue out of the extra money," he'd said. "It is truly our wish for you to accept it. Money can never become an issue between us, Press. I have learned to accept this idea as well, you know, with my being married to Dorene. Her wealth is just a reality, and as a subject, it's completely off of the table between us. We've chosen to serve our government, not to dwell on our riches. The fact that we can travel and serve abroad without worry is a blessing. I need you to join me in this thinking. You're my right-hand man. We can be a team."

"Okay," I had said, just before he'd gone into a riff about race, which told me he was still pained over the conversation he'd had with Bullitt behind the car that day.

"I can't stop thinking how much I wish it were as easy for you to become a diplomat as me," he'd gone on. "Segregation and overall racism is ubiquitous—and evil! But let me help you navigate through it until, God willing, we can come upon a better day. This apartment is certainly fit for a diplomat. Plus, helping you live in this fine establishment so that your wife can do her art is the least I can do. The least you can do is accept."

This conversation had left the two of us feeling even closer. Since then we'd been engrossed in our jobs, working nonstop on the passport issue plaguing so many American expatriates. It was exhausting work that required lots of research and document reading. But, as we'd anticipated, I was now being summoned to the ambassador's residence to help advise on the new ballroom, an assignment that irked the hell out of Bobby. But what could he do about it?

I arrived for my first day of work at Spaso House on a Monday morning and was led through the chandelier room into an adjacent area where several walls had been knocked down. The floor was covered in drywall dust, and so were the eight men standing around a large worktable arguing about logistics.

"This one shows that we cannot knock that west wall down because it is essential to the house's structural support," said a tall, fat man who appeared to be the lead contractor. His Russian words bellowed out in a deep baritone.

"Excuse me!" I said, interrupting.

"Yes!" said the fat man.

"I'm Prescott Sweet. The ambassador has hired me to help as a technical advisor."

"Ah, yes! Comrade Sweet! Please! Come join us! I am so glad to hear an American speak Russian. My name is Makar."

A couple of the men moved aside and created some space for me to join them around the table. Then they all introduced themselves.

"Don't take this personally," said Makar, "but I have been going back and forth with . . . let me whisper . . . with your ambassador about my electrician. He will not even allow Egor in the building because he has demanded that one of *his* men do the job. I assume that is you."

"That is correct," I said, trying not to act surprised at this news.

"He told me, Comrade Sweet, that no power can be shut off until you've had a chance to study the drawings and inspect all of Spaso House's wiring. He claims that the lights go out at night all of the time and that the phone often doesn't work. He also claims that all of the food in the refrigerator keeps spoiling because of these late-night power outages. My electrician, Egor, could easily fix! If I sound angry that is because I am! Not at you, but, you know, this is your ambassador showing that he doesn't trust me."

"No!" I said, preparing to defend the ambassador as best I could.

"What do you mean . . . *no?*"

"I mean . . . I think it has more to do with him feeling like a brand-new set of electrical materials will need to be ordered from America, and that I can recommend the highest quality ones. America's made new advancements in wiring technology.

He also believes I'll be able to determine what's causing things to short-circuit so often. I'm an expert in that area. It probably has to do with the house's outdated system not being able to support the amount of wattage being regularly used, especially at night, when so many lights are turned on. The last thing the ambassador wants is to be hosting a big social event, only to have a blackout."

"I think you Americans don't believe we are smart enough," said Makar, lighting a cigarette.

"Where exactly is the circuit breaker?" I asked, studying the drawings and ignoring his comment.

"We are smart, too!" he said, exhaling.

"Also," I said, "can someone give me a tour of the house? I need to get an intimate understanding of the layout, etcetera."

All of the men looked around at one another, seemingly uncomfortable with my request. This quick little lie I'd told reminded me of how easily I'd always been able to fool people.

Even when I'd originally been hired at the University of Paris and had shown them my diplomas, they'd asked why the name on them read Sidney Temple instead of Prescott Sweet, which was on my passport. I'd told them that upon moving to Paris, I wanted to completely embrace France and leave all of America and its backward ways behind me, to become an entirely new man. They'd liked my insult of the United States and it probably helped me land the job.

The reason I'd been okay with showing them my original diplomas was simple: I knew the name Sidney Temple would never be uttered aloud in the future for any British Intelligence spy to get lucky and overhear. And the odds of said spy unprovokingly visiting the university's human resources department to inquire about some American named Sidney Temple was highly unlikely. At best he'd check the faculty listing and see no such name.

Moments later, I found myself in the bowels of Spaso House being given a tour by Sergei, the caretaker. He was in a foul mood to say the least. I got the distinct feeling he viewed all of us visiting Americans as intruders who'd overtaken the mansion he'd long considered partly his own. When we reached the actual basement, all he would show me was the circuit breaker. He claimed that the main room down here was his living quarters, and that it was locked and would stay that way as long as he lived there.

"Why are you so insistent that no one is allowed inside?" I asked.

"I am the caretaker of this house and the least you Americans can do is allow me to maintain a private space in which to live. There is nothing in there for you to see. There is a bed and a couch and a washroom. It is where I live. Do I ask to come to your house and look around your bedroom? No!"

"Very well," I said. "Is this the only circuit breaker?"

"Yes."

"I have to inspect this panel thoroughly. I am going to need some time here. Feel free to carry on with your daily routine. I can manage alone now."

He looked at me with a bit of a frown before nodding and heading back upstairs.

"Oh!" I said, stopping him, as he was about halfway up. "I am going to need to get back up in the attic after I'm through here to begin inspecting the wires. I will need you to unlock that door again. Will you be around?"

"Of course! I never leave Spaso House. Where else did you think I'd be?" He began to head up again and I heard him mutter, "Stupid Americans!"

Before he reached the top step he began descending again, rapidly approaching like he wanted to come hit me.

"Comrade Sweet, let me show you the other, smaller circuit breaker at the far end of the basement on the other side. It's a bit of a maze getting there."

"Thought you said this was the only one."

"I meant the only one that you need as far as the power that will involve the new ballroom. This is a big house, comrade."

"Uh, I need to be the one who decides which breaker needs to control which sections of the house. I need to make all of the

technical decisions based on a completely thorough understanding of the house's electrical system. So, I'm going to ask
you again . . . are these the only two circuit breakers. Or is there
one inside your living quarters?"

"Excuse me, comrade! You think because you are speaking
Russian to me with such confidence that this gives you the right
to make accusations? According to Ambassador Bullitt, you are
not a diplomat of any sort. You are an assistant. You are no
higher than my level. Nor are you any higher level than the ambassador's personal butler, Jean."

"Just show me the breaker!" I somewhat angrily said. "I need
to get on with it."

"This way!"

As he and I continued winding through the dark basement
hallways again, I kept thinking of what Ambassador Bullitt had
said about hidden tunnels and secret passageways. Sergei's insis-
tence on not allowing me to see inside his living quarters had
me all the more curious. I didn't necessarily want to find any of
this out for the ambassador, either. It was simply a personal curiosity, one that was actually becoming more of an obsession
with each step we took.

I thought back to my spying days in Harlem and the time I'd
drugged one of the UNIA Legionnaires so I could break into
Marcus Garvey's private file cabinet and sift through his documents. Now I found myself staring at the ring of keys dangling
from Sergei's waist, jingling with each step he took. How could I
get my hands on them? My immediate dislike of him had me far
too determined.

Later that evening, having brought Loretta home an assortment of fresh flowers, I sat with her and the children at the dinner table and we dined over baked sturgeon, mashed potatoes,
and steamed carrots. This was my favorite thing in the world,
eating peacefully with my family, listening to them carry on
about the day's happenings, speaking both French and English
to one another. And Loretta seemed particularly enthused on
this evening.

"*Aimez-vous l'esturgeon?*" said Loretta.

"C'est délicieux!" we all three answered at the same time, as it was customary to praise her cooking and mine.

"My goal is to learn Russian in one year," said Ginger. "Then I'll be trilingual. That's what Mrs. Stapleton said to me."

"Trilingual?" said a jovial James. "Well, I am going to be a poly . . . a poly . . . a *polyglot!* Yeah! I will speak ten languages. More than you, Daddy!"

"Une langue à la fois, le fils," I said.

"Yes," said Loretta. "One at a time, James. Being able to speak two already is very good for an eleven-year-old."

"Anyway," said Ginger, "what I was *trying* to say is I really want to set a goal to learn Russian in one year. And I'm serious, James."

"That would be wonderful, sweetheart," I said, savoring the warm fish. *"Ce sera marveilleux!* Or, in Russian . . . *Eto budet zamechatel'no."*

"I love when you speak Russian," said Loretta, smiling, then turning to the children. "If your daddy will speak Russian at the dinner table more often, we can all learn faster. Lord knows it would help me navigate the art scene here!"

"Will you, Daddy?" said James, anxiously swinging his legs under the table and bouncing up and down.

"Yes, son. Stop jerking like that, though."

"Changing the subject," said Loretta. "Simone says she's never seen anyone with a more natural feel for Socialist Realism painting than I," she said.

Simone Dragic was a painter from Switzerland who'd married a Russian dentist and had lived in Moscow for ten years.

"But isn't that particular form too limiting for you?" I said, forking my fish.

"Perhaps," she said, "but it's actually the first time in my career where I've been in a classroom full of students and been singled out by the teacher as the premier painter."

"Wow, Mommy!" said a smiling Ginger.

"The fact that a woman as brilliant and well-trained as you is still taking classes is puzzling to me," I said, pouring her some more water from the pitcher.

"An artist never stops trying to learn specific new forms, love. And ever since we arrived in the Soviet Union, I have been learning that Socialist Realism . . . not to be confused with *social* realism, by the way, can be powerful. This form is unique to this country and is the preferred style of Joseph Stalin."

"Preferred?" I said, sarcastically. "He's not actually giving you all a choice. I mean, the mere fact that other forms are prohibited and—"

"That's a temporary thing, love. Stalin is simply trying to encourage artists to help move the social revolution forward. He feels that we artists play a vital role in making sure communism stays healthy, and that those backward-thinking individuals who are still clinging to the czarists' ways of life are rooted out of society. This country has to heal, and we painters can help by depicting communist values, like the emancipation of the proletariat. We can also do paintings that support the aims of the State and the Party."

"Since when did you become an admirer of communism?" I said, bewildered at the almost hypnotic way in which she was speaking. "Sounds like you're taking classes in Soviet politics, not painting. I mean it. When did you become—"

"I haven't!" she said. "Become an admirer! I'm just learning more about it. But I'll have you know, Mr. Prescott Sweet, that many of America's most successful citizens are saying good-bye to capitalism and hello to communism. Men like Paul Robeson and W.E.B. Du Bois to be specific. You adore both, don't you?"

"Yes, but Du Bois is certainly not a member of the party. He's just expressed views that lead one to think he appreciates it."

"Well, then!"

"Just go slow," I said. "I have a tad more faith in the aims that Lenin and Trotsky had in mind. Stalin's approach has my eyebrows raised. I know nothing specific of him yet, but let's not go allowing him to indoctrinate you overnight."

"Are you gonna be famous, Mommy?" said Ginger, eating only her mashed potatoes. "I think you are gonna become famous."

"Yeah!" said James, his plate almost completely cleared. "I want—"

"Stop tapping your plate with that fork, son," I said.

He quickly set his fork down before continuing. "Um . . . I want you to become famous so I can tell all of my friends at school."

"Oh!" said Loretta. "Become famous so you can brag to your schoolmates. In that case, I must make it happen at once."

"Your mother's kidding you, son. We never brag . . . about ourselves, or about members of our family. Especially in the Soviet Union! Such antics are frowned upon. And it's actually one of the values here that I believe should be applied everywhere. Humility is a beautiful thing. Haven't your American teachers hammered that message home yet, son?"

"No, they just—"

"Yes, they have!" said Ginger. "Mrs. Jones said everyone is supposed to be treated equally at all times. No one is rich or poor. No one is smart or dumb. No one is strong or weak. No one is ugly or pretty."

"Hmm!" said Loretta. "Where is Mrs. Jones from again?"

"She's from Boston," said Ginger.

"Ah, yes!" I said. "She's the woman who's married to the Ford factory engineer. I actually met him. Told me that autoworkers from the U.S. are flooding here. The pay is better. The housing is darn near free. America's Depression is turning the Soviet Union into the Soviet States of America. The only man in America who's had a penny to his name in the last five years is John Dillinger. And he's been dead for two months."

"Really!" said Loretta. "What happened?"

"Cover your ears, kids." Both obeyed my order and I spoke softly to Loretta. "Hoover's agents shot him dead at the Biograph Theater in Chicago back in July."

"Oh my!" she said.

I motioned for them to uncover their ears.

"Who is John Dillinger?" said Ginger.

"He was a bad guy, honey," I said, moving her plate closer to her. "A bank robber. Eat your fish and carrots, too, sweetie."

"I want to go to Chicago, Daddy," said James. "I want to go back to America on the *Trumpet* and see the Statue of Liberty again with Uncle Bobby and Aunt Dorene. And I want to see Milwaukee, where you were born, and I want to see Philadelphia, where Mommy was born. And I want to see the Mississippi River and compare it to the Seine in Paris. Please, Daddy!"

"You will, son. Someday. You will."

"Mr. Fort-Whiteman said America is the worst place on earth," said Ginger. "He said here, in the Soviet Union, they treat brown people like human beings, not like animals the way they do in his hometown of Dallas, Texas."

"What?" I said. "Why is he talking to you about this sort of thing?"

"Isn't he your chemistry teacher?" said Loretta. "What does any of that have to do with science? Did he really tell you that?"

Ginger nodded big and chewed her carrots so we could all see them.

"Close your mouth, Ginger," I sternly said. "You know better than to chew with your mouth open. You're eleven, not three."

James grinned at my scolding of his twin sister, who always overplayed her sadness whenever I so much as hinted at being upset with her. This time was no different. She put her fork down and just stared at her plate. Loretta and I ignored her, certain she'd be back to normal within seconds.

"I need to go have a talk with this Mr. Fort-Whiteman," I said.

"Maybe you should let me, your much gentler wife, go pay him a visit. I've spoken to Lovett several times already."

"Who?" I said. "Lovett? You're on a first-name basis, huh?"

"Yes, Lovett Fort-Whiteman. He's a colored man from the U.S. He's usually out in front of the school greeting parents in the morning. And I'll have you know . . . he most certainly is a proud, card-carrying communist, a formal member. He couldn't wait to tell me all about it. Said he won't stop until every American he meets is converted. And he's even a leader of some sort within the American branch."

"You learned all of this during those brief visits?"

"Who said they were *brief*, love?" She smiled. "He *is* awfully handsome."

"Oooh, Mommy!" said James, crinkling up his face, embarrassed that his mother had hinted about another man's attractiveness, the entire back-and-forth prompting Ginger to perk up and chime in, too.

"Yeah, Mommy! Oooh!"

"I third that!" I said. "Oooh, Mommy!"

Loretta reached across the table and took my hand. "Now come on, love. I said he was *handsome*. I didn't say stunning and breathtakingly gorgeous. Only you fit that category." She kissed my hand. "You hear that, children?"

They both smiled and nodded, overjoyed at seeing her being affectionate toward me. This sort of loving playfulness between Loretta and me always tickled them. We were all so close and happy, so completely connected.

11

I'D BEEN BACK AT THE TRANSIT CAMP FOR A WEEK NOW, REUNITED with my son and the other four comrades from my compartment. My right hand was stitched up and wrapped, and my left arm was in a cast, as Leonid's kick had fractured the humerus bone about two inches above the elbow joint.

I'd found it interesting to learn during my visit to the Camp Z hospital that the man who'd fixed me, a Dr. Smirnov, like all of the other doctors and nurses within Stalin's entire camp system, was a prisoner as well.

I was still waiting for someone official to tell me that my sentence had indeed been reduced to eight years. But after the officers at Camp Z had learned of my injuries and inability to do any more forestry work, they immediately sent me back here, never showing me any papers or holding a private meeting with me to discuss a sentence change. I was just left to wonder. These men were shamelessly unethical and dishonest. Nothing they'd ever tell me from this point forward would mean a single thing. It was the land of empty promises.

What struck me upon my return to the transit camp, having been away for two and a half weeks, was how much thinner my son and the other four appeared. On the other hand, they were shocked to see how strong and normal I looked, save for the obvious injuries and cuts to my face and arms. I'd made it back just in time, because car number twenty-eight's men were scheduled to board a ship and head north to Kolyma in two days.

I was back in the same civilian clothes I'd been wearing the night of my arrest back in Moscow. It appeared that someone at Camp Z had attempted to wash them before reissue upon my release. They were still stained with blood, but they had held up nicely since Moscow, a far cry from the raggedy, civilian garb many of the other *zeks* still wore. Some at the transit had come with suitcases, but my compartment lads and I had not.

It was morning and I lay in my bottom bunk still, James asleep above me, the old man, Abram, on the next lower bunk near my feet, coughing uncontrollably. Yury was above him.

"Can I help you somehow, Abram?" said Yury.

"I'll be fine," he groveled.

"Your cough sounds much deeper," I said. "When did you last visit the hospital?"

He didn't answer me straightaway. He just coughed for a long spell.

"They told me I shouldn't have smoked my whole life," he finally said. "Then they gave me a shot of something and sent me back out. I had tried to also explain to the nurses that I, like so many others, am suffering from night blindness."

Again Abram went into a coughing fit before continuing.

"One of the nurses gave me some cod-liver oil for it. We'll see if it helps. At least I don't have pellagra or scurvy like so many I saw in there. My God, the bloated legs! That medical compound is loaded with diseased souls. The good news is, when you all leave in two days, I will remain here. They told me that next week I can begin serving out my ten years here at the transit cleaning latrines and washing prison uniforms."

"They most certainly will not have you cleaning shit for ten years!" said Yury, his Russian so proper sounding, as he was very well educated and also seemed to pride himself on giving off an air of a distinguished gentleman.

"Of course not!" said Abram. "I won't be doing it at all, boy. I'll be dead within five days."

"Tell me you won't," said James, who'd awoken, his Russian words dripping with sadness. "You can't die, Abram."

My son climbed down from his bed and approached the old man. He leaned down and hugged him. He stayed there and began to cry.

"There, there, boy!" said Abram, reaching his frail arm around James and tapping him repeatedly on the back. The two had obviously grown close over the past few weeks.

"It is conceivable that you could survive here," said Yury with sudden optimism in his voice. "It's cleaning shit, yes, but at least you won't freeze to death."

"Come here, son," I said.

James reluctantly let go of Abram and sat with me on my bed. My unbroken right arm around him now, he rested his head on my shoulder. Still teary-eyed, he began touching the dirty bandage wrapped around my hand.

"Dying naturally can be a gift to man from God," said Abram. "Hear me. I am not being shot or hanged or stabbed. I am choosing to let go and die. I want to. I am old enough. I had my uninterrupted life for so many good years. And now a madman has overtaken my country. I will not die at his hands. I will choose to die at God's."

"But your children," said Yury.

"I have written a letter to my daughter in Poland. She will receive it and send word to my other daughter and three sons. It has been made clear to them. Besides, they know I was ready to go when my wife died two years ago."

"That's one of the many sick aspects of Stalin's prison system," said Yury. "He allows us to write letters to our families, after they've been read by NKVD, of course, but still, it is as if he wants our loved ones to know of our misery, and to also live in fear."

"Or, perhaps he does it to trace their whereabouts," I said.

"It doesn't matter," said Abram, now coughing blood into a white rag. "He can find whomever he wants to find. He can round up the entire country. I wrote the letter to my daughter in Poland. She is safe there. And she's smart. She will notify my other children in Leningrad in a safe way. Besides, we cannot live in terror of this man. Whatever our destinies be, they shall be. Stalin tried to rip away our religion, but I still have God in my heart."

I looked around the filthy barracks and saw most of car twenty-eight's men still sleeping, including our two other compartment mates, Boris and Mikhail. I always wondered which prisoners were actually asleep or dead, as we'd lost several since being here.

"I wish Stalin had never been born," said Yury. "I wish Lenin had lived longer. He is rolling over in his grave right now. I am hoping Trotsky will somehow return and bring sanity back to my Soviet Union."

"You keep talking out loud about such things and one of these *zeks* is going to tell on you," said Abram. "I am much older than you, boy. You are so full of passion, but you must keep your political opinions to yourself. There are always spies within our midst. Do you understand me, Yury?"

"I want to do it your way," he said, the tone in his voice emoting deference to the old man. "I just had such belief in Trotsky. But I will stop and do it your way, Abram. Just promise me you will try to stay alive. I don't want to go to Kolyma with the thought of you being dead in my mind. You remind me of those Russian people from our history who are beautiful, not ugly. You make me believe that I, too, can live a long life, have children, a wife, read books, grow wise, and someday . . . educate young men the way you do. Don't die, Abram."

"When you all get to Kolyma," said Abram, coughing, "make sure you do one thing for me. And I want you, young James, to pay particular attention here. I want you to do exactly as the guards say. Never talk back or delay in responding to their orders. Understand?"

We all nodded and he went into another coughing fit, this time followed by heavier breathing. Then he continued in an even weaker voice.

"I want you to wake up every day and look straight up to the sky and past it. I will be there with my wife and God looking down on you. You may not know why this horror is happening right now, but don't examine it for another second. Accept it. Focus on that day's work. Treat that day's soup or bread as if it were a king's feast. When you lie down at night on whatever hard, freezing board they provide, think of me and let my voice put you to sleep at once. You can make it. I don't care if you have to sleep in one of those holes dug in the ice. You can make it. You are all young, strong, smart. Your spirits are free. They can't touch it. They can't break you. No matter how thin and weak your bodies become, stay alive. See your families again, my boys. I love you dearly."

It was on those last words that he took several deep, labored breaths and closed his eyes. I sat up and approached him, placing my hand on his neck to feel for a pulse. The beautiful, old man had gone to see God. And in two days, when the five of us would finally take our ominous ship ride north, we wouldn't have to wonder if our gray-haired sage had died yet. He'd left us with some lovely last words. But now he was gone.

Three days later, we were still adjusting to having been crammed into a cargo ship like a bunch of sardines for about twenty-four hours now. The waters were choppy and many of the men had been vomiting from seasickness. The smell throughout was deplorable. There were men and women on the ship, but we were not together. We were packed in the lower hold, and they were on the deck above us. The hold smelled of ammonium nitrate, and it was fairly dark, but not completely like the train had been, because two dim lamps hung from the ladder, one at the top, the other at the bottom.

"I'm guessing there are at least a thousand men in here," said Yury. "While you were at Camp Z, the old man told me that other ships on this Kolyma route are much larger, three or five thousand onboard. The holds are different, too. They just threw us in here like dogs, but the bigger boats have three-level holds filled with mattress-less bunks so the *zeks* can lie down."

"You can lie down on the deck there," I groaned.

"Would rather have a bunk."

"It feels like the sea is very angry right now," I said, my bandaged hand on my sleeping son's leg.

"The old man told me that many ships have capsized trying to make this journey," said Yury. "He said the route is difficult because of the La Pérouse Strait, which is a twenty-five-mile-wide stretch of sea dividing two islands: Hokkaido and Sakhalin."

"I want to thank you, Yury," I said, my stomach rolling, the nausea intensifying as I sweated and kept my eyes closed, the back of my head pressing against the sticky, wooded bulkhead behind me. "I want to thank you for not being sick. It allows you to keep talking, which keeps my mind busy. And your Russian diction is so crisp, so soothing. Thank you. I envy your resilient stomach."

"You're welcome. I have eaten many bad things in my life. I am immune. As I was saying, according to the old man, the edges of the strait are made up of rock hazards. So the ship has to fight the choppy waters and at the same time keep it from pushing it toward the edges. But this is tricky, Prescott, because the more the ship tries to stay in the center of the strait, the more it also has to avoid the big monster in the middle. Not easy to navigate."

"Monster?" I slurred.

"Yes, right in the middle of the strait is a rock monster named the Stone of Danger. Many boats have smashed right into it. When it's dark out, they actually can't navigate around it. They can't see it. They have to basically guess where it is and try to avoid it. So, you see, we may be in luck after all. The ship will probably run aground. We may die at sea."

"That'll be nice," I mumbled, sour stomach acid bubbling up to where I could taste it now, the fish soup we'd eaten some twenty-four hours earlier still refusing to digest. Perhaps it had been made of rotten bream. I wondered because I hadn't gotten seasick on the *Trumpet* yacht during that journey to Nantucket, but these were extremely turbulent waters. Fishy bile burning your throat while you're on the verge of vomiting ranks near the top on the misery list.

"Not a single guard has come down here," said Yury. "I'll bet it's because of the choppy waters. They are all up in their cabins sick as dogs. Or they know we are all too weak and sick to cause any commotion. Still, with all of these animals among us, free to move about as soon as their seasickness subsides, I've got my guard up. And there were reports of some *zeks* breaking into the women's barracks while we were at the transit camp. There were rapes. That was the word going around while you were at Camp Z, Prescott. Apparently the suspects were all shot, though."

"Don't repeat that story in the company of my son," I slurred, just before the lamp at the top of the ladder went out and left us all in an even less visible hold, many of the men moaning louder as a result.

"Of course not, Prescott," he said, oblivious to the change in light and the agony surrounding him. "I know James is asleep. But you do want to know such details, yes?"

"Yes, thank you, Yury."

"How long before your fractured arm heals?"

"The doctor said four weeks. So, should be almost healed upon our arrival."

"Yes, we should be there in nine more days," he said.

"And then, in about another week after, they will have me digging with you all, Yury. If I'm kept back at camp during those first days, make sure to try to watch over my son out there while you're mining. I know it may not be possible, but try to stay close to him. Please."

"You have my word, Prescott."

"Check on Mikhail and Boris," I said.

Yury, sitting to my left, stood and walked to the right, past me first, then James. Boris was next to my son, and Mikhail was to his right. All of us *zeks* were covering the deck throughout. We lucky ones at least had our backs to the bulkhead, but others had to sit back-to-back or lie down and curl up tight. The last good light we'd seen had been on the deck when the guards had given us soup prior to our climbing down the ladder. There was one toilet hole in the corner near the bottom of the ladder, but getting to it required squeezing through the knot of *zeks*, so unless it was vital, one was best off holding it.

"They are both breathing," said Yury. "But Mikhail feels too hot."

"Wake him up," I said.

"Why?"

"Because you need to ask him exactly how he feels. If he has a fever and it gets too hot, he will simply allow himself to die. Many of these groaning men are only minutes away from letting death overtake them. He's probably not actually asleep, but rather passed out. Wake him up."

"Mikhail!" said Yury, shaking him. "Mikhail!"

All we heard was him moan.

"Talk to me, Mikhail," said Yury. "How do you feel?"

"Water!" he slurred. "I . . . need . . . water."

"Here, Yury!" I said, handing him my canteen. "Give him mine. All of it! Have him drink it all."

"But we don't know when they will give us more," said Yury. "You are going to need—"

"Now!" I said, still feeling dizzy. "I will be fine."

Yury took my canteen and tried to hand it to him.

"Here, Mikhail," he said. "Take the water."

Mikhail just moaned louder and louder.

"He won't take it, Prescott."

"He's delirious," I said. "Put your fingers to his lips and force open his mouth. Force-feed him the water. Hold his head and make sure he swallows. Do it carefully. He might throw it up at first but talk him through it."

I listened to the ordeal for a few minutes. Fortunately, he drank and kept it down. Besides the old man, Mikhail had

seemed the weakest of us six for the last week. He'd been beyond distraught about not being able to witness the birth of his
child, his wife all alone back in Moscow.

Boris, on the other hand, was a damn tenacious Swede. In
fairness to Mikhail, however, Boris didn't have to worry about a
wife or child. And I was quickly learning that surviving these
seemingly insurmountable conditions was largely based on ge-
netics, one's chemical and mental makeup, regardless of their
food or water intake. It was ultimately survival of the fittest, and
in the recesses of my mind, I knew my son would be okay because he had my blood coursing through his veins.

"Slap his face, Yury," I said. "Lightly! Make him talk to you."

"Can you hear my voice, Mikhail?" said Yury, slapping him a
few times. "Say something, Mikhail! Are you there? What is your
wife's name?"

"Galina!" he whispered.

"Your baby! You and Galina had probably chosen names.
What was it to be if a girl was born?"

"Dominika."

"And if it is a boy?"

"Anton."

"Good!" said Yury. "Either Dominika or Anton will be waiting
for you in Moscow when you get out. Stay alive. Remember what
the old man said. Stay alive!"

Over the next two days the hatch had only been opened
twice, both times to drop nets full of black bread down. The
guards had been too afraid to enter the hold, as many criminals
were amongst us. *Zeks* ripped through the nets and we were left
to scurry after small loaves like rats. Many skirmishes ensued, as
it was supposed to be one piece per *zek*, but some refused to
abide. Luckily the fights had subsided rather quickly, the prisoners too weak to engage in a prolonged back-and-forth. I feared,
however, that if the women's hold had in any way been accessi-
ble, some of these pigs might have done the unthinkable.

The guards had also lowered buckets of water down by rope for us to dip from, hardly an easy task, as we'd been issued one tin cup per five *zeks*. Those had been our only two meals in forty-eight hours. And they hadn't replaced the top lamp.

Now, four days into our blind odyssey north, Mikhail's condition had grown much worse. As we sat there in the dark, he began to mumble bizarre phrases. And the four of us tried our best to make sense of them.

"I want to walk alone and then the chair will do the body bleed, bleed, bleed!" said Mikhail, as I fought back my own pain and tried to interpret his Russian drivel. It was as if he were going from coherent thought to speaking in tongues.

"Body bleed, bleed, bleed!" he continued. "The dove, the dove! Ah, the dove! Ah, the dove! There are five, ten, a thousand. Look at the dove. Look, look, look! Many, many, many, many, many, many! Body bleed, bleed, bleed! We're gonna ride away to the liver parade. The moon, the moon, the moon! Shoot that frog! Shoot that frog parade and all the flowers and cake! You orange juice engine maker! Kill the chocolate teeth and jelly! Look! Look!"

Mikhail stopped and began to soothe himself with long, drawn-out moans. There was no need to talk to him, for there was nothing we could offer.

Hours later, the guards felt it a good idea to open the hatch and point their hoses down at us. Within seconds there was frigid seawater spraying men, the guards' version of bathing us.

With bright flashlights flickering on different faces throughout the hold, the guards hadn't told us to close our eyes, so the first poor souls to get sprayed felt a salt burn that must have been excruciating. Sure, the five of us felt some sting, but having been able to close our eyes and brace for the lathering made all the difference. And it was only after the guards had closed the hatch that we'd dared to even peek at the dark chaos.

Some of the men had already been dead, others, I was guessing, had typhus, pleurisy, or dysentery. And now, whatever filth had washed off of these moaning, bony, infected, withering souls was left for us all to slosh around in until it slowly made its way down the drainage.

"Is everyone okay?" I said to my comrades, the other lamp going out now, leaving the hold black. "Son, talk to me. Are you okay?"

"I think so," he said.

Boris and Yury answered yes as well.

"Talk to me, Mikhail," I said, but there was silence.

"He's dead," said Boris. "I'm holding his neck. My comrade is gone."

He began to weep, but it only blended in with the other cries throughout.

"My beautiful comrade is gone," Boris continued. "I have nothing now. No one! This was my brother. This was my new family. His child is fatherless now. His wife is without her husband."

"You can visit them when you get out," I said, the darkness not allowing me to catch even a glimpse of him. "You can be the strength they will need, Boris. And until then, I will be your brother. Stay with me. I will be your family. You hear me, Boris."

He wept even louder, the madness finally overtaking him. And James, taken by the scene, began to cry into my shoulder. I'd feared that death was becoming too normal to him, but he was still not immune.

"I want to die now," said Boris, trying to control his cry. "I cannot go on. Mikhail was so young. He was so strong. How could he die?"

"Stop!" I said. "The only thing you can do is accept this hell. We are in hell, Boris. My son here is but fourteen years old. He will never be the same. And I have to accept that. But we can survive! For the love of God, Boris, we can survive."

"Prescott is right," said Yury. "You must do as the old man said and think of your parents back in Sweden, Boris. You've only known Mikhail for a short while, but your parents have been there your entire life. They will be waiting for you."

Those words silenced Boris. I didn't know if he had given up or not, but I knew he was a strong enough young man to endure the agony we all had in store for us, if only he would search deep within himself and try to block out all of the fallen victims. But he'd need to find his focus quickly, for death was trying its damnedest to pay us all a visit.

12

Moscow, Russia
September 1934

O N A FRIDAY MORNING I LOADED THE FAMILY IN OUR USED MA-
roon Ford Model A and headed straight to the University of
Toilers, where Loretta was scheduled to meet with an enroll-
ment counselor about taking some history courses. She was
dead set on learning about the roots of the Bolshevik Revolution, the rise of Lenin, the history of the kulaks, the origins of
Stalin's anti-religion campaign, and the split between Trotsky
and Stalin. She also wanted to know what was making so many
people from around the world want to discover the Soviet
Union. She figured if she could capture the essence of whatever
that was, she'd be able to reveal it through paintings. I feared
that she would only learn the version of history Stalin had instructed his professors to teach.

Once I'd dropped her off, I headed straight for the Anglo-
American School to make sure the twins made it to class on
time. I also needed to pay a visit to Mr. Lovett Fort-Whiteman,
the science teacher Loretta had gone on and on about.

As soon as we pulled up I spotted him. He appeared to be
about my age and was hard to miss with his high cheekbones,
angular face, big smile, and jovial demeanor. He was a toffee-
skinned man of maybe six feet and was wearing a long-sleeved,

belted blue shirt that came all the way down to his knees. The golden belt was a wide, ornamental one, pulled tight to accentuate his narrow waistline and muscular upper body. His tan pants were tucked into his black pointy leather boots, and he sported a white fur hat. I could have sworn I was looking at a Cossack. The only thing missing was a *shashka*.

This was a man whose appearance screamed classic, proud Russia. Perhaps if he were a native, his flamboyance would be frowned upon as czarist flavored, but as an American, it could only be appreciated as a rejection of the U.S. and a full-throated endorsement of Mother Russia.

"Good-bye, Daddy!" both kids said, hopping out and closing the back doors, book bags in hand.

"Have fun at school!" I said, getting out myself and walking toward Mr. Whiteman, who was engaged in conversation with a blond woman.

"Ronald has an acumen for this stuff, Caroline," he said. "I mean, he's digested the periodic table of elements with ease."

"Well, thank you, Lovett," she said. "I'll be sure to tell his father."

"Have a nice day now!" he said, and she walked away.

"Excuse me!" I said. "I wanted to introduce myself. Name's Prescott Sweet!" He removed his hat and we shook. "You have my two—"

"Of course!" he said, grinning. "Ginger and James Sweet are your kids. I've been wanting to meet you. Fantastic children by the way!"

"Why thank you."

"Your wife tells me you work at the embassy. Impressive! And it sure is nice to meet another American brother."

"Likewise," I said, already certain that I liked him. He was so charismatic and full of energy, to the point where it damn near made me want to run to join the Communist Party right then and there.

"You'd *have* to work at the embassy to wear a blue suit like that," he said. "Looks to me to be the finest I've ever seen. Expensive! Don't let anyone from the Politburo see you."

"Excuse me!"

"I'm messin' with you. Looks like you got something on your tie there, though." He leaned in with his sharp nose and pointed. "Right in the middle there."

"Hmm," I said, chin and eyes down. "Ah, yes! Made the kids *kolbasa* sandwiches this morning to pack for their lunch and put plenty of mustard on the bread."

I licked my right thumb and rubbed at the red silk.

"Damn yellow stuff stains like crazy, too!" I continued.

"Oh, yeah! That Russian mustard is a beast."

"Thank you for pointing it out, Mr. Fort-Whiteman."

"Ah, call me Lovett . . . please!"

"Okay. And you can call me Prescott."

"Will do! What a time to be working at this particular embassy, Prescott."

"Yes, it is fascinating work. Quite an influx of Americans here with the unemployment rate back in America being what it is. I understand you teach chemistry."

"Yes! But you'll have to forgive me for dabbling in current events from time to time with the students. I'm sure your children have shared a few of my passionate stories with you. I'm a very political man and find myself teaching civics sometimes when I should be teaching chemistry. Something about being in the Soviet Union and not feeling colored all the time has liberated me to the point where I want to shout it to the world."

"Amen! I've had the same feeling since arriving here."

"Where you from?"

"Born in Chicago. Raised in Milwaukee. Educated in Vermont. Employed in Harlem. Liberated in Paris."

"Ha, ha! Harlem! I moved there after finishing school at the Tuskegee Institute. Tried to become an actor. Tried!"

"You have the gravitas for it," I said, studying how his sallow-brown skin, shaved head, and pointy features almost gave him an Asian, Buddhist monk look.

"Wasn't deep enough," he said. "Acting! Didn't help heal things. Nah, but even before that, after I was done at Tuskegee, I tried to be a doctor. Got into medical school in Nashville. Wasn't for me. That's when I went to Harlem and tried acting. Wasn't long before I left that and went to Mexico for a few years. Got to see up close the Mexican Revolution. Affected my thinking!"

"I'll bet."

"Inspired me to head back to Harlem and seek change. Yeah, I was there when it seemed like every brother and sister I ran into had come there seeking refuge. But I didn't find it. Didn't find it anywhere in America. It was only when I joined the Communist Party that I began to see a way forward."

"When did you join?"

"Only secretively in 1920, then publically . . . officially . . . in 1924. I rose up quick. Started recruiting other coloreds, too. Now I'm workin' on you!"

"I see!"

"Was that year, 1924, when I came to the Soviet Union for the first time. Found my soul. Ain't never looked back! Had a lot of colored folks say to me, 'Don't you know the U.S. Government has declared the Party their number-one enemy?' I said, 'Give me a choice between communism and Jim Crow, and I'll sign up the same way every single time.' My daddy and momma back in Dallas taught me too good about the evil of Jim Crow. Got to know it all too well! Oh, yeah! That Crow is an awfully ugly bird."

"Ain't that the truth!" I said, thinking about my old friend James, whom Lovett reminded me of. The longer he spoke to me, the looser his talk became, as if he had been sizing me up, seeing what kind of brother I was.

"Ya know, Prescott, stayin' on Jim Crow for a second . . . lotta folks knew *only* that ugly thang and nothin' else from cradle to grave!"

"I like the way you said that. *Thang!*"

"Us Texas niggas don't never get *too* far away from what we done got used to! Come on now! Guess I feel like I can talk to you straight, just like I could when I was around my two Communist Party USA brothers, Harry Haywood and Otto Hall. Been a while since I ran into a brutha like you. But I'm like a

chameleon. I can talk real white for those high-and-mighty mutha-
fuckas who like to sit up high. But then I can get on down with
my country family like you. Feel like you the type who mighta
done ate a chitlin or two! Ha!"

"Oh, yeah!" I said, laughing and purposely slipping into his
way of talking. "My aunt Coretta and my momma used to cook
the mess outta them things back in Bronzeville. Would throw
some hog maws in there, too. Had the whole damn house . . .
hell . . . the whole damn neighborhood smellin' like . . . like—"

"Like shit!" he bluntly said. "Go on and say it, boy! Shoot! Can
eat me a whole pot of them thangs! A whole mess of 'em! I been
known to slap the hell out a nigga who tries to take the last
chitlin out my momma's pot! Uncles, cousins! Shit! I ain't one
to play!"

We both giggled aloud, his words tickling me to the point I
had to bend over. It had been a long time since I'd felt this kind
of deep, sidesplitting laughter burst out of me. I'd gotten used
to being around such formality for so long, and he was taking
me back to that essence of old, black-folk comfort, the kind that
never leaves you, the kind that bonds people. A *momma's pot of
chitlins* was familiar to all of us colored Americans.

"You should come by this shindig I'm throwing next Saturday
night, Prescott. There'll be other fun-loving members of the
Party there as well. I know you might have to keep it hush-hush
in terms of your embassy colleagues, but I think you and your
wife would find the company quite enlightening and spirited."

"I just might do that."

"Everybody there will be dressed up in their finest, but here's
the catch . . . bring your suits, fine dresses, makeup, and jewelry
in a suitcase. Then get dressed once you're inside. Stalin's
NKVD tend to keep a watchful eye on us foreign Americans
when it comes to our nightlife."

"You're kidding?" I said. "Look at me now."

"But they know you work for the American embassy. I'm talking about the masses. They're okay with the way I dress flamboy-
antly because they think I'm making a positive statement to the

U.S. They actually think I'm protesting the U.S., and that brings a smile to Stalin's face. I've been told as much by a member of his Politburo."

"You've met one of them?"

"Of course! *Time* magazine didn't label me the 'Reddest of the Blacks' for nothing. I was the first organizer of the American Negro Labor Congress that got this damn flood of coloreds-to-Russia *thang* started. Back in 1924, I actually spoke to a large contingent here in Moscow during the Fifth Comintern Congress, and Joseph Stalin was in attendance. The Comintern is simply the international organization that advocates world communism. I like to call it the League of Nations for communists. Damn near every country in the world has its own party, and representatives from each gather in Moscow quite often. Headquarters is here! But, yeah, in 1924 I spoke in front of Stalin."

"I'll be damned!" I said.

"I spoke about America's Negro problem being a *race thang* and not a *class thang*. Stalin and company didn't like that too much. His men made it clear to me that dealing with class always came first. Shoot! These Soviets still don't know that being colored in America ain't got a damn thang to do with class. It's race first! The wealthiest nigga in the U.S. is still a lowlife nothin' to greater America."

"Preach, Lovett!"

"Shoot! I wanted to tell Stalin that the poorest white man in the U.S. is treated far greater than said wealthy Negro. You don't see any poor white men being lynched all over the South. We're far away from it over here, but lynchings are still rampant back home. I wanted to make Stalin understand that if he snapped his fingers and all at once, every American suddenly became of the same *class*, Negroes would still get lynched. But these Soviets just don't get the complexity of our homeland. Our *color-land*! Shh! Let me watch my tongue!"

"It is a color-land!" I said. "But tell me again about us needing to bring our fine clothes in a suitcase to the party."

"Oh, yeah! Nothing too bad would ever happen if you didn't

do it that way, but we like to show up to our parties dressed real plain, just so we don't draw any attention. Such is the way in Moscow these days. I'm a communist, but unlike Stalin, I don't equate nice dress with being bourgeois. Being a communist is about the way you treat people, your moral compass and vision of an everlasting, equal society, not about dress codes."

"You married, Lovett?"

"Yes, I married a Russian woman. And nobody here even raised an eyebrow. Imagine that back home. Me with a white woman wouldn't go over too well. But we feel as comfortable here as a couple could ever hope."

"I look forward to meeting her."

"You know, back to what I was meaning to tell you earlier. If the Comintern can be as effective as many believe, the revolution here in the Soviet Union will spread across the globe. And U.S. Negroes would benefit the most. Gotta believe, brutha! Or in this case . . . *comrade!*"

"Yup!" I said.

"You were raised in Milwaukee, huh?" he said.

"Yes, the Bronzeville section."

"Well, shoot! I'm gonna have to call you Bronzeville Sweet then!"

He didn't know it, but Lovett already felt like family to me. He was an impressive, spirited, and lovable man. He actually reminded me of my late friend, my son's namesake, James Eason. I missed him dearly, still, after over a decade. *My God, how the time had flown by.*

Later that day at Spaso House I found myself with a flashlight in the portion of the multilevel attic that was only three feet high. I was crawling on all fours. All of the wire was old and shoddy. As I neared the area directly above the ambassador's bedroom, I stopped, thinking I'd heard something in the distance. *Maybe it was a rat*, I thought. Still, it spooked me.

Again I heard a noise, like someone was crawling. I scooted forward, my belly scraping against the dusty wood, beads of sweat dripping from my chin. Holding the flashlight up and pointing it straight ahead, I heard a *clank*, like someone had dropped perhaps a metal object.

"WHO'S THERE?" I yelled.

No answer. I froze and waited. Nothing. I crawled forward really fast a few feet and abruptly stopped, hoping to provoke more movement. Nothing.

"Are you there, Sergei?" I said in firm Russian, knowing I'd just seen him downstairs. "*Vy tam*, Sergei?"

I waited there a few more minutes and then made my way back out of the shallow attic. I needed to pay the ambassador a visit. He'd told me not to be shy about interrupting him to share any tidbits of conspicuous news.

I searched the entire mansion until I finally found him outside in front of the garage smoking a cigarette and, of all things, polishing his beautiful sports roadster—the little dog, Pie-Pie, sitting in the driver's seat, and Stewart, the U.S. Marine, standing guard beside the garage door.

"Excuse me, Mr. Ambassador," I said, only to have him remain focused on the wax he was wiping from the rear bumper.

"Stewart!" he said without looking at him. "Give us a moment here."

The big marine nodded and walked toward the main house.

"What can I do for you, Prescott?" he said, the white rag circling.

"I heard someone up in the attic just now above your bedroom."

"Yeah?" he said with no surprise, his eyes fixed on the paint as if it were gold.

"Yes, sir. I believe your suspicions are correct. I didn't see anyone in the flesh, but my instincts tell me someone was there, and they certainly didn't want me to know they were there."

"It was Sergei," he said. "I'll bet the farm on it."

"Well, I had just seen him in the kitchen five minutes earlier."

"What were you doing in the kitchen, Prescott?"

"Excuse me?"

"Never mind."

I frowned at his remark, but he didn't see it. Hell, he never so much as peeked my way.

"As I was saying, Mr. Ambassador, I'd just seen him five minutes earlier."

"And when he saw you, Prescott, he rushed upstairs and removed the microphone that was placed there yesterday."

I waited for him to say something else, but he was transfixed on the polish. I could sense he had the weight of the Soviet world on his shoulders. Or maybe he was thinking about his ex-wife, Louise Bryant, or some other woman in his life. I wondered. He was so mysterious. The rag circling harder with every second, he finally continued talking to *it* rather than me it seemed, and his jaw clinched tighter and tighter.

"They're so damn stupid to think I'd say anything of value while in my study. Boggles the mind! They honestly believe I have absolutely no fucking idea they've ever been up there piddling around. They're so scientifically smart that it has rendered them socially inept. No proper instincts whatsoever!"

"Either that or they simply think we Americans are wholly ignorant people, sir."

"Stay on top of this," he said, as if not hearing a word I'd uttered. "I don't want to catch them. Ever! Does us no good! I just want to be completely aware of their entire setup. It will serve the next ambassador well to know exactly how they're spying on us."

He stood and walked around to the front of the car, lifting the hood. "Carl is not here at the moment, Prescott. What do you know about engines?"

"Plenty," I said, walking over.

"Good. It may look beautiful, but it won't start. And it's not the battery. Just had a new one put in."

"Do you mind?" I said, signaling that I'd like to take a look.

He nodded and moved aside. I leaned over the engine to get a bird's-eye view, looking in every direction before jiggling various wires. "Could be a problem with the electrical portion of the ignition switch, a short or something," I said. "Or, maybe even a plugged exhaust system. I'll need some time to diagnose."

"There's a toolbox behind you just inside the garage there," he said, and I immediately went to retrieve it.

"There you are, William!" said an approaching Bobby. "We've been searching every room in Spaso trying to find you."

"Well, you found me," said Bullitt, rag still in hand. "What is it?"

"You called a meeting, William," said a confused-looking Bobby, who was accompanied by four others.

"I sent Charles to the chancery to tell you that I'd like to move the meeting to tomorrow," said Bullitt, gazing at his watch. "You didn't get the message, Bobby?"

"He never—"

"It's fine," said Bullitt. "You're all here. We may as well take advantage of it. That damn Charles! He probably got side-tracked."

"I spoke to him this morning," said Bobby. "He mentioned nothing of a changed meeting time, but did say he was planning to fetch your ballerina friend for you, William. Maybe he—"

"He's not *fetching* anyone for me. Her name is Lolya Lepishinkaya and she happens to be one of the finest dancers in the entire Moscow Ballet. She's giving private lessons to Anne. Is that okay with you, Bobby?"

"Sorry, William. Your daughter is fortunate to have such a willing teacher. And Charles did indeed say she was a brilliant performer."

Charles Thayer was whom he was referring to, the ambassador's very young, "do everything" assistant and interpreter.

"Anne loves the performing arts," said Bullitt. "She and I recently attended a play called 'The Negress and the Monkey.' She thoroughly enjoyed herself."

Upon hearing Bullitt's comment, I damn near dropped the flashlight I'd just taken out of the toolbox. Something about the words *negress* and *monkey* thrown together so casually didn't fall

easily upon my ears. Nevertheless, I ignored it and began digging through the toolbox in search of some fresh batteries.

"Chip found you some more wooden coat hangers, William,"
said thirty-year-old George Kennan, a nice, handsome gentleman I had met already at the chancery, one of the ambassador's
third secretaries. I'd met all of the staff. The other third secretaries were Bertel Kuniholm and Chip Bohlen, both in their
thirties, both in attendance.

"Ah, yes, wooden hangers!" said Bullitt, walking around to the
driver's side door, Pie-Pie panting behind the wheel. "Did you
find any more of that good vodka we had last weekend, George?"

"Indeed."

"Excellent!" said the ambassador, actually cracking a smile.
"Nothing like drinking vodka in Russia! When in Rome, right,
gentlemen?"

We all nodded, Bobby placing his hand on my shoulder, his
big grin signaling how happy he was to see me. I was still thinking about the oddity of the ambassador asking his third secretary to fetch wooden hangers for him.

"Or in this case . . . when in *Russia*!" continued Bullitt. "Their
vodka is about the only thing I can find worth praising at the
moment. Can you handle this, Prescott, maybe get her up and
running for me?"

"I'm sure I can, sir," I said, turning the flashlight on and leaning over the engine again.

The ambassador smiled. "You're a lifesaver, Prescott. You may
never get him back, Bobby. I hate to tell you that."

Bobby half smiled, all six of the men now standing beside the
driver's side door while I continued examining the engine. Of
course I positioned myself so that I could still see them through
the space between the open hood and frame. How could I not?

"I can't help but be envious of you, William," said Loy Hen-
derson, admiring the white roadster. Loy was the second secretary. He was balding and had a rather egg-shaped head. Booby
had informed me that Loy was forty-two. In fact, he'd informed
me of all of the top staff's ages.

Bullitt actually put some more polish on the rag, squatted down, and began shining the door again, his five staffers standing around him. It was as if the ambassador was suffering from some sort of compulsive disorder. He started talking to the rag again. "I cabled Washington at five this morning and informed the president of the latest regarding Stalin and his hopes for a partnership with us against Japan."

"I fear the Soviet leader has expectations that most assuredly will never be met," said Bobby. "Am I correct?"

"Yes," said Bullitt.

Kennan shook his head in subtle disbelief. "It's like talking to a wall. Does Mr. Stalin somehow not see—"

"Again," said Bullitt, "it is Maxim Litvinov whom I'm dealing with here. He may have the title of People's Commissar for Foreign Affairs, but he's actually just Stalin's mouthpiece. He continues to ask if the president will somehow agree to a pact of nonaggression between the U.S., Japan, China, and the Soviet Union. I told him, very diplomatically, that the answer was *no . . .* again. Still, as it stands today, they are insistent on securing a partnership in the Far East."

"And what of their end of the original promises they made last year?" said Bobby. "Have they paid a penny yet of the war debt they agreed to finally make good on?"

"No," said Bullitt, still squatting. "Back in January I thought Litvinov was about to crack and pay up. I believed they were so worried about an immediate attack from Japan that they'd pay us in the hopes that we'd protect them. But now it seems Litvinov is duplicitous in his thinking—still fearful on one hand, but on the other, of the belief that there will be no such attack. He's halfway convinced himself that Roosevelt will prevent any such attack anyway, or side with Stalin if war did break out. And as far as promises go, Bobby, theirs are all empty it seems."

"This is not going as we'd originally hoped," said Chip Bohlen. "We're spinning our wheels."

Bullitt stood and flicked some lint off of the right sleeve of his fancy blue suit jacket. As fine as my suits were, all of them made in Paris, his were even finer. I'd learned that his had also been tailor-made in Paris. He was the first man I'd met who actually primped more than I, and I'd even overheard him telling his French servant that he didn't give a damn about coming across too bourgeoisie in the eyes of the plain-dressing Soviets.

"I'm still hopeful, gentlemen," said Bullitt, throwing the rag down and lighting a cigarette. "We're not as prejudiced under Roosevelt as we were back in 1919 when Republicans were in charge. As a result, however naïvely optimistic I may be acting, I'm hoping the Soviets will see this new *us* and begin engaging in more honorable . . . truthful talks."

"Then again," said Kennan, "you're not dealing with Lenin like you were back then on your secret visit. This is Stalin, who appears to have been born without a conscience. And didn't he and Litvinov also agree to allow Americans here the right to freedom of religion and security of status? Seems hardly to be the case!"

Kennan, who sounded the most intellectual of them all, cleared his throat, as if summoning up the courage to continue offering his rather gutsy opinion to Bullitt. And he did.

"Why isn't the president being more assertive here, William? I worry that he's more concerned with assuaging the *feelings* of our countrymen rather than actually untangling these knotty problems of war debt and Communist Party interference in America's domestic affairs. Does he simply want to massage his relationship with Stalin so as to make Americans *feel* safe and not grow more fearful of this rising madman, Adolf Hitler? I mean, it's one thing to—"

"You're wrong!" said Bullitt. "The president is depending on *us* to handle this. You don't think he has enough on his plate domestically, George? Americans are standing in fucking soup lines! You don't think he's losing sleep over that, George?"

"Yes! But Germany and Japan are not going to just quietly go away because the president is friendly with the Soviets."

"Friendly my ass!" said Bullitt. "I just told you we're continuing to say no to any nonaggression pact. Litvinov is actually worried that Japan may be picking up signals that Roosevelt's relationship with Stalin is strained. In fact, he has asked me not to say anything publically that might suggest such, as that would embolden Japan. As a result, I've made him no such promise. I'm saving it as leverage."

"Smart," said Bertel Kuniholm, who'd remained rather quiet to this point. "Perhaps dangerous, but . . . smart."

"Our government," said Bullitt, "will never give either a straight loan or an *uncontrolled* credit to the Soviets, and Litvinov never suggested that he wanted either. But now . . . *oh now* . . . he has the temerity to say he wants either a straight loan to make purchases anywhere, or uncontrolled credit to make purchases in the U.S. I told him a loan was off the table, and that at least ten percent interest would have to be built into any credit agreement. Still, he's fixated more on a cash loan."

"Yeah, so they can buy weapons with it," said Kennan.

"Shit," said Bullitt, smoking. "This entire problem hinges on the way a memorandum was written up during the initial agreement. The president uses the words *loan* and *credit* interchangeably. In this case, however, he used the word *loan* when he was strictly meaning *credit*. So the actual word *credit* was never written down, only the word *loan*. Litvinov is quick to point that out."

"Hell," said Bobby, "Litvinov knew we meant credit."

"There's this to consider," said Bullitt. "The Soviets owe England, France, Germany, and others far more than they owe us. So, in Litvinov's defense, he feels that they cannot just pay us off or other nations will demand immediate pay as well. He reasons that if, however, we give them a loan that is double the debt they owe us, the other nations will see it as a type of deal they simply can't afford. He says the interest rate we agree to build in will ultimately leave the U.S. and Soviet Union on agreeable terms."

"Ah!" said Loy. "So their idea of progress with these other countries is to kick the can down the road and hope that they magically forget what is owed them. Brilliant!"

Bullitt took a drag and frowned. "We're not worried about these other damn countries right now, Loy. It's about getting *our* debt settled. Focus! Can you do that for me, Loy?"

"Yes, but forget about the nations they owe money to for a second here. Besides the obvious concern regarding Germany, I'm growing weary of the aforementioned Japan and the ever-so-enigmatic Italy. I just can't help but envision men like Emperor Hirohito and Mussolini doing the unthinkable. I'm hoping like hell we can keep the Soviets with us, regardless of what happens."

Bullitt threw his cigarette on the ground and picked up Pie-Pie. "Well, the good thing is, in terms of Litvinov and me, things are still fluid. He may not admit it, but he knows that the 'gentleman's agreement' was signed between him and Roosevelt last November, in which they agreed to have ongoing talks about payment of debt. He can't run from it. Changing the subject, men, what's the latest on the Christmas Eve party? I want it to be mainly comprised of American guests, but let's invite the French, German, and U.K. ambassadors as well. And try to get Litvinov and maybe some members of the Politburo there. They probably won't attend, but give it a shot. How's the planning coming along with Charles? Talk to me, George."

"It's full steam ahead, William. Charles has had no hiccups. The event will show Spaso House off like nothing they've ever seen before."

"Good. But it's the party in the spring that I want to really be our main event. We'll call it the Spring Festival. We have seven months to plan it, so everyone should be able to come. And at the Spring Festival, I want every damn important Soviet in the country to attend, including Stalin. I want them to have the best time of their lives. When they think of America, I want them to think of bliss. I want them to equate America with a big, fucking, never-ending party."

"With seven months to plan," said Bobby, "I'm sure everyone will indeed be there. But I'm looking forward to the Christmas Eve party for now."

"I wish I were going to be here to see it myself," said Bullitt. "I'm sure you'll fill me in, George."

"Most assuredly. When do you leave for Washington?"

"October 10th," said Bullitt. "I understand the famous Negro actor, Paul Robeson, is planning to be here in Moscow in December as well. You should invite him."

"He won't come," said Bobby. "Some members of Stalin's Politburo being here is understandable because it's viewed by the public as two nations simply gathering on a leadership level. Robeson, on the other hand, is of the people, of the revolution. Our capitalist government is part of the problem in his eyes, and his supporters would find it unacceptable for him to be hobnobbing with us. It's really quite simple."

I continued listening to the men ramble on about the Christmas Eve party, all the while thinking about Paul Robeson's pending visit to Moscow. I figured Lovett might know much more about the details and I couldn't wait to find them out.

13

Magadan, Russia
November 1937

WE'D SURVIVED THE LA PÉROUSE STRAIT AND THE STONE OF
Danger, barely it seemed, as there'd been one day that had sent
us *zeks* tumbling from one side of the hold to the other, many
left to pick stiff bodies off of them in the dark. But the tilting,
rattling ship slamming into violent waves had little effect on us,
for the mental anguish we'd already survived left us half wishing
the boat would run aground.

Beginning from the Sea of Japan and ending at the Sea of
Okhotsk, our ship had finally entered the Nagaev Bay, where
we'd disembarked near the town of Magadan, a place that, according to the old man, had been built for the sole purpose of
advancing Stalin's Dalstroi, his Far North Construction Trust. In
fact, when James and I had first boarded the train back in
Moscow and met the old man, he'd already known exactly
where we were all going. He'd just decided not to tell us until
we'd arrived in Vladivostok.

According to the old man, the Dalstroi was developed to have
prisoners mine for gold that would line Stalin's pockets. "He's a
filthy, soulless animal," he'd said of Stalin while we were lying in
our bunks back at the transit camp. "He has created a forced
labor system in the far northeast called *Sevvostlag* that serves the

needs of the Dalstroi, and it will leave more than I can imagine dead eventually. And don't be so sure that you and your son will be mining for gold. You may be forced to continue the construction of the Kolyma Highway, a road that begins in Magadan and stretches to God knows where. Prisoners started building it in 1932."

"It sounds like another planet!" I had said.

"If they do put you and your boy on road detail, you must know that you are building a road that is designed for the sole purpose of making it possible for future prisoners to more easily access areas rich with gold. Maybe they won't have to walk someday, as you will."

"He's using us to explore new lands, Abram."

"Yes, there have been stories of men literally making a path for a future road by exploring the mountainous terrain on foot, creating footprints for others to follow, many falling to their deaths because of the unexplored area. They were the . . . how do you say in English . . . the—"

"Guinea pigs!" I said. "Sacrificial lambs!"

"Yes."

"I refuse to believe that this will be our fates, Abram."

"The terrain will be horrible, the mountains, the ice . . . rock-hard, the frigid air . . . unbreathable. Whatever thick clothing they provide, take good care of it. Keep the snow out of your boots by tucking your pants into them and tying a sock around the tops tightly. Never take your *ushanka* off, if they give you one. Try to keep your mouth closed and breathe lightly through your nose. Keep your head down and dig."

"We will."

"They don't call that highway the Road of Bones for nothing, Prescott. Many have, and will, be buried right under it."

It was very cold and windy when we disembarked, but not nearly as cold as the old man had said it would be in December. Nor was it as cold as it would be at the mines, which were located near the distant mountains and far beyond the closer hillsides, both of which were currently being smothered by a thick fog. Still, the old man had painted a picture.

After walking inland about four miles on a road that had been partially carved through the high Nagaev Bay cliffs, we arrived at Magadan, a lonely, depressed place that resembled nothing I'd ever imagined. And it certainly wasn't a town in any traditional sense whatsoever. It consisted of a snow-cleared dirt road, watchtowers, barbed wire, fuel tanks, and barracks. According to the guards, thousands were being held here temporarily, and it appeared that thousands more would follow, maybe millions.

At the entryway of the camp was a large sign above that read: WORK IN THE USSR IS A MATTER OF HONOR AND GLORY. Of course, I saw it much differently. The sign was missing two key words. "Forced" at the beginning and "not" after "is."

Based on what I'd seen upon arrival when they opened the hatch and brought in the lamps, I was guessing that at least a hundred had died in the hold. There were only nine hundred of us now. We marched through the dark clouds that had fallen, the seasickness still in our legs. We passed by columns of shabby barracks. I wondered if *zeks* were asleep inside or if the buildings were empty. Whatever the case, it looked like a snowy ghost town on the moon.

Walking behind us in the distance toward a different area of the camp were the women from our ship, maybe a few hundred of them, some holding babies. The old man had said there were nurseries and maternity wards in the camps. Stalin hadn't missed a thing.

Continuing to discreetly gaze back at them, I couldn't help but try to find a couple of black faces, but it was pointless. My wife and daughter had gone north from Moscow.

As we walked deeper inside, there were guards with big-eared, pointy-faced, mangy-looking, vicious dogs on chains patrolling everywhere. We passed by one wooden structure after another, all of them properly built actually with solid foundations and sturdy beams. A food barracks on the left that smelled of cabbage had a poster on the front door with an image of a hand clutching a snake near the head. At the bottom it read: WE WILL ERADICATE SPIES AND DIVERSIONISTS, AGENTS OF THE TROTSKYITE— BUKHARINITE FASCISTS!

With smoky fog feeling like it was coming up from the ground, we approached a nicer-looking structure where the NKVD might be stationed. Or perhaps this was also the Dalstroi head-quarters, because it looked official, the red and yellow state flag blowing high above. An officer stood in front in the distance and held a megaphone.

"Davai! Davai!" he said. *"Bystrey! Bystrey!"*

We sped up, but he kept repeating those same words in his violent Russian. "Get going! Get going! Faster! Faster!"

With our accompanying guards repeating his command, we began to run until we arrived at the stone building, which was painted white. "Catch up, you lazy *zek*!" the commander said through the megaphone. I turned and, through the fog, could barely see a prisoner laboring behind in the distance. He was limping but trying like hell to join the rest of us.

"Ubey yego!" said the commander, looking up at one of the watchtowers and nodding.

An NKVD man stationed up high pointed his rifle downward and fired two shots at the *zek*, dropping him to the permafrost. He lay there facedown. Dead.

"Welcome to Magadan, *zeks*!" the commander said through the black megaphone, as if nothing had happened. "I am Commander Drugov. You are part of the new system. We may be several time zones away from Moscow, but the Central Committee has spoken to us. They have been coddling the *zeks* for years here in the Sevvostlag system. But our great Stalin has replaced all of the Sevvostlag commanders with new, more knowledge-able ones. There will be no more wasting time and money."

I gazed to my left at James and was hoping he'd grown accustomed to hearing lectures that sounded far too intellectual for him. He knew I'd explain things later.

"The Central Committee has voted to make Kolyma more productive," he continued. "The mines and roads are not being worked hard enough. The loggers are not sufficiently cutting the trees down in the taiga. The women are not harvesting peat beside the river fast enough, or washing clothes, cooking, cleaning, and sewing rapidly enough. They are being scolded for such things over in their camp."

He pointed to the right in the distance.

"But that will all change now," he continued. "You will get your daily ration, but it will consist of hand-sized black bread for the day, hot soup in the morning, gruel for lunch, and hot water for dinner. You are henceforth to be known as Lagpunkt Seventy-Nine. Your ship was supposed to only be for hauling ammonium nitrate, but they managed to squeeze your little unit in."

He put the megaphone down and was handed a sheet of paper from a guard. I was still thinking about being several time zones away from Moscow. It seemed we were closer to Alaska.

"Kolyma is called 'the island,'" he continued. "Not because it's an actual island, but because it is all alone away from the mainland. Once you are out there some three hundred miles minimum from here, we won't try to stop you from escaping. Just know that no one has ever made it out. Never! Understand?"

"DA!" we yelled.

"Fortunately for you, however, for the time being, you are being assigned to build more barracks here in Magadan, structures that will further serve our ever-growing Dalstroi headquarters. Nice offices for our great Stalin to sit in whenever he visits! Yes?"

"DA!" we screamed.

"Your thirty-day slog through the ice and snow won't begin just yet. As you can see, this holding camp is very large. There are many thousands here, all with their own schedules for departure. But within the camp, there are a few cordoned-off sections for smaller communities to live as separate *lagpunkts* and remain here indefinitely. Magadan itself needs a myriad of jobs done for its own community. Yours will be to shut your fucking mouths and hammer nails while most of the *zeks* come from the ships and head straight to the mines. Yes?"

"DA!" we shouted.

"Stand in line and wait for the guards to check you in, *zeks.* Oh, and one more item. If you decide to break into the women's camp and rape a female *zek*, you will be shot in your mouth straight away. Stay in your lines now!"

James and I waited and waited until finally a short officer with a clipboard approached. "Give me your papers!" he said, his Russian rather high-pitched, his breath, rotten.

"Prescott Sweet!" he said, searching his list, flipping pages, his short, little finger running over the names. He'd actually pronounced my name, *"Sveet,"* like every other Russian, as the *w* sound didn't exist in the Russian language, but I always immediately translated it to the proper *"Sweet"* as my ear took it in.

"You are now number 22-AA," he continued. "Don't forget! Now . . . what was your profession?"

"Engineer," I said.

He looked at me sternly. "Go line up at building nineteen. It is there!" He pointed south. "Past the top commander's office."

"This is my son."

"Shut up, *zek*! Shut up now! He can stay here in line. Go to nineteen!"

I reluctantly left James behind, but it had given me encouragement to see him nod for me to go. It was like he was becoming a burgeoning young man, almost fifteen. He was more confident in himself, and I hadn't noticed until now how tall he was getting, maybe five-eleven.

There were about ten men lined up when I arrived at nineteen. When we were finally let inside, I made note of how much warmer it was, as this was one of the meeting barracks for the officers, equipped with rows of wooden benches and a podium up front.

"Come and sit," said the commander, walking up to the lectern. "So many things will be changing in the coming years in Magadan. The state has not even given it town status yet, but that will likely happen next year. Meanwhile, you have all claimed to have been professional engineers."

He surveyed the ten of us and half smiled. I was glad to be in the company of a man who enunciated his Russian words with calm precision. He was intellectual sounding, his green uniform well kept, and his Nordic-looking face clean-shaven.

"I have been put in charge of structural and mechanical development for Magadan," he said. "Prisoners will continue to flow in from Vladivostok, and this port location will need to keep expanding. Shipments of gold, tin, etcetera, will be trucked in from the mines and shipped out more rapidly with each passing year. We do not have the adequate infrastructure to handle the quick pace at which the Dalstroi is growing. We need to meet the demands of our great Stalin. Understand?"

"Da!" we said.

"Most of the engineers, doctors, nurses, dentists, and paramedics are what we call 'freely hired' men and women. But others in these disciplines are *zeks* like you. If you were to be working alongside a freely hired man, you must listen to him, for he has authority over you. Raise your hand if you know how to build an engine from scratch?"

Only four of us raised our hands.

"Raise your hand if you can do land excavation."

Only five of us raised our hands.

"Raise your hand if you can do all of the following: load fuel and oil tanks, design irrigation and pipe systems, operate heavy machinery, design and assemble buildings from ground to roof with the proper installations, and with zero supervision. Before you answer . . . just know that a lie could cost you your life. I don't say that to threaten you, I say it because it's the truth. Raise your hands."

Only one of us raised his hand. Me.

"Very good," he said. "What is your name?"

"Prescott Sweet, sir!"

"Comrade Sweet, I would like for you to stay here and complete a written examination. The rest of you sign your name on the paper beside the door and then go back to the lines. I will have an officer retrieve you when it's time to assign jobs."

After they exited, the officer stood at the lectern studying some documents. I sat in the front row with my back straight, hands resting on my knees. I was nervous.

"Comrade Sweet," he finally said, looking up, "can I see your passport? Bring it here."

I immediately stood and walked up. Handing it to him, I stood there waiting while he read.

"You can go back and sit now," he said, still reading while I quickly sat down. "I am certain you will do well on the examination, as it simply consists of math and physics, but it is important for you to know something. For the past six months since I arrived here, every time a new shipment of men comes in, only a few are chosen to lead a construction team. It is a fortunate assignment because it's a way for you to avoid the dreaded Kolyma highway and the frozen mines near the river. Yes?"

"Yes, sir!" I said.

"Men like you are too valuable to send out there to die within weeks. Eighty percent of the men who leave here don't survive. Our great Stalin can always bring us new labor, but he also understands the importance of getting value out of uniquely skilled *zeks*. Why waste you, correct?"

"Yes, sir!"

"Call me Commander Koskinen. I am talking to you as though I already know that you can do the jobs you've so claimed you can do. That's because you will be shot if you can't. You are so lucky to be an engineer. Of course, there are other good jobs a *zek* can be given to do. Some are cooks and clerks. But most are simple hands, waiting to die. They have no useful skills. They are all intellectuals or simple kulaks who've known nothing but tilling soil and milking cows. I have one piece of advice for you, as I'm not the head of the Dalstroi or the Sevvostlag camps by any means. Work hard!"

"Yes, Commander Koskinen!"

"It certainly isn't customary for a commander or anyone else in the Dalstroi to speak to a *zek* with such decency. It's a good thing you were educated as an engineer. It might keep you alive. Of course the examination is only part of your being put in this position. I will be looking into your background to confirm your profession. Do you have any questions before the exam?"

"I have a son. He is fifteen. He is very good at science and math. Might he be able to work alongside me?"

"If your work is pleasing to me and the other Dalstroi heads, maybe we can make arrangements for that in a couple of weeks. It will certainly keep him here for as long as you are, if you can learn to be trusted."

A month passed and I'd already impressed Koskinen enough to make him assign James to my team of one hundred. I'd scored a perfect score on his examination and had since been able to turn a set of Koskinen's architectural drawings into a rectangular, sixty-by-thirty, one-story shell. This after having leveled the site, put up wooden forms, dug the holes and trenches, installed footings, poured concrete, and allowed it to cure. The shell would soon serve as an office building for some Dalstroi heads.

With limited winter sunlight, it was still grueling, sixteen-hour-a-day work, as the camp lights were turned on when the sun disappeared around four p.m. I'd been given the same daily rations as the others—herring head or animal lung soup with bits of cabbage for breakfast, tasteless gruel for lunch, and hot water for dinner. But there was one difference. Obviously the cooks had been told something, because my morning soup had more fish or lung in it than the others.

I'd actually been skipping my breakfast every other day and saving it for James to eat at night. I was making sure he'd been getting a bit more protein. Why they made us have the soup for breakfast and the gruel for lunch puzzled me at first, but then I realized they wanted the protein in us first thing.

The only difference between me and the other *zeks* was that I was in charge of a work crew. But I still had to do the same labor. There were a few other *zeks* like me who'd come here recently and were highly skilled engineers. I could hear them barking orders to their men, too, across the frozen alleys at the other worksites, NKVD men patrolling the maze of barracks. But most of the engineers were free hires.

Even though I was still just a *zek*, there was something encouraging about Koskinen taking a bit of a liking to me. Of course, I assumed it was all because I was making him look good. I was still trying to gather up the courage to ask about my wife and daughter. Based on what the old man had said, I still figured they were in a camp all the way across the country.

Barracks five of our *lagpunkt* is where they'd quartered sixty of us off back on that first November day, after we'd been quarantined, Boris having been placed in nine. The only word I can use to describe my situation was *lucky*. It had all come down to good old-fashioned, pure luck—my being assigned to possibly remain in Magadan with my son whenever the rest of Lagpunkt Seventy-Nine headed for the mines.

The temperature here hovered around five below zero, a far cry from the horror that awaited the others inland. It was on Christmas day that we were allowed to remain in our barracks and not work, only because the officers wanted the day off. We'd been given our normal ration of gruel for lunch, but with this unforeseen rest, it tasted like ham, stuffing, and sweet potato pie.

I lay there on my middle bunk with no mattress, James above me, Yury below. All of our appearances had changed dramatically with the extreme weight loss. And besides James, we'd all grown heavy beards. My normal weight of 200 had dipped to maybe 180. But we were surviving, and if this were to be our lot for the next several years, we would live. It was the minus forty-degree Road of Bones that we all feared, including me, as one mistake would cost me.

"This *doska* is too hard to sleep on with no mattress," said Yury.

"Sleeping on a sheet of wood is better than the floor," I said.

"I wish I'd been assigned to your team, Prescott. The head contractor of my team acts blind. Too many of the *zeks* are getting away with being lazy. Plus, he's a free hire and knows it will be us who pay for this, not him. As soon as we leave this *lagpunkt* and arrive at our worksite, the boss just stands at his worktable reading plans and smoking."

"I need to talk to the top commander, Mr. Drugov," I said, leaning down toward Yury. "I'm guessing you will be leaving here in no more than three months before the road turns into a quagmire. Trucks may not be able to deliver supplies then. And they'll want you and Boris to reach the mines when the ice starts to melt in April so you can more easily explode new caves."

"I see," said Yury.

"Yeah, they'll want you to walk that road for at least a month while it's still frozen. I did the math. I'm guessing, of course, as I'm sure they walk along the sides in the summer, too. Who knows! I'm sure they mine year-round, but perhaps the winter months are spent digging inside already exploded caves rather than grappling with trying to survey rock that's many feet below solid ice. I'll bet they rinse the gold in the Kolyma River during the summer, too. Let me stop speculating."

"What in God's name can you possibly say to Drugov?" said Yury. "I haven't even seen his face since the first day we arrived. Maybe he's traveling. Besides, Commander Drugov only oversees *this* camp. The real boss is that madman I've heard about named K.A. Pavlov. He runs the entire Dalstroi. And every Sevvostlag camp official throughout the region answers to him. Still, what would you possibly say to this Drugov?"

"I want to ask him about my wife and daughter. They might be freezing to death somewhere. They might be starving. Maybe if he sees that I have done good work as an engineer, he'll be inclined to listen. And maybe once he sees that I'm an American who speaks Russian, just as I'm easily doing to you right now, he'll warm up to me. It will be a small request to ask about my wife and daughter's whereabouts."

"Forget that, Prescott! You can't make *any* requests. Don't even go meet with him. You will be shot. I promise. You can't! Besides, it is much warmer on the western side of the country. Your family is okay."

"I also want to ask about you and Boris staying with my crew once the others leave for the mines."

I leaned down and called him closer with my index finger, noticing the missing tip of my thumb and the scarred webbing next to it. Yury sat up and got close.

"You will certainly die in *that* cold," I whispered. "In a few months, not years! You will die in the taiga cutting timber or breaking apart rock along the Kolyma Highway. I must find a way."

"I don't even believe we can walk through those trees and mountains for weeks, Prescott. We are going to die in *days* just getting there."

"No!" I whispered. "Keep your feet dry and just walk. That's a simple thing. I was talking to the nurse back when they removed my cast and stitches. She is from Estonia. She and her husband were arrested five years ago and he was shot shortly after. She said Sevvostlag officials will no longer be issuing the fur and wool clothing we received upon arrival."

"My God, Prescott! It is far too cold not to have such things."

"No more rubber galoshes to cover the felt boots like those under our bunks right now. Apparently, because of the new regulation ordered by Stalin, they will begin issuing canvas shoes along with wadding jackets and trousers. No more coddling! And even though Koskinen claims James and I will remain here, I've been taking great care of our garments. You should do the same. We are lucky to have them."

January 9th arrived and we'd been working seven days a week still, cutting wood and hammering cold nails, Magadan completely covered in ice and snow. Work never stopped because of weather. To say it was freezing cold would have hardly told the story. Chicago, Milwaukee, Vermont, and New York City could get cold, but this was an entirely different beast. It was sixteen below zero, but the ocean wind made it feel even colder.

I had never gone to visit Drugov, too worried about him putting a bullet through my head on the spot. There was simply no talking rationally to these bloodthirsty men.

The gray and brown shirts, pants, gloves, and socks that they'd distributed to us back in November were serving us well, and we were fortunate to still have the wool items. I kept reminding myself that the newer arrivals would have no such luck. And at least our old coats and *ushankas* were made of fur. Plus, I wasn't worried about my feet getting frostbitten because they'd let us keep our felt boots. The Dalstroi heads weren't ones to waste a thing, other than humans.

This was the day I was going to meet with Koskinen in his office. He wanted to go over the drawings for a massive storage facility they intended to construct. It would be used to house some new dump trucks, tractors, and cargo trucks that had been ordered. The Dalstroi was becoming more and more profitable it seemed.

I was called to his office during lunch. When I walked in, he was sitting at his desk eating a large, wooden bowl of fish soup that looked absolutely delicious. I eyed the glowing wood that was burning in the corner stove to his right.

"Come in and sit, Comrade Sweet. I will call you that when it's just the two of us. Yes?"

"Yes," I said, sitting across from him, the frost on my eyelashes already melting.

"The men from Lagpunkt Seventy-Nine will be leaving next week for the mines. You will be staying here with your son. You have pleased me. I want you to take these drawings." He picked up the roll from his desk and handed it to me. "And I want to give you this cost sheet." He put it in my other hand. "I want you to determine how much lumber, steel, cement, tar, etcetera, will be needed based on those measurements, and then I want you to cost it out. Yes?"

"Yes, Commander Koskinen," I said, surveying the books covering the shelves along the right and left walls, a large picture of Stalin hanging directly behind him.

"Then I want to meet with you and the other engineers and compare your estimates. Maybe you *zeks* will give better estimates than the free hires." He gave a wry smile. "We are all just Dalstroi employees waiting to be *zeks*!" He put his finger to his mouth. "Shh! It is only between you and me. Many of my comrades have disappeared. None of us can do the right thing for too long. Please! You can speak. Please!"

"Thank you." His demeanor confused me because it felt genuine, like he was sure he would die, perhaps sooner than later. I carefully continued. "When I was at a place called Camp Z in the forest well north of Vladivostok, I was told my sentence would be reduced."

"I can find out more about that. Continue."

"My wife and daughter are in the prisons."

He picked up a pencil. "When and where were you all arrested, and what are their names?"

"Just back in August, in Moscow. My wife's name is Loretta Sweet, my daughter, Ginger Sweet."

"Is your wife a Negro, too?" he said, writing down their names. "Yes."

"My sister is married to a Negro from Nairobi, Kenya. They live in Toronto, Canada. He is a medical doctor. I have not seen her in five years."

"That's a long time."

"The five months you've been away from your wife and daughter feels much longer, I'm sure."

"Thank you."

"Don't speak of any of this. You would be shot. I will look into it." He leaned in over his desk. "Of course," he whispered, "it would be easier to predict how my request might be received if my beloved Trotsky were our leader and not Stalin. Like Lenin before him, Trotsky is a brilliant man with much foresight and creativity. He would most certainly be able to outsmart this Hitler. We are all going to be *zeks* when that powerful man takes over the world. I know such things. Do I sound like it?"

"Yes, Commander Koskinen."

"Stalin believes it is all about exporting food to the West and importing machinery into the Soviet Union. As Stalin has said about his continuing Five Year Plans, 'Technical skills and machines will decide everything.' So . . . you see . . . you *zeks* are nothing to him. *I* am nothing to him. If only my Trotsky would return from exile. A dream!" He sat back. "Well, Comrade Sweet, anything else?"

"I . . . I must ask. Two other comrades of mine in the camp here, Yury—"

"I cannot help them. You are trying to see if they can stay here?"

I nodded.

"I cannot do that. It is logical regarding your boy. Your comrades . . . no."

"Yes, Commander Koskinen."

"Your Russian is excellent, Comrade Sweet. But how do you feel about your America?"

I was guessing that my answer would carry significant weight. And I was certain that he, like most Soviet brass, detested my country. Even if he didn't, I couldn't afford to say something positive.

"I hate America," I said. "That is why I moved to Moscow and learned your language. They treated me like trash back in America. It was only when I got to Moscow that I felt like a human being for the first time. I was all too surprised when I was arrested, for I love the Soviet Union."

"Good," he said. "Me too!"

Later that night I lay in my bunk talking to Yury. I was devastated that he and Boris would be leaving soon, much earlier than I'd previously guessed. But I could do nothing about it.

"Koskinen says it will remain Lagpunkt Seventy-Nine when you all leave," I whispered to Yury in barely audible Russian. "But a freshly shipped-in batch of *zeks* will replace you. This cycle will continue until Seventy-Nine is full of a thousand highly skilled laborers. *Zeks* who know contracting! How is Boris?"

"I don't know," said Yury. "I hope he is holding up. I could see the bones in his back too much when I last saw him. I could see far too many bones."

"Once you all depart, you've got to maybe figure out an escape. Maybe after you stop and set up camp—"

"There is no way out. They have guns. And Drugov told us that no one has ever escaped the Sevvostlag prison system in this area. You know this! And even if we can manage to escape the camp, the bears will kill us. Many have met such fates."

"Don't talk about bears," I whispered.

"It's true, Prescott. I would rather work all day and even sleep in a big ice pit at night if need be. The old man said he'd heard of such sleeping conditions."

"What!"

"I'm just telling you what he said. Maybe it was a form of punishment. Maybe it was because they ran out of tents."

"I don't believe that, Yury. Sounds like an old wives' tale."

"Believe it! I'm sure they do such things."

"Or not!"

"I'm just thinking of the worst-case scenario, Prescott. The old man said to start from thinking the worst and then work your way back from there. No surprises!"

"Makes sense."

"I am no longer afraid to die, Prescott. The old man is with God. I am not afraid because I can go see God, too. I am happy for you and James. But I am not afraid to go see God now. I have accepted my fate. No one survives the Road of Bones."

14

Moscow, Russia
December 1934

SINCE THE TIME I'D FIRST MET LOVETT FORT-WHITEMAN BACK IN September, I'd gotten to know him much better. Loretta and I had attended the shindig at his apartment and had been introduced to several interesting people, many of them colored.

Perhaps the most fascinating was not colored, however. His name was Karl Radek, a friend of Lovett's, and a close associate of Stalin's. Radek wrote for *Pravda*, the official newspaper of the Communist Party of the Soviet Union, and he was actually helping to write the Soviet Constitution. Much controversy surrounded him, as many wondered, especially Stalin, if Radek had lied his way back into the Soviet Union by swearing he was no longer loyal to Leon Trotsky. Meeting the editor had been fascinating, as this was a politico who not only conversed with Lovett and Stalin, but also Bullitt. According to Lovett, the ambassador had been trying to get Radek to help him convince Litvinov and Stalin to make good on the debt issue.

I'd still been trying like hell to make progress on finding the hidden microphones in the bowels of Spaso House, but to no avail. Luckily, I wasn't getting constant pressure from the ambassador, as he was back in the U.S. and might not be back until April. Nevertheless, much to Bobby's dismay, Bullitt had assigned me to remain at Spaso and help with technical issues until the new ballroom was complete. And he'd made me swear I'd do my best to locate the hidden microphones. So, I'd had my hands full trying to figure out a way to get the keys away from Sergei.

It was now Christmas Eve and I had quite an eventful day in front of me. Loretta and I were on our way to hear Paul Robeson speak. Apparently he was beyond excited to visit Moscow for the first time and wanted to say a few words to us American coloreds. After we were finished hearing Robeson, the plan was to meet Dorene and Bobby at Gorky Park so the four children could play in the snow and drink hot cocoa. Then the four adults would get ready for the big Christmas Eve party set to take place at Spaso House.

Both of us wearing black wool trench coats, Loretta and I arrived at the Theater of People's Art at around noon. When we entered the lobby, a racially mixed crowd of folks were mingling. There was an excitement in the air—everyone bundled up in long coats, hats, and boots, as the light snow had been continuous for days.

"There's Lovett!" said Loretta, pointing across the lobby and removing her gray fur *ushanka*.

"I see he's in full swing already," I said, as we slid our wet gloves off and made our way through the throng.

"I SEE YOU TWO!" shouted Lovett through the noise.

"You holding court?" I said, shaking his hand before he kissed Loretta on the cheek.

There were handshakes and kisses all around, as many familiar colored faces were surrounding Lovett. One thing we'd quickly learned since arriving in Moscow: all of the colored folks knew one another, even if casually. And whenever an event came up that involved anything they might be remotely interested in, everyone seemed to show up, just as they had when we'd first arrived in Moscow at the National Hotel.

Taking off my black fedora, I took inventory of the folks surrounding Lovett and was glad to see these folks again. All of them, again, were noted individuals, here in Moscow because of their talent as performers, scientists, artists, or engineers. There was Robert Robinson, Lloyd Patterson, Homer Smith, Oliver Golden, George Tynes, Coretta Arle-Titz, Robert Ross, Wayland Rudd, and William L. Patterson. Other than Lovett, the only ones I knew fairly well were Robert Robinson and Homer Smith, as we'd conversed on several occasions. Robert was a popular engineer, and Homer was a journalist and postal worker.

"Where is that lovely wife of yours, Lovett?" said Loretta.

"B isn't feeling well at the moment," he said. "She has a cold. I've got my Russian queen locked in bed with hot tea and biscuits."

"I'm sorry to hear that," said Loretta. "Tell her I send hugs and kisses."

Lovett placed his hands together in a prayer position and mouthed a "thank you" to her. Then he took my arm and gently led me away from the group.

"Pardon us for a moment, y'all," he said, never one to shy away from doing exactly what he wanted to do, right when he wanted to do it.

"What is it?" I said, the two of us settling near the entry to the theater.

"Let me whisper somethin' to you, Bronzeville," he said, referring to me by the name of the town where I'd grown up. "I wanted to ask you what the embassy is saying about the death of Stalin's first secretary in Leningrad, Sergei Kirov."

"No one is speaking openly about it," I whispered. "All I know is that when his death was announced on December 1st, it was hard to imagine that some random person shot him."

"Kirov was rising in power. Stalin was certainly threatened by him." Lovett leaned in real close to my ear. "Stalin ordered the killing. I know because my friend Karl Radek has told me as much. Radek says Stalin will try to blame the murder on the exiled Trotsky. I don't know anything more specific, Bronzeville, but you can bet your bottom dollar it was Stalin."

Before he could say another word, loud cheers and clapping

in the lobby began. We turned to the front doorway and in walked a tall man in a long, cream-colored wool trench coat. Accompanying him was a beautiful woman, a young boy, and two handsome men. The woman was colored, but perhaps had some Spanish blood in her.

"That's his wife," said Lovett. "Her name is Eslanda Goode Robeson. And the boy is Paul Robeson, Jr. Pauli! The two men are her brothers, John and Frank, who actually live here, but I haven't seen them lately."

"LIFE IS GOOD, COMRADES!" shouted Robeson with a deep, powerful voice. It was as if these words had rained down on us from a make-believe giant, not a man.

"LIFE IS GOOD, COMRADES!" the crowd yelled back, and continued clapping for at least two minutes, as there was no bigger colored celebrity in the world than Paul Robeson.

"COME!" said Robeson, squeezing through the crowd and making his way into the theater.

I found Loretta, and we all funneled in like happy schoolchildren, each of us grabbing the first seat we could find. My friends Homer and Robert waved for Loretta and me to join them in the back row, so we gladly did, as Lovett continued on toward the stage. It wasn't three minutes before the theater was packed to capacity. With his family sitting in the front row, Robeson took the stage and stood beside a man I recognized from the newspapers, a renowned filmmaker whose name escaped me. I hadn't seen him enter earlier, but he was obviously here to introduce the star.

"My name is Sergei Eisenstein," said the relatively young-looking Russian, whose English was fine. "I invited Comrade Robeson to Moscow because I want to work on a film with him. And I wanted to make sure our American comrade gets to see all of the splendid things Moscow has to offer. Last night I took him and his family to see a play by Nikolai Gogol called *The Government Inspector*. We are so proud of our Gogol."

Everyone clapped and Eisenstein turned to our guest of honor.

"Did you like it, Comrade Robeson?" he continued.

The star grinned, nodded, and raised his hand, as if overjoyed by the experience he was having.

"I'm glad," said Eisenstein. "And tonight I will be taking our guest to a Christmas Eve party at Maxim Litvinov's house."

Litvinov was obviously a name I recognized, as the ambassador was in a constant back-and-forth with the Soviet leader. As I held Loretta's hand and sat back to get comfortable, I thought about how Bobby had told the ambassador that Robeson would never attend a party at the embassy. He couldn't be seen fraternizing with the American dignitaries, but today I was learning that meeting with the likes of Litvinov wasn't a problem. And as I'd come to understand it, Litvinov was due to attend the Spaso House celebration. Now I assumed he wouldn't be.

"But I will not keep Comrade Robeson from you any longer," continued Eisenstein from the stage. "Come talk to your comrades."

Robeson stood and we all clapped again until he interrupted us with a baritone, "I FEEL LIKE I'M HOME!"

The crowd came to a hush and he continued. "For the first time in my thirty-six-year life, I feel like I'm at home. Soviet society is fantastic. And all that I've read about it . . . the good stuff . . . pales in comparison to what it actually is. Never has a Negro been able to walk the streets with such freedom. My wife, Eslanda, and I have never felt happier and more comfortable. I see white and colored in this audience, and you all appear the same to me . . . very comfortable. You know, it tickles me! I was swarmed at the train station by what seemed like a thousand Soviets. I knew they liked me, but WOW!"

The crowd laughed at him raising his long arms and making a funny face, eyes wide open, brows raised.

"I knew they loved me for my folk music here, but WOW!" he shouted through the laughter before it finally died down. "But seriously, it's nice to see so many Americans here, some of whom I know, some who've been fighting the battle for Negro freedom for years. Lovett Fort-Whiteman! William Patterson! I see y'all!"

He pointed to the two who were off to the side standing, and they saluted him back. Patterson was a lawyer and member of the CPUSA who'd actually had his run-ins with Lovett. It was good to see them being civil to each another.

"I want everyone in here to listen to me clearly," continued Robeson. "I want to thank you for taking part in the development of this great, new social order. You are here in the Soviet Union at a time when real world change is beginning to take place. The Revolution has begun to stretch its tentacles to every corner of the globe. You are pioneers. You are freedom seekers. You are proud, determined anticapitalists. And I salute you! TO MOTHER RUSSIA!"

"TO MOTHER RUSSIA!" many in the crowd yelled back, then clapped for a long spell while Robeson watched over them with a large grin.

But not everyone yelled those words. I certainly did not, as it still was a foreign land that I didn't understand. And my friends Robert Robinson, the engineer, and Homer Smith, the journalist, both sitting to my left, felt the same way. They weren't communists. Make no mistake, many American coloreds and whites working in the Soviet Union had by no means joined the Communist Party. And as far as coloreds specifically, most may have loved the freedom Russia offered, but they were not necessarily interested in becoming communists like Lovett or William Patterson. They were here for the good-paying jobs. In fact, according to Lovett, Paul Robeson himself hadn't actually joined the Party.

"Robeson's a damn big man," said Homer, leaning into me, the audience still clapping. "He certainly looks the part of an ex-football player."

"You got that right," I said, leaning across Homer to tap my eyeglass-wearing engineer friend. "I didn't hear you yell 'To Mother Russia,' Robert." I smiled. "What's wrong with you, Negro?"

"The only mother's name I'll ever shout out is my own," said Robert, real proper and serious sounding, as he was a brilliant and studious toolmaker.

The clapping died down and we sat and listened to Paul Robeson for another ten minutes or so before he was whisked away to some other event Eisenstein had lined up for him. Hearing him speak with such conviction about Stalin and the Revolution had an effect on me. I couldn't help but feel connected to all of these people. I wasn't ready to join the CPUSA, but I was proud to be friends with men and women who wouldn't settle for being treated as second-class citizens. These were people who saw communism as a far better option than Jim Crow.

When we arrived at Gorky Park, the Ellingtons and our twins were already there. It was a beautiful picture of white Moscow in the winter, children running everywhere throwing snowballs, adults sipping hot drinks and laughing. I was happy.

"I think James has a future as a baseball pitcher," said Bobby, sitting on the edge of a picnic table, Dorene sitting between his legs on the bench below. "And Ginger isn't a bad aim, either."

"I see you've failed to mention the skills of *your* two little angels," said Loretta, kissing them both on the cheek.

"Ours haven't found their coordination yet it seems," said Dorene, smiling and watching Grant and Greta fling snowballs ten feet over the heads of each other.

"Doesn't seem to matter," I said, kissing Dorene on the cheek and tapping Bobby's shoulder. "Judging by the grins on their faces, they seem to think their aim is just fine. Ah, to be a child again!"

There were hundreds of kids in the park running around like bundled-up monkeys. And the four of us winced and dipped every time one of our babies barely avoided a snowball to the face.

Dorene took out a large canteen and poured hot cocoa into a couple of glass coffee cups for us. Then she opened up a basketful of croissants. She had come prepared.

"Cheers!" said Bobby, flicking some snow from the brim of his brown fedora with one hand and raising his cup with the other, all the while ignoring the powder that was now covering the shoulders of his thick blue overcoat.

We all clinked cups and I sat on the table next to Bobby while Loretta parked herself between my legs.

"To no bloody noses or black eyes!" Bobby continued, his half-worried eyes still on the children. "Apparently, all of the kids have been told repeatedly, at school and in the park, to never aim at another's head. I fear they didn't listen."

"How are your paintings coming along, my dear?" said Dorene, her matching white *ushanka*, gloves, and coat making the snow on her person invisible.

"Perfectly!" said Loretta. "I don't think I've ever been more busy. The ideas just keep coming. It's like there's not enough time in the day. Moscow is pulling the truth out of me. I've actually got a showing next month, and I'm hearing through the grapevine that some high-ranking State officials are coming."

"She's being modest," I said. "It's set in stone and was set up by Claudia Pike, the popular gallery owner from London who's lived here for fifteen years. The showing is going to make her the star of Moscow."

"Fantastic!" said Bobby.

"My goodness," said Dorene. "We'll of course be there! How exciting!"

"I'm nervously thrilled, but enough about me," said Loretta. "We'll see what happens. Fingers crossed! Dorene, Sweetheart, the question is, how are *you* keeping yourself busy?"

"I'm sewing. And I'm loving it! I'm actually having my father ship a new machine here for me. Whom I'm sewing *for*, I'm not exactly sure. The Soviet fashion doesn't exactly scream colorful, linen dresses. So, I guess I'm sewing for the two of us."

"Yay!" said Loretta, the two pressing their cold cheeks together.

"Whomever you're sewing for," said Bobby, "just try to imagine people from other countries wearing it, because we're not going to be here in Moscow forever. Could be a year. Could be two. But it will come. That goes for you two as well, Press. Maybe we'll all end up in Berlin. That's my dream. That's where the action is going to be."

"I can't imagine living in the middle of that Nazi hell," said Loretta. "I mean, I'm sure we'll be fine because of the embassy, but this Adolf Hitler worries me."

"Ditto!" said Dorene. "But that's what this service, this diplomatic mission, is all about. We have to be courageous enough to venture into the hot spots. It's not a calling, but I choose to look at it as a duty. The last thing the world needs is a madman like Mr. Hitler growing in global stature. Not that Bobby working at the embassy there will stop him, but it would certainly be beneficial to have eyes and ears on the ground there. According to Eleanor, the president is becoming more and more consumed with the rise of the Nazi leader."

"I'm hoping Maxim Litvinov is at the party tonight," said Bobby. "With the ambassador stateside, John Wiley and I would like him to lend us his ear on the Nazi matter. I'm sure he'd like to discuss something other than war debt."

I wanted to tell my friend that Litvinov was hosting his own party that night and would not be in attendance for Wiley and him to visit with. Wiley was the counselor directly under Bullitt. But the matter could wait. I figured I'd let Bobby have a glass of wine first at the party before breaking it to him. Or two glasses!

Later that night at about eleven o'clock, the four of us were already two hours into the festive event at Spaso, assembled in the massive chandelier room with roughly three hundred guests in attendance. We'd had a few glasses of the finest champagne, had danced, eaten enough Beluga caviar to feed a large family, and were now being entertained by, of all things imaginable, three dancing seals, compliments of Charles Thayer, Bullitt's young assistant who'd been put in charge of organizing the entire event. He'd been told to spare no expense, but this wasn't what we'd had in mind.

"Am I dreaming?" said a half-drunk Dorene over the laughing spectators. Her black dress, high heels, and gold earrings were stunning. "Are those actual seals, Bobby?" she continued. "Or are they midgets in costume?"

"They've been dancing for minutes now, Dear. You've only just noticed?"

"I've noticed. I just can't believe it still."

"Charles met the trainer at the circus after seeing them perform there," said Bobby. "He tried to get more animals from the zoo but couldn't."

"Thank God!" giggled Dorene, spilling a little champagne on Bobby's black tuxedo.

The room was dark, save for some light emanating from the hallway and a spotlight on the seals, their trainer hidden in the dark, all of us guests positioned on one side of the room. One seal balanced a small, lit Christmas tree on her nose, another, a tray of wineglasses, the last, a bottle of champagne.

"They're so adorable!" said Loretta.

I looked at my wife taking in the entertainment with such delight. She and Dorene were wearing dresses by the same French designer, a woman named Augusta Bernard. Dorene's was a black V-back gown made of crêpe silk, accentuated by peach-colored lamé ribbon along the sleeves and sides of the V-back. The sleeves stopped about three inches above her elbows.

Loretta's was also a V-back gown, except it was sleeveless. It was a shell pink silk, which captured her long, thin frame, the light silk laying smoothly on her brown skin. And what truly made this a stunning dress was how the V-back was outlined with magenta velvet, which captured the beauty of my wife's sexy back and narrow waist. At the point of the V, the velvet tied into a bow and covered the top half of her buttocks. My simple black tux was hardly a match for her, and rightfully so. The women were front and center.

"Take a look, Press," said Bobby, nudging me. "I see that France, the U.K., and Germany are in attendance. Those are their three ambassadors drinking and laughing on the far left near the hallway—Charles Alphand, Lord Chilton, and Schulenberg, respectively. I wonder if they're enjoying their Soviet postings more than Bullitt! I'll bet they are. At least at the moment! If only Stalin were here. Perhaps he'd love the seals, too."

"Perhaps," I said.

As the show continued—the seals now balancing balls, the audience oohing and aahing—I thought about Sergei, the caretaker, whom we'd run into earlier with his wife. It was the first time I'd seen him smile. I figured when the lights came back on and the conversing commenced again, I'd find him and have a little chat. I needed to take advantage of his good mood.

"OOH! The crowd moaned at once, as the largest seal had slid across the floor and was relieving himself near one of the marble pillars. Fully, it appeared.

"Excuse me!" I said to Loretta. "I'm going to go downstairs to the kitchen and see if I can find the whiskey I hid there last week."

"Oh!" she said. "Bring me some, love."

"Where you going?" said Bobby.

"I'll be right back."

When I got to the kitchen, which was full of cooking staff and waiters cursing in Russian, German, Spanish, and French, I found the box of whiskey in the cupboard way above the sink, but I hadn't run into Sergei in the hallway as I'd hoped. The whiskey was actually a gift I'd gotten for the ambassador for his birthday next month on January 25, but being that he'd still be gone then, I decided to use it for something else.

After nearly knocking over a busboy carrying a massive silver tray full of caviar—freshly shipped in from the Caspian Sea per young Thayer's explicit orders—I began searching the mansion high and low, but couldn't find the son of a bitch. I knew he was out and about because when I'd seen him earlier, he was dressed in a suit and shaking hands with all of the Soviet dignitaries who'd shown up, perhaps before they headed off to Litvinov's house.

Grabbing my coat, hat, and gloves, I headed outside and searched the grounds, saying hello to the various marines along the way, one of whom was near the work shed fondling a young woman. I recognized her as one of the many ballerinas who'd been a constant presence at Spaso since I'd arrived some months back. Bullitt was the one who wanted them around, and now, with him gone, they were keeping the marines from doing their jobs. I was betting they were spies for NKVD. How effective they were, however, only time would tell.

I finally headed to the garage, which had no marine standing guard. I opened the side door and it was dark inside. Flipping on the lights, I realized my search had come to a conclusion, for sitting inside Bullitt's prized possession was Sergei; his wife was in the passenger's seat. I was certain the ambassador had not given them permission to smoke cigarettes and drink wine in his roadster, but there they were.

"Comrade Sweet!" said a surprised Sergei, opening the door and hopping out, his olive skin covered in sweat, which was surprising considering it was about twenty degrees outside, though not nearly that cold inside the garage. Even his mustache was glistening with moisture.

"Hello, Sergei!" I said.

"I was showing my wife the ambassador's beautiful car," he nervously said in English. "She never saw such an automobile. She wanted to . . . how do you say . . . *pretend*! Yes! Pretend we were driving real fast in the country! But, of course, we did not start the automobile. No keys!"

He smiled and sipped his wine. I looked at his lips, which had his wife's lipstick smeared all over them. I looked down at her, then quickly away, as she was casually pulling her panties up, her bright red dress still bunched up at the waist, her brown hair much more ruffled than it had been earlier.

"Don't worry about it," I said. "The ambassador doesn't need to know about this. You were simply trying to get away from all of the chaos inside. I can understand that."

"I'm so appreciative, Comrade Sweet." He was practically bowing over and over, begging me with his eyes not to tell on him, a far cry from the short-tempered jackass he'd shown himself to be in the past.

"Yes, Comrade Sweet, it's chaos inside. I've never seen so many people."

"Do you recognize most of the Russian guests?"

"Yes, I mean, I don't know them all, but I have read about them in *Izvestiya*."

"What are some of their professions? What do they do for work, besides the obvious ones who work at the Kremlin?"

"Ah, Comrade Sweet!" He shook his head like he didn't want to tell me. "I don't—"

"You don't want me to tell the ambassador that you were in his car. We've established that. Now just tell me about the guests."

"Okay. Only two are from the Kremlin!"

"Only two?" I said. "Maybe Stalin sent them to take notes."

He half blushed and continued. "Others are local scientists. Some are teachers at the universities. I recognize a couple of artists and musicians, some sculptors. But, of course you know, eighty percent of the people here are just expatriate Americans along with your friends from the chancery. And some of the foreigners are journalists or maybe, you know, diplomats, visiting here to better their relations with our great Stalin."

"Thank you." I held up the box of whiskey and eyed the ring of keys hanging from his waist just inside his jacket. "And now let me tell you why I was looking for you, Sergei. I wanted to give you your Christmas gift. A bottle of Redbreast Irish! For you to enjoy with your lovely wife."

"Oh my! You are far too kind, Comrade Sweet."

I handed it to him and he gladly accepted, extending both arms up at me like a little boy, overjoyed to be receiving a gift from his father on Christmas morning. I was every bit of six-two, but had never felt so tall.

"You must come sit with us and toast to Christmas Eve," he said, smiling from ear to ear and taking my arm. "Come! You can sit behind the wheel and Anya can sit on my lap in the passenger's seat. Come!"

He opened my door and I got in before he circled the front of the car and signaled for his wife to get out, which she did. Then he plopped himself right in her seat.

"We don't need glasses!" he said, opening the box and taking out the bottle. "Get in, Anya. Sit on my legs."

She got in and he began twisting the top off like a drunken sailor.

"In honor of our new American comrade, Anya, I'd like for him to take the first drink." He held the open bottle up while his wife took a handkerchief from his suit pocket and began wiping the lipstick from his mouth. "Please, Comrade Sweet! Drink!"

"I need to run upstairs real quick," I said, opening the door. "I'll be right back."

I headed upstairs and told Loretta, Dorene, and Bobby that there'd been a problem with the circuit breaker because of all the power usage during the party, and that I'd need to help Sergei fix it. I told them to carry on without me for however long it might take and they seemed to be just fine with that, all three engaged in conversation with various folks I'd never met before.

I returned to the garage to find Sergei still holding the bottle and waiting for my return. I opened the door and got in again.

"Please, Comrade Sweet," said Sergei. "Drink!"

I grabbed the bottle and took a fake swig. My plan was to get the both of them very drunk, so drunk that I just might be able to steal the keys off of him. The key would be making sure they were the ones doing the majority of drinking. I'd need to creatively sip.

"Ah . . . that's good whiskey," I said, handing him the bottle.

Without saying a word or handing it to his wife first, he took a big drink.

"Delicious!" he said. "The Irish know how to make the best whiskey."

He took another drink and handed the bottle to Anya, who still had a look of embarrassment, a blush, on her round, olive-skinned face. Based on the behavior of these two, I had a feeling they had downed more than their share of vodka, but this stuff was about to be much more potent.

I'd still had my bouts with sleep over the last decade and had received my last prescription of little white pills from Dorene's doctor back in Nantucket. And as was the case during my Strivers' Row days, they were coming in mighty handy. I just needed Sergei and Anya to enjoy the whiskey along with my crushed-up doozies. Of course, with no work for either of them to do tomorrow, I was betting they would fully partake and empty the bottle.

15

Magadan, Russia
January 1938

TIME DOES NOT PASS FAST WHEN ONE IS WORKING IN THE SOVIET prison camps. It had been exactly one week since Yury and Boris had left the camp here at Magadan and headed up the dreaded Road of Bones, but it had felt like two months. If they had managed to stay alive so far while navigating the frozen tundra, they would now be fighting against forty to fifty below temps.

My standing with my boss, Koskinen, had not deteriorated at all. In fact, I was on even better terms with him. The problem that existed in these ungodly camps was that a man like him couldn't actually help me. He was beholden to a slew of individuals who outranked him, and many of them seemed to disappear and be replaced often. It was a revolving door of bureaucratic Stalin worshippers who made up the Dalstroi, many of them willing to cut one another's necks in order to lay claim to the latest idea of where the newest gold mine might be.

The only thing keeping Koskinen around, it seemed, was his unprecedented knowledge of land and structural development. He was a brilliant engineer and architect, able to design the most comprehensive drawings, most of which were too advanced to use, as they required materials that were not yet being shipped up the coast. His knowledge of state-of-the-art sewage systems, electrical grids, etcetera, was not being completely put to use.

All of the engineers met with Koskinen on Sundays as a group, but it was my biweekly one-on-one meeting with him that kept alive my hopes of one day seeing my wife and daughter again. It was a Saturday in late January when I decided to press the issue further. But first I had to carry a toilet bucket to the big hole.

All of the barracks had five eighteen-inch-high buckets called *parasha* to use as toilets, all set aside in a small room where we were forced to relieve ourselves in front of one another. We used dried leaves from the taiga to wipe—poplar, aspen, or birch. Whichever *zek* topped a bucket off had to carry it to the big hole. Failing to do so would cause a fight. Guards typically let us carry them to the five-by-five, ten-foot-deep hole unaccompanied, but they made sure the bucket was full first.

The big hole was covered by a six-inch-high, square wooden lid, which looked like the roof of a small shed. The lid had handles on each side and a hinge in the middle, allowing one to open it on the right or left. There were many of these *zek*-dug holes within the camp containing waste and leaves. Once a hole was full, it was sealed by covering the lid with a mound of dirt. The hole was then left this way for one year, after which the contents would be used as manure at the nearby Dukcha State Farm, where they were still foolishly trying to grow vegetables in an impossible climate. They were also trying to acclimatize goats, sheep, cattle, rams, ducks, and chickens there, with very little success.

Finished with my toilet duty, I stood in front of the commander's barracks and looked down at my concrete-covered felt boots and galoshes. Still had them, even though they'd already issued me clothing for the still-distant summer, including gray canvas shoes. For the summer they had also issued us long gray underwear, top and bottom, made of linen and old, frazzled, cotton military tunics.

I kicked the lower step of the commander's deck until the almost-dry concrete began to flake off. I took a piece of torn-away sock from my pants pocket and wiped the sawdust and concrete splatters from my face. At least there were no mosquitos to flick away yet. I'd been told they loved the muddy roads and alleys throughout the camp when the summer came, or perhaps it was the filthy sewage holes, the dirty and sick bodies, or the smelly clothes of new arrivals who'd likely be issued garments recycled from the dead.

The small amount of cold water we were given to wash our clothes periodically had little effect. And clothes were never thrown away. They might as well have been gold, too, as far as the Dalstroi heads were concerned. *Zeks* would kill one another over them. We'd seen such things when men awoke to find their coats or shoes stolen.

Water was like gold, too. And it was served randomly in a bucket from which we dipped. We weren't given bowls or cups. We'd been issued a piece of tin to make a pot, usually no more than twenty-four ounces' worth. From this we drank and ate. We'd been given no utensils, as our hands would serve as such. Stalin had more important uses for tin.

If a *zek*'s pot was stolen, he'd have to find another willing to share, a rarity, as each man was only allowed to fill his pot with soup, gruel, or water one time per serving. A stolen or lost pot essentially meant having to cup your hands and have the cooks ladle the food into them. Such *zeks* quickly learned how to overlap their hands to keep liquid from seeping through the natural openings that most bony, knobby hands created. On the rare occasion when the soup or gruel was actually boiling hot, this meant not eating. It always meant not being able to have the nightly ration of hot water for dinner. I felt awful for these poor souls, for I hadn't yet seen a *zek* lose a pot and be reissued another.

But even with self-made pots in hand, water rations were inconsistent. Not counting the ladle portion of hot water we were given for dinner, the most we ever received in a day was a potful. To make matters worse, only sporadically were we sent to the baths with a bucket for ten of us to share. Using our same twenty-

four-ounce pots, we dipped from the bucket and washed ourselves. No soap was provided.

All of these barbaric norms still haunted me, as I remained
standing in front of the commander's small barracks. With most
of the concrete removed from my boots and face now, I stepped
onto the deck and entered.

"I can see that you Americans are always on time," he said
from behind his desk, a lit cigar in hand. "Please sit."

"Yes, Commander Koskinen."

"I do not know how much longer I'll be here," he said. "I may
be going to the mines to construct new camps. They've found
many new mines. Maybe you can come. With your boy! It is
warm inside the mines."

"As you wish, Commander Koskinen," I said, gladly breathing
in the sweet-smelling cigar smoke.

"Do you know about explosives?"

"Yes," I said.

"Good. But you would be building still. Only, it might serve
you well someday in the camps, knowing about explosives." He
paused before continuing. "There has been no record to be
found regarding your sentence reduction. But I have ordered a
new one for you based on superior work. I filed the document
and it will be sent to the proper authorities. It's for your boy, too."

"Thank you."

I felt a warmth run through my body, a good feeling I hadn't
felt in a year. I continued breathing in the smoke, actually getting a chemical effect from it, as I hadn't breathed in tobacco
smoke to this degree for such a long time.

"Do you have any free relatives here in the Soviet Union?" he
said, flicking some ash into a tin cup. "If you do, ask them to
send some money so you can buy tobacco once in a while from
the commissary like the other *zeks* do, at least the ones whose
families have money."

"I do not smoke," I said, "but I have written a letter to a close
comrade. I wrote it last week."

"You wrote 'Prisoner Prescott Sweet' and 'Sevvostlag Magadan Camp' as your name and address, as required, yes?"

"Yes," I said.

"Is he an American?"

"Yes."

"Is he here in the Soviet Union?"

"No, he was earlier. He's now in Argentina."

"Then NKVD confiscated the letter. No letters from prisoners are allowed to leave the Soviet Union right now. As soon as they saw the Sevvostlag in the upper left corner and the Argentina address below, they tore it up. Only letters from free civilians can go outside Soviet borders, this after NKVD has read them. Maybe your comrade is a spy, you see?"

I casually nodded, realizing that Bobby hadn't received my letter telling him we'd been arrested. I'd written it earnestly, half believing it would only be a matter of time now before we were released. It had given me the impetus to work hard and remain in decent spirits.

"Was this comrade in Moscow when you were arrested?"

"No."

"When did you last correspond with him?"

"I sent him a letter in August, which he likely received in September. So, maybe four months."

"How often do you correspond?" he said, setting his cigar in the ashtray.

"At least a letter every five months."

"Do you cable each other?"

"We hadn't since he'd left. But it would be something he would do only if it was urgent."

"Sounds like it is about time for him to hear from you to keep him from being concerned. But it seems that won't happen. What do you believe your Moscow friends and neighbors are thinking about your absence now?"

"My wife and I were traveling to Stalingrad and Leningrad a lot. She was . . . *is* . . . a noted painter here. So the neighbors likely think we are away doing showings."

"Neighbors are too afraid to say a word to anyone anyway when they know of an arrest. They are only worried about themselves. You could be gone for ten years and they'd never say a thing. NKVD has everyone afraid of his or her own shadow. Besides, what your neighbors don't know is that NKVD has already emptied your apartment during the night. Your belongings are being stored somewhere and your place has been rented to someone else. By the way, many artists, like your wife, and writers have been arrested. And their comrades won't report it. Believe me. Too terrified that they'll be put on a list also. What does this comrade you speak of do?"

"He's a diplomat."

"Ah. Not good. He will be one to go poking around. Very much not good."

He stood and walked around the desk until he was at a cabinet next to the door behind me. Returning with a bottle and two tin cups, he sat again. The label on the bottle read *ubróvka*, a brand of vodka I recognized, as Bobby enjoyed it.

"Does this comrade think you're still in Moscow?" he said, pouring two drinks and handing me one.

"Thank you, Commander. Yes, he does."

He held up his cup and I followed suit, both of us downing the tasty stuff. It would be the first time since Moscow that I'd perhaps have my emotions numbed a bit, a more than welcome possibility.

"Hear me," he said. "Your comrade needs to keep believing that you live there, as far as NKVD is concerned. Or, even better, I will give you some strong advice that might keep you alive longer, Comrade Sweet. It will keep this comrade from pestering Moscow NKVD about you."

"Okay."

"I am doing this only because I feel that if I help at least one decent *zek* in this world stay alive, especially a black one who makes me think of my sister's husband, maybe my Trotsky will look upon me someday with pride. I am doing this for Trotsky. Understand?"

"Yes."

"Write another letter to this comrade and tell him you have moved with your family to Leningrad. Tell him you are all happy and fine. Tell him, however, that your wife and children are still traveling a lot with her paintings, and that you've been hired to do a quite lucrative engineering job at the port here at Nagaev Bay for at least six months. There is actually construction being done down there as we speak. I say this all to keep you alive. Makes sense, yes?"

"Yes."

"The bags of *zek* mail here at the Magadan post office are kept separate from the free hires' mail. And it is all shipped to Moscow postal before it goes anywhere else. I will drop your letter in the free hires' bags when I take my mail over to the post office."

"Thank you, Commander."

"Moscow postal might then forward it to NKVD, but once they read it and realize you're from Leningrad, and that you're only temporarily working at Nagaev Bay, they will let it go out. There are only a handful of officials in this entire country who know of you. No random NKVD policeman or postal worker is going to recognize your name whatsoever. They deal with millions, you see. But, of course, you'll never receive your comrade's return letters, as you must use a fictitious Leningrad address. I will give you a good one. I used to live there."

"Well," I said, "he probably won't write back until July, especially if he believes I'm busy here at Nagaev Bay. But still, once his letter eventually comes, it will be returned to him. Not good. I mean, maybe he won't write back until August, but then again, maybe sooner, if he thinks Loretta might forward it to me."

"Ah," he said, pouring us both another vodka, "I know what to do. It is now late January. Don't send the letter for two weeks."

He held his tin cup up again and I did the same. Then he nodded and we drank before slamming our cups down, both of us feeling the vodka.

"Now," he said, "one of the free hires here, a medical equipment technician who I know and trust, Kirill, is returning to Leningrad in March. He, like me, is a Trotskyist. A lot of us Trotskyists know one another. There are more than you would think amongst the free hires, guards, and even the Dalstroi and Sevvostlag officials. And we're brave. Not afraid to take risks. We always help one another. Anyway, I know another loyal Trotskyist who works for Leningrad postal named Rodion. I will have Kirill track him down and tell him in person to set up a post office box in your name. Rodion will then check the box weekly while at work, but will simply save the letters for you. He won't write back to your comrade, obviously."

"Thank you, Commander Koskinen," I said.

"Ah, a problem! I will have to first cable Rodion and tell him that my cousin from Moscow is moving to Leningrad and would like to set up a post office box until he gets situated. The cable will tell Rodion this: *'Please assign a number to P. Orlov and cable me back the box number so I can inform my cousin, who wants to begin having his mail forwarded.'* Then I will simply explain the truth of the matter to Kirill and he can relay it to Rodion in person, you know, explain that the box is actually for you. Rodion will switch the name. You see, we have to get a box number before you send your letter. And, of course, I have no cousin in Moscow."

"I can't thank you enough," I said, truly stunned at his kind gesture.

"This should work for a while, until your comrade realizes you're not answering any of his questions. Yes?"

"Yes," I said. "Could work for a year or so before he grows truly suspicious."

"But maybe our Trotskyist takeover will happen before then. It is only a matter of time before we Trotskyists rise up and retake control by force, allowing our Leon Trotsky to return and lead us. Many men with guns across the country, and many inside the Kremlin, are Trotskyists. All of us former and current military men are simply awaiting the Kremlin overthrow. I won't say his name, but a top member of the Politburo is a Trotskyist. He is in position to seize power and send orders to us loyalists. We want a war. Understand?"

"Very much."

"Still," he said, picking up his cigar, "I can't help you beyond this mailbox arrangement. But just know that NKVD would never release you if your comrade learned of your arrest and de-manded such."

"I understand, Commander."

"They would tell him you'd committed certain crimes against the State and then proceed to secretly kill all four of you in order to prevent an ongoing investigation by your government, and that's *assuming* your Roosevelt would even consider such. He has never done so for any other to this date. Why would he concern himself with a Negro? It is this simple."

"Thank you, Commander," I said with a lump in my throat.

"I found out where your wife and daughter are," he said, pick-ing up a sheet of paper and reading. "They are near a town called Kirovsk. It is all the way across the country, up near Fin-land. They're at the MR4 Labor Camp. I know the director of that camp, a pig named Colonel Ivan Zorin. Now *he*, for one, is certainly a devout Stalinist!"

"If I might ask, what type of labor do you think he has my wife and daughter doing?"

"They mine apatite at MR4. Apatite is a pale-green mineral used to make fertilizer. So they are probably doing very difficult hauling and cleaning of the freshly mined stones . . . even if they are pregnant. As you already know, based on this camp alone, many women get pregnant in the camps. And again, this Colonel Zorin is a real pig."

"Do you know anything else about him?" I said, halfheartedly.

He began rattling off all sorts of details about Colonel Zorin, and I was listening astutely, but his previous comment—"even if they are pregnant"—was echoing loudly in my head.

Koskinen finished talking. He then held the thick cigar near his lips and turned it several times before taking a big drag and exhaling directly at me, as if he knew I was enjoying it. "What was something pleasing you did in our beautiful Moscow with your family, Comrade Sweet?"

I took a second to think back, still trying to ignore the image I had in my mind of my sweet wife and daughter being violated. I wanted to jump up and grab him and demand him to do something immediately. I was enraged inside, perhaps even twitching on the outside. Maybe the smoke was keeping him from seeing the impulse bubbling up in me to want to vomit all over his well-organized, wooden desk. But I breathed in deeply and focused.

"There were so many," I said, my Russian words trembling, a tear forming in my eye. "But the most enjoyable thing we did in Moscow was go to the Theater of People's Art and listen to the Anglo-American Chorus. It was comprised of forty-five Americans, men and women. They sang Negro protest songs to a largely Russian audience. Their applause was so grand and heartfelt at the conclusion of 'Dis Cotton Want a Picking.' So grand! So heartfelt!"

I looked at Koskinen and thought about the part of this story that I wouldn't be telling him. It involved how Loretta and I had actually felt that night. We had looked down at our twins as the applause had continued. We realized that our children had never known America. But part of us was glad they had never known that ugly bird called Jim Crow. Still, as the next Negro protest songs had continued from the stage, Loretta and I hadn't been able to help but feel the souls of our American ancestors. We hadn't been able to help but miss some of what our children would never know—the unexplainable, ever hopeful, *good* essence of the United States of America. I missed it.

"Where your wife and daughter are located doesn't get very cold," said Koskinen. "Nothing like Magadan, and certainly not like Kolyma's frozen road. Men who know about what it feels like to work in forty below temperatures will do anything to avoid it, it seems. I can tell you such things. One *zek*, when I first arrived here, refused to join the lines and leave for the mines. He nailed his own testicles to a wood bench in the washtub barracks. It didn't work, however. The NKVD guards yanked him up, sent him to the medic, and a week later he was sent to the mines."

"He truly wanted to stay here," I said, trying not to grimace.

"I think . . . after that visit to the medic . . . you should be saying 'she' truly wanted to stay here, Comrade Sweet."

"Yes, Commander."

"A few more items. Did you know the *zek* in your barracks who killed himself the other night?"

"No," I said.

He was referring to the man who'd bitten the veins on his wrist under his tattered, thin blanket. It had been a disgusting, blackish-red mess-of-an-image to wake up to.

"Such suicides are common throughout the system. But, I must say, every camp across the Soviet Union is its own universe. Every camp has its own culture. Some have . . . they have . . . I am searching my mind for a Western phrase. Some have *minimally compassionate* bosses, a good term, yes?"

"Yes."

"But others have bosses who are sadists. My boss is a sadist. And then there's Stalin. He still doesn't understand that all of us officials are still just humans. Guards throughout the system are corrupt and rape women *zeks*. Camp bosses steal money and gold. Moscow officials could never know what goes on thousands of miles away. They come to inspect, and camp administrators make the camp appear perfect. But as soon as they leave, things return to reality. Can you tell I was educated in Norway?"

"I was going to ask you where—"

"I like talking to you because you're a Negro. Maybe I'm ignorantly convincing myself that I'm getting to know my sister's Negro husband better by imagining that you're him. They have four children who I don't know. I am an uncle. Maybe I see your boy as one of my unfamiliar nephews. Such impulses to consider such things are not under our control as humans."

"You sound like an extremely educated man," I bravely decided to say. "You sound well-read."

He stood and approached the bookshelf to my right. "I shall give you this one to read by Bolesław Prus called *Pharaoh*." He took it from the top shelf, then handed it to me before sitting back down. "Now you have something to read."

"Thank you, Commander."

"It is Stalin's favorite. You should learn as much as you can about the preferences of Stalin. And it will make you look good when the commanders and guards see you carrying it. When you're finished, have your boy read it."

"I will."

"I prefer philosophy books, a broad range of them. As such, maybe I am too philosophical for Stalin's Soviet Union, too nostalgic for the Lenin days that saw the proletariat as actual human beings who mattered. Maybe I read the *Communist Manifesto* too often. Have you read it?"

"Yes," I lied, hoping he wouldn't quiz me, and, at the same time, realizing I'd spent my entire adult life writing my own manifesto.

"A few years back," he said, "*zeks* in Kolyma were actually fed and clothed better, and even worked shorter hours. There was a belief that such would make the *zek* more productive. But then the numbers got too big, so many arrests. Stalin realized that Kolyma *zeks* were like river fish that could simply die and be replaced with fresh fish from a hatchery."

I watched him sit there and smoke for a moment. He was an introspective man, lost in what he perceived to be an ever-growing, unprincipled land. He appeared to be my age, which would have put him in his early twenties back during the dawn of the Bolshevik Revolution. He hadn't been able to shed those Lenin and Trotsky principles that were polar to Stalin's wholly authoritarian edicts.

"I want you to replace the floor in the northwest chamber of punishment isolator number three," he finally said. "The slats of wood and joists are rotting from all of the blood and urine. That last chamber on the right is where we've kept the worst of the worst for the past year. Fifty shipped-in, murderous *zeks* have probably died in that single chamber over that period. I won't go into details about the vicious beatings they endured. No?"

"No," I said.

"I need the slats replaced by noon tomorrow. It is already four o'clock. You can work until late tonight. Then finish tomorrow. Have your boy help you remove the slats this evening. Then use Dima Avdeyev and Roma Galkin to help you two replace them in the morning. Those two work the fastest. You can go now."

It was the best gift I'd been given in the five months I'd been imprisoned, my getting to work alone with James, at least for a day. With the claw ends of our hammers, the two of us stabbed at the bloodstained slats and began yanking the first two up. It was disgusting.

Punishment isolator number three was where they kept the worst of the worst *zeks*. It was a barracks some one hundred yards west of the entire camp, made of thick logs, rectangular like all the others, but it had a long hallway down the middle and a small guard's room at the end. There were ten windowless, eight-by-eight chambers with heavy wooded doors in the isolator, five along each side of the hallway. We were working in the chamber at the back on the right. There was a crazy *zek* in each of the others.

"Make sure you don't let that hammer slip and hit you in the eye, son," I said, noticing the thick, dry blood that had settled on the sides of the slat I'd lifted. "Make sure the claw is dug in good before you pull. And the long nails on these boards are rusty and filthy. Don't let 'em stick you."

"Okay, Dad."

"What's the first thing you're gonna do when we get back to Paris after we leave here soon? You should start working on your drawings again."

I could see his emotionless mood lift a bit at my mere suggestion.

"I think I want to show Ginger how to play chess. She was always wanting to play with my friend Paul and me back in Moscow. We never let her."

"She'll like that."

"Yeah."

I placed the board aside and looked at the grayish dirt ground underneath the four-inch-high joists. I reached down and picked up a handful. It felt like brittle clay, breaking apart easily in my hands. Fluids had managed to seep through the tight cracks and stain portions of it. It smelled awful, hence the reason Koskinen had said before I'd exited, "Take some shovels and wheel barrels and remove the top foot of dirt underneath. Then replace it with fresh soil before replacing the slats." He'd been more than correct to suggest such.

"Hey, son," I said, "did Paul's father ever tell him when they were going back to Seattle? I remember him constantly talking about his family planning to return soon."

"They probably left in December."

"Well, when we get to Paris I'll track them down and we can plan to see them when we eventually move to Denver, Colorado."

"Really," he said, almost trying to crack a smile for the first time since August. "Are we really gonna move to the United States, Dad?"

"That's my plan, son. As soon as Bobby gets us out of here and we rejoin your sister and mother in Paris, I'm going to contact some colleges there. Denver is a place I've always wanted to go."

We could hear the door behind us opening.

"*Bystreye!*" said an isolator guard who'd obviously just arrived to replace the other guard who'd been outside in the cold guarding the front door to this point. "Work faster! I'm here now! It is my night shift now, *zeks*! You Negroes can't be lazy anymore!"

I kept my head down and continued working, trying to ignore the tall, thin man dressed in his gray uniform and visor cap, a rifle hanging from his shoulder.

"You need to finish the entire job today!" he said, taking a wooden canteen from his coat pocket. "You need to finish tonight!"

"Commander Koskinen said that two *zeks*, Dima Avdeyev and Roma Galkin, would be joining us tomorrow morning to help finish," I calmly said in nervous Russian.

He pulled the corked top off of his canteen and I could see the blood rushing to his white bony face. He took a big drink and wiped the moisture from his Stalin-like, dark mustache. He wasn't drunk, but appeared as though he'd had a bit too much for an on-duty guard. He pressed the top back on his canteen and pocketed it.

"Commander Koskinen is not *my* commander!" he said. "He is in charge of building shit for the Dalstroi. The only commander we listen to at this camp is the big boss, Commander Drugov. He's in charge of *zeks*! I spit on your bourgeois Koskinen! You are no different than a fucking *suki*!"

We kept working, our heads down, trying to ignore the word he'd used. It referred to a criminal *zek* who liked to collaborate with the Dalstroi officials.

"You want to go tell your Koskinen who the lazy *zeks* are so he will be nice to you," he continued. "I can tell you're that kind of filth. Look at me, you fucking *suki*!"

I slowly stopped working, both James and I still on our knees. I touched my son's shoulder, signaling for him to stop pulling the wood. Then I looked up at the guard and waited.

"You think because you are not a *zek* with a regular job that you are special, a *pridurok*?" he said. "You think this is so because your Commander Koskinen put you in charge of a brigade? You think that makes you a lucky, Negro *pridurok*?"

"No," I said, hearing this word for the first time. My ability to translate Russian still left me wondering what odd words like this meant. There were many within the camp that I was learning on a daily basis, and many had to remain Russian words, as translating them into English was difficult. The language of the camps was unique.

"Stand up!" he said, removing his shouldered rifle and holding it at his left side, barrel to the floor. "And put the hammer down."

I did both, slowly, and with my heart rate increasing considerably. Positioned no more than three feet from him now, he reached out with his right hand and grabbed my collar, pulling me close, his breath smelling of whiskey, not vodka.

"I don't like you," he said, his mouth an inch from mine. "And I don't like your bourgeois son either, always walking so proper, picking at his bushy hair. Probably filled with lice! And your Commander Koskinen is a spy. This is easy to see. He will be shot and replaced soon enough. Do you understand me, Negro *zek*?"

I didn't answer, so he proceeded to grab my jaw and repeat himself with more force.

"Do . . . you . . . understand . . . *me* . . . Negro *zek*?"

Again I refused to answer, so he backhand slapped me across the face. Hard. I didn't react. I just stood there, letting the sting dissipate. Using only his right, he took the canteen out again, pulling the top off with his teeth, and drank. Enraged, he threw it on the floor and rushed James, pulling him up by the arm and slugging him in the face, hard enough to drop him flat on the floor. It was a punch powerful enough to kill.

At this point, all sense of rational thought exited my mind at once. Watching James lie there on the floor, perhaps unconscious, I transformed into complete, instinctive father mode. A man of my height and age had struck my child.

As if he could sense the rage surfacing in me, he started to raise his rifle. I lunged forward and smashed him against the wall, the rifle falling to the floor. As he bounced off and tried to gather himself, I reached down to pick up my hammer. He came forward, trying to kick it away before I clutched it. But I already had the handle and his boot only clipped my wrist.

I stood and he swung at me with a right, nipping my nose. As I raised the hammer, he swung again and I stabbed his forearm with the claw, yanking it from his flesh as he cried out and stepped back. Seeing James in my periphery still lying there motionless, I raised the hammer again and rushed him. He tried to swing at me, but I kept coming forward, hitting him in the head with the face of the hammer. He fell to the floor and I straddled him, taking the hammer to his head repeatedly until I'd left him unrecognizable.

I stayed there straddling him for a moment while I caught my breath. Then I rushed to James. He was still out.

"Son!" I said, lifting and shaking him.

I shook him a few more times and he began to come to. There was no blood on him, but as I touched all over his face and head, I could feel a knot on his left temple under his hair. He had turned just enough to avoid a square shot to the face. I realized the predicament I was in, so I slid him toward the wall and sat him up.

"Rest here, son!" I said, looking over at the bloody guard.

I stood and approached him, searching for his keys. Finding them in his coat pocket, I also pulled out his identification card and read the name. Returning it to his pocket, I took off his hat and shoved it in my crotch, then grabbed my bloody hammer from the floor and slid it up my coat sleeve, holding it there. I stood and exited the chamber, walking down the hallway to the front door. I peeked out at the dark evening and across the now-invisible, snow-covered land situated between the isolator and the main camp. It was well below zero out.

I clutched his ring of keys, reentered the barracks, and headed for the guard's room straight ahead at the end of the hallway. Using key after key, I found one that opened the door. Inside the closet-sized office were a toilet bucket, a small table, and a chair. On the table was a clipboard filled with papers, some stray bullets, a flashlight, a tin cup, and an almost-full bottle of whiskey. The top paper on the clipboard had "Punishment Isolator" typed along the top, and below it was a long list of names, some circled, as they were likely the current occupiers of the nine chambers. Typed under a line in the bottom left corner was "NKVD Guard," and written above it was "Vladimir Divac." It matched the name I'd seen on his ID card.

Grabbing the bottle of whiskey, I opened it and poured some all over the table. Closing it now, I reached inside my coat and placed it near my underarm, pressing it there so it wouldn't fall. I lifted the back of my coat, picked up the clipboard, and shoved it in my pants at the back until it touched my rear. Sticking my finger in my mouth, I forced myself to vomit all over the table, which was easy. I grabbed the bucket, entered the hallway, closed the door, and headed for one of the big sewage holes near the western perimeter of the main camp.

I arrived there to find no one, luckily, and the only light was emanating from the bright, streaming camp lamps, as the day's work continued throughout. I sat the barely full bucket down and scanned the area. No one.

Removing the bottle from under my coat, I opened it and then lifted the sewage lid enough to pour the whiskey out. I could tell the hole was almost full by how quickly the whiskey hit it. I slid the hammer out from my sleeve a bit and rinsed the blood off of the head with the remaining whiskey. Then I pulled Vladimir's hat from my crotch and threw it in as well, hoping it would float. Closing it and removing the clipboard, I placed both it and the empty bottle near the western part of the lid's hinge, as *zeks* would be approaching the hole from the east, and very few at night. I also kicked a little snow on the items to camouflage them a bit. Looking east, I couldn't detect any guards looking this way, even though they might have been hidden from my view. I picked up the bucket, opened the big lid again, and threw it in.

Looking east once more at the single light above the door of the punishment isolator, I took a deep breath before turning and making my way back. Entering and returning to James, I found him still sitting there.

"You okay?" I said, and he nodded while I set my hammer on the floor.

I approached him and stood him up, steering him to the guard's office. I sat him in the chair and went to retrieve the dead body. After returning the canteen to Vladimir's pocket, I pulled his long coat up at the back and wrapped it over his pulpy head so there'd be no blood on the hallway floor as I dragged him to his office. I placed him behind James's chair and returned to the chamber, taking the three slats we'd removed and returning them to their original position, even hammering the rusty nails back in. I then grabbed the rifle and our hammers and took them to the office. Touching James on the shoulder, I picked up the flashlight from the table and turned it on.

"I'm going to close this door now, son. And I'm going to turn the light off in here. Don't turn around or move. He's lying on the floor right behind you. Just sit right there and wait for me."

He nodded and I closed the door behind me, flipping off the exterior switch for the office, then the one for the chamber we'd been working in. Even though the lights in the hallway remained on, all of the chambers were dark, as I could see the exterior switches pointed down. I found the hall light switch and turned it off, leaving me with only the flashlight to see. Approaching the chamber directly next to the one we'd worked in, I fiddled with the keys until I managed to open the door.

"*Zek!*" I said, pointing the flashlight at the curled-up prisoner, trying my best to sound like the dead guard.

"*Da!*" he slurred, his eyes closed, my light illuminating his filthy face in the dark. "*Da!*" he continued. "It's me, Goran! Is that you, Officer Anosov, or is it Officer Divac?"

"It's Divac," I said. "Come, you can get some fresh air!"

He slowly stood and approached. Taking him by the arm, I led him down the dark hallway, then stopped, just before the front door."

"Wait!" I said. "I must vomit. You can get air later."

I turned him back around and steered him toward his chamber on the right, except I passed it and led him into the chamber we'd been working in. He couldn't know the difference. Leaving him inside and closing the door, I grabbed James from the guard's office before entering Goran's chamber, the light switch inside now turned on. For the next hour we feverishly proceeded to remove enough slats of wood and joists to create a space large enough for us to dig a hole. It had to be wide and deep enough for us to dump the guard's body in along with his rifle.

"The shovels and wheel barrels are out behind the punishment isolator, right?" I said to James, realizing how fortunate we were that Koskinen had suggested we remove the top dirt underneath the slats.

"Yeah," said James.

At some point deep into the night, we had managed to bury him and replace the joists and slats. I then repeated my "fresh air" routine with Goran, this time effectively returning him to his proper chamber, the one with the guard now buried underneath him. If the NKVD ever suspected we'd buried him under our worksite, they'd be sadly mistaken. He'd be in the adjacent chamber, the one where their only plausible witness, Goran, resided. And he'd say he never left his chamber, save for one minute, when the *guard* walked him outside. He might also mention the guard's vomit comment.

James and I returned all of our tools to the original work chamber and finished removing the slats, frantically yanking up the ones stained in Vladimir's fresh blood. Once finished, we used our filthy, wool rags to wipe away any fresh splatterings of blood from the log walls, but it didn't actually matter, because old bloodstains were all over the chamber walls. Still, we were now ready for our two coworkers to join us in the morning.

On our way back to Lagpunkt Seventy-Nine, I dropped the keys inside the sewage hole. Then we returned to our barracks, got into our bunks, and waited for dawn. When the sun rose we'd be ready to return and finish the job as originally planned. I already had my response prepared for when the morning shift's guard asked me where Officer Divac was. I'd say nothing more than, "He approached us looking sick last night with a bottle of whiskey in his hand and said he was heading for the big hole to empty his bucket."

16

Moscow, Russia
April 1935

AMBASSADOR BULLITT HAD BEEN OUT OF THE COUNTRY FOR SIX months but had finally returned in time for the enormous party to be held at Spaso House. It would be called the Spring Festival, and every important person in Moscow had been invited.

With the party still nearly two weeks away, as it was to be held on April 24, I was waiting in the office that I shared with Bobby at the chancery. For some reason he was running late. We were due to meet a very important man at the Kremlin, one Vyach-eslav Mikhailovich Molotov. He held the title of Premier. I was to attend the meeting only to interpret for Bobby, of course. But I was excited to see the Kremlin.

I was still spending half of my days at Spaso House, but that would soon be ending, as the ballroom construction was fin-ished and ready to host guests. Yet, Bullitt wanted me around until the very last Russian worker finished doing touch-up work. I still hadn't had my meeting with him, so I hadn't told him what I'd seen nearly four months earlier in Sergei, the caretaker's, basement apartment. It had shocked the living hell out of me.

After I'd secured the ring of ten keys from a passed-out Sergei, his wife knocked out on his lap, I'd headed straight for his apartment, past the still-packed house of guests and down the stairway toward the basement. His door had three separate locks on it. It took me a while to find the correct ones for each, but I'd managed.

I opened the heavy door and flipped the light switch on, only to find what looked like a normal, small living room—a couch, table and chairs, a lamp, bookshelves, etcetera. It was very clean and appeared to have wooden floors throughout. Closing the door behind me, I made my way through and entered a short hallway, the end of which was part of the underground back wall of the mansion. Flipping on its lights, I noticed a bedroom on the left and a large toilet room on the right.

Continuing down the hallway, I found a small closet on the left, a kitchen on the right. That was all there was to the place— a living room, kitchen, bedroom, closet, and toilet room. I began to fear my quest to find something mysterious would be met with nothing but grave disappointment.

I flipped all of the light switches on and entered the bedroom first. Searching every inch of it, including under and behind the bed and dresser, I found nothing—same with the hallway closet and toilet room. I even tried to move the tub, but it was mounted. I walked to the kitchen and began opening cabinets and trying to move the stove, which was mounted, too. The back wall of the mansion was behind it. I opened its four doors to find nothing. Then I fiddled with the burners and panel on top. No luck. I opened the refrigerator and tilted it to see if a small hatch might be under. Only wooden floor.

Reentering the living room, I began moving furniture around, lifting rugs, and looking behind framed art and pic-tures on the wall, including a large one of Stalin. I looked up at the low ceiling for grooves that might suggest a hatch of some sort, as the ceiling was made of square black tiles with braille-looking shamrock designs on them. I walked the entire place again, looking up this time to see if one of the tile's borders might appear different. No such luck.

I sat on Sergei's bed, thinking. I was blank. Then I thought of an oddity. *Why is the green stove so large?* It was big enough for a family of eight.

I reentered the kitchen and began examining the big green thing. It had two front oven doors and two smaller ones for grilling below. I opened them all and looked inside, pressing my hand at the back walls. A normal stove.

I headed back toward the toilet room and actually decided to relieve myself of all the champagne I'd had. As I stood there listening to water hit water, I heard a tinkering sound coming from the back hallway. Cutting off my stream, I headed down and stopped at the kitchen entry. The tinkering was louder. I approached the stove and realized the sound was emanating from it. As if it were a door, the entire appliance began to move, its back right side pushing away from the wall. The back left side was on a hinge.

I turned and headed for the bedroom. God forbid this was where the intruder was heading, but I slid under the bed and waited. I could hear footsteps passing, heading toward the living room. The footsteps continued back toward the end of the hallway. The sound of something sliding could be heard, then the sound of feet stepping up.

I slid out from under the bed and crawled to the doorway. Peeking left, I could see a small boy standing beside one of the dining chairs at the end of the hallway. Next to it, a wooden ladder extended up through the open ceiling where they'd removed two tiles. The boy picked up what looked like a toaster. Two arms reached down and the boy stepped up a few rungs, handing over the device. He turned toward me, still looking down at the floor, however, and I suddenly realized he wasn't a boy. He was a grown man, but a dwarf, beard and all. Picking up a few tools, he climbed up and disappeared, too.

I stayed there listening for what must have been twenty minutes. I wasn't about to move yet. Time stood still. Finally I heard movement and saw legs climbing back down the ladder. Again I slid under the bed and listened to the commotion.

A few minutes later I heard the stove close and silence returned. I waited a good five minutes before sliding out and heading for the stove. I positioned myself on the right side of it near the back and tried to see how the entire appliance was mounted. It hadn't been connected to the floor but rather the wall. Running my hand along the space at the back, I felt a lever. Playing ever so slightly with it, I realized it was designed to be pushed down.

I decided to wait a few more minutes. I contemplated waiting for another day to explore the secret passageway, but I realized this would likely be my only opportunity. I couldn't help myself. I realized at this moment, some eleven years removed from my having escaped Harlem, how much I got a rush from these types of dangerous situations.

Pushing down on the lever until it clicked, I pulled the stove and it glided open as smoothly as a car door. A square opening in the wall was maybe thirty by thirty inches, and it was dark inside. Pushing it shut again, I began searching the kitchen drawers and cabinets for a flashlight, finding several in the one next to the sink. I pulled the stove open and entered. Before closing it, I made note of the other lever on the tunnel side.

Pointing the light straight ahead, I began walking. There was nothing complicated about the dirt tunnel. It was seven feet high and three feet wide, but it seemed to go on forever, ramping slightly downward.

After at least a hundred yards of walking, I came to the tunnel's end where a ladder was positioned. I pointed the flashlight up through a vertical tunnel that extended some ten feet higher. The base of the seventeen-foot ladder touched the ground at my feet and reached all the way up to a hatch.

I was intrigued but realized it was likely just an entry to the tunnel. Maybe it opened onto the street, or maybe it opened into someone's house. Whatever the case, I couldn't risk what might be on the other side. What I wanted to see was above the tile ceiling in Sergei's apartment.

I headed back and reentered the kitchen, closing the stove behind me. Grabbing a chair from the dining table in the living room, I carried it down the hall and positioned it below the secret tiles. I stepped up and pushed at one of the black squares, sliding it to the side before doing the same to the adjacent one.

Feeling around for the tip of a ladder, I grabbed it and pulled. Made of very light wood, it easily slid down to the floor.

I climbed up and pointed my flashlight. What I saw was an oddity in terms of how structures are built. The top of my ladder touched the bottom of a wide, metal one that was mounted to the wooden wall of a shaft that ran all the way to the roof. It was very narrow, just wide enough for a person to fit through. Studying my surroundings, I realized that this portion of the back wall behind me had been recently added to create this shaft, the outside façade appearing the same.

Many of the windows around the house were inlet, allowing such an add-on like this not to disrupt the aesthetic. None of the exterior walls of Spaso was flat from corner to corner, as there were sections that extended out from the main frame similar to the way a fireplace shaft extends out from the exterior.

I climbed the ladder with my rear to the new wall, my face to the original. When I reached the crawl space that separated the first and second floors, the wall discontinued, allowing me to point my flashlight inside the fourteen-inch-high opening. The joist bay directly in front of me ran all the way to the front of the house, which meant they all did. These weren't your typical joists, either. They were open web wood trusses, the type I'd only seen on bridges back in America. But, of course, Europe and the Soviets were far ahead of us architecturally. The trusses had triangle patterns, like lattice. From a physics standpoint, using them made sense, as they had much more capability for loads, based on span and depth.

I reached inside the bay and picked up a folded piece of paper. I opened it to find an entire floor plan of the crawl space. Each joist bay was numbered and first-floor rooms were labeled. There were measurements and markers that showed exact drilling points. What I was reading told me that the drilling points through the crawl space would allow microphones to be dropped behind the walls of the ambassador's library and office. There were also access holes to the walls behind the oval dining room, music room, state dining room, and even Bullitt's brand-new ballroom.

I looked again at the open web trusses. The triangles were large enough for a small person to squeeze through. The dwarf I'd seen could weave his way all along the crawl space. I was sure he'd been tasked to do just that, probably placing microphones above and below various rooms, as the second-story floor was essentially the top of this crawl space. I placed the paper back where it had been and contemplated entering the joist bay. Unfortunately, I was too big to make my way inside.

Pointing my flashlight up, I began to climb again. Visions of the NKVD dwarf and his partner ran through my head. They had me a bit spooked. In fact, Spaso House as a whole did. I'd learned of its history.

Perhaps parts of the mansion had been reconstructed after the revolution. That's when it began housing the government's Central Statistical Office. It was then used as the reception house for the Central Executive Committee. The People's Commissar for Foreign Affairs, Georgy Chicherin, had only stopped living here in 1930. Maybe all of those years since the revolution had brought with them several "secret" house makeovers.

And as for the tunnel that began behind Sergei's stove, it was probably an original escape route, much older than this corner shaft, which was likely built to spy on the Americans. I was guessing the escape tunnel hadn't worked for Nikolay Vtorov, the original owner, who was a wealthy merchant and had lived in Spaso House from 1913, when it was built, to 1917, when he mysteriously died during the Bolshevik Revolution.

I continued climbing, finally reaching the attic above the sleeping quarters, the one I'd been in many times before. I crawled inside and sat. Pointing my flashlight around, I realized it wasn't the same space. The original attic had been partitioned into two horizontal spaces, one for guests like the Americans to enter from the regular inside door, and this one below it that could only be reached from where I'd come. I pointed my flashlight up and could tell the wood used to divide the attic was much newer. *No wonder the attics are so shallow.*

Still pointing my light, I could see large recorders every-where. I began crawling but had to stop because of a four-inch-wide crevasse in the floor. Running my flashlight along the opening, it was the exact size of the ambassador's bedroom, a large, rectangular crevasse. It was the typical space that sepa-rated one room's wall from another, except the ceiling portions had been carved open. I pointed my flashlight straight ahead into the distance and could see similar crevasses outlining other rooms along the attic floor.

Trying to calculate where I was in relation to the ambas-sador's office two floors below, I began to crawl in that direction. I looked down into a crevasse that outlined two rooms: a guest room on the second floor, and the ambassador's office just below on the upper lobby first floor. My knee almost bumped into a mounted fishing pole. Beside it was a large recorder the size of a suitcase. It was turned off.

Shining my light way down into the crevasse, I could see a mi-crophone hanging from a wire that was running from the pole. *The lengths they'd gone to!* My educated guess told me the micro-phone was hanging right behind the ambassador's desk.

I sat on my behind, legs crossed, and took several deep breaths, the low ceiling reminding me once again that just days ago, Sergei had been bitching and moaning at me as I'd crawled around in the attic just above me. *The real one!*

I loosened my bow tie as sweat dripped from my nose. Part of me was terrified that I'd perhaps put myself in a trapped posi-tion. I couldn't help but wonder if an NKVD spy was coming up the ladder behind me. Still, my desire to see more was driving me, and though both the ambassador and I had imagined such hidden devices, what I was witnessing sent chills up my spine. The extent to which Stalin had gone to embed this mansion with microphones, as if they were no different than mousetraps, was literally beyond comprehension. Spaso House was an in-fested spy complex. NKVD practically lived in these recently constructed spaces.

I crawled back to the vertical shaft and pointed the flashlight straight down. No one in sight. *Are there more secret shafts on the other side of the house? Will this one disappear when the government de-cides to "remodel." Are there hidden microphones in the garage, house-keeping facility, barn, or washhouse?* All I knew was I couldn't touch or remove a single device from this place. All I could do was re-turn to the apartment, replace the ceiling tiles, return every-thing to its rightful position, place the keys back on Sergei's belt, and rejoin Loretta, Bobby, and Dorene. But I couldn't wait to tell the ambassador what I'd seen.

My dotting i's and crossing t's regarding what I'd seen at the Christmas Eve Party some four months earlier was interrupted when Bobby finally showed up at the office, just in time for us to make our way over to the Kremlin to meet with the Premier. We were stopped by at least ten different security guards on our way inside Corpus Number One, and when we finally arrived at his office on the second floor, he was sitting at a large desk made of thick, dark wood. He was wearing a brown suit.

The guard who was accompanying us motioned for us to re-main still while Molotov finished writing something. It gave me a moment to scan the place. The entire office, with its high ceil-ing, was full of thick chairs and rugs and bookshelves. It had four windows that overlooked the courtyard. All of the walls were covered with dark, polished, wood paneling. It screamed of the old czarist times, as both the size and quality of the office was fit for a king. But in reality, the only king was encased in a frame behind Molotov's desk, one Joseph Stalin.

"Your guests have arrived, Comrade Molotov," the guard fi-nally said.

"Good," said Molotov, standing while the guard stayed posted inside the open doorway.

He nodded at us and opened his hand in the direction of the available red cushioned chairs in front of his desk. There were no handshakes. We sat and he followed.

"Thank you for meeting with us," said Bobby, and I translated his words in Russian.

"It is my great pleasure," said Molotov, expressionless, his squatty build and pudgy yet flat face like that of a certain breed of dog. Perhaps I was thinking of a Pug with eyeglasses and a mustache.

"Before we begin," he said, "I would like to express something that brings me great pleasure, Comrade Ellington. Your interpreter is black. This is a very good thing. Our Great Stalin has invited . . . recruited . . . thousands of Americans to come work in the Soviet Union, or to study at either the University of Toilers or the International Lenin School, and we are happy that hundreds are black. It is a shame how your country treats these people."

I translated to Bobby and he responded to Molotov with a simple, "I could not agree with you more, Comrade Molotov. I am not of that prejudiced ilk back home. I never have been."

"The way your America treats its black people is a great symbol, as Lenin himself said, of what is wrong with capitalism. That is why blacks are coming here, many of them skilled laborers. And the whites, too! They can help with our industrialization process. We have no issue with admitting that we need America's industrial technology."

I translated, and Bobby said, "We look forward to building on the relationship we've only recently reestablished. President Roosevelt is sincere in his desire to open the channels of communication even more."

"Do people get arrested in the United States?" asked Molotov.

"Of course," said Bobby.

"And when you see them being arrested, how do you react?"

"I don't react," said Bobby. "I assume they've committed a crime and are being hauled off to jail for it."

"Even if a group is arrested on the streets of New York City?" said Molotov.

Bobby waited for me and said, "Even then. I assume they've been involved in some type of illegal behavior."

"So, then," said Molotov, "why is it that so many foreign men and women seem to be confused when they see people being arrested here for committing crimes? It is no different than your country. People commit crimes . . . and they get arrested. Simple."

"It's eye-opening to look at it from that perspective," said Bobby.

"Do you follow those arrested men and women back in America to the jails where they are being taken, or to the prisons thereafter?"

"No," said Bobby.

"People don't do that here, either. People don't think seeing someone being arrested is odd. Countries have laws and police officers to enforce them. We are no different."

"Absolutely," said Bobby.

"I read in *Pravda* recently where an American writer named Richard Wright expressed his views on our society. He said, 'Of all the developments of the Soviet Union, the way scores of backward peoples had been led to unity on a national scale was what had enthralled me.' This Negro writer is one of your prized possessions. You must read what he said."

Molotov began sifting through a stack of newspapers before handing me one. "Please, Comrade . . . what is your name?"

"Prescott Sweet."

"Please, Comrade Sweet, read and translate this Richard Wright's words for Comrade Ellington. Maybe he can share it with President Roosevelt so he can see that our government is not this evil machine that so many around the world are suggesting."

"My pleasure," I said, flipping the pages and finding the article. "Richard Wright goes on to say, '*I read in awe how the Communists had sent phonetic experts into the vast regions of Russia to listen to the stammering dialects of people oppressed for centuries by the czars. I had—*'"

"Let those words sink in, Comrade Ellington," said Molotov, cutting me off. "They are important. Continue, Comrade Sweet."

"He writes further, '*I had made the first total emotional commitment of my life when I read how the phonetic experts had given these tongueless people a language, newspapers, institutions. I had read how these forgotten folk had been encouraged to keep their old cultures, to see in their ancient customs meaning and satisfactions as deep as those contained in supposedly superior ways of living. And I had exclaimed to myself how different this was from the way in which Negroes were sneered at in America.'"*

I handed the paper back to Molotov, who was almost smiling. I was actually glad to have read the opinion piece, for it shed even more light on a country I, as of yet, didn't fully understand, and it helped that the views being espoused were those of a colored American.

Bobby and Molotov went on to discuss the issue of war debt, and my friend did his best to gauge the Premier's feelings on the subject. We were hoping that Molotov would say something that was in direct conflict with Litvinov. The ambassador had it in his mind that Stalin himself had been kept out of the loop a bit on the debt issue, and that Litvinov had been withholding information from the Politburo. But we soon found out from Premier Molotov that this was not the case. All of them saw the debt issue the same way. They didn't want to pay it for fear that other countries would come trying to collect their claims. "That debt was accrued during czarist times," Molotov had said. "In case you hadn't noticed, Comrade Ellington, we are not czars."

The following months rolled by rather fast and it was now late September. Loretta and I were heading to the Foreign Workers' Club to meet Lovett Fort-Whiteman. Since April, I'd been to several of Loretta's showings, as her paintings were quickly drawing the attention of some powerful people, including Stalin himself. She'd done a grand presentation in Leningrad that had taken us out of town during the big Spring Festival at Spaso. The party had been for the entire diplomatic corps in Moscow.

Part of me was glad to have missed the massive shindig, although I'd heard all of the details about the animals from the zoo—mountain goats, white roosters, a baby bear, pheasants, parakeets, and one hundred zebra finches. It had all been part of a barnyard motif, and apparently Bullitt had successfully pulled off the grandest diplomatic party in Moscow history. Several members of the Politburo drank until the wee hours of the morning, and other than Stalin himself, just about every important man in Moscow had attended. Bobby had raved about it being "so absolutely odd that it was actually brilliant."

Since I'd been out of town during the formal event, I'd pressed Bobby for more details. Apparently Karl Radek had substituted the baby bear's milk with champagne, prompting it to vomit on a Soviet general. One thing Bobby and I couldn't wrap our heads around was why these Spaso shindigs had to have animals present. It all seemed so odd to us.

Besides the party I'd missed, there were other events from the past months to reflect on. After the meeting with Premier Molotov back in April, I'd left Bobby at the chancery and headed to Spaso to meet with Ambassador Bullitt, per his immediate request. I'd arrived to find him arguing back and forth with his French butlers about whether to keep his office where it was across from his library or make the library his office. Apparently he'd already switched back and forth quite a few times since first arriving the previous year because he couldn't get comfortable. He was glad I'd arrived to break up the argument, and so were his butlers.

My meeting with him had been brief. We'd driven along the Moscow River in his roadster, he behind the wheel.

"Their spy apparatus is even more elaborate than I'd thought," he'd said. "But I'm certainly very happy that you found out exactly where the microphones are. You've truly gone above and beyond, Prescott. It gives me peace of mind to know that my instincts are still as good as ever. We'll keep this between you and me. No need to alarm the staff. And when the next ambassador replaces me, I'll decide then whether or not to tell him about the secret tunnel and shaft. But I must say, the story about the dwarf paints a vivid picture. He's probably up there right now squirming about. Gives me the creeps."

"Indeed," I'd said.

"We'll certainly be one step ahead of them now."

Since that meeting with the ambassador back in April, I hadn't seen him even once. I'd heard that he'd been very upset about Litvinov reneging on a key component of the "Gentleman's Agreement." Over the summer, the Communist Party of the Soviet Union had hosted a meeting of the Third International. American communists attended and this was a clear violation of Litvinov's promise to Roosevelt that they'd stay out of domestic affairs. Bobby believed that Bullitt had almost completely given up on Moscow, and was actually looking to leave.

When Loretta and I walked into the Foreign Workers' Club, the place was packed with several white members of the Communist Party, a good percentage of them American, although to be fair, lots of people in attendance were not Party members. This is where folks liked to smoke, socialize, and drink. It wasn't a bad place to be seen frequenting in the eyes of the gun-toting blue tops either. NKVD believed that folks who hung out here could be trusted.

In the lobby, we walked past a large sign that had some very familiar words on it. It was a quote from Stalin, and we'd seen it all over town lately. It read, "LIFE HAS BECOME BETTER, COMRADES; LIFE HAS BECOME MORE JOYFUL." Continuing through, we spotted Lovett and his wife sitting at a corner table near the back, which was unusual. For him not to be holding court was a shock to my eyes. But at least they were smiling and conversing.

"Ain't you two a sight for sore eyes!" he said, standing and kissing Loretta on the cheek before he and I slapped hands. "My brother Bronzeville Sweet is up in the house!"

"Good to see you, Lovett."

His wife B stood and we hugged her before all of us sat. B was a lovely, regular built, brown-haired woman who dressed rather plainly, as most Russian women did. And she always seemed to let Lovett do most of the talking. She was still trying to teach him Russian, but he wasn't taking to it very well. Luckily for him, her English was good enough to allow them to communicate effectively. Their love of science is what had initially brought them together while he was studying fish breeding at Moscow State University, and she was employed at a scientific research institution.

"I'll be right back," said B, leaving.

"She's going to grab us four beers," said Lovett. "My lovely wife is so, so good to me. Love her to death! Anyway . . . you know who I've been thinking about a lot lately? Alexander Pushkin!"

"Why's that?" I said.

"He's the most famous Russian Negro of all time, that's why. And I love his poems. Don't you, Comrade Sweet, my American *brutha* whom I love like no *otha*?"

"I do. I like his poem 'The Gypsies.'"

"Hot damn, me too!" said Lovett, reaching across the table and touching Loretta's hand. "I should not have said I love him like no other, because I love you just as much, Queen Loretta."

"Thank you, Lovett. You're the sweetest."

"When am I going to get you to officially join the Party, dear? Most of the coloreds in Moscow won't join, so you're not alone. But I do understand why you can't, with Comrade Prescott here working for the embassy and all. Still, I'd love to have ya' join someday, girl!"

"I hear you, Lovett. You keep on doing your recruiting. You're so good at it. The Party owes you a whole hell of a lot!"

"Thank you, sista! Congrats on this amazing success you're having with your art! You're a Moscow celebrity. Ain't too many of those around here besides Stalin himself. Socialist Realism is a form of painting that I believe was created just for you. I particularly like your paintings that show mothers holding their babies. You really capture Russian women. B has said as much."

"It's in the eyes," said Loretta. "At least that's what I believe. None of the women are smiling, but the joy is in their eyes. It's the kind of authentic joy that only a mother who has given birth to this beautiful being they're now holding in their arms can truly understand. That's the essence of my paintings."

"You talking about your masterful works of art?" said B, setting four bottles of beer on the table. "Your paintings are hang-ing in some very important houses. I will certainly drink to that."

We held up our green bottles, clinked them, and all took a swig.

"Any concern that the State frowns on other forms?" said Lovett.

Loretta looked at him and contemplated. "No, I have found my calling. I love this form. And I love finally being recognized and appreciated. It's nice to be honored for your art. New to me! And I love the humble way the people of Moscow show their appreciation. It's sincere, but not over-the-top praise or wor-ship."

"Believe me," said B, "they are worshipping you in the privacy of their homes. You are probably going to have Stalin send word that he'd like for you to paint him. I can see this happening very soon because of how your name is being talked about. Moscow is claiming you as its own. You will have to become a Soviet citi-zen very soon."

"Paint a portrait of Stalin?" said Loretta, looking surprised. "No pressure there!"

"And that's my point," said Lovett. "Why should you feel such pressure in such a case? It's because Stalin is too domineering and rules with an iron fist."

"I agree," I said.

"No," said B.

"No," said Loretta. "He is simply trying to create rule of law. There are too many folks who still long for the czarist times. They believe in a system that has a ruling upper class and a starv-ing lower class. Stalin can't afford to let them regain power. His current Five Year Plan is effectively industrializing the entire country, and soon everyone will be operating on a completely level playing field, with equal-paying jobs and equal shares of food, etcetera."

"Sounds good," said Lovett, "but Stalin, the Politburo, and the entire Central Committee are the ones living like czars. Them niggas is eatin' damn caviar! They seem to be the ruling upper class you speak of. I fear they have forgotten to read from the communist playbook. But I digress."

"Perfectly articulated," I said. "I've been trying to tell Loretta this for the—"

"Just stop, Prescott!" she said, somewhat angrily. "Everyone has varying opinions about how the revolution should take form. The Central Committee and Politburo are not some crazy, iron-fisted body. They are clearly in the throes of recreating a societal structure that meets the needs of everyone. They are undoing centuries of evil, barbaric, czarist damage. And they have to operate with some semblance of order and authority. Otherwise the old, fat, set-in-their-ways cats will eat us new, hungry, revolutionary mice, so to speak. Simple!"

"Yes," said B. "Anything new is met with strong opposition. Stalin's ways are new. Collective farms are new. Hiring thousands of foreign workers is new. Bringing in all of this new technology and machinery is new. Strengthening and globally growing the Communist Party is new. We are rebuilding an entire new country. I for one am not afraid of new."

"Neither am I," said Lovett. "Why do you think I'm pining to get out of Moscow for a while and take that job in Kuybyshev. I'm not afraid to try *anything* new."

"Why are you moving?" I said.

"It's not permanent," said Lovett. "I'm just exhausted with some particular members of the CPUSA. They don't seem to share my views about the importance of America's Negro problem as one that is wholly independent of class. I keep telling them that Jim Crow is not a damn class problem. It's a race problem. I need the Party to be more proactive in addressing race as a singular issue. All they say is, 'The Party's aim is to lift all boats, and that includes the impoverished American Negro.' Fuck that! Pardon me, ladies."

"Well, we hate to see you move," I said. "You're like family to us. And the kids will miss your demonstrative storytelling. They adore you, brother."

"Not a move actually," he said. "Just more like a one-year sab-batical from the Party politics here in Moscow. I'm worried I may hurt somebody. During the Third International this sum-mer, I nearly strangled three white members of the CPUSA. No one, including that damn nigga William L. Patterson, shares my sense of urgency when it comes to the Party tackling the issue of race in America. That was the entire point of my joining the Party. Guess I shouldn't say that about ol' Patterson. He sees it my way, but he just doesn't like my flamboyance and the way I aggressively approach the whole thing. I'm not the go along to get along type. And I'll dress the damn way I wanna dress."

"I love that you dress like a Cossack," said Loretta.

"Well, then, go on ahead and paint me, girl!" he said, raising his hands in the air and laughing. "I make a *damn* colorful sub-ject!"

"Yes, you do," said B, kissing him on the cheek.

"A sabbatical in Kuybyshev, huh?" I said, not so keen on join-ing the playfulness. "Will you still be teaching?"

"Oh, yeah! Already have a job set up down there teaching chemistry. Gonna teach some boxing, too. Y'all didn't know I was a boxer I'll bet!"

"No," said Loretta and I.

"Yep! Will be good for me to take a reprieve from all things science and politics. And B is going to keep her job here in Moscow. We'll meet at the halfway point in Glazov about once a month. I just really need this break. Trust me."

17

Magadan, Russia
August 1938

SUMMER HAD COME AND ALMOST GONE. I COULD NOW SAY I'D OF-
ficially been a prisoner for one year, starting from that initial arrest back in Moscow. James and I had been hardened, meaning
we didn't speak much about our condition, we just lived from
minute to minute, thankful at the end of each day that we'd survived to see the sun go down.

As far as my killing the guard in the punishment isolator, the
aftermath had played out as I'd imagined, with NKVD officials
certain that Vladimir had gotten drunk and fallen into the
sewage hole. For months now the hole had remained covered
and sealed. And the guard certainly wasn't missed. I'd even overheard one officer say, "Vladimir was a fucking pathetic drunk,
terrible at his job. It was just a matter of time before he would
have gotten shot by the bosses for being a shitty guard anyway."

Commander Koskinen had been pleased with my cost esti-
mate for the big vehicle storage facility, but he'd also liked some
other engineers' offerings. Regardless, the project still hadn't
gotten under way yet, and I was overseeing a brigade of *zeks*
tasked with constructing a new medical barracks made of stone,
as the current wooden one was so weathered it was about to
blow over from the strong sea winds.

I'd learned some unspeakable news from Koskinen about the group of hundreds that Yury and Boris had been a part of. Eighty percent of them had died along the Road of Bones before making it to the mines, and the remaining twenty percent had passed away shortly thereafter. Why they had even bothered to send them all on such a suicide mission was incomprehensible. Koskinen's answer: "They got at least one good month of excellent mine work out of that twenty percent, and that's lives well spent as far as Stalin's concerned. He reasons that there's an *endless* supply of bodies."

My weight had originally gone from 200 to 180 to now 170, and I only knew this because a nurse had weighed me during a two-day stay at the medical barracks during my bout with dysentery. My recent concern, however, was less about my own health and more about James's. He had developed a cough and dizzy spells that were plaguing him more and more regularly.

After his couple of visits to the incompetent doctor, I was finding it heartwrenching to have to begin telling James, "Try not to show your sickness, son, because if they suspect that you've developed something chronic, God knows what they might do. Close your mouth, grit your teeth, and cough into the back of your throat and the air will expel through your nose. If you feel dizzy, get on your knees and at least act like you're hammering nails into the floor or lower wall. But always remain looking busy. You can cough freely once we get into our bunks tonight."

It was on this last Sunday of August 1938 that I looked at my son convulsing, struggling to hold his cough while helping me frame a wall, that I knew I had to do the impossible and get us out of here. I knew it was a long shot, but I was forced to broach a specific topic with Koskinen during our meeting.

"I need to ask you a very important question, Commander Koskinen," I said about halfway through our conversation in his office.

"The answer is yes, Comrade Sweet," he said. "They are going to execute me before year's end."

My face must have looked confused to him. "Say again, Commander!"

"I make a joke," he said, not smiling, but lighting his cigar. "Ask me."

"I want to spy for Stalin in exchange for my family's release."

He slowly took a puff and leaned back in his chair, a look of deep thought on his face as he blew smoke, for he knew of my serious nature and was already preparing to hear something that would both intrigue and surprise him. I eyed his favorite book, which was lying on his desk, *The Communist Manifesto*. What he didn't know was that at this very second, I had put the final period on my personal manifesto. I wasn't about to make some public declaration to Koskinen or anyone else, but I'd written this in my mind:

> *I declare, from this moment forward, that I will do any and everything required to get my family out of Stalin's abattoir, even with the resolute knowledge that I could very well die in the process. I say today, To hell with Communism, Capitalism, or any other 'ism'! I say To hell with concerning myself with global society, the various races therein—black, white, brown, red, yellow—for I must be wholly selfish in my thinking now. I declare, right here in this Commander Koskinen's office, that I will outmaneuver Stalin and his complicit comrades at every turn. I will summon and utilize every resource within my being to save my family, and I don't care if it is God or the devil who helps me do it.*

"Proceed," said Koskinen.

"Based on the last letter I received in Moscow from my diplomat friend, Bobby Ellington, months before I was arrested, I believe he will be leaving his post in Argentina by this December."

"Why is that significant?"

"Because," I said, "his post will be in Berlin. We both know all too well how significant Germany is in the mind of Stalin. And, you see, I was afraid to mention something to you before. I had only been teaching at the Anglo-American School in Moscow for a little over a year when I was arrested. Before that, I had been Bobby's interpreter and assistant for about four years, two of those at the embassy in Haiti, the other two, at the embassy in Moscow."

Koskinen put his cigar out in the ashtray and sat up straight. His intrigue was obvious. Perhaps because he wanted to be the man who got credit for suggesting such an idea to Stalin, as it might be just the kind of offering that would put him on the dictator's "Good List," even though he claimed a Trotskyist takeover was on the horizon. Or, maybe he just wanted to do this because he actually thought it might help me. Either reason suited me.

"But you worked for this Ellington," said Koskinen. "Therefore, you are loyal to *him*."

"No! He is a friend, but I would cut his throat to save my family."

Koskinen squinted at me a bit and began pinching his chin with his right thumb and index finger. "Cut his throat you say! You would?"

"Yes," I firmly said, lying through my teeth. "He is loyal to America, and I am loyal to my family. And, as I previously said, I was stunned to have been arrested in a country I love more than the United States. If my family and I were to be released, them before the mission commences and me upon its conclusion, we could easily forgive the arrests and remain loyal expatriates, completely at ease with living out the remainder of our lives in Russia."

"Stalin would never agree to release your family prior to any spy mission having been completed. I know nothing of this sort of thing, but I can guess. Your family would be leverage. They'd have to remain imprisoned until you'd gathered any type of intelligence at the U.S. Embassy in Berlin, intelligence that one hundred percent fulfilled Stalin's appetite. And even then, he might kill you all. He might tell you, 'Mission complete. Come back to the Soviet Union and join your just-released family.' But when you arrive . . . bang, bang, bang, bang! A bullet to each of your heads from one of his most trusted NKVD men."

"Then I'll take on the assignment while they remain imprisoned," I said. "All I ask is that the assignment has a specified time length, one that would assure all of our releases in no more than one year. Otherwise Stalin must certainly know they will die in here if kept much longer than that. I can gather plenty of intelligence in twelve months."

"Do you speak German?" he said, busily writing everything I said now.

"*Ja!* I speak German, Russian, Italian, French, Spanish, and, of course, English."

He looked up from his pen with slight surprise. Then he continued writing, as if preparing a report he'd later type, one that listed the details of my history, the proposed mission, etcetera. It was like he knew such a suggestion of espionage would not fall upon deaf ears. I was reminded of just how seemingly orgasmic this whole spy business was to them.

He stopped writing and leaned back, lost in thought for a while. After about a minute passed, I wondered if he'd decided not to consider my proposal, perhaps realizing that taking such a risk could cost him his life.

"Your ability to speak Spanish could be good for us both," he finally said, leaning forward. "I will help you under one condition. And it involves testing your . . . how do you say in America . . . your character. You see, I can't make you do what I'm about to ask, but you can give me your word. Can you give me that, comrade?"

"Of course," I said. "I am going to die in here like the others; my family as well. I'll promise you anything."

"Assuming you are magically able to get out of Russia, you are going to need a job, yes?"

"Yes," I said, watching him take a small slip of paper and jot something down.

"You're going to memorize this name and address because you can't walk around with this paper. Go to this place and see this man." He handed the slip to me and continued. "He is part of the Trotskyist movement. Tell him I sent you and that you speak Spanish and Russian. Then tell him why you hate Stalin. Because of your color, *zek* background, and rare language ability, he may have a good job for you, or he may not. But find out, okay?"

"Okay," I said, handing the paper back to him.

"Is it stuck already?"

"Yes," I said. "I've got it memorized."

"I have your word that you will go see this man if you get out?"

"You have my word," I said, meaning it to my core.

"Then it is between you and your God now. Correct?"

"Yes."

"I will send this letter I'm writing about you to the proper man at the Kremlin," he said, pen scribbling again. "It will likely be relayed to Stalin. But the next phase, assuming it's not him ordering all of you immediately executed, will likely be a serious interrogation of you from some top NKVD men, along with them having you, in some way, confirm that your friend is indeed posted in Berlin and is willing to hire you. Are you sure you want me to send this?"

"Yes," I said, watching him write, his eyes remaining down. "Like I said, we are going to die in here anyway. That is part of their plan, what, with the way they feed us. They don't want us to live, just as you've said. They want to replace us. This possible mission is my only hope."

"Then let me ask some more questions," he said.

"Okay, but first I have one more request. I must be transferred with my son to a camp near my wife and daughter before I leave for Berlin. I must be able to confirm with my own eyes that they're alive. Of course I know that you can't mention that you've already told me where they are. But I need to see them alive. Can you pretend not to know and ask them to find out where they are?"

"I'm writing this all down," he said, talking into his pen, pausing in between each written word. "But . . . in . . . the . . . mean-

time . . . you . . . must . . . survive . . . these . . . next . . . weeks . . .
or . . . months. You know, until we receive word, because, of
course, this is all only between you and me, and those commanders out there overseeing this camp, the ones higher ranking
than me, have complete authority, as you understand, to kill you
or your son without reason. They don't know that I like you.
So . . . stay alive, Comrade Sweet."

Two days later, I saw before me a sight that required the willing suspension of disbelief. I was in the passenger's seat of a
large cargo truck, and we were just beginning to make the short
drive down to the ship dock at the bay, where we were to retrieve
some recently imported machinery. Just as we began to turn
east, something caught my eye to the left. A rather small group
of *zeks* was heading toward our camp from the west. They were
walking the Road of Bones, but going the wrong direction, perhaps returning from mines. And they were all white men, save
for one. I squinted to make sure my eyes weren't deceiving me,
and they were not. Interspersed amongst the *zeks* was none
other than one Lovett Fort-Whiteman.

As we continued toward the bay and lost sight of them, the
lump in my throat stayed with me. My close friend looked
beaten and weathered. I wondered just how and when he'd
been imprisoned. Perhaps they were sending him to my *lagpunkt,* and if not, I certainly intended to speak with Koskinen
about Lovett, to somehow convince him that my friend was as as-
tute as me when it came to engineering, even though he wasn't.
Still, I knew that his expertise in science might be enough to
convince Koskinen to let him work with me. After all, I had a little bit of leverage now.

Six days passed and I'd seen no sign of Lovett, although I
knew he was probably slaving away somewhere within our Magadan camp. I'd told Koskinen about him and he'd agreed to look
into it, but that had only been some twenty-four hours ago, as it
was now Monday.

With the day's work complete and our ration of hot water

consumed, James and I were lying in our bunks resting. Many of the *zeks* in our barracks were loud and constantly instigating fights and arguments with others over the most arbitrary of issues, everything from a missing sock to a stolen cigarette or ruble. And on this particular night, I was on the receiving end of a bothersome false accusation from a *zek* named Max, who was about fifty years old, short, and considerably bonier even than the rest of us. His skin looked like wrinkled, filthy leather, the deep crevices on his face filled with a sort of green-black grime.

"Comrade Sweet?" groveled Max. "Do you know the name of this new *zek* who is sleeping below you?"

"Yes," I said, eyes closed. "Roy. He's an American."

"Okay. Thank you." He kneeled down and turned his attention to Roy. "Hey, Comrade Roy! What is—"

"Don't fucking touch me," said Roy.

"I just wanted to know if you stole my toothpaste," said Max.

"Get away from me!" said Roy.

Max stood again.

"Did you take my toothpaste, Comrade Sweet?" said Max, grabbing my foot and shaking it so I'd open my eyes.

"No, Max!" I said, eyes still closed.

"I think you did," he said.

"I didn't. Why don't you continue making your rounds! I saw you earlier accusing Douglas, Richard, Chris, and Wendell of the same thing. Do you have something against the American *zeks*?"

"How could I?" he raspily said, clearing his throat and spitting on the wood floor. "You know I'm an American, too."

"Yeah," I said, realizing this was the first time I'd spoken English in a long time, even James and I only speaking Russian to each other. "I do know you're American, Max, and that's why I'm puzzled at your choosing to pick on your fellow countrymen first. Go hassle Anatoly or Stanislav!"

"They only steal pencils," said Max. "By the way, where did you get your pen?"

"How did you know I had a pen?" I said, turning on my side and opening my eyes.

"I saw you showing it to James the other day."

"Koskinen gave it to me," I said, looking at his rotten teeth, wondering if he'd ever even used toothpaste in his life. "By the way, where did you get toothpaste, Max? I haven't seen or used any in a year."

"My aunt sent me some rubles from Moscow. She is Russian. That's how I ended up in this shithole. Visiting her!"

"Do they sell toothpaste in the commissary?" I asked.

"Sometimes. Usually the guards buy it all. But I got lucky. But now someone stole it."

"It was probably Timofei or Yegor," I whispered. "They're the ones doing all of the stealing of rubles in this barracks. I heard that *zeks* like them—you know, actual hardened criminals—are being asked to do some of the policing for the NKVD. This has them feeling empowered to steal what they want from us politicals, as they know we can't say or do anything about it. They take what they want."

"Shit!" said Max. "And they already feed the criminals more than us politicals. I'm going to go find them."

"You must have a death wish. I can tell you exactly where they are. They're in the south corner beside the toilet room playing cards with those other eight, as always. Don't you know this?"

"Yes," he said. "I meant I'm going to go find them . . . as in . . . confront them. I'm going now."

"Do you speak Russian? Because that's all they understand."

"No," he said.

"I didn't think so. Good luck, Max."

He walked away and I shut my eyes again, letting the chatter and clinking throughout the barracks put me to sleep. These had once been the sorts of noises that kept me from sleeping, but now, on each night, after having simply survived the day, it all sounded like soothing rain. I knew this must also have been the case for James because he was already sound asleep up above me.

Having earlier sloshed the last bit of hot water around in my mouth to wash it, I lay there rubbing my teeth with my finger, trying to get the gunk off with my nail. A man's gums and teeth rotting was a forgone conclusion in Stalin's prisons. I was just trying to keep mine from eventually falling out. So far they were fine.

About an hour later I felt a tap on my arm. I opened my eyes to see Lovett standing there stone-faced. It scared me, so I jumped up. I knew I wasn't dreaming, though.

"Easy, Bronzeville!" he said, many of his front teeth missing. "It's just me."

"My God!" I said, shocked as could be.

I rolled out of bed and stood. Both of us stared at each other. We were overcome with joy, pain, sadness, and disbelief. I felt tears forming in my eyes and could see some welling up in his, prompting both of us to break down and embrace. We must have stood there hugging for a good minute. My friend, like me, was much skinnier now, his beard bushy, specks of gray in his full head of nappy hair, a far cry from the slick, bald look he'd previously sported.

"What happened to your ear?" I said, both of us speaking English.

"One of those evil, murdering motherfuckers on the ship from Vladivostok bit half of it off when I tried to stop him from killing an Estonian comrade of mine. And his bite worked. He and his partner still wound up killing him. Beat him with their bare fists over a ration of fuckin' black bread. Hell . . . at least I tried."

"Biting is all they do in the prisons," I said, showing him my thumb and webbing. "With no knives or other weapons available on the ships or in the barracks, teeth might as well be switchblades."

"Mm-hmm."

"Don't get me wrong," I said, "More than once I've seen one *zek* kill another with a hammer or saw. But teeth have caused by far the most injuries."

"Speaking of teeth," he said, opening his mouth and touching his upper and lower gums, "another thing that happened to me when I first left Kazakhstan for Vladivostok was the guards decided I wasn't moving fast enough to board the train, so they took a baton to my mouth and knocked most of my front teeth out, as you can see. My lips were split open real good, too, but they had a nurse stitch me up right there on the train before we departed. Had 'em removed in Vladivostok."

I shook my head with disappointment, and again we stood there holding our words, trying to let this stunning set of circumstances settle in. He looked up at James sleeping and half smiled. Then he looked down and past me like he was transfixed on something not present.

"How long ago were you arrested?" I said.

"Too damn long ago," he said, snapping to.

I leaned over and touched the new *zek*, Roy.

"Yeah," he said, opening his eyes.

"Excuse me, Roy. But would you mind taking my middle bunk for a while? I desperately need to sit and talk to my other American friend here. I'd really appreciate it."

"Of course," said Roy, rolling out of bed and hopping up to my spot. In the forty-eight hours he'd been here, the two of us had shown nothing but respect for each other.

"Thank you," I said, Lovett and I sitting on his bed.

"Sure is good to see another colored face," said Lovett, both of us shaking our heads in disbelief.

"I tried for almost two years to find out from B when I could see you after you left Moscow in late 1935. But she kept telling me she had lost touch with you. It was as if your wife had been hurt by you."

"Na," he said. "The entire thing was a lie. That night we met you and Loretta at the Foreign Workers' Club, we had already received some bad news."

"Come again."

"About a week before that night, I'd been at that same club and had gotten into an argument with a couple of CPUSA members about that damn Langston Hughes book of all things. A book entitled, *The Ways of White Folks*. I had claimed that the book did too much pandering to white people. Well, Hughes is a hero to the Soviet Union, just like Robeson. Somebody in the audience reported my diatribe to the blue tops. Subsequently, they paid me a visit the next day and branded me a 'counter-revolutionary' right there on the spot. They visited B and me every day during the course of that next week, asking all sorts of questions."

"That's hardly enough to get you arrested," I said. "Bitching about a damn book by an American!"

"That was just the tip of the iceberg, Bronzeville. They kept questioning me until they found out I was a close friend to Karl Radek, a man the State was also beginning to investigate. So when I met y'all that night, I hadn't been sentenced to the Sevvostlag labor camp yet. I had only been told to leave Moscow and find work in, of all places, Alma-Ata, a small town in faraway Kazakhstan, until the State could sort out just exactly what Radek's crimes were. I was exiled. B was ordered to remain in Moscow. The blue tops had granted me one final wish: to say good-bye to several friends during the course of that last day. We saved you two for last. They'd also ordered us not to tell a soul where I was being exiled. It pained me to lie to you both. No choice!"

"I'm thinking back to that night," I said. "You two seemed so happy and certain of your plan."

"The fear those blue tops put into you will make you believe your own lie, Bronzeville. Make you happy to just still be breathing! That's what you saw that night. And B was also just glad to see me still alive."

"When did you get arrested and sent here?" I said.

"Well, part of my story I told y'all that night turned out to be true. I did end up teaching chemistry and boxing, just in Alma-Ata, not Kuybyshev. Then I was sent to another town in Kazakhstan named Semipalatinsk."

"Did you and B ever meet halfway like you'd said you would?"

"No," he said. "I never saw her again."

"I'll be damned!"

"I'd been in exile under the watchful eye of NKVD officials for two and a half years before they finally arrested me on May 8th of this year and sentenced me to five years hard labor here at Sevvostlag. That's when they'd claimed that I, like Karl Radek, was a Trotskyist. NKVD told me they'd had a big show trial for Radek."

"Yes," I said. "It was all over the papers for months. He was sentenced to ten years in prison. The papers, particularly *Izvestia*, made it appear as though his crimes were fact, that he'd been justly charged with complicity in plots against the State."

Lovett shook his head. "I'm sure I was found to be one of his close confidants. The list of men associated with Radek is far too long. I'm sure they've all met similar fates. Radek is a damn good man."

"*Are* you a Trotskyist?" I whispered in his ear.

"Shit, I'm an American," he said. "Just like you."

His words shook me. *Of course!* All he'd *ever* been was an American seeking to live a life of dignity.

"Am I a Trotskyist?" he whispered, looking around. "Much more so than a filthy Stalinist. That's for sure. And it's no crime."

"Don't worry about these other *zeks*," I said, surveying the barracks. "Most speak no English, and the Americans who do are completely with us in our opinions. Trust me! We are all loyal to one another. We have to be."

"How could we not be," he said, looking up at the streaming lights. "They hang these bulbs like Christmas lights. They ever turn 'em off at night?"

"No," I said. "One thing I've learned, they never leave *zeks* here alone in the dark."

"Does that guard out front ever leave?" he said.

"Only when he comes in here and makes the rounds."

"I see."

"Did they assign you to this barrack?"

"Yes," he said.

"Good. I had it arranged. Commander Koskinen is responsible."

"Thank you, Bronzeville."

"Of course. Question. You told me they arrested you back in May. Where have you been for these past few months?"

"They had me working at this state farm not too far from here called Dukcha. Just temporarily! Had me doing all kinds of experimental fertilization work for twenty hours a day. Lots of work with trying to help breed farm animals, too! All of their experimenting is failing. Can't grow shit in Siberia for more than a month, and that's only in the summer! Can't keep damn calves alive in this frozen land, either! They ship cows in, try to acclimatize them and have them breed. Then think their offspring can survive through the long, frigid winters. Foolish! Can't happen!"

"Of course not," I said.

"As soon as they found out I had a background in studying fish breeding, I was sent there. Guess they thought I might be a magic nigga! They quickly found out I wasn't. After only two weeks they had my behind tilling soil through the rest of the summer. Shit was like quicksand. The lot of us damn near died ten times a day from exhaustion. And, as you can see, I've barely eaten. Now that I'm here and the State's newest band of scientists is in place there, I'm likely headed to the mines very soon. These new scientists are apparently all Soviets and equipped with some mysterious groundbreaking methods. Please! It ain't nothin' but a bunch of damn pseudoscience. But enough about me! How in God's name did you two end up in here?"

"You mean us *four*," I said. "They arrested Loretta and Ginger, too. They're at some camp near Finland. And to answer your question, I still have no clue as to why we were arrested. They simply said we'd been involved in counterrevolutionary activities, a far too common and devastating label it seems."

"This is pure evil . . . what's happening here," said Lovett. "I don't even think the rest of the world knows about it."

"They know people are being tried and arrested, but they have been shielded from the true horror taking place. Can you imagine if a reporter were privy to this? As far as myself, I'd simply allowed myself to become brainwashed by the State. I can't believe it happened to me. Maybe I didn't want to see it."

"Maybe Loretta had convinced us not to see it, that somehow we were on the good side, that the bad guys, you know, the enemies of freedom and revolution, were the ones being arrested. I must admit, Stalin's propaganda machine is extraordinarily powerful and convincing. He has everyone fearing that so many czarist families in exile are plotting and about to return to enslave the proletariat. Shit, he's the one doing the enslaving!"

"Yes," said Lovett. "What he's masterfully done is convince so many that Trotsky is the devil incarnate. It took him a while, but he managed to pull it off. Every single soul in the Soviet Union, including members of the Central Committee and his own Politburo, are scared to death of him. I had an NKVD Trotskyist tell me as much while I was in exile. And I know that members of the CPUSA, both here and abroad, have grown fearful. Stalin's reach, his spies and assassins, are quickly spreading across the globe. He'll soon have one of them kill Trotsky. Mark my words. And the U.S. Government is infested with his spies. Shit, I know some of them. There was a time when I was willing to become one."

"According to my friend Bobby, there are many famous and important Americans who may not have joined the Communist Party, but are unapologetic in their support for communism. If only they knew what was happening inside these fences. They've probably heard hints of it, as we had, but don't believe it. You have to admit it was hard to imagine when we were on the outside. And I certainly had no idea that so many Americans were being purged."

"We see what we want to see, Bronzeville." He touched his half-cutoff ear and looked down at his muddy shoes, his frazzled garments, and filthy hands. "We see what we want to see."

"True. All I can see now is my wife and daughter. I've had

some very disturbing images running through my mind about them ever since Commander Koskinen told me what often happens to women in the camps. It's killing me."

"The only thing that'll kill you is that Road of Bones out there," he said, pointing west.

"I have a plan," I whispered in his ear. "I don't want to talk about it out loud, but just trust me. I'm going to try to get you out of here with James and me."

Later that night, as I lay in my middle bunk, I penned a letter to Loretta—one that Koskinen had said might or might not ever reach her. He claimed that Colonel Ivan Zorin, the head of the camp where she was near Finland, was a brutal, evil son of a bitch. Not allowing prisoners to receive *any* letters was something Koskinen said was "likely" in the case of Zorin.

I'd heard him loud and clear but wanted to send the letter anyway, for I had the distinct feeling that Loretta and Ginger were in serious trouble. Each night, as of late, I'd been having terrible nightmares about their condition, both of them on the verge of death. It was haunting me. Perhaps I was hoping this letter would reach her, if only so it might be the last words she ever heard from me. I'd always trusted my instincts, and they were telling me that time may have already run out for them. So, with the heaviest heart I'd ever had, I put pen to paper and wrote the following:

Dear Loretta,

My God, my love, how I long to see your face, touch your skin, and smell your essence again. Our lives turned upside down in the blink of an eye. Tell my daughter I love her beyond this universe. Tell her to look up at the Russian sky and search for the brightest star, for that is the one I see tonight, and it reminds me of her, my sweet Ginger. I have died a thousand deaths since being ripped away from you two. Yet I must have a thousand and one lives because my heart still beats and my mind still imagines the moment we will be reunited. Your son is so strong, this young man we created. He has seen far too much ugly, cried too many tears, felt too much pain, but he is still whole and full of life and hope because he was raised by you, an awesome, relentless, spirited, artistically transcendent woman. My weakest, darkest, pain-filled moments are always replaced with strength, light, and joy when I think of you, my gorgeous Loretta. I will never give up on you, on us, on the dreams we have for our children. I will stay alive for us. I will hold you again. I will make our family whole again. I will make love to you again. Life will begin again. I promise.

Faithfully,
Prescott

18

Moscow, Russia
May 1936

MAY 16, 1936, BROUGHT WITH IT SOME BIG NEWS. NOT ONLY HAD Bullitt's tenure as ambassador come to an end, much to his delight it appeared, but Bobby had also accepted a higher-ranking post as Minister in Argentina. Loretta and I had just found out and hadn't discussed whether we'd be joining the Ellingtons, even though Bobby had already invited us. Everything was happening so fast.

This was also another important and exciting day for Loretta. Two of her paintings had been chosen to be displayed at Tretyakov Gallery across the river from the Kremlin. Tretyakov was known as the premier depository of Soviet art in the world. Bobby, Dorene, Loretta, and I had chosen this night to dress up and tour the gallery before heading to a black-tie dinner at the French Embassy.

As we walked the gallery, we came upon one painting that Loretta told us to stop and enjoy. It was a work by Boris Ioganson, a famous Russian artist.

"This will go down as Boris's greatest painting," said Loretta. "It's called *Interrogation of Communists*. I believe it has been displayed here for three years now. I actually met Boris a year ago while visiting the All-Russian Academy of Arts in Leningrad. He was so nice to me, and we've been friends ever since. He visits Moscow often. I consider him a mentor."

"Oil on canvas," I said, kissing Loretta on the cheek. "Just like yours."

"How old is Ioganson?" said Bobby.

"I believe he's around forty-three," said Loretta. "Five years older than me. Yikes! That's so weird coming out of my mouth. Feel like I'm getting older by—"

"Stop," said Dorene, "you look twenty-five. Don't worry."

"Yeah, you say that only because you're just thirty-four," said Loretta.

"Hell, you both look eighteen to my eye," said Bobby, smiling and taking his wife's hand."

"God, I love you, Bobby," said Loretta, turning back to the painting. "Kiss him for me, Dorene! Anyway, if I might, this piece represents the new man fighting against the old . . . you know, the brave proletariat not flinching as these brutal czars interrogate them."

"I'm also noticing," said Dorene, "how the faces of the young man and woman who represent the proletariat are lit up, while the faces of the three czarist army officers appear dark. The man and woman appear bold, not afraid of these men."

"True Socialist Realism," said Loretta.

"Hmm," said Bobby. "What exactly is Socialist Realism again?"

"You sound suspicious," said Loretta.

"No, not at all, just curious."

"Well," said Loretta. "It was explained best by Andrei Zhdanov, an aide of Stalin's. Most artists here have his words stained in their brains. And Stalin himself gave Zhdanov's explanation his stamp of approval."

"Tell us," said Bobby.

Loretta cutely closed her eyes and began. "Zhdanov said, 'Socialist Realism, being the basic method of Soviet literature and criticism, requires from the artist truthful, historically concrete representation of reality in its evolutionary development. Moreover, truth and historical completeness of artistic representation must be combined with the task of ideological transformation and education of the working man in the spirit of socialism.'"

Moments later when we arrived at Loretta's two paintings, my heart began to race, as I hadn't seen either. They were nothing like those I'd looked at before, no women holding babies in either. One was a painting of two young proletariat boys in civilian clothing chasing two uniformed czars who had looks of fear on their faces. The other was a similar painting, but the two young chasers were girls. Both were so vivid and colorful, as if they were photographs that had simply been copied. That was how truly talented my wife was.

"Stunning!" said Dorene.

"Truly!" said Bobby.

"My gosh, Loretta!" I said, taking her around the waist and pulling her close.

"You're all being far too kind," said Loretta, such pride washing over her. "They represent the true fear that was instilled in the czars as the revolution drew to an end. They feared the Bolsheviks at this point so much so that even the mere sight of proletariat children scared them to death. They knew that lingering not too far behind these youngsters was likely a heavily armed brigade of angry Bolshevik soldiers. At the same time, these children symbolized this newfound, emboldened attitude that had permeated the whole of the proletariat. This one is called *Proletariat Boys Rising Up*, and the other is called, of course, *Proletariat Girls Rising Up*."

"The color is just stunning," said Dorene. "But it's as if you've used only various shades of red, yellow, black, and white. And still, it pops off of the canvas so powerfully, the girls' lemon dresses, the boys' cherry pants."

"Thank you," said Loretta. "In terms of color, probably the great artist, Konstantin Melnikov, gave me the greatest compliment. He said I must have found a way to paint with molten lava."

"But you've always had a flair for color," I said, turning to Bobby and Dorene. "Our daughter's namesake, Ginger Bouvier, from our Harlem and Paris days, liked to brag about Loretta's talent for creating various shades of particular colors."

"Ah, yes," said Dorene. "I remember her. We actually met her once when we first arrived in Paris, before she moved to Canada with her new husband."

"Oh, that's right," I said. "Of course."

"Where do you go from here, Loretta?" said Bobby. "I mean . . . you've truly reached the mountaintop. Tretyakov Gallery! The pinnacle!"

"Well," said Loretta, "I can tell you what *might* be next. Prescott and I haven't discussed this yet, and I know that you've asked him to join you in Argentina, but a bit of breaking news here, even for you, love." She looked at me and raised her eyebrows. "I've been asked by the State to teach full-time here at the Moscow Painting Academy. Obviously, as you know, only the very top artists in the country are given the opportunity to do such."

"Of course," said Bobby. "Only the masters! Wow!"

"We have a lot to discuss in the coming days," I said.

"I worry about the changing climate here," said Bobby. "Ever since Kirov was mysteriously killed in Leningrad about a year and a half ago, Stalin seems to have made a shift. He's arresting some of his own men. Perhaps justifiably, but still, all of us at the chancery have continued to grow suspicious of these arrests, along with those of regular citizens. And there's an ever-disturbing secrecy about them."

"But he's arresting men and women who've obviously shown an allegiance to Trotsky or the exiled czars," said Loretta. "So many men and women are undermining Stalin. This country is still hanging in the balance in terms of folks who long for yesteryear versus we who want to move forward. It's like the Confederacy never fully embracing the Republic. That battle is still being fought as well."

"Yes," said Dorene, "but Roosevelt is hardly arresting all of the conservative members of Congress who oppose him."

"Maybe he should," said Loretta. "Many of them *are*, after all, responsible for turning a blind eye to mass lynchings, just like the czars were responsible for—"

"Both of you make good points," I said, squeezing Loretta's hand. "Like I said, we have a lot to discuss in the coming days. I think we're all just reacting to the fact that there's a question mark about whether we're all going to be together again in Argentina."

"I hate even the thought of us not," said Bobby.

The four of us stood quietly admiring the paintings, the somewhat sad thought of our maybe not joining them perhaps running through each of our minds. It was a joyful moment mixed with a dose of confusing emotion.

As Loretta and I drove to the French embassy, the Ellingtons' car just ahead of ours, I still hadn't come down from the high I'd felt at seeing the paintings. I was married to a renowned artist.

"Well," she said from the passenger's seat, "what do you think of all this news?"

"It's amazing," I said, one hand on the wheel. "I'm so excited for you. So impressed."

"But I'm sure you're conflicted."

"A bit."

"Well, I hope you can come around to seeing how important this is to me, love."

"Of course," I said. "But you're an artist with a name now. You can work from anywhere in the world. Why not spread your celebrity to Argentina and beyond? I'm sure Paris and London would roll out the red carpet for you."

"I have no interest," she sternly said. "I'm committed to *this* country, to the people who've accepted me and made me a success. My paintings can, and might, be sent to every country in the world, but I want to *live* and *work* here. They love me here. And it feels good."

"Let's take some time this week to think about it all, Loretta. This opportunity at the embassy in Argentina—"

"No! This is about me now. We've always done what you've wanted to do. But now, this is about me. I'm not moving to Argentina. I'm going to stay right here in Moscow, where I'm actually, in case you haven't noticed, becoming somewhat famous. I've finally arrived as an artist. I just wanna shine."

I stayed quiet on those words and realized how different she sounded. I wondered if she'd become a bit drunk off success. I'd never heard her speak of being so happy with being in the proverbial spotlight. I was genuinely happy for her but wanted to make sure this love of fame hadn't usurped her love of our children and me. Part of me felt like she'd become blinded by this newfound celebrity, unwilling to see the Soviet Union for what it might actually be.

"Look," I finally said, "I just want to celebrate you tonight, to brag about you when we arrive at the French Embassy. They'll probably buy some of your paintings, especially considering your connection to Paris. So this is probably not the best time to discuss the complexities of this Argentina decision vis-à-vis global politics. But do you have any idea what's brewing internationally in terms of the Soviet Union's current and future standing in the world? Their standing is anything but stable, particularly in relation to Germany and Japan."

"Here we go with politics!" she said, shaking her head. "But please! Do tell!"

"Not tonight. Please. I just want to talk about your amazing paintings."

"Dammit, Prescott! Just get it out of the way!"

"Fine! None of this concerns colored folk, so let me preface my comments with that little nugget. But the world is run by white men."

"Thanks for the reminder," she sarcastically said.

"Anyway, the Soviet Union finds itself in no man's land, Loretta. Quite simply, there are the *haves* and the *have-nots*, globally speaking, with respect to military power. The U.S., the U.K., and France are the *haves*. Germany, Japan, and Italy are being very loud about their displeasure with the Western Powers, but, still, they remain the *have-nots*. For the time being, albeit! Meanwhile, the Soviet Union is somewhere in the middle, seemingly uncertain as to which group they should join, you know, consumed with what's in their best interest, trying to have it both ways."

"Well, I think Stalin is with us," said Loretta. "With America. I know he's with the Negro."

"Not so sure. I mean, he might be with the Negro, but I'm talking strictly about countries here. Anyway, regarding Italy, Germany, and Japan, they want territorial expansion to create empires. They want to build up their militaries and overthrow the post–war international order. The writing's on the wall! I believe that's why Bullitt wants to be ambassador to France. He wants to work with a true ally if some global war breaks out again. God forbid!"

"But," said Loretta, "Italy, Germany, and Japan also want to destroy, or at least neutralize, the spread of Soviet Communism. Stalin is aware of that. You know I'm right."

"That doesn't change the fact that Stalin *might*, and I stress *might*, be America's enemy for other reasons. He operates quite secretly and selfishly."

"Stop, Prescott! The U.S. is just as selfish in its desires. And Germany, you know, Adolf Hitler, is clearly the enemy of us all. He's always resented the fact that Germany was forced to sign the Treaty of Versailles. He's truly a madman, and I'm sure remains no friend of Stalin's. But truthfully, regardless of any of this, it's my turn to have a say in where our family lives. Do you disagree?"

With both hands on the wheel now, I took in her question and contemplated my answer for a good minute. She sounded resolute in her desire to remain here. I couldn't deny her that. So, I said what I felt was fair.

"Truthfully, no, I do not disagree," I said. "You certainly didn't choose to move to Paris. That was a move forced by my dishonesty, and you know I'll forever be aware of that fact. It *is* about you now. I'll find work at one of the schools or universities here, or maybe at one of the factories. I'll talk to Robert Robinson about maybe getting a job where he works making tools. Hell, perhaps Homer Smith can get me on at the post office. And after all, maybe I've forgotten what my true mission has always been, to seek freedom for colored folk, even if through unconventional means, not to become bogged down in State Department bureaucracy matters. And regardless of my reservations about Stalin, the revolution here and the people behind it are courageous. I'm probably best positioned to affect change from a country where the phrase 'Freedom for the Negro' is actually met with a smile. So . . . I say . . . let's stay."

"Really, love?" she said, cracking a welcomed smile.

"Yes, I want to be nothing but supportive of you. I love you. You're my life."

I took my right hand and placed it on her lap. She covered it with both of hers. Though I had real misgivings about her unbridled adoration of all things Soviet, I was committed to her right to follow her own path, especially given my previous behavior toward her in New York, which had almost cost us our marriage. In her defense, considering the privileged and sheltered childhood she had enjoyed under the Rev. and Mrs. Cunningham, what person would have the tools to deal with the fierce politics of Stalin—or even J. Edgar Hoover, for that matter? I had tried to shield her from Hoover's world. How much more dangerous might Stalin's world be? All I could do at this point, having failed her in America, was respect her opinion, her success, her growth, free at least from the debilitating injustices of Jim Crow America.

Summer and fall dragged on, and I spent most of that time turning down jobs that I just didn't have the stomach for, one as a toolmaker, another at the Torgsin grocery, and a third at the post office. But it was okay for the time being, as we were getting by just fine and Loretta liked me spending time at home with the children.

I'd been told shortly after Bobby had departed for Argentina that I'd have to wait until the new ambassador arrived to be considered for any position at the chancery, which I actually didn't want. Still, when he did arrive in mid-January of 1937, some eight months after Bobby had left, I went to Spaso and met with him. Joseph E. Davies was his name. He was a man quite different from William Bullitt. To put it bluntly, he knew nothing about the Soviet Union or, for that matter, diplomacy in general.

Bobby had told me he despised the man and considered it a joke that Roosevelt had appointed him in the first place. Davies said to me point-blank, "We have no position here for you as an interpreter or as an assistant of any kind." If he thought he'd been hurtful with his comments, he'd been incorrect because I actually was enjoying this long break from embassy work. Besides, I knew the only reason I'd ever received a paycheck from the State Department had been because of Bobby. And I'd saved up enough money to pay two years' worth of rent, excluding Loretta's income.

Other than that brief meeting with Davies, the only news I had heard about the goings-on at Spaso House was from one of the couriers I'd run into at the Anglo-American School while picking up James and Ginger one afternoon. He'd told me that Davies and his filthy-rich wife had ignored Soviet officials and had had a yacht full of food shipped in from the United States, particularly dairy products, all of which had spoiled after being stored in the refrigerators at Spaso House.

Apparently, he had installed so many appliances and packed so much food into them that the power required to service them all had blown the circuits, leaving tons of cream, milk, and butter spoiled. Jim, the courier, had told me that Davies was so scared of NKVD finding out about his secretly imported food that he'd been forced to scramble around and dispense of it, no small task apparently.

It was also on this day at the Anglo-American School when I learned of an open position, one teaching chemistry. The idea of working at the school where my children attended excited

me, so I applied immediately. A week later, I was hired. It was the
same job my friend Lovett had held.

By the time February of 1937 rolled around, our family, particularly Loretta and the children, were in a very good place.
Loretta was engrossed in her work teaching, painting, and traveling around the country to show her newest pieces, and the
children and I were closer than ever. When I wasn't teaching, I
was tutoring them and watching them develop into young schol-
ars. Both were fluent in Russian now and had plenty of friends.

Of course I spent moments thinking about the conversations
Bobby and I had had about him becoming an ambassador or
senator, and I longed to be by his side helping him rise through
the ranks. I remembered his promise to keep fighting for social
change and him telling me I was playing a solid role in it all. But
now I wasn't affecting Negro life at all. Joining the CPUSA seemed
like the only way to do such, but Bobby had told me early on,
"Whatever you do, do not join the Communist Party. It will make
it difficult, if not impossible, for me to ever rehire you."

So, for the foreseeable future, I just had to hold down a job.
And I found myself beginning to feel a bit militant. I was chan-
neling the anger and frustration I imagined my brothers and sisters feeling back home, for even though I was a respected man
in Moscow, I walked around as if I were still back in America. It's
who I was. I found myself ruminating about this thought all of
the time: *The Negro's problem is that he always finds himself wanting
and needing to work full-time at creating a free society, but he is faced
with the reality of having to work a full-time regular job, one given to
him by none other than his oppressor just to stay alive. Quite the di-
chotomy!*

I tried my best, however, not to let all of this completely con-
sume me. I needed to embrace my circumstances, to enjoy
Moscow life. My good colored comrades, Robert Robinson and
Homer Smith, came by our apartment regularly, especially when
Loretta was traveling. On February 15, 1937, they, along with
the colored actor, Wayland Rudd, were visiting for dinner, and
the issue of NKVD arrests came up.

"Where is that gorgeous wife of yours?" said Homer. "You're lucky my friend Langston Hughes isn't here to try to do another film. He was quite the ladies' man on his last Moscow visit. I'm sure he'd have a hard time refraining from flirting with her."

"Just stop, Homer," said the Jamaican-born Robert, adjusting his dark-rimmed eyeglasses.

"Yes," said Wayland, "you need to quit."

"It's fine, Wayland," I said, refilling my wineglass. "I know she's gorgeous. She's in Stalingrad."

"She's no safer down there than she is up here," said Robert. "I can't tell you how many of my coworkers have disappeared from the tool factory."

"Maybe they're criminals," I said. "Maybe they're Trotskyists. Maybe they miss the czars."

"You must be joking," said Homer. "My editors back in America are begging me to investigate deeper into these ever-growing arrests of foreign workers, and if I didn't have to split my time between being a reporter and working at the post office, I'd probably be able to give them more. And apparently the State Department back home is mum on the entire issue, not giving New York reporters a thing. So, my bosses want me to dig. But there's also a side of me that's worried about saying too much. Hell, they might arrest me if I go poking around trying to find out who's been arrested and where they've been sent. And NKVD men are lurking outside of the U.S. Embassy just waiting to see who's trying to get out of the Soviet Union."

"You should keep your mouth shut, Homer," said Robert. "Write about something else. I can only speak for myself when I say I'm becoming terrified that I may be arrested for some fabricated crime. A white American comrade of mine from the factory went to the U.S. Embassy looking to find out what happened to his brother, who'd gone missing, and Ambassador Davies was of no help."

"Not surprising," said Homer.

"Maybe his brother did something wrong," I said.

"And," said Robert, ignoring me, "when my comrade exited

the embassy, NKVD scared the hell out of him, telling him to never be seen there again. Like Homer said, they have all of the embassies blanketed, looking for counterrevolutionaries. Don't ever try to report someone missing! If they go missing, it's not our problem! And these show trials are frightening, too. Important Russians are being tried and convicted left and right. Look at what happened to that splendid writer at *Izvestia*, Karl Radek. Don't you see what's happening, Prescott?"

"Yeah, Prescott," said Homer. "These trials are disturbing. I've attended many at the House of the Unions myself."

"Did you see any niggas on trial?" I sarcastically said, taking a drink of wine.

Homer looked at me crossways.

"I think it's more complicated than we realize," I said. "Yes, people are being arrested, but just as Premier Molotov once told me, people get arrested in New York City, too. There's a battle for the soul of the Soviet Union going on here, the old hands versus the new."

"Two years ago," said Homer, sipping his wine, "you sounded like this man I knew named Prescott Sweet. Now you sound like your wife."

"Well," I said, "she's a lot smarter than me, and this country has done nothing but treat my colored wife like a queen, my colored children as human beings, and *my* colored behind as something more than a nigger, so I guess I'm guilty of being blind, naïve, foolish, ignorant, and maybe even unsympathetic to men and women who are being arrested for committing crimes against a State that knows far more than I about people's loyalties."

"Looks like you've done found a certain mood," said Wayland, crossing his legs.

"I'm tired of *not* being selfish," I said. "The white man built our country, America, off of being nothing but just that—*selfish.* At least here I can have the audacity to be selfish and not get lynched for it. And to your point, Robert, do you ever stop to ask yourself why your black ass is still making tools and going home at night to a warm bed? And make no mistake, when you pull back the curtain in your bedroom, you won't see any burning crosses or white men in sheets on horses yelling, 'You uppity coon! How dare you order other toolmakers around and talk to our white women at the bars! How dare you act smart! You ain't no educated engineer! You're an abomination! Go back to Africa!' "

"Hell," said Homer, raising his eyebrows, "the only thing you have left to say, Prescott, is, 'Can a brutha get an amen?' "

The four of us laughed hesitantly, breaking a bit of the tension.

"Thank you, Homer," I said, looking at my watch, realizing the children had now been asleep for two hours. "Did all of that jive with you, Robert?"

"Yes, I guess. But I don't go to bars."

Homer, Wayland, and I looked at him and wanted to laugh. Robert was ever the engineer, only taking in the facts and calculating them accordingly. I loved him.

"Where did you find this nice furniture, Prescott?" said Wayland, looking around. "It certainly doesn't look like anything sold off by some wealthy Russian of yesteryear."

"No," I said, looking at our empty plates, the fried chicken, mashed potatoes, and carrots I'd cooked completely devoured. "My friend Dorene Ellington has a particular passion for interior design. She considered it her pet project to furnish this place. All of it was shipped in from London and Paris. The Ellingtons are in Argentina now, but when they were living in Moscow, they spent at least two days a week here, so she certainly got to enjoy it."

"It's very bourgeois," said Robert, "which is wonderful, as far as I'm concerned, delightful to look at, but I wonder how the blue tops would interpret it, that's all."

"You've told me this before, Robert," I said. "The last time you were here."

"Please!" said Homer. "It's much plainer in taste than that czarist shit I see in all the supposed proletariat homes of most

State officials. All that gold and maroon! This décor here is nothing but dark wood chairs and floors, brown and cream upholstery, and pristine white walls. Makes for a very clean, crisp look, I must say, quite foreign to Moscow. And shoot! Your wife's framed paintings hanging everywhere provide just the right amount of color to accentuate it all. NKVD would consider it a Socialist Realism paradise."

"This color scheme is what my wife likes, Wayland," I said, sipping my red wine. "Our home on Strivers' Row in Harlem had a similar décor. Dorene also happens to like the chocolate against white, so she and my wife had a ball picking items out. Dorene and Bobby sure are missed. And our children were so close to theirs."

"Speaking of missed," said Robert. "I went by to see B the other day and she acted like I was with NKVD. When I asked about Lovett and when she'd last seen him, the look on her face went cold. She said she hadn't heard from him at all. She said my guess was as good as hers."

"You know," said Homer, "I went by there recently and she said the same thing to me. It's concerning. Sounds like Lovett done found him a new wife down in Kuybyshev!"

"You act surprised," said Wayland. "Y'all know Lovett wasn't ever one to sit still. Shoot, he probably finally got the State to let him leave for Cuba or Canada, places he's been before. Probably found him a Cuban wife. Or, for that matter, he's probably back in Dallas or New York City signing up new Party members. And hell, if there's one thing I've learned about Lovett, he's the last brother in the world any of us needs to worry about."

19

Magadan, Russia
October 1938

IT HAD TAKEN TWO MONTHS FOR KOSKINEN'S LETTER ABOUT MY PO-
tential spy mission to be met with a response. And it had come
in the form of a cable from Moscow. Koskinen hadn't sent the
original letter as a telegram because of its sensitivity, which
made sense. What he probably hadn't expected was to be completely left out of the loop when the Kremlin responded.

I was approached by a guard on a Wednesday morning while
standing in the soup line with Lovett and James. He simply told
me to come with him and I was led to a black vehicle, then driven
down toward the shipping docks. Before we actually reached
them, however, we turned left, well on this western side of the
rocky cliffs. Navigating a narrow, tree-lined road, we stopped in
front of a small, red-painted, stone building and exited. The inside of the building consisted only of a ten-by-ten room, which
was dimly lit and had a large, square table in the middle. At the
far end sat three important-looking men, all of them dressed in
sharp, army green, military-style uniforms and hats.

"Come!" said the guard, leading me to a chair directly across
from them, my back to the door. "Sit, *zek!*" the guard continued,
and as I did, he stayed standing beside me.

"*Ostav' nas!*" said the serious man sitting in the middle.

"Yes, Director Pavlov," said the guard, doing as he'd been ordered and exiting, leaving the four of us alone now.

"*Mne skazali, chto vy govorite Rossii,*" said this man named Director Pavlov to me.

"Yes, that is correct," I said in Russian, noticing how much thicker he was built than the other two. "I *do* speak Russian."

"Well, then you will understand when I tell you that my name is Karp Aleksandrovich Pavlov," he said, the other two staying quiet, all three sitting tall. "I am the director of the Dalstroi. It is not every day that I am asked by the Kremlin to handle such matters as this. The cables I received were very specific. I have received five alone in the past two days. A lot. Yes?"

"Yes," I said.

"This entire situation is unique and complicated. But I'm sure you can help us sort it out."

"I can," I said.

"I have a fairly decent understanding of what you have proposed. But I have a few questions. Where does this Comrade Ellington believe you to be living right now? Does he know that you were arrested?"

Before answering, I thought of Koskinen. Knowing he had helped me send the few letters to Bobby that I'd sent, and being solely responsible for suggesting that I tell Bobby that I was currently living in Leningrad, I had to think fast. I was sure they hadn't a clue of Koskinen's handiwork, and perhaps if they found out, he'd be in big trouble.

"No," I said. "He does not know that I was arrested. He must think I've just finished touring with my wife."

"Touring?"

"Yes," I lied. "Just before being arrested in Moscow, I had sent him a letter telling him that, beginning in December, we would be traveling with our children over the next six months—at least—to attend various art exhibits throughout Europe, and maybe even America, as she'd received many requests from some prominent art aficionados. Dealers! These people were offering to pay for our expenses, too."

"Of course," said Director Pavlov. "She sells one of her expensive paintings in their bourgeois galleries and they take a nice percentage. These capitalists always arrange to come out on the better end. Continue."

"Apparently," I said, "some of the important Russian artists who admired my wife's work had spread the word about her paintings to Paris and London. The requests started flooding in. Socialist Realism was being viewed as a mysterious, fresh form apparently. All things Soviet Union are probably still viewed as mysterious and attractive to the outside world. Anyway, we were set to do a lot of European traveling beginning in December as far as Bobby was concerned."

"I see," said Pavlov, nodding. "Maybe this Ellington thinks you are all in Berlin now."

The three of them looked at one another and wryly smiled.

"Maybe," I continued lying. "I had told him that our plan was to settle down in Leningrad upon our return to the Soviet Union, a country we absolutely fell in love with. So, he might be anxiously awaiting word from me now, but he is certainly not worried. He's a very busy man who's probably been doing a lot of traveling himself."

"The Kremlin would like for you to clarify one thing," said Pavlov. "They need to confirm that he will be stationed in Germany as you've suggested."

"Let's send him a cable," I said.

"Of course," said Pavlov.

"This will be a long and expensive cable message," I said.

"It's okay," said Pavlov. "We are paying for it."

"It should originate from Leningrad," I said. "It should say, *'Dear Bobby, I hope this message finds you, Dorene, and the children in good health. I have finally returned to Leningrad after being gone a bit longer than I'd originally anticipated.'*"

"Stop," said Pavlov, handing a paper and pen to the man to his left. "You must write this down in English while you continue speaking to us in Russian. Then we can cable it to the Kremlin with specific instructions."

As the man with the pen and paper stood and walked around the table toward me, I continued writing the lie in my mind. I knew that when Bobby saw the words "finally returned to Leningrad after being gone longer than I'd originally anticipated," he'd simply think I was referring to the lucrative engineering job at the port here at Nagaev Bay that I'd written to him about, per Koskinen's orders.

"Write down what you've already shared," said Pavlov, as the man set the paper and pen in front of me and returned to his chair. "Then begin talking again when you're ready to add on to the message."

"Okay," I said, jotting it all down quickly.

"You write fast," said Pavlov. "This is good."

"Thank you. I'm finished and ready to continue."

"We are ready, too."

"Okay," I said, my head down, as I prepared to continue writing in English while speaking in Russian. "The message should go on to say, '*Loretta and the children are also exhausted. All of the art exhibits and travel have been taxing on their bodies.*'"

I paused for a second, recalling exactly what Koskinen had ordered me to write regarding Loretta and the children while I was supposedly working at Nagaev Bay. My mind had grown cloudy over what exactly I'd written down some nine months ago. After a few more seconds, I remembered that Koskinen had said, "Tell Bobby, however, that your wife is traveling with her paintings a lot with the children." This, of course, had been supposedly happening while I was working at Nagaev Bay.

"Sorry for the pause, Director Pavlov," I said. "The message will then say, '*I wish you were here in person for me to tell you this next bit of news. It is quite sad, I must say. I've tried like hell to reason with Loretta over the past three weeks, but there's no changing her mind. She has asked for a divorce. No warning whatsoever. She claims to have wanted it for years, but hadn't known how to tell me. Her emotion toward me has gone completely cold. It's clearly over.*

"'*I guess now that her art has taken my place, she no longer loves or needs me. I also found out that she'd been secretly sending postcards to an art professor here in Leningrad from the various towns that hosted her exhibits. Perhaps she loves him. I look forward to going into more depth with you regarding this painful issue, and am actually hoping you will soon be taking that possible position at the embassy in Berlin at year's end, as I would love to assist you. And I need the job.*

"'*The best thing I can do right now is grant Loretta at least a clean separation and leave, because the children can't bear to see us argue anymore. From Berlin, maybe I can meet them every other month in Riga. They love riding the train. Please cable me back straightaway at this telegraph office and direct it to the new Leningrad office I've listed above.*'"

Before I continued writing, I looked up and asked Pavlov, "What *is* the address?"

"We'll take care of that," he said.

I nodded and continued talking and writing. "The conclusion of the message should say, '*I will be stopping by the telegraph station daily until I hear from you. Your true friend, Prescott.*'"

I looked up and set the pen down. The three men were staring at me with deadpan faces. Maybe they were trying to catch up to my thinking.

"You judged correctly," said Pavlov. "You knew we would never let your family leave the prisons with you. But now this divorce explains to your comrade why they will not be joining you in Berlin. Now we just have to cable this to the Kremlin. They will study it and then forward it to the offices in Leningrad. From there it will be cabled to the embassy in Argentina, and then you must hope your comrade is indeed going to Berlin. If he is, your little plan just might get you out of here. Clear?"

"Yes."

"But make no mistake. If you were to arrive in Berlin and decide to have your American government try to negotiate your family's release, all of them would be killed immediately. Just a hint of any sort of inquiry by your government, even by President Roosevelt himself, about the condition of your family, would cause their deaths. Don't ever try to get clever, Negro *zek*."

"I want to say right up front," I said, forming a lie in my

mouth, "that the important intelligence I gather will be worthy of everyone's time and consideration. I am no fan of America. It's a country that will forever hate the Negro."

"They love their ropes and white sheets," said Pavlov. "What else do you have to say about the mission?"

"Well," I said, preparing to ask two questions I already knew the answers to. "Do you know which camp my wife and daughter are being held at? And where is it located?"

Pavlov shuffled some papers in front of him, reading one. "They are being held at the MR4 Labor Camp over closer to Finland. It's near the town of Kirovsk, which is on the Kola Peninsula."

"Thank you," I said.

"What else?" he said.

"I have three requests right up front," I said. "I believe Bobby will respond within the week. And based on his wife's relationship with President Roosevelt, I am almost certain his original wish to be stationed in Berlin by the end of 1938 will be granted. It had been all but guaranteed long ago. Argentina was just a transition posting."

"Your three requests," said Pavlov. "What are they?"

"One!" I said. "As soon as you receive word from Bobby that Berlin is an affirmative, I want to be moved to the camp where my wife and daughter are being held. I want to confirm, with my own eyes, that they're alive. Meanwhile, I can wait at that camp until we receive word from Bobby that he's arrived in Berlin."

"Continue," he said.

"Two, my son must leave here with me and be allowed to remain at the camp with his mother. He is developing one sickness after another, and I worry about his long-term health. Three, I would like for a particular *zek* comrade of mine, Lovett Fort-Whiteman, to be allowed to remain here in Magadan and not be sent to the mines. Once I have completed the mission, I ask that Fort-Whitman be released along with my family."

"The Kremlin will decide whether to accept your preconditions," said Pavlov.

"Thank you. All I ask is that the assignment have a specified time length, one that would assure all of our releases in no more than one year. Otherwise Stalin must certainly know they will die in the camps if kept inside much longer than that. I can gather plenty of intelligence in twelve months."

"Stop," said Pavlov. "You are repeating word for word all of the terms that were in Commander Koskinen's original letter to the Kremlin. You must have it all memorized. I can't blame you, but we know most of this already."

"Sorry," I said, realizing I had indeed memorized everything word for word. Hell, I'd been walking around like a robot for weeks.

"You must know," said Pavlov, "I would very much like to take you behind this building and shoot you in your fucking black face. And if consideration of this mission weren't being handled at the very top level, from our Great Stalin himself, I would do just that. I'm known as a madman. Everyone from the mines to this coast believes me to be so! Have you heard this?"

"Yes," I said, watching him clinch his jaw and turn a bit red. It was as if he hated not being in control of this situation, of having to sit there and listen to me make all of my requests.

"I am indeed a very mad man," he said, removing his pistol from his waist and setting it on the table in front of him. "But . . . you're not to be touched, you see, at least for the time being. In fact, you and your son will be sleeping in a vacant room in one of the Dalstroi barracks until Berlin is confirmed. The guard outside will return you to the camp. You are to finish your day's work. Commander Koskinen will have you work alongside another lead engineer whom you must bring up to speed. At day's end, you will turn your brigade over to this engineer. After you return to your barracks, gather your items and wait with your boy. We will be sending a guard to retrieve you tonight and take you to your new room. Please leave now."

Later that night, my barracks full of tired, smelly, loud *zeks* once again, I sat with Lovett on the top bunk, our legs dangling down to my middle bed, where I'd had James lie and rest. I felt worried, but hopeful, a strange mix.

"We have to talk about this without saying anything that can be understood by any of these other *zeks*," I whispered to Lovett. "It's too important to risk discussing in-depth."

"I understand," Lovett whispered, coughing, his body looking ever more frail and worn down.

"Just know that I intend to get you out of here, too," I whispered. "James and I have to wait at another barracks and may not see you again before we leave, but please understand that the plan I've suggested has gotten the important people's attention, and I aim to secure your release along with my family's as soon as possible. Just try to hold on, Lovett."

"As long as I can stay here and avoid them mines, I shouldn't have a problem doing that, Bronzeville."

"That's up to Koskinen," I whispered. "I haven't been able to speak to him for a while, and probably won't before we leave, but he knows how I feel about you; unfortunately, so does Director Pavlov, and he can hardly be trusted. Still, he has his hands tied."

"If I do get out of here," Lovett whispered, "the first thing I'm going to do is go pick up my beautiful B and take her to Morocco. You and I have already talked about our old friend Claude McKay. I told you how much he loved Morocco. Said it made him feel like writing a new poem every day. B and I could maybe settle down there and live in peace."

"I worry about Koskinen," I whispered. "He is so bold with how he shares his thoughts about Trotsky. And I know that Stalin has commanders murdered all of the time. In fact, Koskinen told me that the last director of the Dalstroi who was replaced by Pavlov, a man named Eduard Berzin, was arrested not long after he'd left here."

"They all fall to Stalin," Lovett whispered.

"Apparently he had just returned from a vacation to Italy. Stalin detests Soviets who leave the country and return. Anyway, Berzin was accused of spying for Britain and Germany and plotting to ensure that the Japanese gain control of Magadan and all of its gold mines. Koskinen said Berzin was shot and killed just two months ago at Lubyanka prison in Moscow."

"Shit," whispered Lovett. "If Stalin is willing to kill Brezin, he damn sure will cut Koskinen's throat. Even though I'm sure Brezin was a murdering son of a bitch, too, he is probably responsible for putting millions of dollars' worth of mined gold in Stalin's pockets. And a bullet to the head was his reward. Cold to the bone!"

"I'll tell you who was on to Stalin's terror early on," I said. "Our buddies Robert Robinson and Homer Smith. They knew something evil was happening long ago. Both of them are probably trying like hell to get out of Moscow as we speak, and I know they're too worried about their own lives to be making a stink about us. I'm sure everybody is just trying to fend for themselves."

"Shit," said Lovett. "I don't blame 'em!"

"I'm gonna miss you, Lovett. Promise me you'll stay alive until I can get you out. You're too valuable to me and every other American Negro to die at the hands of these monsters. You and I both love Du Bois. Maybe we can work with him in the future. But, regardless of what happens, just know that your life's work will never be forgotten. I will make sure of it. You have helped so many Negroes back home come to see that there's more than just Jim Crow. You taught them not to ever be afraid to fight for their rights, to be brave enough to die for them, to choose the CPUSA as an alternative."

"How right you are about us both loving Du Bois," said Lovett, reaching inside his coat pocket and pulling out his passport. "He was always so willing to help and listen. When I was in New York in 1928, just before I came back to the Soviet Union, I wanted to see him and discuss the crisis surrounding coloreds."

Lovett opened his passport booklet and took out an old, weathered, folded-up piece of paper. It looked as though it might break apart, like it had been wet and dry over and over again. He unfolded it and handed it to me.

"Have always held on to that," said Lovett. "It doesn't say anything special, but it connects me to this great man. It reveals the kind of considerate brother he was."

I hadn't ever told Lovett that I had spied in Harlem for over three years, all in an effort to help Du Bois's NAACP stay afloat against Marcus Garvey's UNIA and Back to Africa movement. Seeing this simple letter that had been written some five years after I'd already left Harlem for Paris brought it all back for a moment. I ran my finger over the typed words. The short note read:

> April 6, 1928
> Mr. Lovett F. Whiteman
> 180 St. Nicholas Avenue, Apartment 23
> New York City, New York
> My dear Sir:
> I have just returned from a month's lecture trip and shall be extremely busy until the 15th of April. If you are going to be here after that, I should be glad to see you almost any day. If you are not going to be in town as long as that, I can make arrangements to spare a few minutes, if you will telephone me.
> Very sincerely yours,
> W.E.B. Du Bois

"Nice of him to have taken the time to write you back," I said, handing the note to Lovett.

"Indeed," he said, refolding it. "Because I knew how inundated he was with requests, etcetera, at that particular time. Hell . . . always! But he really understood what I was trying to do—collect data on the American Negro so I could recruit—even though he's not a Communist Party member. I've spoken with him before, but this letter is the only written item I have from him. It reminds me that he is still out there somewhere continuing the fight."

"Du Bois has devoted his life to the race problem," I said.

"You know something sad?" said Lovett. "Even inside the

CPUSA, folks liked to tell me, 'Get over this whole race thing. It's all you talk about.' Shit! I could talk about it from now until eternity, and that wouldn't be long enough. Race! Race! Race! It has been my life's work. And I'm damn proud to have done it!"

"Preach!" I said.

"And when it's all said and done, brutha, everyone should know that I was proud to have lost my life, prematurely even, trying to make things right for the colored folk in the Party back home by being their voice here at the various Comintern Congresses over the years. Don't wanna die, but I'm not afraid to. I ain't lyin'! If that's what it comes down to, so be it. I will have died during this seemingly insurmountable quest to break permanently free from those ugly, heavy shackles of oppression. Sounds ironic sitting here in the middle of a Soviet prison. But that's where the quest led me. This is where my *fellow Americans* forced me to retreat to in order to live at least one day of my life with an ounce of dignity. And in the end, every Negro worth a damn has to be willing to die trying to make our people one hundred percent free. Do you hear me, Bronzeville? *One hundred percent!*"

20

Moscow, Russia
August 1937

The train ride from Leningrad had been a pleasant one for the four of us, and we'd been back in Moscow for three days now. The children and I had loved being alongside Loretta for two weeks while she met with art dealers and prominent painters in the city named after the great Bolshevik legend. She'd introduced us to many of her fellow artists who'd made Leningrad their home. We'd met a different, important person each night it seemed at the Neva River Gallery, as guests streamed through the doors to marvel at her exhibit. I'd enjoyed conversing with the famous Isaak Brodsky. But my favorite back-and-forth had been with the great painter-turned-writer Kuzma Petrov-Vodkin.

It was now the first Saturday of August, and the four of us were taking advantage of a perfect seventy-three-degree day by having a picnic in Gorky Park. We had two large blankets spread out on the grass and were surrounded by other families. Some kids and adults were playing baseball, a sport introduced to them recently by American expatriates, and other folks were engaged in an assortment of other games. I was just happy to be lying in the sun with my family next to a basketful of sandwiches, fruit, and beverages, compliments of the Torgsin grocery.

"You kids don't want to go play?" said Loretta, lying on her back with her eyes closed, her shoulder touching mine.

"No," they said simultaneously.

Both kids were sitting with their legs crossed, bottoms affixed to their yellow blanket, each reading the same book, *Narrative of the Life of Frederick Douglass, an American Slave.* I lay on my stomach and watched them both caught up in another world and realized how they'd become more enthralled with reading than running and playing. But at least it had happened out of choice. They had simply seen their mother and me read every night in bed, this after years of us reading bedtime stories to them back in Paris. Now they, too, were voracious readers.

"This sun feels so nice," said Loretta.

"It does," I said, closing my eyes. "What do you think it means that Japan has just attacked China?"

"You tell me."

"Maybe the beginning of another great war," I said. "Japan and Germany signed their Anti-Comintern pact last year. They want to stop the spread of communism. So I'm sure Germany is pleased with Japan's attack on China. And it looks like Italy will be signing the pact soon as well."

"Can we lighten the conversation?" said Loretta.

"Sure."

She smiled. "Did I tell you I'm going to be spending a lot of time visiting Saint Basil's Cathedral? Something about the powerful aesthetic of the interior has me fascinated. I think I'm going to try painting something that pays homage to it. Subliminally, I mean. People may not get it at first, but because most Russians are familiar with Saint Basil's, their subconscious will be affected by what I'm going to do."

"That sounds like an abstract," I said, my belly moving up and down against our turquoise-colored blanket. "It sounds experimental, too."

"It is."

"I can't imagine you trying to actually paint the interior of Saint Basil's as it is. As soon as I set foot in there it looked like a labyrinth. I thought, *Which passageway is one supposed to take?* It was as if it had been designed to confuse people, to perhaps make it impossible to follow any map or set of directions. Only a man very familiar with its maze of paths and walkways could truly move about with any degree of certainty. It certainly fits the State's modus operandi: complete secrecy."

"Stop," said Loretta. "I don't want to write a dissertation on it. I just want to let its interior design inspire me."

"Sorry," I said. "Good luck."

"Did I tell you I have been corresponding with Natalia Goncharova, the famous Russian painter who lives in Paris? We've been exchanging letters. One was waiting for me when we returned the other day."

"Corresponding?" I said. "No, I didn't know that. But I certainly know the name, even from back when we were in Paris. How were you put in touch with her?"

"I actually met her when we were living in Paris, but it wasn't until some friends here in Moscow began bragging about her past that I took interest and decided to send her a letter. To my surprise, she responded in kind and we've been carrying on a dialogue. She keeps telling me how much she detests how the Soviet Union suppresses the free will of artists."

"But you knew this," I said. "Why is this woman of interest to you all of a sudden?"

"Because she is so brave," said Loretta. "Back in 1910, she and many other artists got in trouble here in Moscow for daring to imitate European Modernism. She didn't let them intimidate her, though. She and the others put together the first radical group of independent-thinking artists. They called themselves the Jack of Diamonds, and they did exhibitions, despite threats. Now that's what it means to be an artist."

"When did she move to Paris?"

"Years ago," said Loretta. "She had to be free. She had to grow. But she can certainly be credited with helping to create the art philosophy known as Russian Futurism."

"And now, she couldn't come back here if she wanted," I said.

"I know. And that bothers me."

"How can this all of a sudden bother you?" I said. "You've known for three years about the State's laws concerning artistic expression. We're only here still because you said this *controlled*, or better yet, *forced* form of art is one you loved. Don't get upset, but you are sounding a bit naïve."

I opened my eyes and looked at the children, both still with their heads in their books.

"You two go play catch," I said. "Take the baseball and the mitts and go play. Your mother and I need to talk. You can read more in a few minutes. Go!"

They knew when I was serious, so there was no backtalk as they stood, gathered the ball and gloves, and ran off.

"I *have* been naïve," said Loretta, both of us sitting up. "I have been naïve because perhaps I was only wanting to hear what they were telling me, that I am a great Socialist Realism painter. I thought the adoration would be enough. It isn't. I need to try other forms. I need to be back in Paris. *We* need to be back in Paris. I've exhausted this form and I'm ready to move on. I can do exhibits in Paris and make a lot of money for us. It's time."

"Then we need to move soon," I said. "I tried to tell you this back—"

"I know, Prescott. I have been on a high for so long that I couldn't see clearly. But everyone eventually comes down from a high, at least if they are sane. Reconnecting with Natalia helped validate the restrictions I was already beginning to feel. This relationship between Russian artists and the State is abusive. I liken it to a woman in an emotionally abusive relationship who is with a man who showers her with gifts, takes her to fine places, even makes her fall in love. But then she realizes she's being controlled and has been for some time. A light suddenly comes on. And she decides to leave."

"I wanted us to leave with Bobby last year," I said.

"And perhaps we should have. I'll take responsibility for it, though. It's my fault we are still here. There! Are you satisfied?"

"Not really," I said. "This was a big mistake we made. People were having a very difficult time getting out of the country back when the Ellingtons left. It's only gotten worse since. I mean, at that time we were under the assumption that it was only Soviets, both regular citizens and State officials, ones guilty of real crimes, who were being arrested. But now I fear they are just sweeping up whomever they damn well please."

"Look around," said Loretta. "There are families everywhere. People are picnicking and laughing and playing. There are folks in boats on the river in the distance. They hardly look worried about being arrested, Prescott."

"That's because Stalin has posted fucking signs everywhere that say, 'LIFE HAS BECOME BETTER, COMRADES; LIFE HAS BECOME MORE FUCKING JOYFUL!' "

"Lower you voice!" she said, looking around, a few onlookers having heard me yell. "What is wrong with you, Prescott? Calm down! Now!"

I sat with my legs crossed on the blanket, opened the picnic basket, and took out a beer. Opening it, I took a big drink. It had all hit me at once, this anger. It was as if I had allowed myself for over a year to become blind to my surroundings, all in an attempt to unequivocally support Loretta and, in the process, rid myself of any lingering guilt I still had over lying to her about being a spy back in Harlem. But I was awake again now and felt the weight of our situation all at once. I knew, even as I watched the children playing in the distance, that we were already smack dab in the middle of a wall-less prison.

"The new U.S. ambassador," she said, "Mr. Davies, has come out and said that the show trials are legitimate. He's witnessed some himself and expressed no worry over them. He has told American expatriates to carry on doing their jobs. Let's not overreact."

"Well, Davies is a damn imbecile," I said. "As far as I'm concerned, he may have blood on his hands someday. And he does President Roosevelt a disservice by making these declarations about a *normal* Soviet Union. Hell, from what I've read while I've been in this unfathomable state of coma, Davies has his nose so far up Stalin's ass, he wouldn't be able to see one of us getting arrested by the blue tops right outside of the U.S. Embassy. His positive statements about the Kremlin probably have Roosevelt, the State Department, and diplomats like Bobby completely in the dark. It will probably be years before they all learn the truth, whatever that is."

"When did you last write to Bobby?" said Loretta.

"Two days ago. I told him we had just returned from Leningrad and would be leaving for Kazan in two weeks."

"Well," she said, "I think you should go to the consulate and see about arranging for us to leave for Paris soon after we return from Kazan. In corresponding with Natalia Goncharova, she says—"

"Here goes that name again," I said. "Why does she suddenly have her hands on the controls of your conscience?"

"Because it took an artist who's already traveled the road I'm on to get my attention. But, then again, she's only confirming what I've already been coming to terms with on my own, Prescott. She has said she thinks it's in our best interest to leave, but I've also been listening to you."

"It's just frustrating," I said. "I'm sure we'll be fine, but I'm just frustrated. Today is Saturday, so I'll go by the consulate on Monday and see to it that they have our passports cleared with the State."

"Good," she said. "I also need to go by the Anglo-American School and check in with the children's teachers. I'll need to make sure they're up to speed with their lessons after missing all that time. At least this trip to Kazan will only be for one week."

"I can do it," I said. "I'm not supposed to be back until Tuesday, but I'll stop by Monday and check in with my substitute. I'll need to tell him that he'll be filling in for me again in two weeks. Hell, he's probably starting to write his own lesson plans as much as I've been gone. It's okay, though. I detest teaching chemistry. I can't wait to turn the job over to someone else. Maybe Robert will take it."

"Robert Robinson?" she said, puzzled. "He has a fantastic job already."

"Yeah, but he hates the politics at the ball-bearing factory.

Still, he is so talented as an innovator that the State doesn't want him to leave. They keep raising his pay. At least that's what he told me. But the look on his face says otherwise. I think he's being forced to stay here, not allowed to leave. I think he just hasn't told anyone, including me, out of fear. Everyone believes that even their friends might be spies for the Kremlin. It's paranoia run amuck, Loretta. I can't believe that subconsciously I've had these thoughts all along but haven't acted on them."

"Stop, love. You can't keep doing this. We've talked it through. We have a plan now. It's not like our decision to stay and live here was some anomaly. For Christ's sake, Paul Robeson's son goes to school here in Moscow. And we both know Paul was just here again this past May to see his son. He expressed no negative feelings about Stalin, the Central Committee, or anyone else. I'm ready to move now, but let's not characterize this place as hell on earth all of a sudden."

I took a sip of beer and noticed James and Ginger running up with grins on their faces, both of them half out of breath.

"Daddy!" said Ginger, bending over, hands on her knees. "James asked me a question that I thought was pretty interesting. But I really don't know the answer."

"What is it?" I said.

"Tell him, James," said Ginger, watching her brother dig through the picnic basket for a bottle of soda.

James popped the cap off, took a sip, and then asked me, "Why do men like to colonize countries where all of the people have black skin?"

I turned to his mother and we both froze. Neither of us could answer this seemingly simple question. I wondered what he'd read that had prompted such a question. I wanted to say something profound and philosophical on him, but no words came to mind. Maybe he was simply becoming more acutely aware of his own skin color. Whatever the case, his question had no obvious answer, so I turned to him and said, "That is a very good question, son. I'll have to think about it."

* * *

The next day, Sunday, I spent the morning at the house with the children while their mother was preparing her classroom at the Moscow Painting Academy. She would be back to teaching Monday morning, and she was anxious to share stories with her students about the successful Leningrad exhibit. I, on the other hand, was looking forward to the day when she would maybe be sharing stories with her students at the *École Nationale Supérieure des Beaux-Arts* in Paris.

At around noon, I took the children to the Torgsin grocery, where they sold a great variety of foods to Americans, one of the benefits of not being a Soviet citizen. I bought a big piece of beef to make a pot roast. I also bought some carrots, potatoes, and onions to cook with it.

Later that night at around six o'clock, I sat at the dining room table with James and Ginger waiting for Loretta to come home for dinner. She had been due home by five-thirty. Six o'clock turned to seven, and then eight. No sight of her and no telephone call either.

I'd asked the children to go ahead and eat their pot roast and vegetables, but they couldn't muster up an appetite, consumed with worry over their absent mother. In the twenty-plus years we'd been together, she'd never been late for a planned dinner. I knew something was wrong.

When the clock struck nine, the children now doing homework, I sent them to bed. Shortly thereafter was a hard knock on the door and I rushed to answer. Two large blue tops stood there stone-faced. Both mustached, one five-eleven and stocky, the other six-three and broad shouldered.

"Is your name Prescott Sweet, and is this your residence?" the stocky one asked in Russian.

"Yes, Prescott Sweet. That is me. What is the problem, officers?"

They looked at each other, obviously a bit surprised that I'd responded in the Russian tongue, something they hadn't expected from a colored American.

"Come with us," the tall one said, reaching out and grabbing my arm.

I flung it free and stepped back into the living room. "Tell me what this is about?" I said. "Where is my wife? Loretta Sweet! What have you done to her?"

"She has been jailed for being a *counterrevolutionary*," he said. "Now . . . come with us."

21

MR4 Labor Camp - Kirovsk, Russia
November 1938

THE MR4 LABOR CAMP WAS FAR CLOSER TO FINLAND THAN THE Soviet city of Leningrad. James and I had arrived in late November, having taken the ship south from Magadan to Vladivostok, and then the weeks' long train ride across the country to Moscow. From there we'd taken a different train north to Leningrad. Once there, NKVD put us in the back of a cargo truck, where we had to endure more travel—a fifteen-hour drive north to Kirovsk.

There had been one big difference in our travel arrangements this time, however. We'd been kept in a decent cabin aboard the ship, and our train rides had been normal, the two of us given our own compartment aboard a car that was carrying free hires going home from the various camps.

The guards aboard both the ship and trains had been ordered to feed us three good meals a day. In fact, we had been accompanied by one particular blue top during the entire journey. He had checked in on us periodically from his adjacent ship cabin and train compartment. It was clear he had one job to do: make sure the American spy reaches his destination in one piece.

Four days after I'd met with Director Pavlov back at Magadan,

Bobby had responded with a cable that confirmed what I'd predicted. His message had been short and specific. He had mentioned how sad he was to have heard about my pending divorce, but had gone on to say, *"I can't tell you how excited I am to see you on the first of January in Berlin. I will have a new visa and all of your embassy credentials waiting for you at Vitebsky Railway Station in Leningrad. You will be departing at 8:00 a.m. on December 29th. We have much to discuss."*

Ever since the Kremlin had learned of my spy proposal, James and I had found life much more livable. Both of us had gained about ten pounds over the last month and a half, but I was still concerned about James's health. He was no longer having dizzy spells or coughing, but every few days he'd have these fits with breathing. He needed to see a proper doctor.

Our first day at the MR4 Labor Camp was spent in a small, vacant room inside a commander's barracks. Our accompanying blue top had turned us over to a young guard named Osip. He couldn't have been any older than twenty, not a hair on his pale face, but the rifle he was shouldering made him look just dangerous enough. And as he sat in the chair by the door, James and I moved about, sorting through the bags full of clothes and toiletries they'd given us. There was one bunk in the room and we had our items placed on the bottom bed.

"I can't wait to trim this thick, ugly beard with these shears and then use this blade and cream," I said to James in Russian, out of respect for Osip. "You haven't seen your daddy clean-shaven in over a year, son."

"There is a small mirror and sink in the toilet closet over there," said Osip, whose soft Russian words sounded like those of a twelve-year-old. "But as soon as you are finished shaving, leave the scissors and blade on the sink for me to take. You can have it again whenever you need it."

"Thank you," I said, running my fingers through my beard.

"Also," said Osip, "there are many guards stationed just outside this barracks. Don't get any ideas."

I nodded and continued sorting through my bag, nothing but

thoughts of Loretta and Ginger on my mind. MR4 wasn't actually in the town of Kirovsk, but rather about half a mile away. And, of course, the men's camp was separate from the women's. Snow-covered mountains surrounded the entire area; the town itself was situated on the shores of a stunning lake. We'd been able to see the town when the cargo truck refueled before dropping us off.

"Excuse me," I said, turning again to Osip. "Would you happen to know when we will be able to see my wife and daughter?"

"I am going to take you to see Colonel Zorin in one hour. He can answer all of your questions. There is a tub room down the hall. After you shave, go bathe. Your boy can wait here while you meet with Colonel Zorin. And make sure you eat a second helping at every meal. Zorin's orders! You only have one month before you leave for Berlin, and you must look normal. Right now you still look very much like a skinny, sick *zek*. Your comrade cannot be allowed to see you like this."

Later that day, Osip accompanied me across the camp toward the north section, my new blue wadding coat keeping me plenty warm in this welcomed twenty-five degree weather. MR4 was considerably better kept than Magadan but had fewer barracks. Osip had told us about the open-pit mines in the surrounding area, and about the grueling schedule the *zeks* were forced to work mining for apatite. The moderate climate allowed for plenty of snow, but a *zek* freezing to death was highly unlikely.

When we entered Zorin's barracks, I could instantly tell this was a man who didn't spend his time worrying about comfort. There was nothing in the entire office except for a desk and two chairs. There was no fireplace, no bookshelves, no pictures on the walls save for the large one of Stalin behind his desk. There were no windows, no rugs, no cabinets, no art.

All I saw when we entered the small barracks was a tall-looking, olive-skinned man sitting and writing with his head down like he was the busiest person in Russia. He sported a thick black mustache and wore a gray tunic with red piping around the cuffs and collar. His visor was also gray, with a red band and red piping, all of which was accentuated with gold embroidery. He appeared to be in his thirties.

"*Perevodchik* is here," said Osip, prompting Colonel Zorin to look up and put his pen down.

"Come and sit," said Zorin. "Osip, please stand outside and wait."

He exited and I sat. Osip had introduced me as *Perevodchik*, which was the Russian word for "interpreter."

"I was told by the Kremlin that you speak six languages," said Zorin in an abnormally deep voice, his Russian spoken so slowly and loud it was easy to understand.

"Yes," I said. "Six."

"That is why your code name is Interpreter. Let me first tell you something that I am certain you would like to know. That way you don't have to ask. The Kremlin has advised me to tell you this. Your wife was originally arrested for a simple reason. She was sending letters to a famous Russian painter named Natalia Goncharova, who now lives in Paris. Did you know she was writing letters to her?"

"Yes," I said.

"Well, here is what she said in the last letter that was intercepted by NKVD before she was arrested." He held up a sheet of paper. "She wrote, '*My husband and I believe in freedom of expression. We have taught this God-given right to our children as well. We love the Soviet people, but the State should not be allowed to repress the ever-evolving, creative ideas of an artist. No one country should have a monopoly on art. You have inspired me with your bravery, Natalia, so much so that I now feel it's in my family's best interest to return to Paris.*'"

He set the paper down and looked up at me. "Your wife went on to say more, but this was enough to brand your entire family counterrevolutionaries. So, now you can focus on the job at hand, spying for our Great Stalin. Yes?"

"When can I see my wife and daughter?" I boldly asked.

"Let me explain this up front to you, *Perevodchik*. The work here at MR4 is grueling. Your wife and daughter spent most of their time hauling stones in wheel barrels. At first they were quite terrible at it, but after I had them slapped around a little, they got strong really fast. You should also know that your wife kept asking about you and your son, too. But, unlike you, she was never told where you were. Why give her hope, you see. Anyway, your wife and daughter learned how to work hard. But your spy plan should have been thought of sooner."

"I don't understand," I said.

"You still have one very important reason to go to Berlin and keep your promise to the Kremlin, though. Your son will be here working in the mines waiting for you. And if you do a good job, I'm sure our Great Stalin will eventually release him."

"The agreement," I said, "was for me to gather intelligence for up to one year and then have my entire family released, along with my comrade, Lovett Fort-Whiteman."

"Oh, yes," he said. "I have it written down right here. The Kremlin did agree to release this Fort-Whiteman after your mission is complete. So, yes, it would be him and your boy."

"And my daughter and wife?"

"I told you, your spy plan should have been thought of sooner. They both died within the last week."

"What did you say?"

"Your wife and daughter are dead," he said. "Your wife died four days ago, and your daughter gave up shortly thereafter. She passed two days ago, too sad after seeing her mother go. But we haven't touched them. We stored them in the meat freezer room at the NKVD food barracks to preserve their bodies for you."

I must have sat there for twenty seconds before what he'd said actually penetrated my inner ear, at which point, all of the blood in my body rushed to my feet, feeling as though it were spilling all over the floor. With each passing second, I felt myself sinking into this now vast pool of blood, then slowly drowning in it. I could not breathe. The visual of this Colonel Zorin before me grew blurry, my eyes watering, my heart beating as if I'd sprinted up a mountain, chill bumps covering my clammy skin. I tried to form a word but could not. I couldn't even lift my hand to wipe at my tears. I was paralyzed.

As the seconds continued ticking by, I could see the image of

Colonel Zorin mouthing something to me. But I couldn't hear him. All I could hear was the sound of my arms splashing at the blood all around me. Then, as if the hand of God had reached deep into this pool and yanked me back up onto my chair, I took one big gasp, begging in air like a man who'd just been held underwater.

"Can you hear me, *Perevodchik?*" I finally heard Colonel Zorin saying.

I nodded and wiped the tears from my face.

"Come with me," he said.

We both stood and I followed him outside into the cold night and across the way to another barracks, Osip remaining behind, standing guard on Zorin's deck. I was floating behind Zorin, my footsteps not under my control, no feeling of my boots actually contacting the ground. I was moving forward, but some force beyond me was orchestrating it.

We entered the large barracks, and I realized we were in the camp hospital, beds full of sick *zeks* throughout, only a few nurses here to attend to what looked like a hundred men. We made our way to the back of the large barracks and entered a hallway, with several medical staff offices located along the sides. We finally reached the last room on the left and he opened the door.

Facing a dark room, he flipped on the lights and we stepped forward. The inside was quite cold. It appeared to be nothing more than a storage room—mops, buckets, brooms, and cleaning supplies having been shoved against the walls. In the middle of the room lay two wooden boxes, both the size of caskets. For some reason, I was expecting to see two people lying inside who were not Loretta and Ginger. I still had hope.

"I know," said Zorin, "that you had asked to see your wife and daughter before going to Berlin. This is the hospital for male *zeks,* but I had your wife's and daughter's bodies hauled over here from the freezer room when you arrived."

He approached both boxes and lifted the lids off. Inside one lay Loretta. Inside the other lay Ginger. The hair had been shaved off and their bodies looked stiff. They were so frail, so colorless, their lips parched and cracked.

"Their eyes were open," said Zorin, "even after they took their last breaths, but I had the nurses close them."

I stepped closer and looked down at them. Flashes of the guard who I'd killed and buried under the punishment isolator ran through my head. The same rage was boiling up in me, and I forced myself not to look over at Zorin, afraid I might kill him the same way. I tried to think of James and the life he'd have to live alone if I, too, were taken from him now.

More tears ran down my face as I stared at my lifeless sweethearts. Then the nightmare overtook me like a gust of wind. I looked up at the ceiling, closed my eyes, and screamed to the heavens. And I couldn't stop. Two guards rushed in and took me by the arms. I didn't fight them off, but continued crying at the top of my lungs while they escorted me out of the room and past the beds of *zeks* and busy nurses. I was absolutely inconsolable and the guards knew it.

"Put him on the bed at the end over there and administer the sedative!" said Zorin, who was walking just behind us.

The guards laid me down and two nurses approached, one holding a needle, the other, a cup of water. I was kicking and began repeatedly shouting, "MY LORETTA! MY GINGER!" But the guards were able to control my movements enough for one nurse to roll up my sleeve before the other injected me. As the drug began to calm me down, one nurse held my head up enough for the other to pour water into my mouth. By the time I had swallowed it all, light had turned to dark, and the nightmare had been temporarily put to sleep.

Eighteen days later, on December 15, 1938, I sat with James in our private barracks room and we ate lunch together with Osip watching our every move. We were finishing off our plates of baked salmon, boiled potatoes, and cabbage. Neither of us had found it easy to eat after learning of Loretta's and Ginger's deaths, but it was Osip's job to make sure the plates didn't leave the room until they were empty.

"There is something I need to tell you, Interpreter," said Osip. "Colonel Zorin has instructed me to inform you that you will be leaving in two days for Leningrad. You weren't supposed to leave until late December, but that has changed."

Before Osip could say another word, Colonel Zorin entered the room carrying two brown briefcases. He looked down at James and me sitting in our chairs like we had stolen something. He always appeared angry, but this was an even more pronounced frown.

"The Kremlin has just notified me that you will be leaving in the morning, Interpreter," said Zorin. "It had been changed to two days from now, but now it is even sooner. Tomorrow morning is also when your boy here will begin working in the mines."

"Okay," I said, no longer even able to summon up any words of resistance to these Soviet animals.

"Don't think for a second, Interpreter, that your son is no longer a fucking *zek*," said Zorin, setting the briefcases next to Osip. "The Kremlin may have ordered me to feed him well over the next year, but he will work like all the others while you are in Berlin."

"Excuse me, Colonel Zorin," I said, "but I have been asking for days that my son here get treatment for his breathing problem. James has told me that his brief visits to the hospital have only resulted in him receiving cough syrup, which is hardly considered treatment. He needs to see a proper doctor, not a nurse."

"What did you say, black *zek*?" said Zorin, angrily.

"I said my son needs treatment. He is having trouble breathing, particularly at night. I would think the Kremlin would like to see him stay alive while I'm gone. He *is* their . . . you know . . . *leverage* after all."

Zorin removed his pistol from his holster and stepped forward, sticking the end of the barrel against the skin right between my eyes. Part of me wanted him to pull the trigger.

"Shut your American mouth," said Zorin. "You think because you are speaking Russian to me, that makes it okay to talk fancy with me? The doctors are busy attending to *zeks* with serious diseases. Do you hear me?"

I nodded, the pistol still stabbing my forehead. James sat still with his plate on his lap. My fifteen-year-old boy was a young man now, unafraid I sensed, able to handle himself if need be.

"I can sense that you are growing brave," said Zorin. "You feel as though you don't have as much to live for now. But maybe if you get a good night's sleep before the morning departure, you'll realize how important your son is to you. Don't you remember that feeling of having your soul ripped out of you when you saw your dead wife and daughter?"

I nodded.

"You don't ever want to feel that again, I'm sure. Besides, if you start acting too bold, the Kremlin will just have one of our undercover NKVD men visit Berlin and kill you, then order me to shoot your son here."

He finally pulled the pistol back and reholstered it.

"Let me have your chair, Osip," said Zorin. "And bring me the briefcases."

Osip stood, slid his chair over, and Zorin sat with James and me. Then Osip placed the briefcases at Zorin's feet before returning to the doorway, where he continued standing guard.

"Pay very close attention to this," said Zorin. "For the sake of this mission, we will call the town of Valga, Estonia, the halfway point between Berlin and MR4. There will be absolutely no cable communication between you and me while you are in Berlin. And make no mistake . . . the Kremlin has made me their official go-between. It is I who will relay all intelligence to them once I receive it from you. Clear?"

"Yes," I said, setting my half-empty plate on the floor while James continued eating.

"This briefcase is yours for now," he said, picking one up and handing it to me. "And the other one is mine for now. As you can see, they are brand-new briefcases, each made by the Kremlin engineers for this specific mission. Steel covered with brown leather. They can only be unlocked with a combination of nine numbers and letters. Both briefcases have the same combination. I was told that you have an extraordinary memory."

"Yes," I said, running my fingers over the seven small, gold, button-like fixtures located just under the briefcase handle.

"Good, because you are *never* to write this combination down. "It is 7-K-6-Z-R-9-9-V-5."

I rolled my finger over the first button and it clicked each time a different letter or number appeared. When the number 7 appeared, I stopped and continued on to the next fixture. I finally clicked button number nine into position and popped the case open.

"On your first try," said Zorin. "Impressive. Now, listen carefully. The Nazis have all modes of communication under strict surveillance. They will intercept anything spoken over the telephone or sent via cable. So, on the first Tuesday of every month, in the morning, Osip here will meet our German contact, Dieter, at the train station in Valga, Estonia. Both men will have boarded their respective trains the day before, obviously on a Monday. Got that?"

"Yes."

"Dieter is a chauffeur for the Hotel Adlon in Berlin. We have lots of spies working at that fancy hotel where so many important international dignitaries stay. And all of our spies there, and within many other establishments throughout Berlin, are German citizens. But, you see, they are proud, loyal communists first. Dieter is also being well compensated for his longstanding loyalty. We have so, so many communist spies around the world! And, now, you will be the best. Yes?"

"That is certainly my plan," I said.

"Dieter will pick up your briefcase on the first Monday of every month and then catch the train to Valga. His two days off are Monday and Tuesday. And he doesn't have to show up for work until Wednesday, late morning. This gives him forty-eight hours to make the thirty-five-hour round-trip. Make a habit of having breakfast at 7:00 a.m. every Monday and Wednesday at the Golden Café near his apartment. He has coffee across the street at the Blue Lion daily. Your first drop-off is to be on February 6th, a day when he will be carrying a simple, empty briefcase, not one of these beauties."

"Got it," I said. "At that point, you will still be in possession of the duplicate."

"Correct," he said. "So, Dieter will see you get up to leave the Golden Café and cross Friedrichstrasse Street at seven forty-five. It is very busy at that time. Once the traffic guard signals and you cross, wait at the corner in front of the Blue Lion in preparation to cross the east-west street of Beck. Set your briefcase down. He will come stand beside you there in the crowd and set his briefcase down. Before you cross Beck Street, pick up his briefcase and he'll grab yours."

"I understand," I said.

"From that point forward, beginning two days later, on Wednesday, February 8th, he will be setting the duplicate briefcase down. It will be important for you to write any questions, statements, requests, news, etcetera . . . on paper and place them inside your briefcase along with the intelligence, because that will be the only communication you will have with us until a month later. Even an emergency question and response will be subject to this strict schedule. Also, don't forget, even the smallest piece of secret information from within your American embassy is important to us. Our Great Stalin is just trying to learn how much he can trust the United States."

"I understand," I said.

"Who are the only two men on earth with the combination to these briefcases?"

"You and me," I said.

"And it shall remain this way. Again, your briefcase will have gathered intelligence inside, and Osip's will have any information from the Kremlin or me that you might need to read, or it might be empty. The key is that the one *you* deliver must always have intelligence in it. Clear?"

"Absolutely," I said.

"Very good, Interpreter. The officials at the border have been informed that an official named Prescott Sweet is to have no problems exiting the country. Kremlin's orders! Your passport is gold. You're a very important man. And just in case you need any further motivation to keep you focused, I have come bringing gifts."

He turned and nodded at Osip, who exited the room. Zorin took his pistol from his holster and pointed it at me.

"Stop eating," he said to James. "Both of you go sit on the bottom bunk."

James set his near-empty plate on the floor. Then we stood and did as he said. Two minutes must have passed before another word was spoken.

"If you move at all I will shoot you," said Zorin.

"The gifts are here," said Osip, reappearing in the doorway.

"Good," said Zorin. "Bring them in."

On those words, Osip disappeared again. Then, a couple of guards escorted two sheet-covered individuals into the room. They stopped behind the seated Zorin, his pistol still aimed at us.

"Remove the sheets," said Zorin.

The two guards yanked the white sheets off of them, and there before us stood Loretta and Ginger. They had risen from the dead. Instinctively I jumped up and James cried out, "MOMMA!"

"Ah, ah, ah!" said Zorin, clicking his pistol.

"It's okay, Prescott!" cried Loretta in English, both she and Ginger weeping, their bodies still frail, their color, yellowish.

I slowly sat back down and pulled James in close. All of us were weeping loudly, our eyes fixed on one another, the guards still clutching their arms. None of us was being allowed to move. It was motionless chaos.

"Now!" said Zorin. "You should know, Interpreter, all of this was done so that you would know what it feels like to have a dead wife and daughter. And now that you have tasted that horror, you can go do your mission with more clarity and purpose. Your aim is clear now."

Each of us wept through Zorin's words, all the while acutely aware of his drawn pistol. My only recourse was to clutch my delirious son tighter and tighter while he cried into my chest.

"No one better say another fucking word," Zorin continued. "Look at me, Interpreter. We just wanted you to appreciate the importance of your assignment. I'm sure you never want to feel that sickness again. You have much to be thankful for now. You have much to lose again, but now it is more engrained in you. That is why we drugged them and staged the entire death scene. You will come to see that it was very good for you in the end. It will make you sharper, more trustworthy. You might choose to call it a sick game us Soviets played, but we feel that these types of maneuvers work very well."

Zorin nodded at the two guards, prompting them to haul Loretta and Ginger away, each of them showing tremendous restraint and strength. I could tell by the powerful, stern look Loretta gave me just before exiting that she was saying, "I will continue to fight for our family!" I just knew that was what she was saying. And Zorin had been correct. I *was* going to carry out my mission with more clarity and purpose now. And my aim was indeed clear.

22

Berlin, Germany
January 1, 1939

AS SOON AS I STEPPED OFF THE TRAIN AT LEHRTER BAHNHOF, I looked left and right in search of a face I had been longing to see for two and a half years. And as if he'd been sensing my anxiousness for some time, Bobby came briskly walking through the bustling crowd of white faces, almost all dressed in business attire. My best friend was grinning from ear to ear.

"Holy fuckin' shit!" he said, spreading his arms wide, as I set my two bags and briefcase down before he bear-hugged me.

Right when he let go and stepped back, I tried to muster up a smile, but it wasn't in me. The still intense pain had an unrelenting grip on me. And I couldn't stop ruminating over those last words I'd said to James: "Keep your head down and your mouth shut. Do your work and I will be back to get you, son. I promise. I love you." All he'd done was nod like a good boy.

"I see you're still as busy as ever buying new suits," said Bobby, looking me up and down. "And I love the fancy black topcoat. Looks like mine."

"You know me," I said.

I wanted to tell him right then and there that the fine, new brown suit I was wearing, along with the four others in my hanging bag, had been tailor-made for me in Leningrad just days be-

fore my departure, compliments of the Kremlin. They'd also
had three different colored fedora hats made for me, along with
several ties and two pairs of patent leather shoes. They'd spared
no expense in making certain I looked the part of an embassy
employee.

"You've gotten so damn thin," said Bobby.

"Well, you can imagine how—"

"I know," he said. "I'm sorry. Of course! Your appetite has
probably gone to shit since the whole split from Loretta. I've
been so down in the dumps about that news, Press."

"Look," I said, "I want to tell you all about it, just maybe not
right here."

"Of course!" he said, picking up one of my bags. "I have a car
parked out front. Let's go."

Moments later we got into a black Mercedes-Benz and he
took the wheel.

"Some of the embassy staff is still operating out of Bendlerstrasse 39 in the Tiergarten area," said Bobby, beginning to
drive. "Others are finally beginning to move into the refur-
bished Blücher Palace, which is located on Pariser Platz. You
and I will work at Bendlerstrasse for the time being.

"Currently, there is no U.S. Ambassador in place. Hugh Wilson had only served for eight months before being summoned
home by the president this past November. Roosevelt felt it necessary to call him back to the States after the Nazi attacks on so
many Jews during the Night of Broken Glass. They call it
Kristallnacht here in Germany. Actually, it was Assistant Secretary
of State, George Messersmith, who persuaded Roosevelt to recall Wilson."

"I'm surprised Roosevelt didn't shut down the entire embassy," I said, looking out the window at the cold city, uninter-
ested in its stunning architecture, so much of it appearing to be
made largely of glass, concrete, and steel—Modernism on full
display.

"It looks," said Bobby, "as though a gentleman named Alexander Kirk will be here by May to serve as the chargé d'affaires."

"Then who's running things now?"

"Yours truly," said Bobby. "Actually, to be fair, there are three of us holding down the fort for the time being. It's only for a few months. But with the climate the way it is, the Nazis tightening the screws, Lord knows when Adolf Hitler will do the unthinkable. This is a man who is wholly evil."

"Sounds like Joseph Stalin," I said.

"Believe me," he said, "Hitler's much worse."

"Maybe they're equally evil."

"No," he said.

"Then I'll just put it this way. Stalin has shown me, very clearly, how absolutely evil he is. I'm glad you didn't notice earlier the piece of my ear that is missing."

"What in God's name are you talking about?"

"Let's just say you should completely disregard the cable I sent you, Bobby."

"Come again."

"Loretta and I are not getting a divorce. We never moved to Leningrad. And I have just gotten out of hell. I can't waste another second not telling you this. The unthinkable happened to my family beginning seventeen months ago—August of 1937. We were all arrested for being so-called counterrevolutionaries. Stalin has had me, Loretta, and both children locked up in his barbaric labor camps for almost a year and a half—James and I in Magadan, Loretta and Ginger on the other side of the country in Kirovsk. It was only days ago at a Leningrad hotel that I took a proper bath for the first time since leaving Moscow. I should be dead."

Bobby pulled the car to the side of the road, busy morning traffic buzzing past. He kept both hands on the wheel and we sat there with the engine idling. The shock on him was obvious; his eyes fixed straight ahead, his mouth agape. I looked down at my damaged hand and reminded myself once again what I'd always believed. Stalin was never going to release my family. He was going to use me up, call me back to the labor camp with the promise of releasing Loretta and the children, only to then execute us all. I felt it in my bones.

I also believed he was going to eventually kill Commander Koskinen, Director Pavlov, Colonel Zorin, and everyone else working for him, just as he had executed Sergei Kirov and the previous Dalstroi director, Eduard Berzin. According to Commander Koskinen, Stalin had also executed other prominent political leaders: Grigory Zinoviev, Lev Kamenev, Nikolai Bukharin, and Alexei Rykov.

"Listen," I finally said. "I know you are shocked to have heard all of this, but I want to be very specific. Time is of the essence, Bobby."

He turned to me, tears in his eyes, the blood gone from his face, and slowly nodded.

"I will tell you all of the details about what exactly happened—the camp I was in, the beasts I had to brawl, the commander who helped me send letters, a guard I had to kill, how a sick bastard made me believe Loretta and Ginger had died . . . and whatever else you want to know, but right now I need to ask you something."

"Ask," he said. "Please."

"Do you have any contacts who deal in international undercover work?"

"Yes."

"I need the best person you can find," I said.

"Talk to me."

"While you and Dorene were living in Moscow, we all knew about the arrests that were taking place, but they are much worse than anyone who hasn't been inside the labor camps can imagine. A great man, a Trotskyist named Commander Koskinen, told me that in 1934 there were approximately five hundred thousand people in the prison camps. But, he told me that beginning in 1937 at least one in every twenty people in the Soviet Union was being arrested."

"Good Lord," said Bobby.

"He referred to it as the 'Great Terror.' Just before I left Magadan, Commander Koskinen claimed that their census showed that, as of the end of 1938, approximately two million people were in the prison camps. And the number of people who'd already been executed by then was even greater. Ambassador Bullitt couldn't have known of the earlier number, and Ambassador Davies certainly must not have known of the latter."

"I would think not," said Bobby.

"In fact, I read where Ambassador Davies reported back to Washington that he'd seen some of the show trials. He claimed they were legitimate, and that only real criminals were being tried and convicted. Davies seemed all too keen on kissing Stalin's ass. I guess Davies simply didn't want Americans back home to know what was happening in the Soviet Union. But he did the president a disservice. His ambassadorship was an absolute embarrassment, and I believe he has blood on his hands. Son of a bitch!"

"My head is spinning, Press," said Bobby. "Those numbers are astronomical. This is a fucking extermination."

"It involves a company called the Dalstroi, and Stalin's plan to do a myriad of things, which I'll explain later. But it's insanity. And somehow, someway, I managed to get out. I don't for a second expect you or anyone else to negotiate my family's release, as the politics—"

"Screw that!" said Bobby. "We're going straight to the embassy to cable the president."

"No! We absolutely can't! If our government even broaches the issue, I've been told they will execute Loretta and the kids. Besides, Roosevelt can't open that can of worms. There are many Americans in the prisons, Bobby. And I'm smart enough to know where securing the release of American expatriates ranks on Roosevelt's long list. He got reelected in '36 to handle the Depression. And he's also got this monster named Hitler to deal with. Hell, you spoke of extermination earlier. Koskinen says Hitler wants to exterminate everyone on earth who isn't part of the Aryan race. I'm sure the president sees the value of having Stalin on his side as Hitler threatens the world. I understand the politics."

"I don't want Loretta and the children to spend another second in prison," said Bobby, wiping his wet eyes. "And just how did you manage to magically talk your way out—"

"I agreed to spy for Stalin. I told the Kremlin I would gather information from within the U.S. Embassy and have it delivered via train on the first Monday of every month. I have a contact here, a German communist who'll deliver a briefcase to Valga. But, of course, I have no intention of gathering legitimate intelligence. I just need to buy time until I can execute my plan."

"What plan, Press?"

"That's where your international man comes into play. But first, can you help me buy time? Can we manufacture some plausible intelligence to hand over to Stalin?"

"Of course," said Bobby. "We can send them some fabricated shit every month that will be solid enough to keep the waters calm. Just tell me your plan."

"It involves trying to track down some targets in Riga, Latvia. I've written it all down while I was on the train. I'm still working through the logistics of the entire idea, but I know I need help finding these Latvians. If memory serves me correct, I recall the U.S. having good relations with Latvia. Has anything changed since '37?"

"No," said Bobby. "We have an Envoy Extraordinary and Minister Plenipotentiary there now named John C. Wiley."

"Who is your international man?" I said.

"I'm thinking of an old Military Intelligence veteran named Dallas Conrad. He does off-the-books intelligence work for high-paying clients."

"I'll pay you back. Just make sure—"

"Don't you dare say that," said Bobby. "I will take care of this, and I will spare no expense. Just tell me what you have in mind."

"I've actually said all I want to say about my plan at this juncture. Saying anything more today is pointless, because if the targets don't exist, the plan is dead. If they do exist, I simply need this Dallas fellow to locate them."

"What if they don't exist, Press?"

"I have a plan B, but I don't want to even discuss it until we exhaust this one. I'm afraid if I tell you anything more about either idea, you'll try and stop me. And I can't afford a moment of delay."

"Done," said Bobby. "I'll track Dallas down through some Military Intelligence friends of mine. I'll cable them today. I believe the old veteran works out of Paris now. But once I make contact with Dallas, I'll have him meet us in Brussels. We can do no communicating regarding the specifics of this via cable or telephone. The Nazis have all modes of communication under surveillance. Besides, Dallas knows that anyone from a U.S. embassy contacting him about a sit-down is code enough for it to be worth his time."

"Excellent," I said. "I know that you are here to do a very important job at the embassy. Try to focus on it. Try to be present with Dorene and the children, too. Tell them the divorce story and I'll play along. I'm here to be your interpreter and assistant as planned. I just need something in that briefcase every month."

"There is nothing in this world that could stop me from exhausting every option possible to help you, Press."

"Thank you," I said. "Judging from how Loretta and Ginger looked, and how sick James has been, I don't think they'll make it much longer. Plus, I don't believe the head of their camp, a man named Colonel Ivan Zorin, will treat them well. Zorin is the head of MR4 Labor Camp where Loretta and Ginger have been all this time. James is there now, too. And he's having trouble with his lungs, something that truly has me worried . . . but back to Zorin. He is an animal of a man, the worst—a notorious executioner. I don't think he cares if my family lives, even though the Kremlin sees them as leverage. They have every reason to believe I will do legit spy work based on this. Why wouldn't they? They know I can't have you all negotiate anything."

"True," said Bobby. "As far as they're concerned, they've got you by the balls."

"But back to Zorin," I said. "He knows that even if my family dies because of his inability to keep from being a monster, he'd just lie and tell me they were still alive. And let's say they do live, and I complete this job, and Stalin releases us, he'd never let us leave the Soviet Union. We'd be monitored for the rest of our lives. He wouldn't want me, an embassy employee, to tell the world about his death camps. I know I'm risking it all with this move, but it's all I've got. I'm desperately trying to hold on here for dear life and the big clock is ticking."

When February 6th arrived, I sat outside on the patio at the Golden Café sipping my coffee and finishing up a plate of toast, scrambled eggs, and cold salami. The entire block was busy, just as Colonel Zorin had predicted, and across the way at the Blue Lion, I assumed, sat my contact, Dieter. Wherever he lived wasn't far from me. I had secured a tiny, furnished apartment just up the block.

Taking a bite of toast, I looked down at my German-made Aristo stainless-steel watch, a gift from Bobby, and made note of the time: 7:30. I then eyed my briefcase and imagined how the Kremlin would react when they opened it to find notes I'd written regarding a fictitious correspondence that had taken place between U.S. Secretary of State Cordell Hull and Bobby.

The fabricated lines by Hull that were certain to feed Stalin's massive ego were the following: "President Roosevelt was most disturbed to see *Time* magazine list Adolf Hitler as its 1938 Man of the Year and feels that the editor's rationale for doing so remains unpalatable. As a result, folks within his administration are pressuring the magazine to make sure Stalin is named 1939's Man of the Year."

Bobby had typed up the fictitious note from Hull on U.S. State Department letterhead and had signed the Secretary of State's name on it. Then he'd had me photograph the letter, as if I'd stolen it from his desk. The idea worked because actual mail was indeed being sent back and forth between D.C. and Berlin, and embassy couriers had been hired to both pick up and receive it directly from our American ships. Such precautions were required due to German officials combing through the regular mail.

What gave this particular briefcase delivery a hell of a lot of credibility involved some notes I'd taken regarding an actual meeting that Stalin was trying to organize between his man, Maxim Litvinov, and Germany's Minister of Foreign Affairs, Joachim von Ribbentrop. But Hitler was only willing to consider the meeting if Litvinov was replaced. His reasoning? Litvinov was Jewish.

I figured Stalin would love finding out that his desired meeting just might happen if he were to simply replace Litvinov. And once said meeting did take place in the future, I'd have all the more credibility. Stalin would wonder how the hell I'd found out about this, but unless or until he asked, I wasn't going to worry about it.

I was, however, impressed with how Bobby had actually found out about Stalin's desired sit-down with Germany. He'd been receiving messages from a top-level informant who was embedded within the German government, a man who was part of a team of folks who wanted to oust Hitler. Bobby had learned of the informant from another anti-Nazi, German diplomat who'd been stationed in Argentina with him.

"Don't think for a second," Bobby had said, "that the United States doesn't have its own spies in many nations, including Germany and the Soviet Union. And they're not Americans, but rather, locals who oppose their country's politics. Our German spy is an anti-Nazi."

"How does he communicate with you?" I had said.

"There's a certain dry cleaners that has the most amazing owner. He would poison Hitler if given the chance. Our mole and I love having him clean and press our suits. I'll leave it at that."

"Fair enough," I had said.

"We can thank President Roosevelt for realizing the importance of America's need to begin matching Britain, Germany, and the Soviet Union when it comes to international spying. During his time as Assistant Secretary of the Navy, Roosevelt's interest in the spy business was born. And now, I believe he only intends to grow his global, covert apparatus. Maybe he could use you and your multilingual abilities, Press. But that's certainly a story for another day."

Again I looked at my watch and then the briefcase. The Kremlin would also find two fictitious lines about Poland of interest, the first in which Hull says, "The President understands that Hitler anxiously wants to attack Poland from the west, and he's hoping like hell that they won't, all the while, remaining steadfast in his belief that the U.S., Britain, France, and the Soviet Union will continue to show that they are the real world powers." The second in which Hull says, "We believe Hitler is envious of Stalin's calm and resolve, and rightfully so."

The following information was not going to be put in my briefcase, but one thing I had come to learn since arriving at Bendlerstrasse 39 was that the U.S. was already keenly aware that Stalin and Hitler were preparing some sort of an alliance, one in which they would share in the carving up of Poland. In fact, we had no intentions of stopping them from attacking Poland, even if our allies, Britain and France, decided to defend them.

The two countries had not signed any official pact yet that made official their intentions of protecting Poland; still, embassy folks could smell one coming. But again, zero information I'd ever send would make this known to Stalin. Bobby and I only intended to nibble around the edges. Nothing sent would affect Stalin's decisions, one way or the other. Whatever he intended to do, he was going to do.

I'd also included in my briefcase a letter requesting that the Kremlin look into having Lovett transferred from Magadan to MR4 so that he could eventually be released with my family. I was looking forward to their response.

When the clock hit 7:45, I stood and walked toward Friedrichstrasse Street, leaving some money behind on the table. Waiting for the traffic guard's signal, I stood amongst the crowd of suited men and we finally crossed over and stationed ourselves in front of the Blue Lion. Then, just as planned, I sat my briefcase down, and before we began to move, Dieter approached, setting his next to it. I casually looked at him, his black fedora similar to mine and the many others who were hustling off to work. He was my height, thin, fair-skinned, with a sharp nose and chin.

The traffic guard finally stopped the vehicles and the throng began to walk again, Dieter and I following protocol. Not a word needed to be spoken. The first delivery had been set into motion.

23

Brussels, Belgium
February 9, 1939

BOBBY AND I HAD WANTED TO MEET DALLAS CONRAD EARLIER IN the week, but I'd had to be in Berlin from Monday to Wednesday to make the briefcase exchange. As a result, we were taking the Thursday morning train to Brussels. Bobby had been able to organize the fourteen-hour trip by setting up a meeting with none other than Joseph E. Davies, the current U.S. Ambassador to Belgium. It was too ironic that he'd be visiting with the man I despised for having been a deplorable ambassador to the Soviet Union.

We arrived at around 10:00 p.m. and checked into two rooms at the Hotel Metropole. Bobby's meeting with Ambassador Davies wasn't due to take place until the following afternoon. Meanwhile, our man Dallas Conrad would be joining us for breakfast downstairs at 8:00 sharp.

Both of us woke feeling well-rested and anxious. We sat down at a corner table in the busy hotel café at around 7:30, each of us ordering coffee and oatmeal. All Dallas had mentioned was that he'd be carrying a little black dog—a Pomeranian to be specific.

"Thanks again, Press, for trusting me with your entire plan," said Bobby, stirring some milk into his coffee. "I hope you believe I was never going to try to stop you."

"I do," I said, adjusting my tie. "I just needed some time to think it through a bit more before completely filling you in. I needed to get that briefcase in Dieter's hands for the first time. That simple act cleared my mind quite a bit."

"What else did you send?"

"I asked Colonel Zorin to give me details on my family's well-being. And I specifically asked for a doctor's report regarding James's breathing issue. Problem is, the medics at the camp are awful. He needs to see a proper physician."

"Do you know how fucking handcuffed I feel right now, Press?" He sipped. "I sort of blame myself for all of this. How could I not have been more proactive about looking into the arrests while living in Moscow? All of us diplomats were so damn busy romanticizing about the damn place. Even still, I believe many of our government officials live vicariously through white rebels like the late Jack Reed, along with current so-called Soviet sympathizers like Max Eastman, James Burnham, and Max Shachtman."

"Please don't blame yourself," I said.

"I've been walking around in a constant state of shock for over a month; in utter awe of not only how you managed to survive the camps, but the specific acts of barbarism you had to endure, the friends you were forced to watch die. I can't grasp how you had the strength or wherewithal to think up an escape plan in the midst of the entire mess. And again, I can't help but beat myself up over it."

"Don't," I said. "I'm focused on what's ahead, on Dallas."

"He's going to stand at the entryway so that we can see him," said Bobby, opening a notebook and scribbling something. "I'll go retrieve him when he appears."

"Then you should probably stand up," I said, sipping my coffee. "I believe that's our man with the silver head of hair standing next to the maître d'."

Bobby took a sip of water, wiped his mouth with a napkin, and stood. I watched him walk across the large café, winding his way through the many tables until he reached Dallas, who was standing about twenty feet in the distance. The Military Intelligence vet appeared to be in his late fifties or early sixties. He was average height, trim, finely tailored, his silver hair fashioned like Bobby's, in the mode of one Clark Gable. The two shook hands and then headed my way. Just before they arrived I stood.

"Prescott," said Bobby, "this is Dallas Conrad."

"Thank you for coming," I said, shaking his hand. "It's nice to meet you."

"Likewise," he said with a deep smoker's voice.

"Please," said Bobby, offering Dallas up a chair, the three of us sitting. "Coffee, Dallas?"

"No, I'm fine," he said, petting his perfectly behaved dog.

"I don't want to waste a second of your time, Mr. Conrad," I said, taking a file from my briefcase and placing it in front of him. "I think you'll find the plan clear and concise."

"Good," he said, taking a pen and blank card from his suit pocket before opening my file and beginning to read.

Bobby and I sipped our coffee and watched Dallas carefully running his finger down my typed outline. I scanned the café and wondered if Stalin had designated someone from day one to shadow me, a person who had perhaps traveled on the same train from Berlin to Brussels. It didn't matter if Stalin had done such. All this possible spy would be witnessing was my boss meeting with some important-looking official.

"Anything in Latvia is possible," Dallas finally said, jotting down a note, his clean-shaven, pinkish, rough-skinned face remaining completely calm.

"Good," I said.

Dallas looked at me. "My men can start by poking around the secondary schools. Not to state the obvious, but every one of us was a child at one point."

"Your men?" I said.

"My men," he said, writing again. "The next phase of your plan sounds like a job for . . . I don't know . . . say . . . two young officials from the Central Statistical Bureau of Latvia. My men can certainly look the part. I'm sure when they knock at the

door with their proper-looking badges, your targets will welcome them in for a cup of tea and a nice chat about their family.
Most Latvians speak Russian. So do my men. Any covert opera-
tive worth his salt these days has to speak it."

"Good," I said. "And I'm assuming they can pick most locks?"

"In their sleep. But back to the idea of them dressing as Central Statistical Bureau officials. My men will simply say that they
are updating the country's census. Questions surrounding this
topic never draw the target's suspicion. This process should
allow my men to specifically identify all of the players involved
here, their histories, their relationships with one another,
etcetera. Believe me, my men will ask the right questions."

"How long?" I said.

"Could be two weeks. Could be two months. Hard to say.
They'll stay in a simple apartment until your targets are confirmed to exist or not exist. If they do exist . . . then . . . as you've
suggested here in your outline, they'll rent a two-bedroom
apartment somewhere off the beaten path, a real secure one.
Easy. They operate with plenty of cash on hand."

"Speaking of cash," said Bobby, sliding an envelope full of
money across the table toward Dallas. "This is triple what I was
told you might require. And there's more to come as the job
progresses, and certainly when it's finished."

"I've got one shot at this," I said. "All I ask is that your men
take that into account."

Dallas nodded. "Look, my men are highly skilled, highly
trained professionals. They're not choirboys. They're not hired
assassins, but they've killed. Bobby here is an American diplomat. That's all I need to know to trust him. It's obvious that this
isn't some sort of damn game to you, Mr. Sweet. My men will see
the job through until you and Bobby are satisfied. No one needs
to die, but if it means protecting either of you, that is certainly
part of their job description. They're private contractors."

"When your men finish their investigation, Dallas," said
Bobby, "cable me at the embassy with a standard message regarding how your wife and children are doing, etcetera. Act as if

we're long-lost friends. And, if it is indeed confirmed that the targets exist, make this one of the sentences in your cable: 'My family is looking forward to our annual trip to London on the *blank* of April.' You fill in the actual date, Dallas. That date will signal to us when Prescott is to meet your men in Riga. Where do you suggest?"

"The Riga Hotel," said Dallas. "And they will have with them what you've requested."

"Fine," said Bobby. "They will meet Prescott in the lobby. He will likely be the only person of color staying there. If not, they can walk up to the other few and ask if their names are Prescott Sweet. The time of this meeting, no matter what, will be noon."

"Got it," he said, petting his dog. "You've got me wishing I actually had a wife and children."

"Sorry," said Bobby.

"Not a problem." Dallas half smiled.

"Continuing," said Bobby. "If, on the other hand, your men confirm that no said targets exist, or that they exist but not in the nature we need them to, make this one of your sentences in your cable message: 'Unfortunately, my family will not be taking our annual trip to London.' And if our plan does not bear any fruit, I'll be cabling you thereafter about our next idea. We would convene here again in that case."

"What if my men hit a snag?" said Dallas. "A myriad of things can cause delay or hang-ups. Targets could be traveling. If two months roll by and there's no news either way, then what?"

"Send a friendly cable that doesn't mention London," said Bobby, "one that has a line in it somewhere involving your wife not feeling well lately and being in and out of the doctor's office."

"Good," said Dallas. "If and when my men meet you, Prescott, what will be that day's next order of business?"

"For your men to show me where their apartment is."

Two weeks later Bobby and I found ourselves at the French Embassy sitting down with Robert Coulondre, France's ambassador to Germany. He had actually invited Bobby because he wanted to share some news with him in person. We hadn't heard from Dallas yet, but I was thinking positive and trying like hell not to dwell on it.

The middle-aged, mustached, dark-haired Mr. Coulondre sat down with us in his library—a fire ablaze in the corner. Bobby and I parked ourselves on a velvet-covered maroon couch in the middle of the room, and Coulondre made himself comfortable in a thick, leather chair just on the other side of a coffee table.

"Thank you for your hospitality, Mr. Ambassador," said Bobby after we had already shaken hands and introduced ourselves.

I translated. *"Vous remercie de votre hospitalité, Monsieur l'Ambassadeur."*

"De rien, Bobby," said the ambassador. *"S'il vous plaît appelez-moi Robert."*

I translated. "He says you're welcome, Bobby. And he says to please call him Robert."

Bobby nodded and smiled.

"I don't want to waste any of your precious time," said Ambassador Coulondre in French. "I just want to look you in the eye and tell you that not a day goes by when our country takes for granted its special relationship with America."

I translated.

"The feeling is certainly mutual," said Bobby.

I translated.

"If you wouldn't mind," said Coulondre, "I have changed my mind. I was expecting heavy snow today, but it is clear out. I shall have my chauffer drive us to the Tiergarten and the three of us can enjoy some cold, fresh air. I would much prefer a walk through the beautiful, tree-lined garden today, even if we have to see and listen to the Nazi soldiers marching all over the damn place."

I translated and Bobby agreed.

Minutes later we found ourselves strolling along the eastern portion of the massive park, myself in the middle, the ambassador to my left, snow having been recently shoveled off of the sidewalks.

"I feel," said Coulondre, "it must be made clear, once again, that we intend to back Poland if Germany attacks her. Prime Minister Chamberlain agrees with us on the matter. We understand that President Roosevelt will not be joining us in this pact, but, nevertheless, want to reiterate how welcome he is to change his mind. The French, British, and American friendship is everything to us. And speaking of attacks, we both know it is only a matter of days before Hitler moves on Czechoslovakia. He was certainly shameless in violating the Treaty of Versailles last year by annexing Austria."

I translated.

"President Roosevelt," said Bobby, "respects yours and Britain's position here. For God's sake, if it were Mexico and Canada being threatened today, we'd be forced, like you, to consider force, based on their simple proximity to us. We understand how you and Britain feel squeezed. But, as you are fully aware, Congress has already spoken. America's Neutrality Act remains in place. Besides, our economic situation all but demands that we not get embroiled in a second world war unless the sovereignty of our nation is under direct threat."

I translated, and I also thought about what Bobby had told me privately, that Roosevelt actually wanted like hell to get Congress to repeal the Neutrality Act passed in 1937. He wanted at least to send military aid to European countries that were likely to be attacked in the near future by the Nazis. With each step we took, I couldn't help but see the desperate look in the French ambassador's eyes. All of us here in Berlin could feel the strength of Hitler growing daily. And if I wasn't walking around scared to death about what might be happening to my family back in Stalin's hell, I'd certainly be more worried about walking the streets of Berlin.

"What's happening here is insane," said Coulondre. "The walls of Berlin are closing in on us all. I will be leaving for France sooner than later. I assume all of the embassies will be closing within months. Acts of aggression by the various players have already occurred. But a global war is inevitable. And we may soon find ourselves trapped in Hitler's inferno."

I translated.

"I would like to think," said Bobby, "that we are here to try to stop that kind of war from breaking out."

"We can't stop it," said Coulondre, responding to my French. "And here, our families are no longer safe. Is your wife here, Mr. Ellington?"

Bobby waited for me and answered, "Yes . . . and my children."

I translated and Coulondre said, "You can't feel that they are safe. If you don't leave soon, there will be no way to get out. Think about it. Communicate this to President Roosevelt."

Bobby listened to me and responded with, "Perhaps if Hitler attacks Poland we will be recalled. But with each day that passes, I grow more concerned, more fearful. It is much worse than any of us could have imagined. Everyone is walking around in total fear. And my God, to be Jewish! The Night of Broken Glass was likely just the tip of the iceberg."

Coulondre watched my lips and then nodded. "If I may, Mr. Ellington, I must ask our interpreter friend here if he knows what Hitler is doing to the local blacks, most of them of mixed race. He calls them 'Rhineland Bastards.' They are mainly the children of white German women and African soldiers who fought alongside the French when they controlled the Rhineland area during the Great War. These black children are being subjected to Hitler's mandatory sterilization process. They'll never be able to have children of their own. Adolf Hitler doesn't want them mixing with the Aryans. Sick, sick man!"

24

Riga, Latvia
April 9, 1939

On a Sunday, some two months after I'd met Dallas in Belgium, I found myself sitting in a two-bedroom Riga apartment accompanied by two of Dallas's men. The train ride from Berlin had taken me two days.

Dallas had finally sent his positive cable to Bobby on Friday, March 24, but I hadn't been able to leave straightaway because my next briefcase exchange had been just ten days away on April 3. But now that I was here on the 9th, I had at least two and a half weeks to accomplish what I needed to before heading back to Berlin in time to make my fourth exchange on Monday, May 1.

The second exchange had gone smoothly, the briefcase filled with false information about U.S. submarine technology. I had typed up several reports using strictly physics and mathematics terminology—reports that partially detailed new types of S-boats called *X-boats* that America was on the cusp of introducing. Of course there were no renderings included, no actual math equations or physics specifics. It was strictly conceptual, my best attempt at theorizing. What I'd articulated could only describe a submarine that might be able to exist in the distant future, not 1940.

The size, speed, range, and depth of these futuristic sounding war machines would leave the Soviets scratching their heads and wanting to know more details. But in the end, I was certain Stalin could only worry at best, for he knew my access was limited and that I was merely relaying a small piece of a much larger and more complex mechanical breakthrough. That's what *he'd* think at least.

I'd explained to the Kremlin that I'd accessed portions of a broader set of documents from the suitcase of a visiting Department of War official named Bob Wilmoth. Of course, there was no Bob Wilmoth. Still, it had been fun using my engineering skills to dream up something that didn't exist.

The briefcase Dieter had given *me* during the second exchange included confirmation that the Kremlin was going to make sure Lovett was transferred from Magadan to MR4. They had confirmed that he was alive but said he wouldn't be transferred until May, when a large group of free hires were set to ship home. I was just happy he wasn't dead.

The third briefcase I'd delivered had information in it involving the same X-boats, but focused on who was involved. I'd reported that two men were responsible for aiding the U.S. in this engineering breakthrough, both with code names. I'd reported that the code names were probably being used so that various U.S. officials could comfortably correspond with one another about their two well-compensated, secret geniuses. One was a fictitious Australian mathematician being referred to as Warren Press Lord. The other was an engineer from Singapore I'd code-named Lee Rodgers Lincoln.

I'd told the Kremlin that a team of scientists from America would be having their next meeting with the two geniuses in Honolulu, Hawaii, on August 30 at 8:00 p.m. It would be held in Fountain Lecture Hall at the University of Hawaii. I was guessing some Soviet spies would be dispatched to Hawaii in order to try to place recording devices throughout the lecture hall. I was sending the Soviets on a wild goose chase, all the while knowing I'd need to be long gone before this August 30 date. And I had to keep telling myself that this entire escape plan wasn't some ill-conceived fantasy.

Regardless, now that I'd arrived in Riga, I needed to deal strictly in reality. The apartment I found myself in was bare, old, and drab—several mattresses and blankets having been placed in the bedrooms and living room. The unit was on the first floor of a brown five-story Gothic-style complex. There were four apartments on each floor. I had met Dallas's men as planned at the Riga Hotel and the introduction had gone smoothly.

Both men, Luc and Xavier, were in their thirties, from Paris, and spoke fluent English. They were clean-shaven, fit, and tall, and one could easily imagine either playing the role of a businessman or soldier. How they'd ended up working for Dallas was of no concern to me. I needed them. They had driven me to 105 Stabu Street in a green Ford Deluxe Tudor, and though my body was tired, my mind was fresh.

"Listen to me very carefully, you two," I said, the three of us sitting on the wooded floor in the living room with our backs against the wall, all of us dressed in suits. "Change of plans. I know what I told you in the car, but I want to move on this tonight."

Xavier and Luc nodded, suggesting that was absolutely fine with them. Images of my son lying in a hospital bed ran through my head. All I'd received in Zorin's last briefcase, besides a letter telling me how pleased the Kremlin was with my work so far, had been a brief note informing me that James was doing much better. I knew it wasn't true.

"Before I forget, Xavier," I said, reaching for my leather bag and taking out one of two envelopes full of cash, the other being for my own upcoming expenses. "This is for you to give to Dallas when you see him next, which may be a while. I'm assuming he'll give you your share at that point."

"We will be here until you tell us to leave," said Xavier, placing the envelope in his small suitcase.

"We brought what you asked for," said Luc, taking a pistol from his briefcase and handing it to me.

"Do you have the camera?" I said.

Xavier nodded. "And the flashlights, and the paper, and the pen."

"Did you have a telephone installed?"

"Yes," said Xavier.

"We'll wait until 3:00 a.m. to head out," I said. "One of you can go grab food for us." I pulled down my black fedora a bit and fiddled with the pistol. "I see you're both wearing brown suits."

"We know," said Xavier. "We are all to wear black suits tonight. Clear, Mr. Sweet."

"Do you have their names written down, a list of who's who?"

Xavier took a paper from his pocket and handed it to me.

"What is the address?" I said, reading the names.

"3 Maza Pils Street," said Luc. "It's a three-story apartment building. There are five units on each floor. Our targets are in a second-story unit at the end of the hall, number six. The place is approximately one and half miles from here. The door has a typical brass set; typical keyhole below the knob, easy to manip-ulate the inner cylinder, easy to pick."

"There can be no screaming," I said. "We have to execute with precision."

The narrow, cobblestone streets were completely bare when the three of us pulled up some twelve hours later, the dark morning leaving us practically invisible. We exited the car and entered the main door of the building. Inside was a small, well-lit lobby with mailboxes to the right, a stone stairwell to the left.

Luc led the way and the three of us climbed to the second floor, quietly making our way to the end of the dimly lit hallway. Stopping at the apartment door, Luc sat a large leather bag down. I nodded at him and he calmly jiggled the handle. It was locked, so Luc took a tiny tool from the backpack Xavier was wearing. Then he began doing what Dallas had claimed he could do in his sleep, pick the lock.

A few minutes passed and then a *click*. Luc returned the tool to Xavier's backpack and proceeded to remove three flashlights, Xavier and I each taking one. All three of us removed our holstered pistols. Then Luc slowly pushed the door open, darkness awaiting us inside.

As the two moved forward, I picked up the leather bag, set it just inside, and closed the door behind us. With our flashlights dotting the living room floor and walls, Luc led the way deeper inside. We knew that the apartment had three bedrooms. I was to head to the one at the rear of the hallway on the left. Xavier and Luc were to split the other two.

Each of us positioned ourselves near the respective bedroom doors and I held the flashlight up to my face. All of the bedroom doors were open. We were to enter the rooms slowly as soon as I dropped the light from my face. So with my heart pounding and our targets presumably sound asleep, I did just that.

Pointing my light straight ahead into the room now, I could see a man and a woman lying in a large bed. I stepped inside and closed the door behind me. When I flipped on the light, both of them wrestled about, affected by the sudden brightness. It was as if they hadn't been sound asleep. They both sat up and squinted.

"Audra!" the woman said.

As soon as she realized I wasn't Audra, that I was a stranger who had a pistol pointed at them, she let out a single scream, but the man stayed quiet, holding his arm up in front of her, signaling for her to shut up. I could tell this wasn't the first time he'd stared at a pointed gun. According to Xavier, both were in their late fifties.

"Do not scream again or I will shoot you!" I said in Russian. *"Ne krichi! YA budu strelyat' v vas!"*

The woman pressed her back against the headboard and tried to hold back another scream, all the while moaning and beginning to weep. I stayed calm and kept my eyes on him. He knew I was serious.

"Good," I said. "Just stay quiet like that and no one will get hurt. I am not here to kill you. I am not even here to lay a finger on you. All you have to do to stay alive is stay calm and do *exactly* what I tell you to do. Do you understand?"

They both nodded.

"Now, I want you to both get out of bed and get dressed. Then I want you to walk down the hallway and sit on the couch in the living room. That is all. I will stand right here and wait."

Minutes later, the man, woman, and their two twin daughters sat on the living room couch, Luc and Xavier sitting in chairs while I stood. Both girls were crying. I focused my attention on the father.

"Do you love your son?" I said.

"Da," said the salt-and-pepper-haired man, Zigfrid.

"Very much!" said his wife, Karina, her dingy red hair pulled back in a ponytail, her Russian barely audible.

"And Xavier has reason to believe that your son loves you all, too," I said. "Is this true?"

They all nodded.

"I read in Xavier's report that you young women are sixteen," I said, looking at the plain-looking blond daughters. "And do you love your older brother?"

"*Da,*" said Audra.

"*Da,*" said Jana.

"I have a wife, a daughter, and a son," I said. "And ironically, they are twins just like you. I love them dearly. But they are in Joseph Stalin's prison camps. I'm sure you can understand how painful this must be for me."

Again they all nodded.

"I'm sure you can understand that I am willing to do anything to get them out. I would rather be dead than live without them. And I can't sit idly by while they die a slow death. How old is your son?"

"He is thirty-two," said Zigfrid.

"And yet your daughters are so much younger," I said.

"They were a surprise," said Zigfrid. "My wife got pregnant at forty-two. We had already seen our son grow to be twenty-six years old at that point."

I walked over to Xavier, unbuttoned his backpack, and removed a pen and file. I took a blank sheet of paper from it.

"Which neighbors are your closest friends?" I said.

"The Krols," said Zigfrid. "They are downstairs in number three."

"Good," I said, setting the paper and pen on the coffee table in front of his wife. "I want you to write a letter to them explaining that your family has been invited to Leningrad to stay at your son's new big house. Tell them in the letter that your son is very sick. Tell them that because you may be gone for several months, you would like for them to collect your mail for you. Tell them you received a telephone call early this morning and didn't want to wake them, hence the reason for leaving the letter and mailbox key under their door. That's all."

Karina sniffled, nodded, and began to write, her hands shaking in the process.

"When you are finished writing that letter," I said, "I want you all to go pack a suitcase. We will be taking you to a different location here in Riga. My plan is for you to be there no longer than two months. Don't worry. You will be fed and taken care of. Meanwhile, I have to return to Berlin. You see . . . I have to send a briefcase to your son on May 1st. He's expecting some spy information. But this briefcase will have no such thing inside. It will have letters and photographs and instructions, telling Ivan's young assistant to meet me in Leningrad on May the 10th. When did your son first fall in love with Stalin?"

"He didn't fall in love with Stalin," said Zigfrid, his daughters still lightly crying. "He fell in love with Lenin and the Bolshevik Revolution when he was a ten-year-old boy. He swore he would leave as soon as he was sixteen to live in Moscow and join the Red Army. And he did."

"Well, this son of yours, Colonel Ivan Zorin, has shown himself to be ruthless. I am not going to belittle him any more than that in front of you, but you would not be proud of his actions. He has taken very much after Stalin."

"Maybe he lost his way," said Zigfrid, making a cross on his chest and looking upward.

"I first found out about your son while I was in a labor camp on the far northeast side of Russia. A good man named Commander Koskinen said he knew your son, this after he'd just told me where my wife and daughter were. He then proceeded to tell me that they might have gotten pregnant from one of the guards or commanders or *zeks*. With my head ringing, I asked him to tell me more about your son. Koskinen said he'd met him in 1933 at a Dalstroi training academy in Moscow. He also told me that your son was from Riga, Latvia. And right then and there I began to hatch this plan."

With all of them having attentively listed to my story, I walked over to the front door and removed the camera from the leather bag. I handed it to Xavier. Then I walked over to the mother and picked up the written letter.

"Thank you, Karina," I said, reading her Russian words. "When we get to the other location, I am going to need you to write a detailed letter to your son, explaining the terrible situation you four find yourselves in. You will lie and tell him that I almost killed your husband. You will lie and tell him that it is only a matter of time before I do the unthinkable to all of you. You will write about his childhood, telling him only things that you, his mother, could know. And you will mention each of my family member's names, pleading with your son to do exactly as I say immediately. Understand?"

"Da!" said Karina.

"I need you all to scoot over and make room for me," I said, waiting for them and then sitting next to Karina. "Luc over there has his pistol loaded and ready, so none of you should try anything stupid."

I began taking the bullets out of my pistol and setting them on the coffee table.

"I want you to all look," I said, holding up my empty gun. "This is only a pistol for show now. Xavier is going to take a few photographs of the five of us. Again, let me reiterate, I have no intentions of harming you. But I have to do everything I can to make your son believe I will. So, when we are finished with this group picture, I am going to sit with each one of you individually. I am going to hold this empty pistol next to your head. And Xavier is going to photograph it. I am sorry. But I have to put the fear of God in your son. Now, look at the camera."

25

MR4 Labor Camp - Kirovsk, Russia
May 11, 1939

COLONEL ZORIN'S YOUNG ASSISTANT, OSIP, HAD PICKED ME UP AT the Leningrad station right on time. From there we had gotten into a white Ford Coupe. And now, with the long drive behind us, we approached MR4 Labor Camp once again.

Seven days earlier, Stalin had actually replaced Maxim Litvinov with Vyacheslav Molotov. Bobby had rushed to tell me, reiterating that it had been done for the very reason we'd suspected, Litvinov being Jewish. Now it was surely only a matter of time before Germany and the Soviet Union had their important sitdown. My work had paid off, and in Stalin's eyes, this single piece of information had probably warranted my having been used.

Osip drove me up to Zorin's barracks and the two of us entered. We found him sitting at his desk doing nothing but staring down as if he were daydreaming. Another young guard was sitting in a chair against the wall to his left.

"The Interpreter is here," said Osip.

"Come and sit," said Zorin. "Both of you."

"How is my family?" I bravely asked as we sat.

"How is mine?" he said, his Russian words filled with anger, his jaw clinched.

"They are fine, Colonel Zorin. So far!"

"I will just say that yours haven't died yet," he said.

"And they better not, Colonel."

"Your son is in the hospital as we speak. He is having the same problems with his lungs."

"I figured as much," I said.

"They are giving him lots of strong syrup."

"Keeping him knocked out is not treatment," I said.

His look suggested he wanted to stand and slap me.

"This is my other assistant, Roman," said Zorin, looking to his left at the young guard. "Only myself, Osip, and Roman are privy to this sensitive undertaking."

"What would the Kremlin do if they knew you were being blackmailed?" I said.

"They can't know," he said.

"They'd execute you and you know it."

"Let me worry about that."

I looked at Osip and Roman. "And you trust these two?"

"They have been with me since they were sixteen. I trust them more than anyone on this planet. They understand my predicament. Besides, you filthy blacks aren't worth losing my precious family over."

"Just know that if they try anything stupid, hurt any of us, my men in Riga will even the score. They are far less compassionate than I. More like you!"

He shuffled around in his chair, uncomfortable with the pinch he was in.

"Your instructions were very clear," he said. "I immediately cabled the Kremlin when I received your last briefcase and told them that you were demanding to return to MR4 in order to see your sick son before continuing to spy in Berlin. Of course they cabled back and said it was okay."

"Even if they hadn't," I said, "you still would have sent Osip. We just would have had to work the plan differently. But this makes it cleaner. I'm assuming you informed the Kremlin that I intend to return in three days, on the fourteenth?"

"Yes," he said.

"Then that is when you will tell them how sick my boy has become. That is when you will tell them that I am unwilling to return without my entire family. They will balk at that and then you will offer to execute us."

"Yes," he said. "They love for me to execute people, especially ones who make impossible demands, and in your case, especially someone who they've already used up. I mean, I'm certain they would love to squeeze some more out of you, but once they know you are serious about demanding your family's release, they'll give me the go-ahead to put all four of you in the graves."

"I'm assuming you will be informing your briefcase man, Dieter, that I've been executed."

"He will come to know this soon enough. Yes."

"I'm also guessing that Lovett Fort-Whiteman is here now," I said. "He was due to be transferred in early May."

Zorin stuck out his lower lip and then cracked a bit of an evil-looking smile.

"Not everything the Kremlin has been telling you is true," he said. "When they told you that they'd tracked your comrade down in Magadan, and that he was alive, they lied. He was sent to the Kolyma gold mines right after you left back in November. But he only lasted a little over a month. He died on January 13th of this year. According to his official death certificate, he had apparently starved to death and was found frozen with no teeth. But . . . I have no more details other than those I'm afraid."

Learning that Lovett was dead came as a massive slug to my gut. But I sat up straight and glared back at him. I just swallowed deep and didn't allow myself to feel anything yet. I had to stay present and focused and strong. I couldn't let him see an ounce of weakness. He was trying to hurt me one last time, his constant smile signaling how much he was delighting in this news.

"So, you see, Interpreter," he said, putting his hands together at his chin and tapping his fingers together, "your good comrade has been dead the entire time you've been in Berlin. He was only alive in your mind."

He looked at Roman and Osip, and they all half smiled.

"Let's just hope," I said, "that your lovely mother stays alive . . . both in your mind *and* in reality."

He paused. I could sense him trying to figure out one last possible way of getting out of this trap I had him in. But in talking to his mother, I'd been able to sense how much he loved her. All of these men like Zorin and Stalin exhibited no feelings when it came to murdering people, unless, of course, it was their own family members.

"I want you to know," he said, "that both Osip and Roman will be with you the entire time and will have guns on them. You and your family will be searched and have no way of defending yourselves during the trip."

"That's fine," I said. "I brought my suitcase and have my suits, but did you have the fine clothes made for my family like I asked for in the letter?"

"Yes. When you arrive at the hotel in Riga and check into a room, only then are you to phone your men. And Osip will be listening. What hotel will it be?"

"That part you don't get to know. That's part of the deal. Your men get to pick a room and check in under a name I won't be privy to, but I get to select the hotel."

Three days later, at around 10:00 p.m., my family stood near a freshly dug pit. It was the latest in a long line of others that had been covered up already, thousands of dead *zeks* having been buried underneath them. This pit was large enough for several people. All four of us stood there knowing what the plan was. Zorin was going to be the man who shot each of us. He would do so while two guards and another high-ranking officer bore witness. The only other witnesses would be Osip and Roman, and they were also the only two people besides Zorin and my family who knew that Zorin would be using blank cartridges.

We had been driven to the massive graveyard in the white

Ford Coupe, Osip behind the wheel. Roman had driven an identical beige Coupe behind us, while Zorin and his witnesses had been in a black sedan leading the way. The graveyard was situated about a mile from the main camp. More *zeks* than we could even begin to imagine had been driven out here and executed by Zorin on far too many occasions. We could smell death all around us.

I had been able to be with Loretta and the children the entire time since I'd arrived from Berlin. Zorin had put us all in a private room. The emotions had been overwhelming to say the least. They looked terrible, their spirits completely broken, their bodies even more withered—Loretta and Ginger's hair having grown back only a bit. And they had barely said a word, too tired and broken to even imagine that my plan might work. We must have spent that entire first day together just holding one another and crying and resting, particularly James, whose breathing issue wouldn't relent.

It was in this private room that I'd explained to them what the escape plan was. I had reiterated how important it was for them to drop to the dirt as soon as the gun was fired. I'd even demonstrated how they needed to fall. "Don't jerk backward," I'd said. "Just fall straight to the ground and come to rest wherever your body's natural movement stops. If you're still on your knees and slumped over, fine . . . just stay there."

"I will have no problem falling, Daddy," Ginger had said. "I've been wanting to drop to my knees and rest for almost two years."

The feeling of guilt I felt for not having kept my daughter safe was uncontrollable. She and James were sixteen now, she as tall as her mother, and James only an inch shorter than I. They were all grown up, but with real-life educations that were far too advanced.

Our rehearsal had gone well, but I also knew that the darkness would aid in our dangerous skit, making it difficult for Zorin's witnesses to see details. I spent most of my time telling Loretta and the children not to scream or react when Zorin fired his gun. "He's going to shoot at me first," I'd said. "Just stand there and wait for your turn, as if you've completely accepted your fates. Trust me! This is our only chance!"

I'd also made it very clear to Zorin that his family would be killed on May 21st if I didn't confirm our release with Xavier sometime between now and then. And I'd gotten the sense that the colonel knew I wasn't bluffing. Still, as Zorin raised the gun and pointed it at me, I couldn't help but fear that he had decided to use real bullets.

We were lined up almost shoulder-to-shoulder, me to our far right next to Loretta, James on the far left next to Ginger, the only light emanating from the white Ford Coupe's headlights that had been left on in the distance. Zorin pulled the trigger and *bang*! Then another *bang*! I dropped to the dirt like a sack of potatoes and lay there on my left side about five feet in front of the pit, relieved that the bastard had actually kept his word. I was alive and well.

I listened to the next two shots ring out and then felt Loretta's arm slap against my shoulder. And as the next four blanks were fired, we listed to our babies fall to the ground, doing everything in their power to act out the scene like seasoned thespians. *God bless them!*

"*PROSHCHAY!*" yelled Zorin, which meant, "Good-bye, Americans!"

"*PROSHCHAY AMERIKANTSEV!*" yelled the other men.

"*OSIP!*" yelled Zorin. "You and Roman take their pictures and then throw them in the graves and bury them!" He turned and began walking toward his car. "We have some steak and potatoes to eat!"

"*Da!*" said the other high-ranking officer, following him. "And some good vodka!"

The two nameless guards joined them, the four getting into Zorin's black vehicle and driving away. As soon as they were out of sight, Osip approached us.

"Stay lying there," he said, as I opened my eyes a bit and watched him take the small can of animal blood from his bag. "Go get the camera and lamp from the white Ford, Roman."

Roman nodded and walked away, while Osip continued rummaging through the bag. When Roman returned with the brightly lit lamp and set it near our bodies, Osip dipped a paintbrush into the can and let a drop of blood fall to my forehead. Then he let another one drop to my chest. After he'd done the same to the others, he took the camera from Roman.

"Go get the shovels from the trunk now, Roman," he said.

After he'd taken several photos of the dead Sweet family, he wiped the blood from our faces with a wet rag.

"You can stand now," he said.

As we got to our feet, there was no hugging or talking, for the situation was still very much fluid, our hearts and minds racing. The six of us began shoveling dirt into the pit until it was completely covered. When we were finished, we returned to the white Coupe and I removed several bags from the trunk. Inside them were their new clothes, fancy hats, and one of my suits. We quickly removed our raggedy, bloodstained *zek* uniforms and got properly dressed. Osip and Roman then patted us all down and checked the bags.

After they were finished, James and I hopped in the white Coupe, myself behind the wheel this time, James in back, Osip in the passenger's seat with a loaded pistol. Roman was driving the beige Coupe behind us with the ladies sitting in the backseat. A long drive to Leningrad awaited us.

The following afternoon we pulled up to the beautiful Hotel Astoria in Leningrad. We would be spending one night here, checking in as the Robeson family, all of us sporting our new clothes and fancy hats. Before I'd left Berlin, Bobby had given me our new, fake passports. He'd had them made way back in late January before we'd ever met with Dallas Conrad, as part of my plan involved us leaving the Soviet Union disguised as the famed Paul Robeson's family. The international Negro star was now a true hero to the Soviet people. There was no one more beloved in the country, save for Joseph Stalin.

The next morning, after James and the ladies had covered

their drab faces with lots of makeup, we drove to the train station, parked the vehicles, and approached the terminal. As we
stood in line and waited for our turn at the ticket counter, folks
began staring at us, obviously curious to know more about the
foreign-looking, well-dressed colored people.

Osip and Roman took our passports and placed them on the
ticket counter. The young agent seemed to be enamored with
the names he was reading, so he turned to the guard standing
behind him, signaling for him to approach. Both continued
reading the passports.

"Robeson?" said the guard. *"Vy svyazany s Pol' Robeson?"*

"Yes," I said in Russian. "I am related to Paul Robeson. He is
my brother." I grabbed Loretta, James, and Ginger, pulling
them in close. "And this is my wife and our children."

The guard smiled real big, holding my passport up as if it
were a piece of gold.

"Can we take a photograph of you and your family?" he said.
"No one here has a camera, but I can have one retrieved from
the east office. It will only take five or ten minutes."

"Well," I said, "we don't normally—"

"I am the Robeson family's military host," said Osip, chiming
in. "Their tour guide! We really don't have time. Besides, they
have been constantly swarmed during their tour of the country.
And if you start taking pictures of them, a huge crowd will
gather and it will be chaos." He looked at Roman. "This is my security aide. If some of your staff would like to take a quick photograph with the Robesons, we could come inside one of the
administrative offices back there and organize a private session.
Roman here can use his camera and send you all a picture in the
mail."

"Very good!" said the guard, he and the ticket agent smiling.
"Please come around to the side door."

Minutes later, the four of us stood in one of the back rooms,
several guards and other staff members surrounding us as
Roman clicked away. Of course these were pictures no one
would ever see. Still, you would have thought I was Paul Robe-

son himself the way these Soviets were treating us, huge grins pasted on all of their faces. The reach of the famous colored American was on full display.

When we arrived in Riga later that night, we took a taxi from the station to the Riga Hotel, a destination Osip had just now learned of. We all sat in the busy lobby while Roman checked into a room.

"When we get everyone settled in the room," said Osip to me, "you and I will go call Xavier. He and Luc are to drive here with Zorin's family and park out front. They are to wait until nightfall."

"It's my plan," I said. "I know."

"I know," said Osip. "I'm just going over it again. Besides, I don't trust you. I would never trust you. You're always scheming. We will release family members one at a time as you've suggested. You last! And you will be explaining this to Xavier on the phone. Yes?"

"Continue," I said. "You've got it down well so far."

"When Xavier and Luc get here, they will not know which room we are in. Besides, like you said, Roman is checking in under a name even you won't know. Your men will wait outside in two cars with the Zorin family. I will be waiting here in the lobby with you."

"That's correct," I said. "But they won't actually be entering the large, circular driveway out front. They will be pulling up to the narrow side street at the east end of the hotel. That is where they will wait. Now, continue, Osip."

"As soon as you see Luc enter, you'll tell me. Then you will nod at him, signaling for him to return to the vehicles while we go back to the room. I will then take your daughter out to the cars for the first exchange. I will be bringing the mother back inside first."

"No," I said. "The mother is brought in last. Period! And don't push me, motherfucker! The last thing you want to do is mess this up. All you have to do is return to Leningrad with

Zorin's family. We're doing one at a time, but the mother goes last. You already knew this. So did Zorin. Paranoid son of a bitches! Why would any of us, on either side, try to pull some funny business at this point?"

Roman approached and signaled for us all to follow him. We made our way through the lobby and down a long hallway to room 122. Moments later, Osip accompanied me to a phone in the lobby and I called the hideout. The operator connected me. Xavier picked up and listened to my instructions, then said he'd be arriving at 9 p.m.

Osip and I returned to the room where we waited for the time to pass with the others. When it was 8:55 we returned to the lobby and sat again in one of the fine chairs atop a large golden rug, travelers hustling about with their luggage. When Luc entered I nodded at him. It was time.

Several minutes later, I found myself sitting in the room with Colonel Zorin's father and two sisters. Roman was standing near the doorway with his pistol out. It was all playing out perfectly. When Osip returned and signaled that it was my turn, I stood, looked at the father and sisters, placed my hands in the prayer position, and wished them peace with my gesture.

As we approached the two Ford Deluxe Tudors—one green, one black—Xavier opened the door of the green one and let the mother get out from the backseat. Luc stood near the driver's side door of the car behind us, his hand under his suit jacket, his pistol loaded and ready.

As I passed the mother, I gave her a warm smile and said, "God bless you!" Osip took her arm and led her around the corner toward the hotel entrance. His last exchange was complete.

As I got into the car and sat in the backseat next to James, I thought about Lovett. I believed he was indeed dead, but still, part of me wasn't sure. And as Xavier began to drive, I wondered how I'd ever be able to confirm his death. I figured Bobby would help me find a way.

I turned around and watched the Riga Hotel's lights disappear in the distance. I believed that Zorin would kill both Osip and Roman when they returned to MR4. They were too young to know how the Soviet brass operated. I also couldn't help feeling that Colonel Zorin himself would be executed sooner than later, as Stalin seemed to know nothing but finding reasons to off his own confidants.

I turned to James and realized I needed to get him in to see a proper doctor as soon as we arrived in Brussels en route to the port in Le Havre, France. My best guess was that he was suffering from treatable asthma. But, as planned, I wasn't about to return to Berlin for fear that Zorin might have some men waiting for us at the station. And we needed to get out of Riga as soon as possible.

The last thing Bobby had told me was that they believed Stalin would soon be moving troops into Latvia, and the embassy believed it was only a matter of weeks, if not days, before Hitler attacked Poland. We needed to leave Europe right away. War was likely fast approaching.

"Dad," said James, as we motored down the street.

"Yeah, son."

"Where are we going?"

"To America, son. To the United States of America."

BENEATH THE DARKEST SKY

Jason Overstreet

ABOUT THIS GUIDE

The suggested questions that follow are included to enhance
your group's reading of this book.

DISCUSSION QUESTIONS

1. Why do you think Prescott, an engineer by training, continues to be drawn to working for the U.S. Government?

2. Discuss the friendship between the Ellingtons and the Sweets, and give some reasons Ellington might need Prescott to work with him in Haiti.

3. All of the figures whom Prescott and Loretta meet at Moscow's Hotel National in Chapter 6 are actual historical figures. What circumstances do you think enticed African Americans to immigrate to the Soviet Union during the first half of the twentieth century?

4. This novel presents thorough research of *factual* events that occurred in Stalin's Russia. Discuss the plausibility/implausibility of the following *fictional* events that happened to the Sweet family given what you know of the history of the period.

   - A black man working for the U.S. foreign service
   - Loretta's artistic style and fame in the Soviet Union
   - The way Prescott finds the bugs placed in Spaso House by the Soviets
   - Incarceration of the entire Sweet family
   - The Sweets' disguise as they leave Russia

5. Loretta perhaps shows the most growth across the two novels, *The Strivers' Row Spy* and *Beneath the Darkest Sky*. Discuss her path to becoming a famous Soviet artist.

6. Why do you think the author dedicated the novel to Lovett Fort-Whiteman? How is Lovett's dream similar to or different from Dr. Martin Luther King's dream?

7. In what way did Lovett Fort-Whiteman's view of racism in America differ from that of the Communist Party's view?

8. Discuss the political/economic reasons for Stalin's gulag system. What event that occurred while Prescott was imprisoned did you find most egregious?

9. Thousands of Americans left the States during the Great Depression to accept jobs in the Soviet Union, an estimated 10,000 in 1931 alone. Many of them were eventually swept up in the purges and died in Stalin's gulags. Why has this fact been virtually ignored in American history books?

10. Many expatriates living in the Soviet Union during the purges were not allowed to return home, and more than a few Americans were also imprisoned in the gulags. Why didn't FDR exert more pressure on Stalin to protect these Americans' rights?

11. Discuss some aspects of history that you were not aware of before reading this novel.

12. The author uses chapter juxtapositions between real time and events that have already occurred. Discuss the effectiveness of this literary device.

13. Given how this novel ends, can you predict what may lie ahead for the Sweet family?